**THEY WERE BOUND TOGETHER
BY POWER AND AMBITION,
TORN APART PASSION
AND VIOLENCE...**

Alexandra Fleury—Beautiful and talented, she vowed to follow the story of a lifetime, no matter where it led—even into the arms of the one man who could destroy her. . . .

Phillip Carriere—Cardinal of Washington, he gambled the souls of millions of American Catholics in a daring power play with Rome—only to risk his own soul in the bargain. . . .

Father John Leighton—A handsome, idealistic young priest, he was torn between his passionate love for the Church and the woman whose passion taught him another kind of love. . . .

Richard Easterling—The charismatic, hard-driven junior senator, he had an insatiable appetite for power and sex that could drive him over the edge. . . .

Lindsey Easterling—The senator's wife. Her husband's infidelities drove her to desperate measures—and into the bed of one of Washington's most powerful men. . . .

MORTAL SINS

**Dianne Edouard
and
Sandra Ware**

BANTAM BOOKS
NEW YORK • TORONTO • LONDON • SYDNEY • AUCKLAND

MORTAL SINS

A Bantam Fanfare Book / May 1991

FANFARE and the portrayal of a boxed "ff" are trademarks of
Bantam Books, a division of Bantam Doubleday Dell Publishing
Group, Inc.

ISBN 0-553-28929-2

Published simultaneously in the United States and Canada

Bantam Books are published by Bantam Books, a division of
Bantam Doubleday Dell Publishing Group, Inc. Its trademark,
consisting of the words "Bantam Books" and the portrayal of a
rooster, is Registered in U.S. Patent and Trademark Office and
in other countries. Marca Registrada. Bantam Books, 666 Fifth
Avenue, New York, New York 10103.

PRINTED IN THE UNITED STATES OF AMERICA

OPM   0 9 8 7 6 5 4 3 2 1

For Kent, Carol, and Cary-Stuart . . .
  and for the Hals

Acknowledgments

It's continually amazing, the magic in the words: "We're authors. And we're writing a book." Even the shyest people smile and open up, sharing ideas and experiences that bring truth to the fiction.

Special thanks to Hart Roussel, John Ed Bradley, Joan McKinney and numerous others who helped along the way.

To our wonderful agent Faith Childs, who daily lives up to her name. And to Barbara Alpert, our creatively "on target" editor.

For bed and board and lots of love, Royce and Jane, and Gerrie.

CHAPTER ONE

Tragedy should have a darker beginning. And yet there was a warning of decay in the cracked, unleveled sidewalk fronting the three-story Greek-revival that rose, white and elegant, amidst choking ferns and dark green aspidistra. One might have expected Blanche DuBois to walk out upon the upper balcony to catch a breath of fresh air; but Blanche, poor fallen creature, would have seemed out of place here tonight, meandering about. No one at all could be seen moving outside in the rich light shafting from the first floor windows, not even on the wide veranda. The characteristically high temperatures of early June in New Orleans kept everyone inside, where the air was cool and civilized.

"Another shot... this time one on each side of the portrait." The man bent his knees and snapped a photo. "One more... for insurance." *Click*. "Good..."

"Enough, George. Alexandra, I think, would rather like to enjoy this party. It *is* her birthday." Margaret Venée had pulled her daughter closer and kissed her lightly on the cheek.

"Please, Mrs. Venée, one more shot. You'd both hate me if the newspaper had to go with something you didn't like. And how often do our readers get the chance to see three generations of such beautiful women...?"

"George Laborde, I am the least vain woman I know...."

1

"Stop talking, Mrs. Venée, and smile."

"Listen to the man, Mother, or we'll never get finished." Alex pinched her mother playfully on the arm.

"One more... It's a wrap." George lowered the camera. "You know it's remarkable how much Alexandra looks like her grandmother, Mrs. Venée. Even more than you. If Alex's eyes were blue..."

Alexandra Venée was a beauty whose honey-blond good looks leaped out so forcefully that most were unaware that it was actually the vitality of her personality that made her compellingly attractive. A miscalculation that she found exceedingly irritating. The comparison with her beautiful grandmother, which had started years ago, had by now begun to annoy her. It wasn't that she didn't enjoy being beautiful, it was just that she'd become aware of the disadvantages. She frowned as her mother turned to join the photographer in studying the portrait.

"Yes, the resemblance is rather uncanny...." Margaret almost whispered the words as she stood staring at her own mother's image. It was always if she were seeing it for the first time.

"And what's so strange about a granddaughter looking more like her *grand-mère*?" Alex heard herself asking, as she invariably did when someone pointed out the likeness. The whole exercise had by now become ritual.

"My two favorite girls"—Alex's uncle had come up behind them—"and easily the two most beautiful at this party." He lowered his head, kissing each on the cheek.

"Why, that's not such a compliment, Phillip." Margaret turned toward her brother, scolding. "Just the two most beautiful at this *party*..."

"A thousand pardons, madame." He feigned an apology. "The two most beautiful women in the world."

"You stand corrected, Phillip." Margaret smiled. "But after I've made such a fuss over my complete lack of vanity to George, I'm afraid you've made me quite the liar."

"I hardly think that a little vanity qualifies as a mortal sin, Margaret. Or a bit of lying for that matter."

"May I quote you on that, Uncle Phillip?"

"You better not, Alexandra. That comment is strictly off the record. How about a picture of the three of us, George?" Phillip pulled the two of them closer and smiled.

Cardinal Phillip Camélière was an elegant man with refined patrician features, dark where Margaret, his twin, was fair. To everyone, friend and foe alike, it seemed that he was the epitome of old-world charm and polish, and the trappings of his office did little to discourage this. Neither did Phillip himself.

"Send me a copy, George. Mail it to the residence," he called back over his shoulder as he maneuvered Margaret and Alex into the dining room.

"I can't believe you won't stay the week with us, Alex. I thought you had ten days of vacation time coming to you."

"I do, Mother, but I explained that there's something really special I'm working on right now."

"I just bet this is your idea, Phillip," Margaret teased. "You get to see Alex all of the time. Can't you share her?"

"Yes, Phillip, can't you share her?" Alfred Venée's words, as he appeared beside them, were low and even, and his rather plain middle-aged face showed not a trace of humor.

"Alfred, I was only joking. . . ." Margaret's hand loosened its hold on her brother's arm and fell limply at her side.

"Oh, Daddy, don't you start in on Uncle Phillip." Alex moved forward and circled her arms about her father's neck. "Besides, it was Uncle Phillip who convinced me to come home to celebrate my silly old birthday." She kissed him on his forehead. "And you know what? He was absolutely right— birthdays are for families. I wouldn't have missed spending this one with you and Mother for all the world."

"Alfred, darling, now, don't be so grumpy. We'll have Alex in New Orleans for three more glorious days before she flies back to Washington." Margaret joined her daughter at her husband's side, locking her arm through his.

"Come on, birthday girl." Davey Davidson had materialized to clamp a firm hand on Alex's elbow, her open freckled face as wonderfully impish and warm as it had been in their academy days. "It's time for the show," she said, smiling. "And

don't try to fool me with that look, Alexandra Venée. You love
opening presents just as much as the rest of us."

"Okay, okay..." Alex surrendered gracefully, letting herself
be dragged away to where her friends waited.

Alex had finally worked her way through the pile of gifts
when her mother appeared with still another. "From us,"
Margaret said simply. Alex looked up, surprised. She had
already been given Grandmère Camélière's emerald engagement ring this morning at breakfast.

"This one was your father's idea," her mother explained
smiling. "I had nothing to do with it."

Alex laughed and tore into the wrappings. "It's beautiful
Daddy," she said, rising to embrace him. "Really beautiful."

"An important writer for *The Washington Post* needs the
proper briefcase." His pride and pleasure were evident as she
reached up to kiss him. "Look inside," he whispered.

She opened the case. At the bottom lay a check. "Daddy..."
she began.

"Buy whatever you want, baby. You're so far away we don't
really know what you need."

"The case was perfect, Daddy. You didn't have to—"

"One more, Miss Alex." Sarah was calling everyone's attention to a very large and elegantly wrapped package. As always
her uncle's present had been left till last.

Alex looked up at her father a bit anxiously, but he was still
smiling. He patted her on the shoulder, and she reached up
with another quick kiss before walking over to where Sarah
stood. She really did love getting presents, and was as eager
as always to discover what Uncle Phillip's surprise would be
this year. Quickly she knelt and, cutting through the ribbons
pulled the paper away.

"Oh..." It came out as a gasp. "Uncle Phillip, how...?"
For a moment she could only stare. Then, resting the canvas
against her chair, she walked to where her uncle stood
smiling beside her mother and father. He opened his arms for
a hug.

"How after all these years could you even have found it?"
she asked him.

"Phillip works in mysterious ways, his wonders to perform." Alfred's words were heavily ironic.

"Aren't you confusing me with someone else, Alfred?" Phillip laughed.

"I assure you, I am not."

Alex had caught the raw edge, sharper than usual, in her father's answer, almost a note of warning. Her eyes flashed to her mother's strained face.

At that moment the doorbell rang.

Everyone turned, expecting some new arrival, but Sarah came back from the front door with only another package.

"A gift for Alex?" Margaret asked too brightly.

"No, ma'am," Sarah answered, puzzlement in her voice. "The taxi driver said it was a gift for Cardinal Camélière." She stepped forward to place the box in his hands.

"Thank you, Sarah." He smiled graciously.

As always, he seemed completely serene, as unruffled by this unexpected delivery as he had been by his brother-in-law's obvious antagonism. Alex watched him with the others as, gracefully and without haste, he undid the packaging, handing aside the string and coarse brown paper. The box was deep and the lid had to be worked off slowly, but finally he was inside, peeling back the crisp white layers of tissue. And now there was almost a moment of hesitation, the slightest of movements about his lips that might have been the beginning of a frown. But he smiled, and his laugh, so charmingly self-deprecating, drew them all warmly into his circle. "I fear," he said, looking up at them, "that we have all been made the victims of some foolish practical joke." And reaching into the box, he brought out a baby doll, the more shocking in that it looked so very much like the real thing.

CHAPTER TWO

"You still haven't told me how you got that painting, Uncle Phillip." Alex settled deeper into the first-class luxury of her airplane seat.

"Now Alexandra, you won't have me give away all of my secrets, will you?" He had turned from the report he'd been reading, and removing his glasses, he fixed her with his gray eyes.

"You know you can't keep anything from me, Uncle Phillip, your favorite niece."

"My *only* niece, I would remind you."

"You're positively awful. Stop teasing me. How in the hell did you get that painting? It's been ten years for chrissakes."

"Alex, watch your language. And in front of a man of the cloth."

"Uncle Phillip . . ."

"Okay, okay, I surrender. I can't keep a thing from you." He turned back to his reading and began leafing through the pages. "I stole it."

"What?"

"I stole it, Alex. Now, stop asking questions."

"You are the most exasperating person I know. I guess you will never tell me. Well . . ." She leaned over and kissed him on the cheek. "I adore it anyway."

"I'm so glad you have it now." His face came closer to hers, and for an instant the gray eyes became more intense as he pressed his hand over hers. "And did you enjoy seeing your old friends again?"

"Yes. I'd forgotten how much I miss Davey. You know I think she and old Butler have something going."

"Ah, Butler. Your father's handpicked husband for you."

"That's not true, Uncle Phillip. It's just that Daddy..." She hesitated, not really wanting to say anything more. "Uncle Phillip, I wish you and Daddy would get along better. If only for Mother's sake..." She stopped, this time determined to let it go.

"Alex, you make more of this than there is. And so does Margaret. Alfred and I do just fine. Acutally I rather like your father." He had closed the report and slid it into his briefcase. "Now let's change the subject. How do you like John Leighton?"

"I haven't met him yet."

"Oh, I thought that the interview had been arranged and the two of you had already talked. Any problems?"

"No... and don't you get involved. I'm meeting with him next week."

"Now, Alex, you're getting upset."

"I'm not upset... not yet. However, I better not find out that His Eminence Phillip Cardinal Camélière of Washington, D.C., had anything to do with my getting this assignment."

"You *are* angry." He spoke cautiously, reacting to the fire in her voice. "Alexandra, I understand how important your independence is to you. You know I would never do anything to hurt you. Alex..." He reached out and touched her cheek lightly. "Alex, you do believe that, don't you?"

She lowered her eyes and cupped his hand against her face. "Yes, Uncle Phillip," she whispered. "It's only that I know you sometimes do things... *for my own good*." She found his eyes again.

"Forgive me, my darling, forgive an old man... for this, the least of his sins?" And seeing her smile, he patted her cheek, withdrawing his hand. "Now, what about this book that Leighton is writing?"

"A work intended for the masses, according to the press kit I received from his publisher. A display of condescending pap, as I see it, meant to draw the battle lines in this little religious war that is about to break out. And in this corner . . . we have the Pope. And in this corner, we have . . . Cardinal Camélière." She stared at her uncle, looking to see if her last words had found their mark.

"I'm afraid, my dearest Alexandra"—her uncle laughed—"that you have given me far too much credit. And far too little to Father John Leighton."

"I think not, Uncle Phillip. It sounds to me like Father Leighton is nothing more than a shrewd priest with a good instinct for making a fast buck. I detest how he is staying safe and cozy out of the line of fire, keeping his sweet ass on the fence while the two sides fight it out to the death. How dare he not have an opinion."

He watched her for a moment before he said anything. Then his mouth formed that half-wicked smile for which he was famous. "Well, *you* certainly are not without an opinion."

"Yes, I . . . I guess I have formed an opinion," she stammered, suddenly embarrassed and surprised by the force of her own convictions.

"You know, Alex, such a strong position so early in the game can be dangerous."

"Yes, yes, I know all about objectivity. It's just that . . ."

"I know John Leighton." They were the only words that he spoke for a moment, allowing the hum of the engines to fill up the cabin's late-night stillness. Then: "Although I've only really spoken with him on one occasion, John Leighton is the most innocent man I've ever met. I don't believe he is capable of what you think he is doing. He's not manipulative, and he does care . . . in his own way. Don't mistake his neutrality for lack of commitment. I think he is simply trying to bring some sense of rationality to this thing. If the truth were known, I think that John Leighton would be more than a little saddened if the old Church died. He's been quite happy there for a good number of years now."

"Happy . . . or protected?"

"Perhaps it is all the same thing. For all of us..." His last words sounded weary, somehow forced out of him. "Yet I don't think you will have to wait too long to see Father Leighton move his ass off that fence, Alexandra."

She looked down, feeling uneasy at hearing her own words thrown back at her.

"Brian Donovan," he went on, "has suggested that John serve on the secretariat to the Doctrine Committee for the Bishops Conference."

She looked up surprised. "Why would you want him, if he's so tied to the old Church? I would think you'd want someone more in line with your own position."

"Actually, John's moderate stance works in our favor, Alex. Appointing John to work with the Doctrine Committee will serve notice to Rome that this is an open convention."

"I know that no one now envies your position as president of the Conference, Uncle Phillip. Are things as bad as they seem?"

"It has never been easy to take on the Pope, Alexandra. He seems to have all of the right connections."

She laughed quietly at her uncle's effort at humor. "Doesn't the other side have the same connections?"

"Oh, I think we aren't so well placed, Alex. And despite what most people think, Pope Stephen will do whatever is necessary to preserve the virginity of the Holy Mother Church."

"What?"

"Check the raping hordes of doctrinal liberals." He smiled.

"And how will he do that?"

"By pruning the tree, my dear Alex. By tossing out the bad apples from the barrel. In other words, those who fail to follow the party line will have to go."

"Like the excommunication of Bishop Vanderveer?"

"Yes, and all seventeen of those women priests he ordained."

"Will the Conference recognize those ordinations?" She knew that it was the right question, but she also realized that she had very little chance of getting a straight answer.

"And what's the talk on the street, Alexandra?" He moved

closer to her again as if her reply held some real interest for him.

"That you'll not only accept those ordinations, but praise the Dutch bishop for his seeing the moving hand of God."

He relaxed back into his seat, but seemed to be holding his breath. "If the Church does not change," he began quietly, "soften her position on certain critical moral issues, she will cut herself off, grow into a withered old woman, and... she will die.

"Yet"—he exhaled slowly—"if she does change, becomes something else, something new, some say she will become a painted whore. And then the Church becomes something not Catholic at all, something that even those of us who have cried out for change will not possibly recognize. Or, in the end, want."

She watched him as he closed his eyes. It was his way of saying that he wanted to be quiet for a time. She hoped that he would sleep. She reached up and shut off the small overhead light, then turned to stare out into the thick well of darkness through the small cabin window.

"I'm not asleep."

She turned back at the sound of his voice. "We'll be home soon." She spoke with no particular emphasis.

"So Washington is now your home. Not New Orleans?"

"No, Uncle Phillip. Not New Orleans."

"You are so grown up, my darling, I hardly know you anymore."

"Not so grown up..."

"Good." He smiled, and even in the shadows she could see his bright clear irises as he stared into her face. "I like thinking of you as a little girl."

"I love you, Uncle Phillip."

"And I love you... most of all."

She sat quietly with her own thoughts for the rest of the flight. And then a disembodied voice, instructing them to put their seat backs in an upright position and fasten their seat belts securely, drew her back.

"Uncle Phillip, I'd almost forgotten." She pressed the small button to raise her seat back. "Who could have sent you that doll?"

He looked down then to check his seat belt, so that she could see only the vague outline of his profile, but she heard the joking tone in his voice. "Oh, I don't know. Probably some anti-abortionist who read about my visit to New Orleans and is out to let me know what she thinks of my so-called liberal position."

"You think it was a woman?"

"Oh, I don't know why I said that. I guess it could as easily have been a man. It just seems the kind of thing a woman would do."

"What did you do with it?"

"Do with it? I threw it away, Alex. Why would I want to keep a thing like that?"

"I don't know. The child you never had?" she teased.

"But Alex, you are the child I never had."

Alex leaned back in the tub. It was one of the old claw-footed kind, really long and deep. Along with the heart-pine floors and high ceilings, the tub was one of the major attractions of the apartment. Even in the summer she loved a hot soak.

It was good to be back. She felt comfortable here. She had found for herself what she'd come looking for two years ago when she'd left her job at the *Picayune*—a space apart, a life away from the easy existence that had begun to close too snugly around her.

She thought of Davey. Her friend was happy to remain in New Orleans. But then Davey was strong, "comfortable in her skin" was the phrase which came to mind. Davey would make her own way anywhere. Alex hoped it would work out with her and Butler, and that Davey had understood that she had her blessing. She had thought it was clear to everyone that it was over between her and Butler. He was a part of that world she had left behind.

She closed her eyes, letting the water soothe away the travel weariness from her body. It was a short flight really from New Orleans to D.C. But the packing, the farewells, the drive to and from the airport . . . She flipped open the drain and stepped out of the tub. She had work to do tonight, but there was one more pleasant task she would allow herself before beginning. She would hang Uncle Phillip's painting.

Wrapped in a white terry robe, she padded barefoot into the living room. The air-conditioning was at last beginning to take hold and the smooth wood felt cool under her feet. She sat on the comfortable sofa and pulled the protective wrapping from the painting. The nude figure of an adolescent girl sketched simply but adeptly in shades of blue reminded her of Picasso's early works.

She walked to the fireplace and replaced the print that hung above the mantel with the painting. She stepped back. It was perfect. And to think Uncle Phillip had somehow found and bought it for her. A painting she had only once told him about and hadn't seen since she was a teenager. But why be so surprised. Anyone who could charm hard-nosed politicians and bottom-line businessmen into funding his ever-growing list of charities was by definition a miracle worker. "Thank you, Uncle Phillip," she said aloud. "It's the most wonderful gift ever."

She thought of his other gifts then, not the least of which had been his help in getting her the job at the *Picayune* after college. She had known, of course, about the letter of recommendation he'd sent to the personnel office. She hadn't objected to that. It was the little personal talk he'd had with the publisher, something she'd finally found out about only two years later, that had angered her. That was when she'd applied for a position with several large papers. She still wondered about the speed with which the *Post* had contacted her. Her work for the New Orleans paper had been good, maybe even very good. She'd gotten a lot of attention nationally for her pieces on voodoo cults, and the *Post* was known for its talent scouting. Yet the suspicion that Uncle Phillip's influence might have been a factor haunted her. She had told her uncle nothing of her plans to leave New Orleans, but he always seemed to know everything. She could have turned down the job, of course. She'd had several other offers. But it was the *Post* for which she'd most wanted to work. And despite everything, she was as glad to be near Uncle Phillip as he was to have her near him. There could be no denying the truth of that.

So, had she truly escaped? The uncomfortable question rose in her mind. Was she really standing on her own feet, or only playing at it? She had a sudden urge for a cigarette. But she had given that up almost as quickly as she had developed the habit after coming to the District. Uncle Phillip hated her to smoke. She hated it, too, although from time to time she still wanted one.

She settled on the sofa again, still admiring her painting, and reached for the answerphone on the end table. *Rang you three times this week before I remembered you were on pilgrimage;* Lindsey's distinctive tones survived even the tender mercies of the machine. *What about lunch on Tuesday? You can tell me how it all went. Give me a call.* There was the click as Lindsey hung up, then the tone, and Frank came on. *So, Alexandra, you finally got out of that tub.* She laughed aloud at the accuracy of his guess. He was beginning to know her a little too well. *If it wasn't for this damn assignment*—his voice boomed out at her—*I'd have been there to greet you in person. You wouldn't have needed a hot bath to get the kinks out. Be back in town Wednesday at the latest. See you then. Oh yeah, before I sign off. Look under your pillow...a little surprise from the tooth fairy.* She heard what might have been his short dry laugh, and then the tone. No other messages. She reset the machine.

In the bedroom she pulled back the coverlet. If Frank had been at the apartment in her absence, he'd been neat enough. She hadn't suspected that anyone had been in here. But there *was* something under her pillow. A videocassette. Wonderful! It must be the *Nightline* she'd wanted. He'd come through for her again. There was a lot more print material to be read through in her preparation for this interview with John Leighton, but first she'd just have a look at this.

The light from the TV flickered raggedly in the darkness as she ran the tape through. Could it be possible that this man was what he appeared to be? Was he what her uncle had said—an innocent? A little guiltily she realized she'd been hoping to have her suspicions about him confirmed. She liked to cling to her comfortable prejudices just as much as the next person. She forced emotion out of her thoughts and concentrated.

This late-night interview had taken place just after the trouble in Holland. Brian Donovan, chairman of the theology department at Catholic University and the network's favorite authority in such matters, had been unavailable. And so Father Leighton had been tapped to answer Koppel's questions on the Pope's decision to excommunicate Bishop Vanderveer and the women he had ordained. She had missed the show, but knew that it was on the basis of this one short appearance that John Leighton had been approached to do a popular book on the problems confronting the Church. She had been certain that he was simply an opportunist who couldn't resist the ego satisfaction of cashing in on instant notoriety. Now she wasn't so sure, but she wasn't yet ready to grant him in reality the sincerity he undoubtedly projected from the tube. Of one thing she was certain—the publishing house that had snared him had known exactly what it was doing. In these days of media hype and promotion, Father John Leighton was an editor's dream. In a market where women bought the greatest percentage of books, his publishers had found themselves a priest with all the little-boy-lost sexuality of a screen hero.

"Dammit. Dammit," she cursed under her breath. John Leighton made her mad. Mad at herself. Where *was* her objectivity? She had faulted him for trying to do the very thing that was the essence of her own job: to try to present all sides of an issue, then let the reader or the viewer make his own judgment from the facts. From what she was seeing tonight, John Leighton was very very good at doing just that. Still, the issues he dealt with were moral ones, and he was a priest and a theologian, not a reporter. He did have, or should have, a vested interest in the outcome of such a debate. It still seemed to her, despite Uncle Phillip's defense of him, that it was somehow cowardly, an abdication of responsibility, for a theologian not to declare where he stood.

With the remote control she froze his image on the screen. He seemed to look out at her, the quick intelligent eyes bright with humor as he emphasized a point.

"You won't get around me so easily, John Leighton," she said to the face. "I still don't think I much like you. But I do promise that I will do my homework. It's going to be one hell of an interview."

CHAPTER THREE

Lindsey Darrington listened to the slapping of the water against the walls of the stall. Richard would be cooling down now. The entire shower taking exactly ten minutes. He never lingered, not even to relax on those days when he came home dead tired. His shower, like everything else he did, was closely regulated, part of a tightly set schedule. She closed her eyes, and for a moment the spraying of the shower became splashing rain—the rain that had fallen on the two of them that early spring evening when they had first met.

She had been only half-serious about her career, although her editor thought she showed promise. Now she waited in the falling rain for the candidate who would at last bring the Massachusetts Democrats to their knees. She ran up the steps with the other reporters to meet him, watching for a moment as he pushed away an umbrella an aide sought to angle over his head.

"We might as well all get wet," he said. "And who says Republicans think they're privileged characters." Everyone had laughed. A nice touch, she had thought then, softening the disgruntled media people, who had been kept waiting for over an hour for the candidate his political foes called "Pretty Boy."

And she could easily understand the label as he stood

looking almost elegant with the rain falling into his golden
blond hair, across the chiseled planes of that almost too-
perfect face. But as he fielded the tough insistent questions
smoothly—never once losing his cool, smiling, showing
off incredibly white teeth—she knew that the charm, the
solid good looks were just components of a beautifully
complex machine that worked at maximum precision all of
the time.

She had gotten in a question, something about his plan to
trim social programs. He had turned to match the voice to
the face, looking directly into her eyes, as though she had
asked him something personal, something just between the
two of them. "Well, Lindsey..." He had called her by name,
this Greek god of a man standing in the rain, running for a
seat in the U.S. Senate, addressing her as though he had
known her all of her life.

Two weeks later she had handed in her resignation to the
paper and gone to work in the senatorial campaign for Richard
Darrington. A month after his election they were married.

When she opened her eyes he was watching her, standing
just inside their bedroom, a towel wrapped around his waist.
She smiled, dropping her gaze from his face. "It seems
extraordinary, Richard, but I don't think I've ever seen you
completely naked in broad daylight." She looked up to see
his expression, and then watched as his hands moved to
loosen the towel. He walked slowly toward the bed, and
stopped. For an instant the machine shut down and his
blue eyes seemed curiously unguarded. His hand reached
out across the small distance between them and brushed
against her cheek, his thumb testing the softness of her
lower lip.

Then he was inside her, his body moving hard, driving into
her, his mouth forming words she could not make out. She
bit her lip as at last she circled her legs around his hips,
digging her nails into his back. "Yes..." she whispered long
and low. "Fuck me."

He was fixing his tie before he spoke to her. "What are
your plans today?"

"I'm treating Alex to lunch for her birthday." She watched

him in the mirror draw the knot tighter. "And yes, I like Alex a lot."

"What?" He had turned to face her.

"I said that I liked Alexandra."

"Oh." He reached for his coat.

"I'm also fucking the President."

"For God's sake, Lindsey, what in the hell are you talking about?"

"What I'm talking about, Senator Darrington, is that you don't really give a goddamn what I do."

"Shit, Lindsey. That's unfair. What the truth is, is that you don't really care what I think."

She slid deeper between the covers and drew up her legs. "No, Richard, the real truth is that neither of us cares."

He stared at her for a moment and then walked over toward the phone. He picked up the receiver and dialed. "Tony, Richard Darrington here. Is he back? Good. Then we are set as scheduled for this afternoon. See you then."

She watched as he held the receiver against his ear, then replaced it in its cradle and walked toward the bed.

"Lindsey, you're wrong. I do care. I care. . . ." He stopped and took her head in his hands and pressed her face against his chest. "Let's keep it here, Lindsey, in this bed, where we were twenty minutes ago."

When she heard the door slam she remembered whom he would be seeing this afternoon. And rolling over onto her side, she clutched a pillow to her stomach, willing herself not to cry.

"Don't look now, Alex, but your favorite 'out of the way' restaurant had just been discovered. It'll be 'reservations only' after today."

Alex quite naturally disobeyed, following Lindsey's gaze to a nearby table where Claude was seating another large party. "Surely, Lindsey, you can't believe that Claude would ever turn away his, quote, most beautiful patrons, end quote. . . . And one the wife of a U.S. Senator."

"Ha!" Lindsey's eyes blazed. "You've been in this town

long enough to know that the only commodity which really counts is power. And wives are notoriously short on that." She stabbed at her salad. "It's different in New Orleans, isn't it? It's family that gets you points there... breeding." Her next words sounded almost like an accusation. "You were a debutante."

"Yes..." Alex began, somewhat puzzled by her friend's tone. "I 'came out' as they say. It was boring really, just something to be gotten through to please the family. None of us took it seriously. Well, almost none of us." She laughed. "I remember my friend Davey once asking silly Emilie Whitting why she supposed it was only homosexuals and debs who came out." Then, catching the hardness in her friend's face: "It's just a game, Lindsey, a pointless ritual; it doesn't mean anything anymore. Not really."

Lindsey made a sharp sound. "It only feels that way if you're on the inside," she said.

"I don't understand." Alex leaned forward. "You're not exactly one of the have-nots."

Lindsey glanced down at her plate as if suddenly embarrassed. She took a deep breath. "What do you really know about me, Alex?" she asked finally.

"I know you went to a rather exclusive college."

"A scholarship. You know, throw a crumb to a poor country girl so that everybody feels better. I got my first pair of shoes that didn't come down from my cousin that year I went off to Vassar."

"I... I don't know what to say, Lindsey. I still don't understand." She stopped. "I'm not getting this right, am I?"

But now Lindsey gave her pleasant deep-throated laugh. "I'm sorry.... Eat. Your food is getting cold. I know it's hard for you to understand, Alex. You were born to all this." The motion of her head encompassed the casual elegance of the restaurant and the whole of the city beyond. "But I can never quite shake the feeling that at any moment someone is going to recognize me for the fraud I am and demand to know just what the hell it is I think I'm doing here. So," she went on quickly, allowing no comment, "what's with the emerald? Not a gift from Frank?"

"It was my grandmother's." Alex's eyes went to the ring as Lindsey turned the stone toward the light. "My parents thought it was time I have it. Part of my birthday present."

"So you were suitably rewarded for making the trip. . . . It's really beautiful," Lindsey added, to soften the previous remark. "What else did you get?"

Alex picked up her fork before answering. "A wonderful briefcase from Daddy. I think he's really proud of my working for the *Post* and all. And"—she paused waiting for Lindsey to look up again—"a painting, the most beautiful painting. I can't wait for you to see it."

"Another present from your parents?"

"No . . . no. This was Uncle Phillip's gift. Every year it's something special."

Lindsey's eyes shifted away. "Special . . ." Her voice was low. She smiled over her wineglass. "Like the gift of our friendship?"

"You know I've never thanked him for that . . . for introducing us," Alex said thoughtfully. "In fact I was a bit angry with him at first for interfering, for thrusting me at you. He was worried, he said, because I hadn't made any friends in Washington. He just couldn't seem to understand that I was enjoying my solitude away from New Orleans. Uncle Phillip thrives on being surrounded by people."

"Don't you think that even Phillip . . . Cardinal Camélière," Lindsey corrected herself, "likes solitude . . . to get away from it all sometimes?"

"You *can* call him Phillip, you know," Alex said, smiling. "Richard does. Besides, Uncle Phillip likes his friends to call him by his name. Though I do think it amuses him that you seem to insist on formality. I've seen his eyes twinkle at your always proper 'Cardinal Camélière.'"

Lindsey sipped at her glass, seeming to forget that the wine was all gone. She put it down carefully next to her plate. "Maybe it's because I'm a Protestant," she said with a small laugh. "I don't know what's correct."

"Just treat him like you would any friend. That's what will make him happy. And to answer your question: Uncle Phillip likes his privacy. But total solitude? I guess he must sometimes, mustn't he? All intelligent people need to be alone sometimes with their thoughts. And Uncle Phillip's the most intelligent man I know."

"More intelligent than say... Frank?" Lindsey probed not too subtly.

"Frank? Frank *is* very intelligent. One sometimes forgets that his blustering overconfidence isn't *over*confidence at all. He's disgustingly self-sufficient, self-motivated... and too damn smart."

"And...?"

"And...?" Alex repeated blankly.

"Well, what's happening with the two of you?" Lindsey asked at last. "You don't have to tell me, you know. This isn't an interrogation... or an interview."

"It's not that I don't want to confide in you, Lindsey. It's that anything I say, even to myself, sounds like a cliché. Or worse, like antifeminist backsliding."

"What was that?" Lindsey laughed. *"Antifeminist backsliding?"*

Alex had to laugh, too. "You see what I mean about clichés." Then pushing away her plate: "I know we're supposed to be two mature independent career people, but it bothers me that Frank doesn't really... *need* me, Lindsey. No dammit, that's not it." Inhaling sharply she tried again: "There's no passion."

"That's not the impression I got," Lindsey said.

"You're thinking sex," Alex shot back. "No, there's nothing wrong there... but I'm talking *passion*. See, I told you I couldn't explain it." She sighed. "It's just that Frank is always joking about everything. Nothing's ever serious with him. If he found me in bed with another man, he'd probably hit him with a one-liner instead of a blunt instrument."

"Don't be so sure of that."

"No. No, I'm not sure. But I'd be afraid to ask him how he would feel about it."

"Why?"

"Because the truth is, Lindsey, I don't want to know how Frank feels about me, because then I'd have to know how I feel about him."

"Want some advice?"

"No." Alex let a slow smile light her face. "Yes."

"Leave it alone. If it ain't broke, babe, don't fix it. You say the sex is good. And heaven knows, with his connections, Frank could be a tremendous help professionally."

"Good Lord, Lindsey, don't you think that's just a bit cynical?"

Lindsey shook her head. "My sweet innocent." She laughed. "When will you ever remember? This is Washington, Melanie Wilkes. You're not on the plantation anymore."

Tony always wore the Roman collar to work, even though the Cardinal had from the first given him permission to wear civilian clothes. "Out of uniform" simply wasn't his style. On many days he even donned the outmoded cassock, finding the black flowing gown with the splash of magenta cummerbund at his waist more suitable to his mood.

The Cardinal had teased him at first, saying that he was a throwback to the days of the Medicis and Borgias, when the vestments of clergy were indistinguishable from the trappings of royalty. Yet he wasn't offended, in fact he regarded his superior's words as a distinct compliment. He had even jokingly embroidered upon the Cardinal's observation by saying that he "wore the purple proudly." The Cardinal had countered that it was propitious that he wore it at all, pointing out that the title of monsignor was a relic of the old order and that he had probably gotten in just under the gun.

Yet despite the pompous veneer, Cardinal Camélière's secretary still looked like a satyr, his blue-black hair curling softly about his forehead and temples, his golden brown eyes tilting slightly upward at the corners beneath slashes of fine dark brows. Monsignor Anthony Campesi was a decidedly sexy man.

He flipped through his appointment book. It had already been a full morning—the Cardinal starting his day at breakfast with what he now referred to as the "clique," the inner-circle clerics who were executing some behind-the-scenes maneuvers in preparation for the upcoming Bishops Conference. Then an unscheduled visit by the Pro-Nuncio right on the heels of that earlier meeting. He frowned to himself. Old Mantini's spy network was more effective than he'd guessed. No one outside of the clique knew about these gatherings, but the shrewd hard-line Vatican politician had found out, and had come on a fishing expedition for the Pope. Still he doubted whether Mantini had gotten even a nibble. The Cardinal could beat the best, even at their own game.

Then there had been Sister Catherine, flying in with her usual exuberance, making pleas for higher budget allotments for her halfway houses, and Superintendent Fleming with his regular litany about the problems plaguing the archdiocesan schools.

As hard as he tried to pluck these nagging little bureaucratic thorns out of Phillip's side and hand them to Chancellor Beatty in the Pastoral Center where they belonged, he sometimes failed. And the Cardinal didn't help—wanting everyone in the system to feel he could always be counted on to lend a sympathetic ear, to show that he was still the master of his own house. This, despite the fact that Phillip had technically reorganized himself out of the bothersome mechanics of actually running the archdiocese.

And now this afternoon, the meeting with Senator Darrington. He looked down at the large black X he had made through the rest of the day. From past experience he knew to reserve ample time for any appointment with Richard Darrington.

It was all such a delicate balance. But he loved his job. Juggler, diplomat, watchdog. He had never expected to be any of these things when he had gone for his law degree after ordination. Yet he knew that he was ably suited to his position. Indeed, his skills as an attorney had come in handy, and more, his expertise in tax law and finance had made him invaluable to His Eminence.

He glanced at his watch: 3:00. Senator Darrington would be coming through the door at any moment. He closed the appointment book and folded his hands across his desk and waited for the door to open.

"Senator Darrington." He rose to his feet and extended his hand. "Punctual as usual."

"Is he in, Tony?" The senator returned the handshake.

"Yes, Senator. One moment, please." He walked around his desk and disappeared behind the double doors leading into the Cardinal's office. When the doors reopened, Cardinal Camélière stepped out.

"Richard." Phillip walked forward and clasped the man's arm as he shook his hand. "It's good to see you. Come in. How about something to drink? Coffee okay with you?"

"Coffee sounds good."

"Tony, see if Madame Elise can manage a pot for us," the Cardinal directed over his shoulder as he led Richard Darrington into his office and closed the doors.

"Here, make yourself comfortable." Phillip spoke as he drew a large wingback chair closer to his desk. "Just push that thing out of the way," he said as he pointed to one of the straight hardbacks.

"Save these for an inquisition, Phillip?" Richard joked as he moved one of the chairs.

"An astute observation, Senator. I mustn't allow my enemies the luxury of feeling, shall we say, too relaxed. Still . . ." Phillip paused before seating himself, considering his next words carefully. "A bit of comfort might cause them to let their guard down."

"If they're smart, they won't make that mistake," Darrington's tone held only some of its former lightness.

"Why Richard, you sound positively . . . untrusting."

"Cautious."

"Spoken like a true politician. But we are friends, Richard. There is no need to be cautious with me. I'm quite harmless."

Richard did not answer but watched the Cardinal's mouth twist into that small mocking half smile that he almost found irritating. Then he laughed. This initial sparring match had now become a familiar ritual between the two. "I like you, Phillip Camélière. I like the hell out of you."

"Yes, I'd say we haven't done so badly—a conservative Republican senator from Massachusetts connects with a liberal Democratic cardinal from Louisiana."

"And the senator happens to be Protestant to boot."

"A High Church Episcopalian. That's not the same as Protestant, Richard." Phillip looked toward the doors, hearing the light knock. "Come in, Tony."

Tony came in, balancing a tray, and walked to a small sideboard. "Madame insisted on sending croissants with the coffee. I told her that neither of you would probably eat any. But you know Madame Elise." He set the tray down and began pouring the coffee. "Black with one teaspoon of sugar, Senator?"

"You remembered." Richard took the cup, and raised a hand to beg off the croissants before Tony could offer.

"Your Eminence, I don't suppose you're going to humor Madame." Tony had placed a cup of black coffee in front of Phillip.

"You know better. But I'll pay for it. She won't speak to me for three days. I should fire that woman . . . too temperamental. But she's the best cook in the District. I stole her from the French embassy."

"*That* Madame Elise! I thought it had been the White House who had enticed her away from the French. Shows you how much a U.S. senator knows about the really important things that go on in Washington."

"Your Eminence . . ."

"This is fine, Tony. We'll probably need you in here as we wind down." Phillip stood and walked his secretary toward the doors. "Thank you, Tony. Like always . . . no interruptions."

Phillip paused a moment in front of the wide expanse of the closed double doors, then moved to sit on the edge of his desk. "How is Lindsey, Richard? I don't see her nearly enough."

"Fine. She and Alexandra were going to have lunch today."

"Good. I'm glad they've gotten to be friends. Alexandra needs women friends."

"So does Lindsey. She needs something to occupy herself. She doesn't seem to be really interested in anything."

"Oh . . ." Phillip reached for his cup and held it to his mouth, the thin porcelain rim pressed against his lower lip. He watched his friend for the briefest of moments, then turned and replaced the cup in its saucer without taking a sip. "I thought there were all sorts of things that wives of senators did."

"Oh, she does all of the required things. But nothing she does seems to really interest her." Richard spoke almost to himself. Yet his next words were deliberate and seemed to have been worked over in his mind for some time. "You know, Phillip, you might be able to motivate Lindsey."

"Me? How can I possibly motivate Lindsey?" Phillip's tone was a mixture of surprise and skepticism as he walked around to the back of his desk and sat down.

"Well, first of all, she likes you. She's never actually said it, but I can tell. I know Lindsey. Second, you have millions of interesting things that she could really get involved in. Third, and most important, Phillip Camélière, you are the most persuasive man I know."

Phillip's face opened up with laughter. "Thank you, Senator Darrington. Although I'm afraid you highly overestimate my abilities." He clasped his hands together beneath his chin, the index fingers pointing upward as if supporting his head. "And now, Richard, I assume that you have all of the four hundred thousand in the briefcase. . . ."

Ashes and roses. The air from her apartment swept out at her as Alex opened the back door into the kitchen. The late-evening rain had been unexpected, and she stood wet and dripping just inside the threshold, staring at the flowers that flopped over the sink, onto the draining board. With a wry smile, she stepped out of her shoes and followed the scent of tobacco to the bedroom.

Frank sat up smoking in the big antique bed, the dark horn rims an odd contrast to his bare chest above the rumpled sheet. He had been watching the *Nightline* tape and hit the remote switch as she entered, muting the sound of the TV.

"H'lo, Frank." She greeted him straight-faced. "Why don't you make yourself comfortable."

His eyes were hidden in the glare of the bed lamp on his glasses, but she saw the blond brush of his mustache curl over the even teeth. "Sorry. Especially about the mess in the bathroom. I hit National at the rush. Never would've made it here if I'd gone home first. And the roses were wilting."

"They're beautiful." She allowed a smile.

"Happy birthday," he said. "There are twenty-six of them, one for every year. Now, why don't you get those wet clothes off, and I'll give you the rest of your present." He threw her the towel that lay crumbled at the side of the bed.

She dried her hair, then began undressing, watching him watch her. She moved unhurriedly, laying each piece of her damp clothing neatly over the back of a chair. When she was finished she went to him, slipping beside him between the cool sheets.

Carelessly he tossed his glasses on the table, switching off the lamp as he turned to her. His eyes shone clearly now in the flickering light from the set, and even in the semidarkness she experienced the now familiar shock of those naked gold-flecked irises. He reached for her, pulling her to him, and she smiled as she caught the scent of her perfumed soap on his skin. She had a fleeting image of his tall solid frame jammed into the claw-footed tub. It was incongruous and dear, and now suddenly she wanted him.

He kissed her, and she clung to him, her lips opening beneath his. Her body relaxing, anticipating the easy familiar pleasure of their lovemaking. But his kiss took on a rare urgency and he thrust her almost roughly beneath him.

"God, Alexandra, you feel so good. I missed you, baby." His tone, so different from his usual casual manner, surprised her.

On his knees, hands gripping the brass spindles of the headboard, he entered her quickly. Then he was full over her, pounding hard within her, his thick straight hair brushing the pillow at her shoulder, his breathing so ragged and intense that she was shocked into a cold awareness. Clasping her hands about his back, she strained upward against his thrusts, wanting to help him. She held him tightly till he fell heavily upon her at last, shuddering violently, his face buried in her hair.

He rolled onto his back, staring upward at the ceiling. "Sorry." He turned his face toward her. "But you shouldn't stay away so long." He leaned forward on one elbow to kiss her breast, then gathered her closer, his hand slipping between her thighs.

She lay back against his arm, closing her eyes, letting herself feel again the warm lazy pull of desire. Wanting his touch, wanting him to bring her to the edge... "No." She sat up, not understanding her own resistance. "It's not necessary." She pushed his hand away.

"Alex." Smiling, he drew her down to him once more. "I think it's highly necessary." He tried again to contain her within his arms.

"Look, you're exhausted." She pulled away. "And I know you're dying for a cigarette. Don't worry, Frank," she said lightly, "you're not getting a grade. Besides, when are men going to learn that for a woman, there doesn't have to be the big O every time. Closeness and cuddling are just as important.... So just cuddle me."

Without comment he let her crawl again into his arms and settle her head against his chest. Then: "Let me get this straight, Alex," he said, holding her. "If a man neglects a woman's pleasure, satisfying only himself, he is without doubt a 'grade A' asshole. But on the other hand," he went on, "if in the heat of his own passion, he lets his lady go unsatisfied, and then tries to make amends, he is now a patronizing bastard.... Seems fair." He shrugged.

She tried to pull away but found herself giggling. Then laughing. He could always make her laugh. She turned toward him. "Spend the night," she said, offering amnesty. "I'll let you make it up to me in the morning."

"Done." He grinned. He released her and reached for his cigarettes. "How was your trip?" he asked, lighting up.

"Fine. The usual family visit. How was your New York assignment?"

"It was okay. Got some decent stuff. But I also went to meet with someone that Alfie put me onto."

"Oh..."

"Yeah, but I'm not sure yet where that's going. Still, if it pans out, there's a good possibility of a tie-in to the drug story I'm supposed to be doing." He leaned back heavily against the pillow. "The main trouble is, everyone's done a major story on drugs. Hell, I've done three. You wonder what there could be left to write. Still, it's a problem that won't go away, and the research department claims public interest has never been higher. So that's why Bob wants this new piece. 'Get me a fresh slant, Frank. Something really explosive.' Shit."

"You don't sound very enthusiastic." She lay on her side, watching his face. "That's not like you."

"I'm getting cynical, baby. Occupational hazard." His eyes focused idly on the screen, where John Leighton mouthed silent words. He drew hard on the cigarette. "I tell you, this drug thing's a fuckin' mess. I'm going to be putting my ass on the line again, and for what? I can't see anything I write having any kind of real impact. Hell, look at the stuff I already dug up on the CIA involvement in distribution. It hasn't changed a thing." He stubbed out the remains of his cigarette. "What about that interview you're supposed to do?" He jerked his head toward the screen.

Her glance followed his to the television, settling on John Leighton's face. "He's not quite what I expected. Uncle Phillip seems rather impressed with him. He told me that Leighton might be asked to do some work for the Bishops Conference in November."

"Tell me, when exactly are you supposed to do this interview?"

She didn't answer at once. She recognized from Frank's tone that this simple question was somehow loaded. "I'm going to meet with him next week," she said finally.

"Good. You'd better latch onto him quick. I was listening to some of Koppel's interview with him before you came in, and I can see 'martyr' written all over him. He's the type who always gets crushed in these kinds of situations. You can take it for what it's worth. But it's my opinion that no matter how neutral he intends to stay, before it's all over, your Father John Leighton will have been neatly drawn and quartered. If you hang with this guy and stay in for the kill, you could come out with one hell of a follow-up."

"Frank, if it goes well, I do want more than just another

feature out of it. I'm going to try and parlay this interview
into some front-page coverage of the Conference, with Leighton
as my source. What do you think? Will Murray go for
it?"

Frank nodded slowly. "He might...he might. But you
know, babe"—his tone was reluctant—"there could be a
problem. Murray could take a lot of flak for assigning you hard
coverage with your uncle being president of the Conference.
It might be smarter to wait for another chance to move into
hard news."

"But I don't want to wait. I'm sick of covering society
weddings and ambassador-row parties. Sure, I've gotten to do
some really good feature work, but it's all soft, dammit. I was
supposedly hired because of my hard-news stories for the
Picayune. So what am I doing on Style? And what if Phillip
Camélière *is* my uncle? I know it's not going to influence
what I write. If anything, my background should make me
the perfect person for the job. And besides, do you even
think Murray knows?"

"Alex, the *Post* is a newspaper, remember? The gossip
mill is extremely efficient. You can just bet Murray and
everybody else knows that you're Cardinal Phillip Camélière's
niece."

"Are you telling me not to try?"

"No, I'm not. That's a decision for you to make. And you
know that if you want, your old buddy Frank will put in a
good word for you with Murray."

"Thanks, Frank." Her tone had softened. "I'll let you
know."

She watched him later as he slept. Without his glasses he
looked like a boy, despite the thick mustache. *Getting cynical*, he'd claimed, but it wasn't true. Frank was a romantic.
She lay beside him, remembering what he'd said about John
Leighton's potential for "martyrdom." It had been his rounda-
bout way of warning her that it was a cruel world, and that a
reporter had to stay tough and unemotional. She wondered,
and not for the first time, how Frank really saw her. His offer
of help had been sincere, but she was uncertain of just how
seriously he took her as a colleague...as a woman.

She turned away from him. God, she was tired. Why couldn't she sleep? She fumbled in the sheets for the remote control. Some time ago she had hit the pause button, letting the comforting electronic glow act as a kind of night-light. Now, before switching it off completely, she glanced up at the screen. John Leighton was still there waiting, his serene face hanging in the darkness like an icon.

CHAPTER FOUR

Father John Christian Leighton walked unheedingly across the university grounds. He had passed this way thousands of times since his first days here as a graduate student. But if he didn't any longer see the beauties of the campus with the sharpness of fresh sensation, he experienced them as something altogether more satisfying. He experienced them as home.

The campus was quiet, the Gothic stone buildings basking in the June sun as he made his way toward the theology department offices. Uppermost in his mind was what answer he would give to Brian concerning the Doctrine Committee, but as he passed in front of University West, his look of intense concentration gave brief way to a smile. He was recalling a conversation he had once overheard in the basement rathskeller, the "Rat," as the students called the campus pub. Two young women at the table next to his had been arguing whether it was the fatherly gray-haired priest in *Boys Town* or *The Bells of St. Mary* of whom Monsignor Donovan reminded them. He had known at once that it was Barry Fitzgerald and not Spencer Tracy that the two intended. For despite the fact that Donovan's family was several generations removed from the old country, one could reasonably expect that a brogue might accompany the round rosy cheeks and the Gaelic twinkle in the blue-blue eyes. And yet, if the

young women had a very imperfect knowledge of forties film
stars, it was apparent that they knew even less of Brian
Donovan. Certainly they had never enrolled in his classes.
Barry Fitzgerald, indeed. John almost laughed aloud. From
experience he knew that Brian's students characterized him
in a far less kindly way.

Seventeen years ago, when he had come to Catholic University from Mundelein to earn his first two pontifical degrees, it had been Brian Donovan who had been his principal
professor. . . and his nemesis. Yet if at first he had thought the
man hard and unsympathetic, he had soon recognized that
Donovan's toughness served as a focus for his students' ener-
gies, and that this kind of channeling was precisely what he
himself most needed at this point in his studies. He had
stopped resisting and found himself welcoming the discipline,
even welcoming Donovan's unsentimental appraisal of his
talents.

Now that he was himself a tenured professor in theology,
the two were friends, and more than friends. Donovan, as
chairman of the department, was his immediate superior, and
was also his chosen confessor. Others might not have found it
an agreeable arrangement, but for them it seemed to work.
He had never felt that Brian took advantage.

And yet he knew well enough that Donovan was quite
capable of using any knowledge of his colleagues' weaknesses
in gaining something that he wanted. It was part of what
made him such an effective administrator. John acknowledged
the usefulness of the technique, but still it made him uncomfortable, seeing that brilliant mind used so cunningly, often
behind a mask of ingenuousness. So perhaps it was a mark of
their special friendship that this particular talent had never
been turned on him.

He pushed open the heavy wooden door at the front of
Caldwell Hall. The familiar neo-Gothic ambience of arched
wainscoting and worn mosaic floors hit him with a surprising
rush of nostalgia. His sabbatical would not even officially
begin till the opening of the fall semester, and already he was
missing his classroom and the daily contact with students. He
passed through the double doors at the end of the foyer,

acknowledging the greetings of the two seminarians who passed him in the corridor, and walked downstairs, still undecided as to what he was going to say.

Donovan, pipe in hand, glanced up as he entered the cluttered, book-lined office. "Got an answer for me, John?" was his greeting.

He dropped into the less-than-comfortable chair in front of Brian's desk, wondering if it were not the same one he'd occupied so often as a student. He smiled inwardly and looked up. Brian was leaning forward, regarding him closely as he drew deeply to light his pipe. He didn't repeat his question, but with two quick flicks of the wrist the match was extinguished and tossed expertly into the corner trash can. Then very deliberately he tilted back in the deep leather desk chair, his cold blue stare unwavering through the haze of smoke.

"I just don't feel I'm the right person for this, Brian." He knew he was hedging, and was amused to rediscover that the whole act still had the power to intimidate him. "As you've many times pointed out"—he smiled, continuing more evenly—"scholarship is my strong suit. If this position with the committee were only a matter of research and interpretation ... But dealing with people, trying to play the mediator between opposing factions ... You know what kind of circus this conference could turn into." He heard himself stumbling again and pulled himself up short. "I'm not a politician," he finished.

"You're a solid teacher, John. And your students love you. Ergo, you must be *something* of a politician." Brian chuckled appreciatively at his own joke. "But you're looking at this all wrong. The Committee needs you precisely because you're not a politician, and not known as one. We need a man who has a solid reputation as a moderate. A man above petty factionalism. We don't want Rome to claim that the Doctrine Committee is the puppet of Cardinal Camélière."

"It won't be, Brian, will it?"

"Camélière's puppet?" Donovan's shaggy eyebrows had risen fractionally over the hooded eyes. "If that worries you, John, the one way to make sure that the Committee is not in the Cardinal's pocket is to be there yourself, take the job. You can keep us all straight." He laughed again.

"I don't know, Brian. I've got the book to finish. A semester's not a long time. And the work of the Committee will go on even after the Conference meeting in November."

"When's that interview with the *Post*?" The question was sudden and seemingly unrelated.

"It's tomorrow. The reporter's coming to my office at two."

"Better watch yourself, John." Brian's tone was suprisingly serious. "You don't want any bad publicity before your book is even published. Especially now, with the Committee..."

He forced himself to look straight at Brian. "I haven't said I'd take on the Committee," he reminded him. "And anyway, I don't intend on saying anything controversial. I'll only be repeating pretty much what I said on television, just giving a straightforward account of some of the critical issues that face the Church."

Brian shook his head. "You're being naive, John. Koppel already had his juicy item—the excommunications. He just needed you for window dressing. It would have been bad form to try and trip up his own guest expert. But you're fair game in this situation. That reporter will be looking to stir up some trouble."

"Oh...I don't think so, Brian. She's a feature writer for their Style section. She sounded young and very nice on the phone. She'd seen the *Nightline* interview and heard about the book contract. I know it was checked out with my publisher before she even called me, and they wanted me to do it. I'm sure it'll be fine."

"Just remember, John, this *nice young girl* is a reporter. And it's not the kind of moderate position you intend to present, which will interest her. She'll be trying to make you take a position, looking for a way to stoke the rumors of a possible schism between the American Church and Rome. *That's* the kind of thing that sells newspapers."

"Maybe," he began, "but I just don't think Ms. Venée—"

"Venée!" Brian sat up straight in the chair. "Alexandra Venée?"

"Yes. Do you know her?"

Brian was looking at him strangely.

"Obviously you don't know, and you should always know your opponent, John." Then: "Your Ms. Venée is the niece of His Eminence."

"The reporter is Cardinal Camélière's niece?"

"His twin sister's child." Brian had relaxed back into his seat to better enjoy the effect of his revelation. "I've met the girl myself several times, and I know Phillip's very close to her." He smiled, pulling comfortably on his pipe. "She's quite a beauty. And independent, John. I don't think the fact that she's Phillip's niece will make a damn bit of difference in how she handles this story. So I say again, tread carefully."

"Yes . . . I will."

"And, John . . ." The blue eyes fixed him again, the Gaelic twinkle hardened to glass. "I have to know now, this afternoon. The position with the Committee. Will you take it?"

For a moment he hesitated. Truly he had no inclination to get involved. But he was a priest and his obligation was to serve willingly where he was most needed. His personal desires were hardly relevant to such a decision. This was his friend and superior who asked, and the man who surely knew him better than anyone. If Brian Donovan felt he could be of use . . .

"You win," he said at last with a sigh. "I'll do it."

Archbishop Giovanni Mantini, papal delegate to the United States, stretched out in the padded chair and drew deeply upon the fat cigar anchored between his teeth, his black pupilless eyes squinting through the blue haze of smoke that curled out from his mouth. He always lit up when he felt particularly satisfied with himself.

He straightened his back and retrieved the cigar, angling it in the long crystal ashtray made especially for cigar smokers. He reached now inside the pocket of his pants—a rather awkward effort for a short man who weighed well over two hundred pounds—and withdrew a large ring of keys. His stubby fingers plucked at the jangling mass until he found the key he was looking for, a slender gold one that would open the top left drawer of his desk.

He turned the key in the lock and slid open the drawer. Immediately he drove his arm deep into the recess, groping until his fingers clutched at the familiar object—a small leatherbound book. Opening it, he leafed through its pages, his eyes scanning what few had ever seen—the private telephone numbers of some of the most powerful men in the world.

His index finger stabbed at the page he wanted, and he wondered, not for the first time, how many even within the elite inner circle had this particular number. He smiled at the prospect that the group was no doubt very small. Then as quickly, his smooth round face cracked into a dark ugly scowl.

For all his power, for all of his talent for winning when the stakes were the highest, he still had not scaled the top. This telephone call, like all the others he had made over the long weeks, would go through another channel, filter through that single man who stood between Giovanni Mantini and the summit.

If he hated Cardinal Jean-Luc Flancon, this emotion had probably been spawned from the considerable envy he felt for the man who held the most privileged of ecclesiastical positions. And the sentiment was likely nurtured by the petty chauvinism that branded the tall aristocratic Frenchman as an outsider in a world that should have been the exclusive domain of Italians. But the real cause of that hard lump that sat uncompromisingly in the center of Giovanni Mantini's chest came from the cold realization that he must acknowledge, if but to himself, the absolute superiority of the papal secretary of state.

Yet he had done well and in the most difficult of times. Long ago he had realized that his appointment as Pro-Nuncio to the most powerful nation in the world had indeed been an enlightened pontifical decision. And he was convinced that he had done nothing since that contradicted the correctness of Rome's judgment. The red hat would surely not be long in coming.

It was still early morning in Rome. But he knew that Flancon was an early riser. He dialed the number and listened to the particular set of clicks that would ensure a direct connection. As always, he would ask to speak to His Holiness, and as always he would be told that His Holiness was unavailable. Of course, the Secretary of State would gladly relay any message to His Holiness. It had now become a little game between the two men. Archbishop Mantini salvaging a measure of pride; Secretary Flancon allowing him to do so. All the while each playing by those rules that kept the whole system afloat.

"Ad maiorem . . ." The Secretary's cool voice gave the code phrase.

"Dei gloriam."

"Yes, Archbishop Mantini. How may I be of service to Your Excellency?"

Mantini let the tight knuckle of anger pass. He had never fully analyzed why Flancon's recognition of his voice always gave him such an intense rush of displeasure. "Good morning, Your Eminence." He spoke in his most condescending tone. "I hoped that I might speak with His Holiness. I have some information which I believe the Holy Father would wish to hear."

"I am most sorry, Your Excellency, but His Holiness is unavailable. I would be most happy to convey your message to him."

"I hope that His Holiness is in good health."

"His Holiness is blessed with the best of health, Your Excellency. I will tell him of your kind interest."

"Yes, Your Eminence, please tell him that he is always in my prayers."

"Likewise, Your Excellency. Never does our Holy Father speak of Archbishop Mantini without concern for his Pro-Nuncio in Washington."

"I am most unworthy of His Holiness's concern, Your Eminence. Yet I am most humbly grateful that I am in his thoughts."

"And of what matter did you wish to speak to His Holiness?"
The game had ended.

"It concerns the *Lucifer* affair, Your Eminence."

"Yes." The word was quick and hard.

"The Leprechaun, it appears, is keeping to our schedule.
He called in today to report that the invitation to serve on the
Doctrine Committee has been issued to the Archangel. And
the priest has accepted, Your Eminence.... When will His
Holiness ask the Archangel to join *Lucifer?*" The question
was risky; it went too far.

"I cannot answer that, Archbishop Mantini."

"May the Holy Spirit guide His Holiness."

"And you. Good day, Your Excellency."

Cardinal Jean-Luc Flancon caressed the receiver for a
moment, staring at the web of blue veins across the surface of
his hand.

"So the Archangel has agreed to assist the Doctrine Committee?" Pope Stephen XI put down the extension phone.

"Yes..." Flancon's reply was little more than a whisper.
When he turned, the Pope was standing before him. "Yes,
Cesare." The secretary's voice had grown stronger, but he
looked away from the sad dark eyes.

"Jean-Luc..."

The Pope's thin urgent voice brought him back. "Do not
speak it, Your Holiness. Do not question..." Flancon's voice
trailed off as he lifted the pontiff's slender fingers to his lips.

Withdrawing his hand, the Pope patted his secretary on his
shoulder. "I know, Jean-Luc, I know we have no choice. Yet I
had hoped for another way."

"There is no other way, Cesare."

"I know." The Pope spoke softly, his delicate hands fluttering
in the air like small wings. "Perhaps I am no more than what
they first thought... a weak and frightened old man."

"You are not that... never have been. Everyone realizes
that now."

"Ah, now... at last. Oh, but how the Curia laughed behind
my back at first, made such a joke of my election. 'Poor
simple Cesare Sersone. Pope, you say. Hah, you mean
puppet... *our* puppet.'"

"But you showed them, Cesare...with your strength, your courage."

"It was but a small victory...we were all on the same side from the beginning." The Pope paused, lowering his head as if he suddenly had the need to examine his shoes. Then he looked up, his eyes once again pleading with the tall handsome man who stood before him. "Can she be saved, can this Church I love be saved, Jean-Luc?"

"If *Lucifer* goes well, we have a chance."

"Ah, *Lucifer*. Back to *Lucifer* again. One man's life is a small price to pay—eh, my dear friend. Shall we simply say that the end justifies the means?" His words bit sharply.

"But if that life is...unworthy?"

"I am not God, Jean-Luc! I don't want to judge Phillip Camélière!" The Pope was trembling now, his dark eyes unnaturally bright. He shook his head and passed a hand across his brow. "I'm sorry."

"You are His Holiness, Pope Stephen XI." Jean-Luc's voice was soft, measured, speaking gently as though to a child. "You are God's representative on this earth. Into your care was placed that Church founded by His only Son, that Church which was ordained to bring men to salvation and to carry them into eternal life. Do you wish to see all of this destroyed?"

"Oh..." The pontiff strangled upon the sound as he glanced up. Clearly it pained him to look upon this man who had become his strongest ally, his dearest friend. What did it exact of Jean-Luc Flancon to speak these words, to stand before him with such unwavering resolve, to chain himself to this absolute orthodoxy, when always in the past that noble mind had tested, explored, challenged? What thing had kept him from crossing over to the other side? "Jean-Luc, it is not easy for you."

"I have found the truth, Cesare. There are no more questions." Then more quietly: "I, too, love her...my Church."

"Yes..." The Pope moved away from his secretary and walked to stand before one of the large windows. He reached outward and pulled upon the latch. A warm wind billowed the heavy drapes into swollen scarlet sails. "Vanderveer gave me no choice. Excommunication was the only path left open to me. And now... the others... they will support him and the women... and it will not stop there... but go on and on... until..." He turned sharply, a movement that seemed to contradict his frailty. "Will the Archangel do this thing that we shall ask of him, Jean-Luc? Will John Leighton do it?"

CHAPTER FIVE

"Come on, Father Leighton. Aren't you being just a bit of a Pollyanna? Wouldn't you concede, in light of the very serious problems that divide the Church, that the unthinkable could happen—a schism between the North American Church and Rome?"

He stared at her. He had thought it was going well. Alexandra Venée had seemed much as he'd expected. But if Brian had been right about her beauty and intelligence, he had also been right in cautioning him against her. Their seemingly innocuous chat on the problems facing the Church had turned without warning into a kind of cross-examination, as she insisted rather abruptly that it was his own opinions on these troublesome moral issues that she wanted. And when he had patiently explained that his *personal* views were of little consequence, she had begun almost immediately to badger him about the possibility of an "all-out war" between the American bishops and the Vatican.

He was becoming angry, he realized, as he confronted her coldly expectant face. Angry at the hostility he felt directed at him personally. Why should she be so mad at *him*? Or was this only part of some professional technique to rattle him, to make him say something he would have held back upon more sober reflection?

She was still waiting. He took a deep breath and found his

usual calm returning. "Perhaps you might better ask Cardinal Camélière your questions about the likelihood of schism, Miss Venée," he said. "Your uncle's in a much better position to answer that than I."

The point had definitely struck home. He saw the dark pupils grow larger in the amber eyes.

"I assume you are making some kind of issue of the fact that I am the biological niece of Cardinal Phillip Camélière," she said with a frozen evenness. "I am a reporter, Father Leighton, a representative of the *Post*. My relationship to Cardinal Camélière is totally irrelevant to this interview with *you*, a self-proclaimed authority on the issues which affect the solidarity of the Church. Issues on which you, as a practicing theologian, might be expected to give an educated opinion..." She went on before he could reply: "However, since it is clear that we have reached a dead end, I'll ask you something else. Something which you may find easier to answer. Do you intend to accept the offer to serve on the secretariat of the Doctrine Committee of the National Conference of Catholic Bishops?"

For a moment he was simply relieved that his decision to join the Committee had indeed been made—glad to have something to which he could give a simple and unambiguous reply. And then he realized that the question was distinctly odd. How could Alexandra Venée have known that he'd even been asked to serve as a consultant to the Committee? He looked sharply at her and saw the realization dawn that she had betrayed herself, that her protestations of professional detachment had been a sham. Though it was marginally possible that she could have heard it elsewhere, her reaction confirmed his guess. The Cardinal had told her.

He smiled and saw spots of hot color deepen in her cheeks. "Yes, Miss Venée, I can give you an answer," he said mildly. "I have agreed to assist the Doctrine Committee in its work."

The interview went more smoothly after that.

I don't think you understand, Miss Venée. My book will *deal with these modern challenges, but it will not take sides.*

*It's meant to give some historical perspective on the issues
which will be dealt with at the conference. It's a guidebook, if
you will, for the concerned layman.*

The phone rang. Alexandra hit the pause switch on the
tape recorder, stopping John Leighton's carefully patient voice.
Rising from her seat behind the small desk, she moved
quickly to the sofa, collapsing into the oversized cushions in
time to catch the phone on the third ring.

"Hi, babe. Busy?" It was Frank's nightly call.

"Yes, but glad for a reprieve."

"Oh! Didn't it go well today?"

"As a headline it would read 'Girl Reporter Makes Total Ass
of Herself.'"

"That bad, huh." Frank chuckled. "Want to tell me about
it?"

"I just blew it. No objectivity. I don't know... I've had
trouble getting the proper distance on this project from day
one. It's like I have some hidden agenda, some ax to grind
with this poor guy. And I don't know why. Dammit!"

"So you're human just like the rest of us."

"But I'm a reporter. Or supposed to be."

"Yeah. Well, we're human, too. Or did you think otherwise."

"Oh, I know. But I was just so... unprofessional. And he
was really very nice. Not out for publicity or a fast buck. I
was totally wrong about that. But I just kept pushing him.
It was almost as if I wanted to make him as angry as I was.
As if I wanted to drag him down, to make him be that person
I had thought he was. And then the worst..."

"Well, what? Come on, Alex, it can't be that awful."

"He knew I was Cardinal Camélière's niece. Frank, you
know how sensitive I am about that. It was the worst thing he
could have said."

"Yeah, and..."

"Well, I very coolly informed him that my biological relationship... I actually said 'biological,' Frank. I was being
so fucking technical."

Frank laughed. "Sorry. But it *is* funny, baby. I can just hear
you up on that New Orleans high horse. So, go on."

"I told him that being Cardinal Camélière's niece had nothing whatever to do with my position as a reporter, or with the present interview. I let him know in no uncertain terms that the one thing had no bearing on the other."

"So?"

"I thought it was true. That's the horrible thing."

"What happened, Alex?"

"I asked him if he was going to accept the post he'd been offered with the Doctrine Committee. He realized right away from whom I must have learned that little piece of inside information. I saw him realize it, and he saw me seeing it. I've never been so humiliated."

"Alex, Alex, Alex!" Frank's voice was mildly exasperated. "Your skin is gorgeous, my love. But it's too damn thin. As you keep repeating, as if maybe you don't believe it, you *are* a reporter. You have contacts. You have sources. So what if one of them happens to be your very powerful uncle? That's just your good luck."

"But I want to stand on my own. You should understand that."

"Why? Grow up, Alex. None of us stands alone. I've had help. We all have. It's called the old-boy—excuse me, the old-*person* network." The humor had returned. "Anyway, you know what I'm talking about."

"Yes. I know. But I wouldn't ever like to think I *used* people to get what I want."

"Maybe you're in the wrong profession."

"That sounds so cynical."

"It isn't cynicism to take help that's freely offered. And look, you'd still love your uncle, you'd still have a good relationship with him, even if he had no influence, wouldn't you?"

"Yes, of course."

"That's it, then. Your reaction to him as a person would be the same. That's the difference between *using* in the bad sense, and just taking advantage of a fortunate situation."

She couldn't answer at once.

"You still there, Alex?"

"Yes . . . and Frank?"

"Uh-huh."

"How'd you get so smart?"

He laughed. "God, I wish I had this on tape. It's just the years, babe. Unless you're plain hopeless, they teach you something. You'll see."

"I'm twenty-six, Frank. It's just seven years difference."

"They're seven big ones. And I'm a man." It was a deliberate provocation.

"Oh no, you don't." She smiled. "I'm not taking *that* bait. I've got a story to salvage tonight."

"Go to it, then. I'll check in tomorrow."

"I never got around to asking about your day."

"The headline would read 'Boy Reporter Goes to Bed Horny. High Hopes for Weekend.'"

"Good night, Frank."

"Good night, Alex." He was laughing as he hung up.

She replaced the receiver carefully in its cradle and was still for a moment, looking at nothing. Then she went back to the desk, pulling a manila folder from one of the drawers. Inside was the press kit from Leighton's publisher. She should be able to use the picture with the feature she was writing. Her own photographer had gotten sidetracked and missed the interview.

John Leighton's face in glossy black-and-white looked up at her from the publicity still. The photograph captured the movie-star handsomeness but not that inner quality that had come through on television, and even more strongly as he sat across from her today. She struggled to define it. What was it about him exactly that made her believe in his essential innocence?

"Blessed are the peacemakers"—the familiar phrase rose almost as an answer in her mind. And she relaxed, feeling her frown of concentration softening to a smile. She had the title for her feature. "Blessed Are the Peacemakers." It wouldn't be the attention-grabbing piece she had envisioned, and certainly after her performance today, there would be little chance of having John Leighton agree to be her source for future stories tied to the Conference. But the interview could still make a very nice feature, a nice contrast to the more extreme items that had been surfacing since the excommunications. She looked again at the picture on her desk and her smile broadened. Yes, she would do a very nice piece on Father John Leighton. She owed him that at least.

The room was dark except for the faint light coming from a small lamp. His tall body made a long thin shadow upon the wall as he walked from the chair to a far corner to pour himself another brandy. Phillip Camélière rolled the caramel-colored liquid around the glass. Breathing deeply, he closed his eyes and sipped. For a long moment he held his head back, savoring the taste, reminiscing.

From the very first day of his appointment to the archdiocese, Phillip knew that he would be unable to live in the drab little apartment fitted out for him on the second floor of the Pastoral Center. He had never been strong on the virtue of poverty, not even at a pretense of it. But more critical to him was his privacy. Living *on the premises*, as it were, made it impossible to isolate himself from the petty bureaucratic grind of the archdiocese. So one of his first tasks had been relieving himself of the cumbersome job of administration—a responsibility he happily surrendered to his chancellor, Monsignor Beatty. A strategy that also freed him to do those things he judged to be really important. Then, out of his personal funds, he built a separate residence, a lovely Georgian mansion nestled among the trees on the large tract of Maryland land that surrounded the Pastoral Center.

He turned now and looked about the study. It was his favorite room, filled with his favorite things. He memorized its precious image, friendly and safe. Like an old tintype, it seemed at this moment yellowed and indistinct in the soft golden glow of the single lamp. He moved out of the shadows and walked about silently, the glass still held in one hand, touching, caressing those objects that had come to mean so much to him—an ancient netsuke, a porcelain vase, his books. He stopped before a chest and gazed down. He smiled at the faces looking up at him—his grandparents, his mother and father on their wedding day, Margaret at sixteen, at thirty . . . Alexandra. They were all there, enshrined in the beautiful old frames he had so carefully chosen—all there, all the people he loved.

He reached out and took one of the pictures—a photograph of Margaret and him taken on the day of his ordination. He ran his thumb over Margaret's delicate features, the fall of golden blond hair. He was in profile, smiling into his sister's face. She had tried to get him to be serious but he had been hopeless that day. He studied his twenty-five-year-old face—noting the decidedly square jaw, the high cheekbones above deep hollows, the straight nose. It was an almost too-thin face, made up of too many angles. Yet it was miraculously saved from severity by slanting gray eyes that crinkled in laughter, and a mouth already practiced in that now famous smile. He noticed his black hair tumbling rakishly across his brow, and had an instant memory of Margaret's hand passing against his forehead to smooth it.

He squinted and tried to recall where he had so recently seen such a face, a face somehow reminiscent of his twenty-five-year-old one. The image had been on videotape, played out on a flat two-dimensional television screen. But the man being interviewed, laughing, showing off the handsome outline of his well-defined profile, had been anything but two-dimensional. He had never before noticed Father John Leighton's resemblance to him in his younger days.

He sipped the brandy, thinking how successful John Leighton had been until now in shutting himself away in his ivory tower. Keeping himself pure, unsullied. But now Donovan had convinced the priest to serve on the Doctrine Committee. A real victory considering Leighton's abilities and his reputation for avoiding controversy. His prophesy to Alex had come true—John Leighton would indeed now have to move his noncommittal ass off the fence. He smiled, recalling how effectively the priest had handled Koppel. He wondered how his niece had fared.

He turned his back on the cache of photographs and walked across the room to stretch out upon the couch. He closed his eyes, allowing his mind to drift back to his privileged youth . . . to New Orleans a thousand lifetimes ago.

Everyone had been surprised when he had decided upon the priesthood after graduation from Tulane. A move mysterious to everyone except himself. The Church was to be his salvation—his salvation from himself. Perhaps it had been as far back as that day when he was nine years old and had persuaded Danny Humphries and Billy LeClerque to steal Cary Beason's bike, that he first became aware of his terrible power. It had been a masterpiece of manipulation. Danny and Billy finally being convinced of the absolute moral rectitude of their actions.

From then on it had all been so easy.

Then, on the day of his twenty-second birthday, amid the celebration, he quietly and inwardly acknowledged for the first time a sincere and precise fear of himself. With an almost detached consciousness he analyzed the causes and effects of this growing discomfort, and with a characteristic certainty he came to a decision that would forever alter the circumstances, if not the substance, of his life.

Never once did he consider another path, another way. The choice was immediately and absolutely obvious to him— the Church of his misspent youth would save him from himself. That sweetest Most Holy Mother Church would strip him naked, force him into a life of humility and sacrifice, whip him into submission, form his conscience, bend his will for good. Yet on that fateful day of his twenty-second year of life, he did not know that his Roman church would fail him, did not understand that he would ultimately be left to himself in a system that would allow him to manipulate in God's name, in an institution that would eventually make him a *prince*.

He was first made an assistant pastor under old Father Bordeleon in the distinctly Cajun parish of St. Gabriel, though his actual assignment was the pastoral care of a small south Louisiana mission, an impoverished settlement strung out along the bayou. He found that he was almost instantly happy there, at peace among the moss-haired oaks and silent-running waters of the bayous. His pontifical degrees

suddenly seemed a bit of cumbersome baggage. There were
more basic tasks than the teaching of dogma that needed his
fine Catholic priest's touch. But his people were a distant and
stubborn lot. Going to Mass on Sunday, receiving the sacra-
ments were not common practices and, if done at all, were
acts wholly left to the women. The birth of a child, a desire to
get married, a death—these might bring some of them to
him. But most often in the small makeshift hovel of a church,
he faced empty pews on Sunday mornings.

So the fundamental hardware of Roman Catholicism was
put on the shelf for a time, and Phillip Camélière forgot
that he was a priest, and remembered that first and foremost
he was a man. He loosened his Roman collar and took to
visiting. Most often he went in the interval between day and
night when the whining of the cicadas beat against the thick
warm bayou air. He would take a seat on the porch, spreading his legs comfortably, and accept a mug of the blackest
coffee he had ever seen, all the time struggling to make
sense of the curious mixture of Cajun French and English
he was automatically expected to understand. Once in a
while they asked his opinion on something, and he answered
honestly, but never too honestly, remembering that most
often people wanted to be told what they wanted to hear.
Soon they were arguing among themselves at whose house
he would be having dinner the next time he came down the
bayou, or who would carry him catfish so that Father
Bordeleon's old Negro could fry up a batch for the two men
for supper.

At first he had traveled back and forth from St. Gabriel's
rectory to the bayou, the priest's house at the mission being
little more than a shack. Then one morning as he drove up
the winding dirt road to the house to get some things he
stored there between visits, he saw them—like a swarm of
bees, hammering and sawing and painting. They thought
that he would like to stay the night once in a while. He
smiled, and rolling up his sleeves, he said he thought that
was a good idea, and wondered why he hadn't thought of it
himself. It wasn't too long before the poor excuse of a

church also bore the brunt of their hammers and saws and paintbrushes.

And so it was that the people of the bayou began to trust and like Father Phillip Camélière, and slowly, very slowly, in twos and threes, they came at last to hear him say Mass on Sunday in that little church they had worked so hard to fix.

He observed the brandy snifter now, balanced upon his chest, rising and falling with the slow measured intake and release of his breath.

A deep sigh, and . . .

He slept upon the still and silent waters of the bayou. His shoulder slumped, his arm trailing like a dead man's over the edge of the pirogue into the murky thick depths. He jerked up, startled into wakefulness by a sharp nibble upon his fingers.

He cradled the injured hand, sucking at the small tear in his skin, all the while attempting to steady the now rocking boat. Then, above the lap-lap-lapping of the water . . . a new sound. Soft low laughter. He grasped the sides of the boat, and searching the tangled growth of trees, he spied a ghost of movement behind one of the cypresses. He half raised his body, straining to see what was now no more than the languid sounds of the bayou, to see what was only the same familiar sleepy landscape. Then . . .

A splash! He twisted around, his eyes catching but the foamy edges of whirlpooling waves. And then she was there, inches away from him, half-submerged, her dark hair like black ribbons swimming around her face. Her white dress pressed wet and rumpled across her breast, so that there were wrinkles of cloth and tantalizing stretches of skin showing smooth and dusky beneath the thin fabric. He reached over the edge of the boat.

In a moment her hand was in his, grasping, pulling him into the water. He heard her laughter as he finally floated upward into a spume of brown bubbles. But when he was able to focus, her face had grown solemn and he watched her run her tongue across the space between her nose and upper lip, thinking that it was very much like something a child would do. He saw that her dark eyes glistened too brightly, and he couldn't tell if she were crying or if the water sliding from her hair fell into her eyes. He reached out and touched her lower lip. Her small pink tongue made a tiny wet circle around the ball of his finger. Then she stopped, as though waiting for something more he might do.

His mouth opened before it closed over hers. Then he brushed past her lips, needing to find the small throbbing pulse in her throat, needing to convince himself that she was real, that she was truly there with him in the warm sucking water. He pulled away so that he could look at her. But she pushed quickly backward, the oval of her face, like a bright moon, floating away from him.

He fought against her escape. Pressing himself forward, he grasped her ankles, bringing her back hard against him. Gliding his body between the parting curve of her legs, he could feel her warmth pulling at him beneath the rising white billow of her dress. A shot of bright light in his head, and he was like the limitless formless water swirling about him... flowing into her....

The glass crashed to the floor.

He sat up and looked down at the dark liquid pooling like blood across the edge of the rug, shards of glass like crystal daggers shimmering upon the polished floor. He passed one palm across his brow, hoping to erase the dull ache forming in the middle of his forehead.

It was the large painting that finally brought him back to himself. Drawn by the bright splashes of color, the raised dabs of oil, he walked across the room. For a moment he just stood staring before the broad canvas, and then reaching out, he grasped the edge of the frame. The painting swung forward and his fingers fell on the cool metal of the lock, working the combination, spinning, rotating, until he heard a dull rewarding click.

For an instant he had the wild desire to slam the painting back against the gray innocuous face of the safe. But the moment passed and he pulled open the small door. His hand plunged into the dark eye within the wall, feeling about until he found what he wanted. Soft and rubbery, and cold. In the half darkness he saw the sparkle of small glassy eyes opening, and heard the sad ragged whimper of *ma-ma* float across the stillness of the room. His hand trembled as he touched the short brown curls, a single dark lock clinging tenaciously about one finger.

"Angelique," he whispered to the doll cradled within his arm. "Angelique . . . ?"

CHAPTER SIX

Alex wrapped the large towel around her and walked into the living room, a trail of wet footprints glistening in her wake. She stared at the white telephone, resting undemandingly on the small end table at the edge of the sofa. No, it hadn't rung. The room was almost silent. Absently, she glanced down to her feet and saw that a small pool of water had begun to collect on the shiny hardwood floor. She looked up again at the telephone.

No, it was something else about the phone that had pulled her out of her bath. The memory of an earlier conversation with Father John Leighton. She could almost hear his voice now—low and soft, as if it were being filtered through something and had to travel a great distance to find her. It was a different voice than the one he had used in the interview. But then her approach this morning had been different. . . .

"Father Leighton." Her fingers gripped the phone tighter, "This is Alexandra Venée." She covered the mouthpiece and took in a deep breath and exhaled.

"Oh, Ms. Venée. How nice to hear from you. You must have read my mind. I was going to call you. I want to thank you. The article . . ." He stopped short and Alex sensed that he was suddenly embarrassed.

"I'm glad you liked it, Father Leighton." She responded to

his unfinished thought, sparing him the agony of paying himself a compliment.

"You are a good writer, Ms. Venée." His voice was surer now that the topic of conversation had switched from subject to author.

"Thank you, Father Leighton. I had good material to work with." She brought the focus back to him, unwilling to let him off the hook completely. Then she laughed.

"Ms. Venée . . . is there something . . ."

"*Wrong?* No, Father Leighton, everything is just perfect. It's just that . . ." She paused for a moment, not really certain that she should be saying what she was about to say. Then: "It's just that if you could have seen me before I made this call. I must have picked up and put down the receiver at least a dozen times. You see, Father Leighton, I was just a little bit, shall we say, unsure about the reception I would get when I phoned."

Now he laughed. "Ms. Venée, you are to be congratulated. You are far braver than I. The last time I put down the receiver this morning in an abortive attempt to call you, I didn't pick it up again. I confess *I* am the coward."

"Well, then you won't have the courage to refuse."

"*Refuse?*"

"My proposition, Father Leighton . . ."

She reached out now and lightly touched the phone. Like a talisman it felt comforting and safe against her fingers. Yes, she told herself as she caressed the receiver's smooth cool surface, she had finally connected with John Leighton. She glanced up at the clock: 1:00. She was going to be late if she didn't hurry. She dropped the towel to the floor and mopped up the puddle of water. *Damn, I can't be late. Not now when things are going so well.*

It was just before 2:00 when she parked on a side street off Connecticut Avenue and checked her lipstick in the overhead mirror. She would make it. The restaurant was just up the block. Instinctively she reached for her briefcase. No, not this time. This was going to be just a nice friendly chat over coffee. Small talk with John Leighton. No script, no tape recorder. No business transacted this afternoon, except for that one small favor she had to ask of him. She hid her briefcase under the floor mat.

Opening the door, she got out and smoothed the freshly made folds in her straight skirt. *Cotton*, she cursed under her breath. Natural, cool, and comfortable... and wrinkles like hell. She slammed the door and checked to see that it was locked. She looked around—good neighborhood, but she'd learned long ago that bad things sometimes happen in good neighborhoods. She wasn't taking any chances.

As she walked up the street she wondered in which of the Connecticut Avenue apartment buildings John Leighton lived. She guessed he had just leased a place from the way he had talked this morning. What had he called himself—a refugee from Curley Hall? Curley Hall? Probably a residence for priests on the CU campus. Well, he could certainly afford his own place. The grapevine had it that Father Leighton's advance from his publisher was more than liberal.

When she entered the restaurant, she spotted him almost immediately, and he stood as she walked toward the table. She saw that he had on some kind of knit shirt and a pair of faded jeans. Yes, this was a different John Leighton from the one she had interviewed.

"Father Leighton." She took his hand. "I hope I haven't kept you waiting."

"No, I was early." He was drawing the chair back so that she could sit. "I hope you like coffee. I took the liberty and ordered a pot."

"Thank you. The reporter's legal drug... caffeine." She heard him laughing behind her, then watched as he sat down again and began to pour her a cup.

"Cream? Sugar?" He waited to slide the coffee toward her.

"Black as sin, Father Leighton." She let the words slip out and saw that he stared at her. "A joke, Father..." she said, trying to recover.

He smiled. "I'm sorry." He looked down into his coffee. "I... I..." He suddenly seemed self-conscious.

"Father Leighton . . ."

"Please"—he laughed—"it's my fault. I have a habit of doing this to myself. Letting my mind play strange tricks."

"Strange tricks, Father?" She saw that his dark hair fell across his brow, and for one wild instant she wanted to reach out and smooth it.

"You know . . . imagine things about people." He was looking at her again.

"Yes . . ." It was the only word she could manage.

"Just a moment ago . . . when you said 'black as sin,' I was imagining what kinds of sins Alexandra Venée could possibly have committed."

It wasn't what she had expected him to say. It was too intimate, too direct. Yet almost instantly she realized that those strange mind tricks of his were totally innocent, were nothing more than simple curiosity. If there was anything like a pass in Father Leighton's words, it was only in her mind.

He was still looking at her intensely. "For most of my life"—she made her voice matter-of-fact—"my sins were sins of omission. Now, Father Leighton . . ." She smiled, letting it hang.

"Please . . ." He paused as if he were again unsure of himself. "Please call me John."

She didn't respond immediately, but her eyes moved down from his face to his long slender fingers pressing against the sides of his coffee cup. Then she looked up, smiling again. "And please call me Alex."

"And now . . . *Alex*"—he spoke her name deliberately—"what is this proposition you have to make?"

"It concerns the upcoming Bishops Conference and your position with the Doctrine Committee."

"What about my position with the committee?" He spoke cautiously now as he sat up straighter in his chair.

"I just think you have the perfect vantage point." She tried to keep her voice light.

"For what, Ms. Ve—Alex?"

"For seeing the Conference inside out." She could see that he wanted her to go on, that he didn't want to commit himself until he had heard everything she had to say. "I want to cover the Conference, John." His name seemed to stick in her throat.

"Cover the Conference?"

"Yes, front-page stuff—the hard news, day-by-day, minute-by-minute. If this thing's going to explode, I want to be there." She heard the excitement in her voice, and when she looked at his face, she saw that his eyes had grown more serious.

"John . . ." She almost reached out and grasped his hand. "What happens this November at the Conference affects not just Catholics, but anyone who gives a damn about people. These questions that are being raised by the American bishops are not just religious issues, but social and moral ones. And I want to make sure that those who care, even those who don't but should, get the clearest, most objective picture possible of what is happening." She stopped short, afraid she might be saying too much.

"And you want me to help you present that clear objective picture?"

Unlike the interview, there was no defensiveness in his voice, and this time she did reach out and cover his hand with hers. "Yes," she said, "you are on the inside. You will be where it's all happening, at the center. And I want you to feed me what I need to know. Be my expert eyes and ears. No opinions, no interpretation. I promise. All I want from you are the facts." Suddenly she looked down and saw her hand curled about his wrist, and for a moment there was the pleasant sensation of his rapid pulse against her fingertips. She pulled her hand away. "I'm sorry. . . ."

"Don't apologize. I understand your need to tell the truth. To write so that others may understand clearly what is happening. I am doing the same thing in my book . . . if you remember. . . ." He allowed his voice to trail off, and it seemed that he was almost sorry for his last comment.

"Yes, I know." She laughed. His remark had not slipped by her. Yet he had failed to understand that she had needed to apologize not for her over-zealousness but for reaching out and taking his hand into hers. Obviously he had been totally unaware that she had even touched him. "Will you help me, John?"

"I don't know that I can, Alex. You know, technically I'm not on the Doctrine Committee. I'm to serve on the secretariat, as a consultant. I don't even know the protocol for admission of the press at the NCCB. I don't even know if there will be any open sessions."

"I have it from a reliable source that the press will be welcomed on the floor and at the committee hearings."

He laughed, then fixed her with a wide grin. "And I don't suppose you're going to tell me who your source is?"

"You know I don't have to do that." She returned his grin. She knew that he knew who her source was, but he wasn't about to hear it from her. "Well, Father John Leighton, are you going to help me?"

"I'll have to check it out with Monsignor Donovan." He spoke almost dismissively. "And . . ."

"Well?"

"If Donovan gives the okay, I'll help you in any way I can . . . Alexandra."

He had drawn out her name, and if she didn't know better, she would have sworn now that John Leighton was flirting with her.

The force of his orgasm woke him. The dream came with such steady frequency that John had long ago learned that neither nightly meditation nor lingering guilt was any bar against its recurrence. And so he lay tonight, clammy in the narrow bed, staring into blackness, listening to the harsh rhythms of his own breathing, fighting to restore his hard-won acceptance that this was something which he could not control.

In another moment the breaths slowed to quietness but the dream feeling remained in force, image and sensation clinging to his mind like fog. This time it had been different. Though the body beneath him had been as yielding and warm as always, the face, softened in the aftermath of passion, was not her face. Not Brigit's face...but Alexandra Venée's.

CHAPTER SEVEN

Monsignor Brian Donovan watched the backs of his fellow clerics as they filed in a single unbroken line from the room, past Tony Campesi's desk, into the hall and out of view. A burst of laughter and Donovan focused his eyes on its source. Phillip Camélière was standing just inside the outer office patting Auxiliary Bishop Estevez on the back. The bishop seemed to have found something that his superior had said extremely funny. But then, Donovan thought, couldn't His Eminence charm the proverbial birds out of the trees. All except this old bird, he thought, smiling to himself.

When was it that he had begun to distrust Phillip Camélière? The first time that he had witnessed the man's manipulation of a situation to get what he wanted? Or used someone to his advantage? Oh, the man was good. A master of the game. And rarely, if ever, was he held suspect. Always he remained the brilliant, the exquisitely polished, charming, and benevolent Cardinal Camélière. But Donovan had seen through the clever charade. It takes one to know one. He tolerated the self-accusation.

History was full of men like Phillip Camélière, he thought. What name had the Renaissance given to them? Enlightened despots? Machiavellian princes? Whatever the label, the bottom line was that for Phillip Camélière, as for those cunning foxes who came before him, power was the supreme aphrodisiac.

But distrust was never hate. So when was it that his very well-grounded misgivings had turned into something else? When was it that he had begun to hate Phillip Camélière? That wasn't so difficult to answer. He could still see Mantini's little monkey eyes boring into him, hear the heavily accented voice slink out of his mouth like a viper. *And do you know what I have here, Monsignor Donovan?* The Pro-Nuncio waved the sheet of paper before him like a flag. *The list for Rome. The nominations for new bishops. And do you know whose name is absent? And do you know who removed your name from this list?*

He closed his eyes, shaking his head as if trying to dislodge cobwebs from his brain. The past, he reminded himself, all in the past. This is now.

"A penny for your thoughts, Monsignor Donovan."

He opened his eyes and saw Phillip Camélière standing in front of him. "Not for sale, Your Eminence."

"That's what I like best about you, Brian. You are one of the very few people who don't always give me what I want. You are still somewhat of a challenge."

"I suppose I have been paid a compliment, Phillip, and properly I should thank you."

The Cardinal laughed, walking toward the double doors leading into his private office. "I'm glad you're on my side, Brian. You would make a formidable opponent. Tony, the monsignor and I are going to have a little chat and don't want to be disturbed." He had his hand on the door, pushing it open so that they could enter.

"And how do you think it went this morning?" Phillip had seated himself behind his large desk and was leaning back in his chair.

Donovan observed that the gray eyes had grown especially luminous, as if lit from within, lit by the same energy that was powering the complex piece of machinery that was Phillip's brain. He knew that there was no need for him to reply. The question was innocuous. Phillip had already assessed

the merits of this morning's meeting. "Very well." He spoke
confidently. "I think the meeting went very well."

"So do I." The Cardinal had moved forward just a bit in his
chair. "I think our strategy to keep the early focus on those
issues where there is greatest consensus is the best tactic.
This will certainly enable us to get whatever we want later on
down the road. Open in unity. Create a feeling of solidarity in
the beginning so that no one will dare balk when the going
gets tough. Not a single bishop, not even those in the
Kirkpatrick crowd, will want to appear a traitor to the cause."

Donovan noted Phillip's special emphasis on the last word.
"Agreed," he said. "Ordination for women, tied into the
Conference's support of Vanderveer's actions, and the celibacy
issue should establish that united front we need. There are
few American bishops now who don't see the reasonableness
of ordaining women and abolishing celibacy."

"Ah, Brian." Phillip leaned back again in his chair and took
a deep breath. "We certainly have come a long way. I can still
remember when some of our more enlightened European
brothers laughed behind our backs. The Pope's lackeys we
were then. And Rome all the while getting richer off of
American dollars. Oh, American bishops were properly liberal on all the right social issues, but on doctrine, personal
morality... Not an inch would we budge from the Vatican
line." He had shifted forward again, folding his hands neatly
upon his desk. "We were always very good at dealing with
the concerns of the masses, Brian. Their plight was anonymous
enough. It was the intricacies of individual conscience that
made us uncomfortable."

"But that is all changing now." Donovan spoke confidently.
"If everything goes as planned, we'll get more than female
ordination and optional celibacy out of this conference. Birth
control, divorce, homosexuality—all of these issues will have
to be addressed."

"I'm afraid the Roman Church has never liked sex very
much, Brian." Phillip laughed. "But perhaps our old American boys have softened up a bit." Then, inexplicably, his face
grew serious. "Yet not a single bishop will ultimately go
against his conscience."

Donovan shifted in his chair, uncrossing his legs. This sudden tentativeness on Phillip's part was a new twist. But nothing this man did was without calculation. "Surely, Phillip" —he had raised his guard and forced his voice to sound almost complacent—"you don't foresee crises of conscience for most of the bishops. Certainly we're past that point. Perhaps just a little shifting of perspective will be necessary for some."

"Yes, Brian, a little shifting of perspective." Phillip's voice seemed to drift off. Then instantly his gray eyes focused hard, and his words came out sharp and clear. "The Conference cannot fail."

"And so we break with Rome?"

"Rome will never accept what we are about to do. If separation is the only way to get what we want, then separation it is. Besides..." He laughed softly. "I don't think we'll stand alone for long. You know as well as I that the Vanderveer coalition has been holding its collective breath hoping for our support. The Northern Europeans have been waiting a long time for us to catch up with them, although I still consider them light-years ahead of us doctrinally. And lest we forget the Latin bishops... They'll jump on our bandwagon soon enough. They need our money."

"Do we risk schism to secure what is best for the American Church, or what is best for His Eminence Phillip Cardinal Camélière?" He made it sound almost like a joke. Yet it was the first time he had dared speak the truth.

"My dear Monsignor." There was the barest trace of sarcasm in Phillip's tone. "I don't see that there is any difference."

The words hung in the air. Then Donovan saw something flash behind the gray eyes. And for an instant he had the bizarre notion that Phillip knew, knew that he, Donovan, was betraying him. Then the moment passed, and he watched as Phillip rose easily from behind his desk and began to walk distractedly about the office.

"Technically speaking, I don't see any problem getting proposals passed intact out of the Doctrine Committee," Donovan said at last. "It's when they are thrown onto the floor that we may have a bit of trouble."

"And that is where your friend John Leighton comes in."
Phillip spoke behind him, and he found that he had to turn
somewhat awkwardly in his chair to see his face. "John will
have to do his homework," Phillip continued, "present the
scriptural imperative for what we do, clothe the issues in
language that will be acceptable to everyone sitting in that
assembly hall. I control the committee chairmen, but I do not
control the Conference. If there are floor fights in general
session, things could degenerate, get nasty."

"Especially if Kirkpatrick can marshal the support he claims."

"Mantini certainly knows how to pick them."

"Mantini?"

"Monsignor Donovan, I gave you more credit. Don't you
know that Kirkpatrick is the Vatican's boy?"

"No, I didn't." His voice was soft. "I actually thought he
believed in what he was doing."

"But he does, Brian. Yet it is very convenient that his
conscience just happens to follow the party line. Mantini has
been grooming our reactionary Bishop Kirkpatrick for quite
some time in the fine art of sabotage."

"I didn't know. . . ."

"That's all right, Brian." He patted Donovan's shoulder.
"It's impossible for everyone to know everything in this dirty
little war we're fighting. Now, let's get back to Leighton. Can
he do the job for us?" Phillip was moving away to seat himself
once more behind his desk.

"He's perfect, Phillip. To Rome, John looks like a moderate. But philosophically, he's really on our side. He might
hate our methods, but his conscience will force him to write
what he believes. And once we get what we need from him,
he'll have no control over how it's used."

Phillip smiled. "And with John Leighton on staff, no one
will be able to claim that the Doctrine Committee is in my
pocket."

"Exactly. And everything's got to at least look on the
up-and-up."

"I've done nothing wrong, Brian."

It was a simple direct statement. But he didn't understand
why Phillip had even said it. He knew that Phillip Camélière

didn't in any way feel the need to justify himself to Brian
Donovan. Just another of the Cardinal's clever ploys? No,
instinctively he knew that wasn't right. And that rankled him
the most. For despite all that he knew, all that he suspected,
he believed what Phillip Camélière had said. Believed that
he had done nothing wrong, because at rock bottom he knew
that Phillip Camélière believed it.

"Good to see you back, Miss Venée." The garage attendant
gave her his big white-toothed smile as she got out of the car.
"You have a nice vacation in New Orleans?"

"Yes, I did, Joseph. But I've been back in town since last
week working at home. Today's just sort of my *official* return." She handed him a dollar. "I'm not sure how long I'll
be, so don't park it too high up. Okay?"

"Don't you worry, Miss Venée. You get a hot story, we'll get
you outta here real fast." He chuckled, settling himself
behind the wheel of the Toyota.

"I'll count on it."

Smiling, she walked west and swung down Sixteenth Street.
A big jet just taken off from National roared overhead, and
she stopped to watch its climb. She felt good and wondered
at this sudden elation. No not sudden, she realized. She'd
been feeling this way since...when? Since her meeting
yesterday with John Leighton? She shrugged off the thought,
turning into the alley that ran alongside the Russian embassy
and on through to the loading area behind the building that
housed the paper. It was rumored that the Russians had
chosen this rather unorthodox site because the elevation here
gave their microwave equipment a clear shot at intercepting
White House communications. Frank maintained that the
real purpose was to make it easier to intercept the communications at the *Post*—a far more reliable source of information.

She moved along briskly under the gaze of the forbidding
wired windows. Behind them she could sense the hidden
cameras tracking relentlessly the comings and goings of the
alley's patrolling pigeons. Quite deliberately she stopped and
for a long moment simply stood staring upward. Very slowly
she began to stick out her tongue till it curled almost to meet

her nose, and crossed her eyes outrageously. Then, turning casually away, she continued on unhurriedly past the grim stone building. In the loading yard she stopped, bent over, shaking her head, holding back the laughter. She had to get hold of herself.

Deliberately she forced herself to concentrate on what she planned to say to Murray. This whole thing was going to be delicate. She really didn't want to hurt Beverly. The Style editor had been great. But this was her career, after all, and she had to go after the kind of work that would keep her excited about her job—keep that edge that made a good reporter.

She walked around to the staff entrance and took the elevator to the fifth floor. The bright open spaces and high energy of the newsroom surged out at her as the doors opened, and she smiled, glad to be back, eager now for her encounter with Murray. She went to her desk, waving a brief hello to Will Carmichael two cubicles over.

Beverly was nowhere in sight. That was good. She wanted to talk to Murray first. The message-waiting light glowed red on her console, and she hit the key for display. *You can do it* popped to life on the screen. She smiled. Frank must have come in this morning. She leaned back in the chair, staring at the message. She admired Frank. Behind all the kidding lay a deep respect for his work. In many ways, since their unlikely relationship had begun, she had modeled herself on him as a reporter. *You can do it*. She left the words on the screen as she rose. A silent mantra.

Murray was in his office—one of the cluttered windowed cages on the periphery of the newsroom that housed exotic types like associate managing editors. Oh, well, Alex sighed under her breath as she tapped on the door.

"Come in, Alex." Murray glanced at her over his shoulder. After two years on the paper, the insecure child in her was still sometimes surprised that people like Murray knew her name, while the feminist part speculated if indeed it was only her pretty face that anyone found memorable. He motioned her to sit down as he swung around in his chair, the phone pasted to his ear.

She hadn't realized he was on the phone. Bad timing? she wondered, taking a seat in front of the work-piled desk. But he gave her his biggest smile and made a face at the receiver as he picked up his cigarette. "Yeah, Mike, hang with it," he said into the phone, inhaling. "Okay, okay. Talk to you Thursday then. And don't let the bastard stonewall you." He blew out an enormous cloud of smoke as he hung up. "Back from vacation, Alex? New Orleans, wasn't it?"

"Yes. A family visit."

He nodded. "So, what can I do for you? By the way," he added before she had had a chance to respond, "that takeout of yours this Sunday on the priest . . . nice piece."

"Thank you . . . Murray," she began slowly, "that's what I wanted to see you about." His face was still open, expectant. "I'd like to be assigned the coverage on the NCCB in November," she said quickly. "This same Father Leighton will be working with the Doctrine Committee, and if he can get an okay, he's agreed to act as my source." She waited.

"I see. And what does Beverly say about this?"

Alex forced herself not to look down. "I came to you first."

"You want to work on National permanently?"

"Yes."

Murray was nodding his head. "You're good, Alex. You're a good Style writer." He paused, puffing furiously on the over-worked cigarette.

Inwardly she sighed. He was going to pat her on the head and send her back where she belonged, doing features on visiting celebs and the First Lady's favorite designer. But he went on.

"And you're rare in that you can bring that same flair to a hard story without trivializing or cheapening it. I read those pieces you did on the voodoo cults in New Orleans back when you were hired."

"Then you'll give me the coverage?"

Murray attempted another hard drag, then crushed the butt into a crowded ashtray. "Alex, there's a problem with that."

Now she did look down, making herself take a long easy breath before she spoke. She knew exactly what he was talking about. Her best chance was to face what was coming head on. "You're referring to the fact that I'm Cardinal Camélière's niece," she said, raising her eyes.

"Yes, Alex. I am." He was shaking his head. "Cardinal Phillip Camélière seems to be the focal point of this whole nasty business that's building between the U.S. bishops and Rome. Your relationship is too close. It can't be ignored."

"It's not anything I chose, Murray. It's a simple biological fact. He was my mother's brother before *I* was born." Keep calm, she told herself. Don't lose it. She forced a smile.

"Why do you want this story so badly?"

God, that was the right question, she thought. Murray wasn't made AME of National for no reason. Now if I could just give the right answer. "It's a great story," she said. "Maybe one of the biggest, if there's a schism. Of course I would want it. And Murray"—she pressed her only advantage— "you've just finished telling me that you approved of both my coverage on religious cults in New Orleans *and* my profile of Father Leighton. I've got the experience. I've got the source."

Murray held up his hand. "Compromise?" he offered.

She didn't speak. Just waited, thinking, I haven't lost.

"Here's the deal." He leaned forward, fishing in his pocket for the cigarettes. "I talk to Beverly, ask her to let you out on loan for a special story . . . a loan that could stretch into permanent." He tilted back in the chair. "You start right away on this thing for me."

"Which is?"

"A comprehensive overview of the issues which this Conference will be dealing with. Our readers need answers to some basic questions." He shook another unfiltered Camel out of the pack. "Is all this turmoil something new, or have issues like these come up at other times in the Church's history? Just how likely is a split between the United States and Rome? Are we witnessing a second Reformation? You know the kind of thing." He stuck the cigarette in his mouth and fumbled on the littered desk for a lighter. "I agree with you that this story could get big." The search stopped as the unlit cigarette became a pointer. "I want *us* to have done our homework."

"And how do you see all this being used?" she asked
soberly. "One big story? A series?" *I'm on National. I'm on
National.* The phrase kept running insanely through her
mind as she struggled to think clearly, to listen carefully to
what Murray was offering.

"Oh, more than one piece for sure." He had found some
matches in a drawer and was finally lighting up. "I want
plenty of stuff for the months leading up to this Conference as
things continue to break. Like those excommunications. See
if you can find out if we're likely to be in for more of that kind
of thing before the big meeting. No other assignments...unless
I have to soften the blow with Beverly and let you finish up
some stuff for Style. Otherwise just get out there and dig.
Come back and talk to me when you've got a handle on it,
and we'll discuss which way we want to go."

"And the Conference coverage itself...I'll get that?" She
couldn't leave it unasked.

"No promises on that, Alex. Let's cross that bridge later.
Okay?"

The phone rang as if on cue. "Yeah," Murray spoke into the
receiver. "Oh hi, Lambert. Just a minute." He held his hand
over the mouthpiece. "I'll talk to Beverly this afternoon...
before tomorrow's editorial meeting." He smiled at her. "It'll
be okay."

"All right...yes. Thanks, Murray." She smiled back. "I'll
check with you...tomorrow?"

He nodded, turning his attention back to the phone.
"Yeah, Lambert. Whatcha got?" He swiveled away. For a
moment she just sat, watching the dark plume of his untended
cigarette diffusing through the already thick air.

She left, closing the door behind her. There were some
curious looks from people drifting back in after lunch. She
felt a little numb. It was a victory. No doubt of that. She was
on National now, working on the story she wanted. She
nodded her head absently as she walked to her desk. Comprehensive coverage. She was beginning to see the possibili-
ties. There was so much she could do with it. The thoughts
came crowding, but she pushed them back. Murray had
hedged on the actual Conference coverage, the front-page

stuff. Still, he hadn't said no. And hell, as much as she
protested, she could understand the sticking point. But she'd
show Murray, prove to him, that she could be totally objective. It was really a false issue, her relation to Uncle Phillip.

Back at her desk, Frank's message still glowed on the
screen. Briefly she wondered if she would see him tonight.
He'd mentioned yesterday that he might be flying to New
York. Switching off the monitor, she grabbed her purse. She
needed to get out of here before she ran into Beverly. Best to
let Murray handle that.

As she hit the street, a rush of well-being washed over her,
and the success of her meeting with Murray at last became
real. She thought of John Leighton. This whole thing had
started with her assignment to do the takeout on him. Why
had she ever felt such antagonism toward poor John Leighton?
Her foolish unfocused anger seemed a lifetime away now. He
was really very nice . . . so open and unaffected. She smiled as
she remembered his sitting across from her yesterday in his
jeans and shirt. She would have to call him right away. His
help was more important than ever with this new assignment.
She couldn't wait to get started.

Frank cursed under his breath as the taxi passed him
narrowly at full tilt. He hated driving in New York at the best
of times. Tonight the black streets were pockmarked with
neon-lit puddles. Any moment it might start raining again.
But at least tonight he knew where he was going. Last time
he'd played hell finding the tiny neighborhood bar where his
contact had insisted they meet. He sure hoped the guy had
something for him tonight besides vague hints that he knew
more than was healthy about the Lambrucis.

Almost he wished that he'd turned Bob down on another
drug story. The stuff he had so far didn't amount to much.
Maybe Alfie's friend actually would give him that new slant
Bob was looking for. He was really sick to death of the whole
drug mess. His personal opinion was that only total de-
criminalization could change things. Drugs were dirt cheap to
produce. It was only their illegality that made them inordinately
profitable, and the problem seemed to escalate in direct

proportion to attempts at law enforcement. It was Prohibition all over again. People never learned.

He stopped at a red light and pulled out a cigarette. Alex was right, he smoked too much. He smiled inwardly, wondering how she'd made out this afternoon with the chain-smoking National editor. She hadn't ever said if she'd wanted him to speak to Murray on her behalf. She was so damn sensitive about that kind of thing.

The light turned green and he shot forward before the drivers behind him could find their horns. He kept to the right lane and tried unsuccessfully to settle back more comfortably in the unfamiliar seat. He was acutely conscious of how much he'd prefer to be with Alex now instead of where he was, here in this rented compact going to meet some two-bit informant in the dead of night in Brooklyn. It angered him, this realization that he'd rather be with her. He loved what he did.

He remembered the first time he had seen Alex at the paper. All long legs, golden skin and hair, she'd stood waiting for the elevator in a light brown suit, simple but obviously expensive. Rich bitch, had been the first thought in his mind. Dipped in honey, had been the second. Those two quick responses had set the pattern of what was to come.

He'd introduced himself later in line at the staff cafeteria, and she'd followed him to a table. It was a surprise to find her open and friendly—experience had taught him that women like Alexandra Venée used their looks like a weapon. He had resisted the impulse to ask her to dinner, which had turned out to be a good move. He'd learned later that she'd already turned down all the other reporters on the make. An easy office friendship had developed over many months before he finally asked her out.

He'd never dated old money before. Hadn't wanted to. It was a world he preferred to view from the outside. But with Alex the privileged background receded. Not that you could ever forget it. It was there in her every look and gesture. In her clothes. Her tastes. The things she loved. *Breeding*. But with Alex you couldn't resent it. You could only admire what it had produced.

Now they were lovers—a "hot item" as they said in the trade. But was that all they were? Just a piece of staff gossip to be discussed over coffee in the lunchroom? "Damn," the word exploded out with his pent-up breath as he cut sharply into a side street. He'd almost driven past the turn. Impatiently he brushed back the hair that had fallen into his eyes and jammed his cigarette into the ashtray. He didn't want to think about any of this now. But lately it kept nagging at him—the light way Alex seemed to regard their relationship. She was what he had always told himself he wanted. A bright, beautiful woman who made no demands, who never complained about his lengthy absences or moaned about the danger involved in his work. Just the opposite of his ex-wife Karen, who had never let up on him for two minutes. Be careful what you ask for, he thought ruefully, you just might get it.

So what *did* he want from Alex? He was suddenly determined to push himself into an honest answer. *Love?* He tested the word in his mind. Was love what he wanted? That wouldn't be smart. Karen had given him that in great quantities, and it had only driven him away.

But it wouldn't have to be the same with Alex, some deeper interior voice spoke within his head. *A woman like Alex could love you and not tear you apart.* Ah, he thought, the great subconscious has spoken. Now we're getting somewhere. Well, let's just push it some more, let's take this motherfucker to the wall. So you *do* want her to love you, huh, buddy? Well then, answer this one. Does she?

The drizzle had started again and he adjusted the wipers, leaning forward to look for street numbers. He wasn't there yet. Still plenty of time for thought. About six more blocks worth.

So did Alex love him? He shoved his glasses up the bridge of his nose and leaned forward as if to see better through the flat harsh slapping of the wipers. Did Alex love him? He didn't much think so. For all the great times they had together, for as good as it was—and it *was* good—there was something... something not there. He couldn't put it into words. His eyes on the oncoming traffic, he groped for the pack of cigarettes he had tossed onto the passenger seat. He

was being a fool. Alex was there for him, wasn't she? She
hadn't said she didn't want to see him anymore? She hadn't
said anything like that. Why then was he always half expecting,
dreading, that she *would* say it? *Now we're getting to it.* He
worked a cigarette out of the pack and punched in the lighter.
She's messing with your mind, pal, said the voice in his head,
on his side now. *The woman is giving you mixed signals.*

Yes, that was true. The lighter popped out, and he brought
the glowing element up to meet the jutting tip of his cigarette. He considered the last thought. Alex *was* giving him
mixed signals. Like the other night. Pulling back from him,
then asking him to stay. Then waking him early the next
morning... *Women. Who could figure them?* He let himself
retreat into cliché. So did she love him? Insufficient data to
support an hypothesis.

But there yet remained the obvious question. He would
give himself points for not attempting to avoid it. Was *he* in
love with Alex? No sense hedging now. He knew that answer.
Poor stupid bastard, he said to himself.

The bar, when he finally arrived, was even less crowded
than on his last visit. Otherwise it hadn't changed. It looked
like it hadn't altered much in over four decades. Dark paneling, peeling photos, red leatherette and chrome. Actually he
liked it. It was pretty much like most of the places he
frequented, only more authentic. He got a beer at the
counter, remembering from the other time that they stocked
Guinness, and walked down to the farthest booth in the
narrow room. His contact was waiting.

"Hi, Jano. Nasty night." He slid in across the table. "I
hope it was worth my coming."

The man sat hugging the corner, his dark eyes hidden in
shadow. Frank caught the brief nervous flash of a smile. "Hi,
Frank. Glad you could make it." He smiled again. "I don't
think you'll be disappointed."

Frank sipped at his beer. "That's good, Jano. Because last
time I *was* disappointed. You let names drop, names like
Lambruci. But you didn't tell me anything that any street-
smart twelve-year-old doesn't know." He leaned forward,
trying to read the shadowed face. "So, I'm not going to be

disappointed, huh? You saying you do know something *worth* telling?"

"Not me. That's why I couldn't really give you anything last time. I was just sizing you up for somebody else. Alfie said you were straight, but I needed to talk to you myself. Get a feel. So I could report back to this other person." He paused as if searching for the words. "This . . . other person. My friend's the one who can tell you things."

"So will this 'other person,' this 'friend,' talk to me now?" Frank picked up his beer. He still harbored the suspicion that the trip tonight had been a waste, and yet he couldn't trust this instinct. The man hadn't answered. "Well, Jano, *is* this other guy going to show?" If there really is another guy, he thought tiredly, angry at his own lack of enthusiasm.

For a moment the man's eyes met his. "No. It's too dangerous. It's all gotta be done through me. That all right?" he added, almost apologetic.

Frank pulled back and set his glass carefully down into the wet ring it had made on the table. None of this was quite right. Jano wasn't right. Not your typical snitch. For the first time since the lead had opened up, he felt a genuine interest. "Look, Jano, I'm not sure what's going down here. Alfie said you wanted someone from the *Post* because there's some kind of Washington connection. I came last week and again tonight because Alfie's played straight with me in the past." He hesitated. He never liked this part, the haggling. "The *Post*, as a matter of policy, doesn't pay for information," he began again. "However, as I'm sure Alfie has told you, he and I have done some *personal* business. And if your information is reliable and steady, I can put you on the payroll as a stringer."

The man shook his head. "No, no money. It's not for money . . . that I . . . that my friend wants to tell you these things."

"What things?" Frank pounced on the halting words, all reporter now. Fuck the reason why, he thought. Just tell me for chrissakes! But he didn't say it. Only watched as Jano sagged forward now into the dim glow from the light above the bar. Deliberately Jano set down his own beer now. He seemed resigned, ready at last to talk. *Wrong.*

"It's not for money." Jano was still stalling. But there was something like anger in his eyes now, and the nervousness was gone. "Let's just say my friend's got an ax to grind. And I don't mind helpin'."

Frank sighed. Now he was beginning to understand. This guy or his friend or whoever wanted revenge. That was believable enough. It wasn't just the narcs who wanted to nail the Lambrucis. The brothers left a trail of misery wherever they took their dirty little business. Yeah, he was beginning to understand, but he didn't like it. He was going to be fed information as a form of revenge. He preferred a more businesslike approach. Fanatics were dangerous.

"Let me see if I've got this straight," he said. "This friend of yours who is no friend of the Lambrucis, has something on them. Something he's willing to give me with the understanding that I'll put it in print?"

"Yes." Jano was nodding eagerly like a teacher whose less-than-gifted pupil has fianlly grasped the lesson.

"Why doesn't your friend just give it to the police, then? It's a more direct route."

Jano's face fell. The schoolboy had turned out to be a dunce after all. "You kidding me, Frank? You got to know how many in the department the Lambrucis have on their payroll?"

Frank shrugged. "Things are better here in New York since the reorganization. It's not like it used to be."

"Sure, and if you believe that, I got a bridge not far from here I'd like to sell you." Jano grinned uncertainly, testing the effect of his joke.

Frank felt himself smile. "Okay," he said, "so your friend's not going to the police. What exactly does he expect from me? I can't print anything I can't back up. Even the Lambrucis can scream libel and make it stick."

"Carl . . ." Jano stopped and swallowed.

It had been a name. For the first time Frank really believed there was another guy involved.

"My friend will give you stuff," Jano went on, "stuff that nobody can ignore. You can check it out. Then when you think you got enough, you print it."

Frank nodded. "Jano, I'm going to be straight with you.

I've done work on this kind of thing before. You don't often get the kind of results your friend is looking for. Most times it just amounts to some bad publicity. And what do you think, that the Lambrucis are worried about their good name?" He shook his head. "And Jano, the Lambrucis are smart. They're wholesalers. Moneymen. And they have a rule. They never touch the actual stuff. No exceptions. That's why it's been so tough for the feds to get anything to stick. So this information. It's got to be primo, you understand. Not just things your friend has maybe heard—"

Jano cut him off. "Don't worry. It'll be good. My friend's on the inside. Deep on the inside."

"Then he knows how dangerous this is."

"'Course. Nobody knows better. Doesn't care. Just wants to get the Lambrucis... And maybe some of their good friends. So," he asked abruptly, "you gonna help us, Frank? You gonna write what I get you?"

"If it can be substantiated."

"Good. My friend will be happy." Jano gave a real smile. "Here's what I got for you so far." He leaned closer. "It's got something to do with all the money they're moving around."

"The drug profits," Frank offered.

"Yeah... well, my friend seems to think that Johnny and Paulo have got some real smart way of shuffling the dough so it don't *look* like drug money. My friend heard them laughing, saying it went out dirty but came back 'pure as a virgin.'"

Frank's mind was working. This could be hot. It was well known that Johnny and Paolo had gotten their start by jumping into the vacuum created when the five major families pulled back from drugs in the early sixties. Business for the Lambrucis had been good from the very beginning, but in recent years their whole operation had become much more sophisticated, and rumor was that the brothers were now fronting for some legit business types who had begun to tap into the huge profits of drug trafficking. If this friend of Jano's actually knew, or was able to figure out how the biggest wholesalers on the East Coast were washing their profits, it just might blast a hole into the higher levels. "So, Jano," he said, "does your friend have any clue at all as to how the Lambrucis are actually moving the money?"

"Don't know," Jano said softly. "My friend hasn't told me yet. But I'm sure we'll find a way to get you what you need."

"How are you communicating with him?" Frank was suddenly anxious. "Phone?"

Jano shook his head. "We're not stupid. This friend and me go way back. We see each other from time to time. Always have. Nothin' different from usual. We talk then."

"What about this place? Is it safe for us to go on meeting here?"

Jano laughed. "Safe as you can get. This whole neighborhood," he started to explain, "it used to be Irish. I grew up here. Oh, I know"—he intercepted Frank's glance—"I don't look Irish. That's 'cause of my mother. She's Siciliano. But my old man, he was as Irish as you can get. Anyway, like I said, the whole neighborhood used to be Irish in the old days. This place was packed then. I started coming in with my papa when I was seven. He and my uncle Mike used to let me sit up on the bar and dip my finger in the foam on their beers. God, I remember it like it was yesterday." He sighed. "Neighborhood's mixed now. More spics than micks." He laughed. "But they don't come here. Nobody comes but the old regulars. The ones who are left. I know everybody who walks in that door, and I'd trust my life with any one of 'em. It's safe."

"Okay, Jano. But you've got to be real careful." Frank crushed out his cigarette against the inside of the bottle.

"Oh, I know. I'm scared. Believe me. But like I said, I know my friend. I guess in a funny way I think my friend's more dangerous than the Lambrucis. Hell"—he gave a bitter laugh—"if it wasn't for... well, for my own reasons, I'd almost be sorry for the bastards."

CHAPTER EIGHT

The palm of Brian Donovan's hand literally itched to make the first of his two telephone calls. But he couldn't give in to his anger. He must calm himself. Think through what he was going to say. What were the old boys in the Vatican up to anyway? Why hadn't he been told about Kirkpatrick? He ran his hand through the gray waves of his hair. "Mantini," he mumbled under his breath. Just like the prideful old bastard to keep something all for himself. He supposed the papal delegate needed to play his little games to make himself feel important. Fuck his ego, he cursed silently. He didn't like being on the outside looking in. He damn well had his own ego to look after.

He picked up the receiver and dialed the embassy number, forcing a civility he did not feel into his voice. "Your Excellency, I hope that this isn't an inconvenient time. Father Ufizi said that you were free."

"Monsignor Donovan, I am never too busy to speak with you." The Italian's voice was thick with condescension.

"Thank you, Your Excellency. I'd hoped that I might speak to you in person rather than by phone but...I'm operating on such a tight schedule these days. But of course you understand." His voice was suitably apologetic but he had made his point. Indeed, the implication was quite clear: Brian Donovan was engaged in matters so important that he simply had not the time to meet with Archbishop Giovanni Mantini. Of course, the implication was ridiculous, since both men were fully absorbed in working on the same project. But the fencing was entirely satisfying, if unwarranted.

"Yes, I understand, Monsignor. I, too, am quite busy."

Donovan smiled to himself. Just the slightest trace, but it was there, that small edge of irritation in the Pro-Nuncio's voice. "Your Excellency, I..."

"What is it that you want, Monsignor Donovan?" Mantini's heavy voice bit into his sentence.

"It is about Bishop Kirkpatrick, Your Excellency."

He thought he heard the low rumble of a grunt, but he was not sure. The silence seemed to drag on endlessly before he finally heard Mantini's perturbed voice growl, "What about Kirkpatrick?"

"I did not know he was—how should I put this?—shall I say *fighting on our side.*"

"I do not understand this 'fighting on our side.' Bishop Kirkpatrick's views are well known. It is no secret that he stands with Rome in its opposition to certain changes."

"I understand Bishop Kirkpatrick's conscience, and I appreciate his motivation. What I was unaware of, Archbishop Mantini, was that he had been actively recruited and mobilized to help put *Lucifer* into operation."

There was no mistake this time, the grunt was real. "I did not think it was necessary that everyone know everything, Monsignor Donovan."

"Since we are playing for the highest stakes possible, Archbishop Mantini, it seems a bit shortsighted not to make critical personnel privy to vital information."

"Ah, Monsignor, you are insulted." The Archbishop laughed without humor.

Donovan cursed himself. It seemed that he had not been as adroit as he had hoped in disguising his anger. The old jackal was a hard one to fool. "No, Your Excellency, I am not insulted," he lied, willing iron control into his voice. "That would make the issue a personal matter, and it is one rather of strategy." He paused for a moment to let his words register. Now that sounded better, he congratulated himself on his clever choice of words. "Truly, Archbishop, I am not offended, only perplexed by the oversight," he went on, pressing his advantage. "Surely I should have been the first to know that Kirkpatrick was a part of *Lucifer*."

He heard a slow exhalation of breath through the receiver, then Mantini's low garbled words. "So now you know."

"Is there anything else I should know in regard to Kirkpatrick's involvement, Archbishop Mantini?"

"No." The word was hard, final.

"Good. I hope that in the future—"

"You will be informed, Monsignor Donovan."

"Very well, Archbishop. Then I will rely in the future on your good judgment in these matters." It was all that he could do to keep the sarcasm out of his voice. But he had won this little sparring match, and he wasn't about to press his luck. He changed the subject. "I think our problem of getting Lucifer and the Archangel together on a more or less daily basis is solved. I've convinced Camélière that Father Leighton could work more efficiently if he had the benefit of the Cardinal's extensive library, not to mention the privacy that having an office at the residence would afford. And of course, there would be Monsignor Campesi to lend assistance."

"And?"

"He thought it was a splendid idea. I knew he would. He would like nothing better than to have Leighton under his thumb. In fact he was so pleased with my suggestion that he volunteered a suite of rooms for him at the residence."

"Good. And how does Father Leighton feel about it?"

"I haven't told him yet. I would expect that he would be slightly reluctant since he is so sensitive about keeping his objectivity. But I can handle him."

"I am sure you can, Monsignor Donovan."

In a perverse way, Mantini had paid him a compliment, and he had to smile to himself again. "When do we tell him what we want him to do for us?" It was a sensitive question, but he could afford it.

"*When*, Monsignor Donovan?"

So Mantini had not conceded defeat. There was still plenty of fight in the old boy, and he wasn't giving another inch of ground to Brian Donovan. Yet there was nothing to do but repeat the question to which he knew there would be no answer, "When do we tell John Leighton about *Lucifer*?"

"All in good time, Monsignor Donovan." Mantini chuckled. "All in good time..."

For a moment Donovan held the receiver cradled against his ear, listening to the dial tone. He was not so anxious to make the second of his calls. He liked John Leighton. Something he hadn't allowed himself for a very long time—to really care about another person. He had learned early on that it was highly impractical to become emotionally involved. It was just so much cleaner if one remained detached. Then if one had to do things, things that were necessary, things that might hurt...

But he had not been able to do that with John. At first he had made a conscious agreement with himself that he would simply avoid the seminarian. But staying clear of John Christian Leighton hadn't proven to be such an easy task. For without warning, this supremely gifted young man had crawled inside of Brian Donovan, crawled into places that he had shut off long ago. And despite all his efforts, despite the considerable strength of his will, he had failed to keep John Leighton at bay.

He felt a sudden sharp twinge of guilt—leading the lamb to slaughter. He hadn't lied to Phillip yesterday when he'd said that John's conscience would force him to work on the Cardinal's side. That much was true. Except for the trump card that would soon be played, John Leighton, he knew, would never agree to become a part of *Lucifer*.

Yet soul-searching served no purpose, and the old wound went deeper than any remorse he might ever feel over John. He had his own score to settle. He dialed the priest's number.

"John, it's Brian."

"Brian, you old sorcerer, you've been reading my mind again. I was going to call you this evening. I wanted to get in a few more hours on the computer."

"How's it coming?"

"Some days it just flows. Other days..."

"Writer's block?"

"Whatever it is, it's a bitch."

"Is this John Leighton I'm speaking to?"

"How would you like it if I recited all the four-letter words I've recently added to my vocabulary?"

"I'd be delighted. Then I'd know you're human just like the rest of us."

"That's not fair, Brian."

Donovan was instantly sorry for his last remark as soon as he heard the real hurt in John's voice. "Come on, Father Leighton"—he made his voice light—"can't you take a joke? So you were going to phone." He changed the subject. "Anything important?"

"I had coffee with Alexandra Venée day before yesterday."

"I liked the article." He knew not to say more.

"Yes, she writes well. At any rate she wants to do some coverage of the Conference, and asked if I could be her contact person."

"Her source?"

"Yes, I guess that's more accurate. I told her that the Conference is really a long way off, not till November. And that I really didn't know the protocol on this sort of thing. But if it were acceptable to all parties concerned, I'd do what I could to help. I said I'd check it out with you."

"Very interesting. The Cardinal's niece covering the NCCB. I wonder how in hell she got the big boys at the paper to go for it. The *Post* is so touchy about that sort of thing. But sure, it's fine with me. There is a clearance procedure she'll have to follow; however, I doubt seriously she'll have any problems."

"Brian, do you think I should do this? I mean I don't want in any way to compromise my position with the Doctrine Committee."

"Of course you should help her. Besides, if you didn't . . ."

"What?"

"Let's say that Alexandra Venée is just about the most important person in Phillip Camélière's life. Or so I'm told. So, you see, anything to advance her career would of course please His Eminence. So you can't lose—you make points with the Cardinal and help his beautiful niece all at the same time."

"Brian, I hate the way you put things sometimes. I'm not out to make points with anybody. I didn't want this job with the NCCB. You asked me to assist the Doctrine Committee and I agreed. I just want to do what's right for everyone concerned. And that includes Cardinal Camélière and his niece."

"God, I know that. Listen, John, I still hold to the premise that the Doctrine Committee needs you—I repeat, to keep us all straight. Please don't take my kidding to heart."

"I'm sorry, Brian. I guess I'm still a little uncomfortable with the whole idea. Maybe I'm not right for the job. Maybe you had better get yourself someone else."

"Chrissakes, John, don't back out on us now. I don't think His Eminence would be very happy if I told him that you've decided not to take the position. God, he has it all planned. An office at his residence. Use of his library. Monsignor Campesi at your beck and call."

"What? I don't understand. I thought that it was all arranged that I would work out of the NCCB offices."

"No, Cardinal Camélière says it's going to be a madhouse over there. He wants optimum working conditions for you."

"Do you agree with him—that I should work at the residence? You don't think that . . ."

"That some people will think that Phillip Camélière is orchestrating everything that you do? Hell, yes, I think that people will say that. But what difference does that make? You will know differently."

"But couldn't even talk like that be damaging to the success of the Conference?"

"John, there is going to be talk no matter what. Cardinal Camélière is a very powerful man. Powerful men have enemies."

"I'm not talking about Phillip Camélière, Brian. I'm talking about the National Conference of Catholic Bishops. I'm talking about the future of the Church."

"Father Leighton, in the most essential of ways His Eminence Phillip Cardinal Camélière *is* the National Conference of Catholic Bishops. He *is* the future of the Church."

• • •

"Your home away from home." Monsignor Campesi switched on the lights to reveal a beautifully furnished room. "There's a TV in the bedroom. That's through that door over there. This one's a closet." He advanced into the room. "Don't you want to see it all?" he asked, turning back to where John still lingered in the hall.

"Forgive me. But I don't understand, Monsignor."

"Tony, please."

"Tony," John corrected himself, remembering that the Cardinal's secretary had asked to be addressed informally. He did his best to return the monsignor's smile, but inwardly he was full of reservations. He had been right to have doubts when Brian informed him this morning about Cardinal Camélière's offer of an office at the residence. This whole thing was going a bit too fast. "I don't understand," he repeated. "I thought you were going to show me where I would be working."

Tony Campesi waved a hand dismissively. "Don't worry. We'll get to it. I wanted to show your rooms first. The Cardinal thought it would be prudent for you to have a place here in the residence. That way, should you want to work late, you needn't worry about driving back to the university. You can remain here as much as you like." The secretary looked at him appraisingly. "You're staying in Curley?"

"I have an apartment," he answered simply.

"I see. Is it far?"

"On Connecticut. Near the zoo."

The Cardinal's secretary nodded. "The rooms were a good idea, then. Bring some things to leave when you come . . . tomorrow?" The last word made it a question.

"I had planned on starting work then. Will it be convenient for me to use the library in the morning?" He made no reference to the matter of the rooms.

"Of course. We'll give you a key. You can come and go as you like. The Cardinal wants you to feel at home here. He is really counting on you, you know."

Yes, John thought, but for exactly what? His misgivings concerning the Cardinal's influence over the Doctrine Committee returned in full force, and he found that he was annoyed at Tony Campesi's implied assurance that he would fall into step with whatever decisions were being made for him. He felt tempted to state here and now that he would not be accepting the Cardinal's kind invitation to "bring his things," but he held back. He might be overreacting. He knew he had been spoiled from years of independence, teaching at the university. I'm being too sensitive, he told himself. It was unfair to make judgments till he'd spoken personally with the Cardinal.

He looked up to find Tony Campesi watching him from the door that led to the bedroom. "Come see, John," the Cardinal's secretary said mildly. "I think you'll find it comfortable."

A few minutes later they took the small elevator to the first floor, emerging toward the rear of the residence. "The library is just down the hallway," the secretary explained, "but I know Cardinal Camélière will want to show you himself. He's very proud of it. The two of you should get on very well." Campesi motioned him to follow. "His Eminence has made church history a sort of personal specialty." The secretary had stopped before a heavily paneled door. "Our offices are just through here."

They walked into a room hardly less elegant than the others they had passed through. The desk that faced the doorway looked antique. He thought of all the sterile post-war, "Catholic Modern" diocesan offices that he had encountered and almost laughed aloud.

At his side Tony Campesi smiled almost slyly, as if he'd read his thoughts. "I sit here if we're expecting visitors," he explained. "We've no receptionist or anything. As I'm sure you know, the everyday business of the archdiocese is still conducted over at the Pastoral Center. These are the Cardinal's private offices. It's just he and I."

"It's very nice." The comment seemed inane, but he was not sure what else was expected.

"Yes, it is." The monsignor seemed pleased enough with the reply. "The Cardinal has impeccable taste. And he believes that a pleasant environment tends to inspire quality work."

He smiled, more warmly this time. "One finds it easy to do his best here."

John smiled back. He could hardly disagree. He had used a similar argument with himself to justify an off-campus apartment.

"Cardinal Camélière's office is just behind us through the double doors," the monsignor continued. "You'll be joining him in a moment. But first I'd like to show you your own office." Campesi gestured for him to follow him down a small hallway. "Of course there's the table in the library, but the Cardinal thought you would also want to have a desk and a phone."

The room was at the end of the short corridor. Tony Campesi switched on the light. "It's not huge. But the chair is comfortable and there are shelves for books. And you might want to hook up that computer." He indicated a PC unit sitting unassembled in a corner. "When the residence was built, the Cardinal thought he might like to have two prelates assisting him. I've since managed to convince him that he needs only one. That's why there's the good luck of an empty office."

"I'm sure it will be fine." Again he felt his reply to be less than adequate. He was experiencing the dull awkwardness that was his usual response to the easy self-mockery of people like Monsignor Campesi. But this time his discomfort went beyond a simple conflict of styles. For despite the man's overt friendliness, he had received the distinct impression that Tony Campesi did not welcome his presence here. Again he felt the familiar qualms about the political overtones of his work within the Committee. With the exception of his class-room, he was never any good in formalized situations. He was beginning to dread his meeting with the Cardinal.

As they moved back down the hallway a buzzer sounded. "Excuse me." The monsignor pushed open a nearby door and reached across the desk for the phone. He punched in a flashing button on the console. "Yes. He's here. Yes, fine. Okay. I'll bring him to you in a minute."

The secretary hung up abruptly and caught him gazing about idly from the corridor into the office. "My sanctum sanctorum. It's something of a mess this week," Campesi said,

snapping shut a large ledger book sprawled next to the
computer, his eyes searching the broad surface of the desk.
Then with a last quick look, he backed into the hall, closing
the door behind him.

Distinctly, John heard the tumblers click, and he wondered
briefly why it should be necessary during the day to lock an
office as untrafficked as this.

"Cardinal Camélière is ready for you," the secretary said as
they continued on down the hall. And John forgot everything
but his fears.

"Hello, John." The Cardinal rose casually as he entered the
office, coming from behind his desk to offer his hand. "It's
been a long time."

"Your Eminence." He wondered whether a simple handshake or the ritual kissing of the ring was expected, and opted
for the handshake. The Cardinal's reference to their one
rather brief personal meeting several years ago seemed calcu-
lated to establish informality. Frankly he was surprised that
Phillip Camélière remembered him at all, and said so.

"You're too modest, John." The Cardinal had regained his
seat and was motioning him to the chair in front of his desk.
"The paper you presented at the seminar was brilliant. And
you were very patient with my ignorance on several points
when I spoke with you after the presentation, as I remember.
That's why I was so delighted that you agreed to work with
the Doctrine Committee. We need you, John. The work of
this year's Conference has got to be based on solid scholarship. It has to be clear that we American bishops, and not the
reactionary forces in Rome, carry the true Christian message."

"But you do want to avoid a schism?" The rather bald
question had slipped out before he thought.

For an instant Phillip Camélière's clear gray eyes seemed
to measure him. Then there was only a kind of sadness in his
gaze and a note of reproach as he spoke. "Of course I want to
avoid schism, John. Could you really think otherwise?"

"I'm . . . sorry, Your Eminence," he stammered. "Truly. I
didn't mean . . ."

"Don't apologize," the Cardinal said. "These are terrible
times for the Church. It's a strain on all of us." Abruptly he

changed the subject. "Are the rooms upstairs all right? Your office? We want you be happy here." He smiled warmly.

"Everything is fine, Your Eminence." He realized he had answered reflexively, and began again, "It's all wonderful, but as I explained to Monsignor Dónovan this morning, I could as easily work out of the Conference offices."

"Ah, but you haven't seen the jam-up over there," the Cardinal answered. "Even in the new building there's still a problem with office space for committee staff. And, John, you haven't yet been in my library. It will probably provide most of what you need. And if there should be something we don't have, it can always be sent over from the campus."

He found himself nodding acceptance. Why argue? It did appear to be a good arrangement. His deadline on the manuscript had begun to loom impossibly near since he'd agreed to do this work for the Committee. Luckily much of the research for the two projects coincided, and working here at the residence might make it all easier. It seemed suddenly foolish to resist the Cardinal's offer. "Thank you, Your Eminence," he said simply. "I think it would be helpful if I could do at least some of the work here."

"Of course." The Cardinal was still smiling. "That was rather a good article about you this past Sunday," he said now. "Alexandra Venée is quite a reporter. Don't you think?"

Again John was caught off guard. He wondered if the Cardinal supposed that he knew Alexandra was his niece. Had she talked to her uncle since the interview? "Yes," he answered at last. "Alex—Ms. Venée is very good. She managed to make a dull subject interesting."

"Alexandra is my niece, you know?" Phillip Camélière was watching him with apparent amusement.

"Yes. I did know," he admitted now. "Monsignor Donovan told me the day before the interview. I really hadn't known before then." He hesitated. "I talked with her Monday. She asked me if I would help her with press coverage of the Conference. I checked it out with Monsignor Donovan this morning. He seemed to think it would be all right. Perhaps I should have waited, though, and asked you."

Now the Cardinal laughed. "As you likely already know, my

niece generally gets what she wants. I wouldn't think of standing against freedom of the press, especially when the fourth estate is embodied in the person of Alexandra. You have my blessing, John."

"Thank you, Your Eminence. I admit to a healthy fear of having to tell your niece *no* about anything." He relaxed back into the softness of the chair. "She certainly knows how to be persistent."

"A family trait." The Cardinal grinned. "Have you talked to her since getting the okay from Donovan? Does she know you're going to agree to help her?"

"No." He shook his head. "I haven't had a chance yet to call her."

"Don't," said the Cardinal, his chin resting in the cradle of his fingers, his elbows propped casually on the desk. "Let's just leave my niece wondering for the moment. That way we can both give her a little surprise. Stay for dinner tonight. Alexandra is coming. We can tell her together."

"Thank you, Madame Elise."

John watched Alex accept the cup of steaming coffee that the tiny gray-haired woman had poured for her.

"Madame makes coffee just like at home," Alex said, turning toward him as she set down her cup. "Strong. Not like the dishwater you get here in the District."

"Why, Alexandra," the Cardinal said, "it seems that just the other day you were claiming the District and not New Orleans was your home now."

"Not when it comes to food." Alex laughed. "We New Orleanians take our food seriously, Father Leighton. Which explains why Uncle Phillip so shamelessly stole Madame here from the French."

"As Madame Elise will tell you herself," the Cardinal said mildly, "I didn't steal her. I simply let her know that there would be a place for her at the residence whenever she became tired of the embassy circus. It just happens that she became tired very quickly." He looked at Madame with a smile.

"The Cardinal is a hard man to refuse," Madame Elise

answered in her light accent. "But it is true I was tired of it all. Here it is quieter." Her hands waved expressively. "Not always rush, rush, rush. And no ambassador's wife to try to tell me how to run my kitchen." She laughed and patted the side of a huge bowl of chocolate. "You must all have more." She stared pointedly at the Cardinal.

"She's something else, Uncle Phillip," Alex said as the woman closed the door behind her. "Everything was fabulous as usual. . . . By the way, where's Monsignor Campesi tonight?"

"He's out. He had some business this afternoon. Then he was going to visit a friend, I think. . . . Please, Alex, take some more mousse. You're staring holes in the side of that bowl."

"I am not."

The Cardinal laughed, ignoring her protest. "Alex has always had a passion for desserts, John. When she was a little girl, old Sarah had to literally hide her homemade ice cream."

"Really, Uncle Phillip." Alex's eyes widened. "Father Leighton doesn't want to hear about my childhood."

"Of course he'd like to hear, Alex. Your childhood was fascinating. But we'll make it even. Father Leighton will have to tell us something about his."

For most of the evening John had sat quietly in the background, simply enjoying the food and company. He had not expected to be so suddenly drawn in. "My childhood really wasn't very interesting," he answered softly. "I grew up in a small town near Chicago."

"What about your family?" Alex was smiling at him. "What are they like?"

"My dad was in insurance. Still is, really, but he's semiretired now. My mother's started doing a lot of church work. She's also taken up her music again. For her own enjoyment. She finally has the time after rearing seven of us."

"Seven? I don't remember that from your press kit."

"One of the last big traditional Catholic families, I guess. You don't see them much anymore."

"Brothers? Sisters?"

She seemed really interested, but it was probably just the reporter's instinct to get the facts. "My sister Marie is the oldest," he answered. "Then there's Will, Charlotte, Barbara. And me. Another sister, Lucy. And the youngest, Thomas."

"It's funny," she said softly, "I didn't picture you as being from a large family. Somehow I thought you were an only child. Like me."

"Did you dislike being an only child?" the Cardinal asked abruptly.

"Sometimes I did. I guess I always wished I were a twin like you and Mother. I thought it would be so wonderful to have another person close like that, another *you* almost. I had a pretend twin." She smiled. "I never told you about that, did I, Uncle Phillip? I guess I never told anyone. His name was . . . Bunky." She laughed. "Funny, but I hadn't thought about Bunky in such a long time." She turned her attention back to him. "Were you very close to your brothers and sisters?"

"I guess I was . . . in a way." John felt himself smiling. "It was a really terrific family to grow up in. Very warm. It made you feel protected." He was amazed to hear himself saying these things.

"You haven't told Alexandra yet about our surprise, John." The Cardinal's words broke in upon his thoughts.

"Another surprise?" Alex questioned. "I thought the surprise was that Father Leighton had joined us for dinner."

"That of course," the Cardinal anwered. "But I would have thought you'd be more interested to know the result of Father Leighton's request to assist a certain reporter with coverage of the Conference?"

"So you know about that." She was looking from one of them to the other. "I'd be *very* interested."

"Well, it seems Monsignor Donovan thought it would be all right. Subject of course to the approval of the Conference president—"

"Uncle Phillip."

"—who after due consideration has generously agreed to allow Father Leighton to assist you." He grinned.

"Thank you, Uncle Phillip," she said dutifully.

"Don't thank me. Thank John. He's the one who will have

to put up with you while trying to do his committee work *and* meet a publishing deadline."

"Hmm, that brings up some news of my own." She was hesitating now. She turned from her uncle to look up at him. "I hope this isn't going to be a problem. I tried to get you earlier. It's just that my editor, Murray, asked me to do some background articles before the conference even starts."

"So Murray Stone's your editor now," the Cardinal interrupted. "That sounds like you're on National, Alex. Congratulations. I know that's what you wanted."

"Yes." She smiled. "I've been wanting to tell you, Uncle Phillip. Murray agreed to give me a shot." She turned back to him. "That's why it's important for me to have your help on this right away, John."

For a moment John was startled. When she had found him here tonight with her uncle, she had addressed him as Father Leighton, perhaps feeling that the formality of the situation required it. Now she had called him John, and absurdly he felt as if he were being invited into some magic circle.

"I hope it won't be asking too much"—she spoke again—"but I'd like to start immediately. I need what you've called 'the historical perspective.' I was hoping you could give me a bibliography—some things I could read and then discuss with you." The words trailed off. Then: "Is that going to be okay?"

He was looking into the wide amber eyes. They seemed almost yellow in the candle glow, like a cat's. "Yes..." He started to say something more.

"You're in luck, Alexandra." The Cardinal picked up the thought. "John will be doing much of his preliminary committee work here, in my library. You can work there, too. If *he* doesn't toss you out, I won't. Well, John?"

"No...I mean, of course Ms. Venée—Alexandra—is welcome in the library. It's a pretty big table," he said, joking at last.

"Oh, this is perfect!" Alex had risen to put her arms around her uncle. "And you love it, don't you, Uncle Phillip, having found this new opportunity to tease me?" Laughing, she kissed her uncle lightly on the temple. But she was looking across the table, and John saw that her smile was for him.

. . .

"No, Eric, I can't stay tonight." Tony was repeating himself, and now he heard what had been mild frustration begin to turn to anger. He hated losing control. It had taken years, but he had learned to rein in that volatile Italian temper he'd been cursed with. He brought his chin up a bit, altering his breathing.

"He always wins, you know," Eric's voice, in contrast, seemed almost complacent.

"Win? This isn't a contest, Eric." He forced a laugh. "I simply have work that needs to be done. I shouldn't have come at all. But I thought we could spend a few hours together and relax. I see that I was mistaken."

"Think whatever you like, Tony, but I'm not going to allow you to make me feel guilty. I refuse to be on the defensive."

"Eric, I . . ."

"No, Anthony. His Eminence Phillip Cardinal Camélière holds all the cards, pulls all the strings."

"I don't even know what you're talking about, Eric. I can't believe this. I tell you I can't stay tonight, and you decide that Phillip is . . . is . . ." He was not doing so well, and he could feel the precise throbbing of his pulse in his throat. He took another deep breath. "I don't even know what you think Phillip is doing, Eric."

"Controlling your life, Tony. I think that is a good analysis of the situation."

He continued to look straight ahead at Eric, trying to focus. He could not answer him. Not because he didn't have a reply, but because it was taking him some time to absorb the fact that it was Eric who was speaking to him like this. He walked toward the window and ran his hand over the blinds, checking for dust. He looked at his fingers, then brushed them against the side of his jeans. When he spoke, he did not turn but kept his back toward Eric.

"The simple fact is that Phillip Camélière is my boss, a man who has taken on tremendous responsibility. And for whatever reasons, he has seen fit to share that responsibility with me. He trusts me. He relies on me. And I want him to." He turned around and looked at Eric. "I happen to believe in what the Cardinal is doing. I respect and admire the man more than anyone else I know." He dropped his head slightly, then met Eric's eyes again. "But yes, you are right—right about what you said before about winning. When it comes down to a choice between you... a choice between anybody in the world and Phillip Camélière, I should choose him every time. If that hurts you, if you can't accept that, I'm truly sorry, Eric."

He had tried to sound firm but compassionate at the last, but he was not sure that he had succeeded and he looked away again. This was all so new for him, this arguing with Eric. *Arguing?* He repeated the word in his mind. Never had the two of them had so much as a disagreement. It simply wasn't in Eric's nature to argue. And if it had been, he, Tony Campesi, would not have tolerated it. He didn't have the time or energy for pettiness or intensity in an affair.

From the first Eric was to be his island, his peaceful refuge from the priesthood. The one person for whom he chose not to play the grand role of monsignor. However satisfying that part was, the Roman collar sometimes bound like a noose. So he had been happy to discover that he was able to build the kind of casual relationship he wanted with Eric.

And Eric seemed more than grateful for whatever he was willing and able to offer. So when his schedule permitted, he drove over to his friend's apartment for a quiet evening. Dinner was usually prepared by Eric, who fancied himself something of a chef. After, there was an hour or two spent drinking wine and listening to some progressive jazz, his musical passion good-naturedly tolerated by Eric. Then some gentle lovemaking.

On rare occasions they went out and did something silly, laughing all the while like two mischievous schoolboys playing hooky. Hardly, if ever, did they talk about anything of any great importance. Never about the two of them. Yet once in a while Tony would feel a twinge of conscience. A pang of guilt that told him that he was the real winner in this relationship— always on the receiving end. It has been very easy to assume that Eric's unselfishness exacted no price of him. But then tonight...

He sensed rather than heard Eric walk from where he had been across the room. "I am not hurt, Tony," Eric said finally. "I am not jealous of your loyalty to Cardinal Camélière. I am not angry at being second . . . or third, or whatever. I would choose to take any place, as long as I was able to fit somewhere in your life." He stopped for a moment. "I just want to know that you are happy in what you do. Sometimes I feel that . . . I don't know exactly. It's so difficult to explain. But sometimes, when I know you're preoccupied with work, I watch your face and it seems to grow kind of hard and tight." He paused again. "You seem all wound up on the inside, driven by something that I can't begin to understand. But I want to understand. Talk to me, Tony, talk to me."

"Eric." Tony turned full around and touched the side of his friend's face with his hand. "If someone you cared a great deal about asked you to do something that most people considered wrong, would you do it?"

"I don't know," Eric murmured hoarsely, touching the hand that rested against his cheek, then pulling it away as if to gain a kind of control over himself. "I guess it would depend on a lot of things—how much I cared for that person, if I really believed the thing I was asked to do was wrong."

"Exactly, there are no clear-cut choices. You have to make your own rules."

"Isn't that cheating?" Eric looked at him hard. "Making the rules fit the game so that you can win?"

"Not if you believe that the end result will be good."

"So the end justifies the means?"

"Yes." The word was little above a whisper and he paused for a moment before beginning again. "And once you establish the rules, you never never question them, never waver, never look back . . . or you're lost. You believe absolutely in what you do. And because you believe it to be true, it is true."

He knew he had gone too far to stop now. He was in too deep and Eric would not be satisfied with anything less than a full confession. "I have created my own truth, Eric. Anything outside of that truth is false. Beyond even that, anything outside of it is irrelevant."

"And if your rules hurt other people?"

He looked at Eric. Oh, you are closing in, he congratulated his friend silently, you're asking all the right questions.

"There are no unwilling victims, Eric."

"How can you say all of this and still be a priest?"

"The same way I reconcile my being with you, Eric. I keep everything separate. The trick is never to allow any of the roles to overlap, and for God's sake don't take any of the roles too seriously. The last is the hardest part. You'll have to be patient with me. Keeping everything in its place, and not taking any of it too seriously, is not always so easy. I'm still working on this aspect of the game."

"Game? It's all a game to you?"

"Yes, Eric." He frowned at the incredulous tone in his friend's voice. Maybe he had been wrong about Eric's level of tolerance. "If Phillip has taught me anything," he said almost flippantly, "it's that it's all a game."

"So it all comes full circle to where we began—to Phillip—doesn't it?" Eric's voice seemed suddenly tired, but his gaze was steady.

"Yes, it does." Tony moved away and looked through the blinds to the sidewalk below. He watched for a moment as an elderly lady curbed her dog, and then laughed softly to himself.

"What's so funny?"

"Life. I'm up here trying to explain to you how I play metaphysical games with myself, and outside a dog is taking a shit in the street." He turned suddenly. "Are you upset? I mean about all of this?"

"Upset? No, Tony, I'm just glad that *one* of you wants to spend time with me."

Tony laughed again and reached out and brought Eric's face close to his so that their foreheads were touching. "You're crazy, you know." And he turned and walked away. "There's something more I want you to understand about Phillip. He cares. Phillip really does care about people. And there are so many people who depend upon him, who need him. Have you any idea of the poverty in this city, the number of kids who are on drugs, the women who are beaten

every day of their lives by their husbands? Phillip wants to
change that . . . even if just a little."

He stopped for a moment, then he moved so that once
again he stood just a few steps in front of Eric. He reached
out with one hand and touched him lightly on the arm.
"Listen, Eric, Phillip knows that all the prayer in the world,
all the volunteers putting in their one and two hours a week,
all of the noble intentions can't change things very much. But
money can, lots and lots of money can make a difference. And
the Cardinal understands this better than anyone. So when
the chance came to get more money for the archdiocese, a lot
more money, he took it. No questions asked."

"No questions asked?"

"No questions asked," he repeated. "But this I can tell you,
Eric. Not a penny of it goes for personal gain once it comes to
us, not a cent. All of it, every bit of it is used for those who
really need it."

He felt Eric's hand upon his shoulder and he placed his
own over his. It felt cool and he wanted to press it against his
forehead.

"Can you be . . . hurt?" Eric's words seemed to break inside
his throat.

"No, nothing will happen to me. I promise." And he
brought Eric into his arms. The lamplight coming across the
room made the tears on his friend's face seem like small
shards of glass. And for moments it was all that he could see.
Then he kissed him in a quiet comfortable sort of way.

"I love you, Eric," he said softly. It was the first time he
had ever said those words to anyone.

The apartment seemed oppressively quiet tonight. The
silence beat against his ears. Restlessly John paced to the
window and looked out. It was very late, but there was still
traffic on Connecticut and the sound of the cars drifted
pleasantly up to him. He remained standing a moment, not
thinking of anything, staring downward at the moving headlights, the signal light flashing from red to green.

He would have to get some sleep soon if he was going to
start early at the residence tomorrow. He pulled away from

the window and walked toward the hallway. Maybe he should take a hot bath. No, he'd just shower in the morning. Some milk? Not that either. Some water might be good, though. He moved into the kitchen, and picking up a glass from the draining board, he filled it from the tap. Two sips and he poured it out, setting the glass down in the sink.

Back in the bedroom he took off the stiff collar. Usually it didn't bother him, but it felt good to get it off tonight. Still in his suit, he paced to the bedside table and picked up his breviary. He liked ending the day with the seasonal procession of the psalms and the antiphon to the Blessed Virgin that completed each night's prayer.

He sat down in the comfortable chair he had bought for himself. The apartment had come furnished, but this was something special he had wanted. It was a wingback, and it reminded him of the chair that still stood in his parents' bedroom. His mother always sat in that chair for mending, something she had done a lot of with seven growing children. He had always been able to talk to her there about anything that bothered him as she sat, her concentration seemingly upon the needle, drawing together the pieces of tattered cloth. She never looked at him while he spoke, which made it easier. But she was listening. And she always answered. Now from this chair he talked to God. Somehow it felt right.

The breviary still unopened, he leaned back within the comfort of the chair, letting it surround him. He thought of his family. Libertyville seemed very far away tonight. Recently, he realized, all his mother's letters had ended with the question of when he was coming home. It would have to wait now until the Conference was over. He really did want to see them. All of them. It had been true, what he'd told Alexandra tonight. They were a close family, yet he'd been the outsider. The quiet one. The scholar. It wasn't that the others weren't smart. They'd all done well in college, even Will, when he'd finally put his mind to it. And they had responsible jobs now. Even the girls managed work and family. But his brothers and sisters, and indeed his parents, had never been "bookish," as his mother described it. And though he'd been rough-and-tumble like the others, had loved the outdoors and sports,

still it was books, books and ideas, that had been the things
he loved best. It had marked him as different, had made his
decision to enter the seminary more acceptable to his father
than if the announcement had come from Tom or Will.

They loved him, his family. They were proud of him. But
except perhaps for his mother, they had never understood
him. He opened the book in his lap and began to read the
psalm. After the first few lines he knew that he was reading
without comprehension or sense. He closed his eyes, breathing deeply, inviting his mind to clear. For a few moments
longer he sat in utter stillness, then he began to read again.
Now the words came together on the page. It was a passage
he had always enjoyed, and at last he relaxed.

With no warning, his focus began again to waver. He found
his thoughts wandering in memories of tonight's dinner at the
residence, catching at images and bits of conversation—the
Cardinal smiling at him from his seat at the head of the table,
Alexandra's face so open as she spoke of her imaginary
playmate.

And then he was seeing the dream as it had come to him
again. *Was it only two nights ago?* he thought. With sudden
force he remembered. *It had been Alex in his dream.*

At first he was only very surprised. He could not recall
another instance when the dream had varied. Always before
it had been Brigit's face that softened beneath him in passion.
But now . . . He found that he was trembling, and unmistakably
he felt the involuntary beginnings of physical arousal. How
could this be happening? he wondered, but he was not yet
unduly disturbed. It was simply an unexpected physical
reaction and he had no real doubt that he could handle it. For
just a moment longer he let the memory linger of how Alex
had looked tonight, how pleased she had seemed to find him
dining with her uncle.

For the third time he went back to his breviary.

CHAPTER NINE

"Good morning, John." Phillip stopped, looking in at the library door. "Getting an early start?"

"Good morning, Your Eminence." John glanced up from the list he was making. "I'm getting settled in. Thought I'd try to get a handle on what you have here and what I'll need to find elsewhere."

Phillip nodded. "Well, I won't interrupt except to give you some idea of how things run around here. It's pretty loose, but there are a few things you'll want to know. Mass at the Pastoral Center is at seven every morning. If you want to be on the schedule over there, talk to Father Chaney. Breakfast here is at eight-thirty. Lunch at twelve-thirty. Dinner is generally at seven, but it varies. Just try to let Madame Elise or Mrs. Jordan, our housekeeper, know in the morning which meals you'll be having here. And let Tony know if you need anything else."

"Thank you, Your Eminence. I will."

"And, John"—he made his voice light—"*Your Eminence* gets very cumbersome after a while. Around here let's just make it Phillip. Okay."

"Okay."

Phillip registered the slight hesitancy. His guest hadn't been quite ready for this particular gesture. But no harm done.

He stopped next at Tony's office, knocking lightly.

"Yes."

He went in, sitting down in the extra chair. "Well, Tony, what's the word this morning on the stock sale. Has it gone through okay?"

"I haven't heard from Miller yet, but I don't expect any kind of hitch. He's acted as broker on these things before."

"Good. I want you to watch the price very closely. As long as it's stable or better yet shows an increase, hold on to it. We don't need the cash right now, and I want to avoid a turn-around sale as long as possible." He spoke seriously. "You've done a great job, Tony. I'm very grateful. We couldn't have accomplished half of what's been done without you. Which reminds me. What about the contracts to build the new halfway houses? I have no doubt that that's what the pile-up of phone messages from Sister Catherine is all about, and I would like to give her an answer soon."

"You can tell her we've about got it wrapped up. She can start breaking ground on the first building in three or four weeks."

Phillip rose and rested his hand for a moment on Tony's shoulder. "Hold my calls unless it's something that has to be dealt with immediately, okay? I need to make some calls of my own. There are some committee chairmen I have to keep on the straight and narrow. Things are getting close now."

"Is Father Leighton here? I didn't see him."

"He's in the library."

"You know, Phillip." Tony seemed to be hesitating. "I'm not sure it's a good idea, his being here all the time . . . in these offices."

"What are you trying to say, Tony?"

"I just don't like having him, or any outsider, around our operation. Especially on a daily basis."

"I've explained to you why it's important for me to have him here. I need what he can give me at this Conference, Tony. It's important to have him on our side. Besides, you're worrying needlessly. What harm can he do? I know I said for you to be alert, but there's no need to worry about John Leighton."

"Maybe. But security's not the only thing that bothers me. He doesn't impress me as an easy target. Even for you, Phillip. If he begins to suspect that he is being purposefully courted, manipulated in any way, he'll dig in his heels. This campaign to woo him could turn out to be very counterproductive."

"Really, Tony." Phillip was genuinely surprised at his secretary's uncustomary bluntness. "I would never wish Father Leighton to go against a sincere conscience. Besides, I've always felt that he would willingly support our position. But you are absolutely correct about one thing, Tony. We must guard against the possiblitiy that John might misinterpret my friendship. What would you suggest?"

Tony smiled. "I don't think for a moment that you need my advice as to how to proceed with Father Leighton, Phillip. I simply wanted to draw your attention to the danger involved."

"Which you did, Tony. And as always, I'm grateful," he said sincerely, turning toward the door.

Tony started to speak, but answered the phone instead. "It's Mrs. Kenison," he said.

Phillip nodded to Tony and went on through to his office. He sat down and picked up the phone. "Lauren? This is a surprise."

"I'm not at the embassy. They think I've gone out for stamps."

"It's something important then?"

"No, not really. I just wanted to touch base. Damn, my Italian's terrible. I don't know whether Mantini hired me in spite of it or because of it."

"It's okay, Lauren. Just keep your eyes and ears open."

"One thing. Bishop Kirkpatrick's name's been bandied about a lot. But that's no surprise."

"No, it isn't."

"Sorry, it's not more, Phillip. But maybe that's because there isn't any more."

"I hope you're right, Lauren, but it's hard to believe the Vatican's not up to something. Every time I look up, Mantini or one of his Italian spies is over here snooping."

She laughed. "I know what you're saying, Phillip. Mantini's

a sneaky old fart, but honestly, I thing you're worrying needlessly."

"Maybe so, Lauren. Keep in touch."

Tony walked in.

"I guess you heard."

"Yes." Tony shook his head. "But I still can't believe nothing's going on.... Oh, Phillip, I almost forgot. I was going to put this on your desk earlier, but I got distracted."

A small premonition warned him of what it would be even before Tony held it out to him. As he reached for the small package, there was no need to look at it to know it would be essentially like the other. Wrapped in brown paper. No postmark. No return address. The lettering in the wide ink of a flow pen, black and childishly drawn.

"How did this come?" He was angry that the words should sound so strained.

Tony looked at him sharply. "I don't know. Mrs. Jordan handed it to me in the hallway." He reached for the phone. "I'll buzz her."

"No . . . no, that's not necessary. It doesn't matter. There's no return address, that's all." He forced a smile. "Thank you, Tony. See you at lunch."

For a moment Phillip considered ringing Mrs. Jordan himself, but he knew already what the housekeeper would tell him—that the package had arrived by private messenger, or by taxi, as had the first one in New Orleans. In either case there would be little hope now of tracing the sender.

As long as there remained no proof, he could pretend not to know who sent the packages. And pretending, he need not guess why, now, after all these years, they should come at all, and to what final purpose. But his memory would not accept that his ignorance was real. He could not block the images that rose up from the past, fresh and accusing. He had known at once in New Orleans. He knew now.

He remembered the shock of so long ago, seeing her walk into the small Sunday catechism class with her uncle. Until that moment he had imagined that his encounter with her in the swamp had been something unreal, mystical. But here she was now, standing before him in the small church. Not a dream, after all, but a creature of flesh and blood, a young girl in a cheap new blouse and skirt. But not ordinary. Possessed of a strange and ravening beauty that survived the tawdry clothes. And the smile. The self-absorbed, secret smile that still haunted him.

"This is Angelique, Père Philippe," the man had said in his thick bayou accent. "My niece. I have brought her to you. I think maybe you can help her."

Her uncle told her story. How Angelique was his sister's girl. God alone knew who her father was. The devil, some said, and he was not one to deny it. His sister was gone. Run off with some worker from the rigs three years ago. And no one but him to take the girl in. He fished and trapped for a living, he said, from a shack way out on the bayou, and he had to come in by pirogue. Now he came to the point. She was wild, his niece, *dans la lune*. He did not himself go to church, but he had been baptized. He believed in God. He had heard about Père Philippe and his classes for the children on Sunday after Mass, and he'd thought maybe a priest could do something with the girl.

Throughout this monologue, Angelique herself said nothing. Just stood there with her head down, so that you could have thought she was embarrassed or shamed by her uncle's words. He couldn't read her eyes, which were shadowed by her hair, but he could see her lips curving in that maddening smile. And he had wondered desperately what she was thinking.

His first thought when they entered was that the man had come to accuse him of violating her. He had felt a shattering thrill of fear. Now, when he knew that he was instead being asked to save her, he almost laughed. She had obviously said nothing of what had happened in the bayou.

He heard himself speaking. Telling the man that he must bring her every Sunday for Mass and catechism. He would do for her what he could. The uncle nodded. Satisfied. He would come for her after the class, he said, and left.

He spoke to her then as he had spoken to all the others, telling her firmly and quietly to take her seat. She lifted her head. And with the sight of those black fathomless eyes, fear returned. Fear and a kind of elation. For in that instant he had glimpsed the absoluteness of her freedom. Never at any moment would he know what she would do. Never would he control her. For a little longer she had stood looking at him, still smiling. Just an ordinary adolescent smile now. Then without word she had turned, walking obediently to an empty pew.

His hands were steady now as he reached for the package. The paper came off easily, and he worked the lid quickly from the small cardboard box. Within the plain white tissue were three long ribbons. Green and purple and gold. There could be no more pretending at doubt. It had to be Angelique. These could only be intended as a remembrance of his first gift to her—an offering brought back from Mardi Gras. Three perfect ribbons to tie in her gypsy hair.

He had been late this afternoon, and now Lindsey lay very still beside him. Just watching. Watching the rise and fall of his tanned naked chest as he slept. He always slept after they made love. She never could. Carefully she reached out and touched his hair, graying now at the hairline. She pulled back her arm and propped her head up with her hand. He looked so much younger in sleep, the small lines that sometimes showed around his eyes and across his forehead seemed to have disappeared. She was tempted to reach out and touch him again, but feared this time he would wake if she did, and he needed his rest. Instead she lay back against her pillow and closed her eyes, not to sleep, but to remember.

Each time was like the first time. His taking endless moments to undress her, slowly, oh so slowly, never hurrying. Touching her skin lightly as if he would somehow bruise her if he were not careful. And when his mouth finally opened over hers, he kissed her long and deep. A young and hungry kiss. But never hard . . . not at first. Then he would stop and bring his face up to gaze down at her. An almost quizzical look. And she would hold her breath until that quick smile of his finally reached his eyes. And then he would take her in his arms and carry her to the bed. She would lie quietly under him, not moving, but pressed so close that she could feel his heart thud between her breasts. Then, reaching to push him away a bit, she would find his pulse strong against the palm of her hand. And almost distractedly he would stare at her fingers trembling upon his chest, till after a moment he would move her hand and whisper, "I'm here."

Feeling him stir at her side now, she turned her head. He had drawn up one leg, and slid it down slowly as if he were testing the smoothness of the sheet. She moved nearer, lowering her head close to his, feeling his warm breath against her cheek.

They never discussed what they felt about each other. It was understood that there could never be more than what they shared here. And she worked hard at keeping up their unspoken agreement. Worked hard at keeping that tight lump that formed inside of her from rising up and bursting, from cracking her wide open so that all that was left was: *I love you, I love you, I love you....*

No, she had been good, had not given herself away, had not spoiled everything. But sometimes it was so difficult, like now, as she lay watching him sleep. She swallowed hard and moved away, resting once more on her side of the bed. She cursed herself silently, hating her weakness, praying that it would somehow become easier, that she would somehow grow to be like him—strong and controlled. Except when they made love and then he would let himself go.

Another movement and she knew that he had awakened. She could sense his eyes upon her. She turned, and for a time she watched him watching her. Then his hand clamped about her wrist and he was pulling her on top of him. She felt him slide hard inside of her, yet for a moment she remained still, resting comfortably upon his chest. Then she pushed up so that her small nipple fit easily into his mouth. When she eased away, he reached up and drew her lips to his, whispering, "Now, my darling, now..." And she began to move against him, slowly at first, then faster and harder, all the while his hands locked firmly around her hips, helping her. Then she heard him cry, "Open your eyes, Lindsey. Look at me. Look at me come, baby, look at me...."

And she looked down into his face, into the shining gray eyes, and smiled. "Yes, my darling Phillip, yes..."

Later, alone in the Capitol Hill row-house she shared with her husband, Lindsey sat quietly at her vanity in the bedroom, listening to the early-evening sounds filter through the constant drone of the air-conditioning unit. She glanced up and looked at her image reflected back at her from the antique mirror. The old mirror was one of the few things that had been worth salvaging from her apartment-living single days.

She leaned forward on her elbows and examined her face more closely—a ritual now after an afternoon with Phillip. From the first she had done this, looked at her face in the mirror, appraised her features carefully to see if those few hours spent with him had in some way changed her. She opened her eyes wider, scrutinizing the large green irises. "Windows of the soul"...or so they said. Yet the eyes that stared back at her revealed nothing.

She laughed softly, swinging the heavy fall of red hair back from her face, remembering how Phillip had told her once that making love makes a woman grow more beautiful. She recalled telling him that he had it all wrong: it wasn't *making* love, but *being in love* that was supposed to make the difference. She could still see that wicked smile spread across his mouth before he asked how in the world was he ever to know which it was with her. She knew he had been teasing that day, and she had kept up the game, saying that he would never know. And now... No, Phillip, you will never know.

She reached for the bottle of cologne, her finger poised, ready to release the scent, and remembered, remembered how it had all begun. With the fragrance...

It was late last October, almost nine months ago. There had been more than a hint of the coming winter in the air that day. And as she read over her shopping list, she congratulated herself. Never had she done a bit of Christmas shopping before Thanksgiving, and here she was standing in the middle of Woodies with more than half of it done. She glanced at her watch: 2:00. She hadn't stopped for lunch. Oh well, if she had lasted this long.

She moved toward the cosmetics section. Something in fragrance was a safe bet for almost anyone left on her list. She smiled as she paused before one of the counters, thinking of the mob scene this place would be in less than six weeks. She had just selected one of the cologne testers when...

"Your favorite?" The vaguely familiar voice came from directly behind her.

She turned abruptly and saw Phillip Camélière's smiling face. "Oh, Cardinal Camélière, I—"

"Please, Lindsey, I'm off today. Can't you see?" And her eyes followed the sweep of his hand, indicating the navy sport coat he was wearing over the light blue dress shirt, opened at the neck with no tie. "Just Phillip will do... in fact, Phillip will do nicely all of the time."

"I'm sorry." She searched for the correct words. "I'm not Catholic and..." She still wasn't getting this right, and she was angry with herself because she didn't understand why she was so nervous. But then she always felt this way around Phillip Camélière. A little uncomfortable, slightly on edge. This, despite the fact that he and Richard had become very good friends over the last few years, and that the three of them had been together socially dozens of times.

"There's no protocol between friends. And we are friends, aren't we, Lindsey?" He fixed her with his eyes.

"Yes, yes, of course..." She was still having trouble.

"Good, then it shall be Phillip from now on. Agreed?"

"I'll try... Phillip." His name seemed to stick in her throat.

He laughed, then reaching out, he took the bottle of fragrance from her hand. "Mmm, I like this. Let's see, what's this one called? Calyx. Interesting name. But this isn't the way to test perfume, is it?" And he moved his hand to her neck and lifted her hair, spraying the side of her throat. "There..." and he leaned over and took a deep breath. "Ah, that's better."

"Is it? I can't really tell." Her hand fluttered to her throat.

"Here." And he took her hand and sprayed a small cloud of the fragrance on her wrist. "There..."

She lifted her wrist to her nose. "Yes . . . yes . . ." She closed her eyes, breathing deeply. "Yes . . ." And when she opened her lids, he was staring at her, his gray eyes intense, the smile gone from his face. "Yes, it's . . . it's nice." She made her voice level, tearing her gaze away, looking over her shoulder at the maze of crystal bottles resting on the counter.

"Excuse me, please." He was saying something and she turned around to look up into his face. "I think that we've made a selection. We want a bottle of this," he said cheerfully, handing the sample to the attractive young woman who had walked over to where he was standing.

"Phillip . . ."

"Shh . . . My treat. I never get to buy anything for a pretty lady, unless it's a relative. One of the disadvantages of being a priest," he whispered.

And before she could do anything to stop him, he had purchased the perfume and was pulling her by the arm. "Now, enough shopping for one day. I'd love a glass of wine. Let's go somewhere where we can talk. I know just the place. It's not far. We can walk."

She never could recall where they went, or what she ate or drank. But she remembered clearly that Phillip had done most of the talking, smiling a great deal, touching her hand lightly every now and then to punctuate something he'd said. More than once, she recalled, he shook his head, mourning the fact that they had not done this sooner. Then she was in his car, driving faster than she wanted to think about, feeling the crisp autumn wind slice through the open windows, listening to something soft and dimly classical on the car's CD player.

When they had come to Rock Creek, he stopped and parked the car. He opened the door and took her by the hand. "We'll walk from here. I want to show you something."

They left the car behind and moved a short distance over sloping ground, then higher toward a small hill where the trees crowded closer together. The sun had begun to set and the air had become colder. When she shivered suddenly, he must have noticed because he pulled of his coat and placed it about her shoulders. "Better?" he asked, smiling down into her face.

"Yes," she replied, leaning against him a bit as he put his arm around her waist.

They stopped at the rise and looked out across the rolling hill. It had grown steadily darker, and the long shadows of the trees made everything below seem somehow indistinct and out of focus. But she could not mistake what she was seeing. The rows of headstones looked like small fragile bones rising from the dark earth. He turned then and whispered against her hair, "One of my favorite places."

She looked up and searched his eyes, still luminous and clear in the descending shadows. The she moved out of the shelter of his arms and circled down among the headstones, careful not to walk across any of the graves. Bending down, she read one of the inscriptions. "This is a very old cemetery," she said with no particular emphasis, glancing back over her shoulder to find him. He only smiled, and she knew he watched her as she touched the stone, her fingers tracing the outline of the name chiseled upon the weathered granite.

Then he was standing behind her. She had heard him move across the carpet of newly fallen leaves, yet she did not turn, did not stand, but remained quiet and huddled before the small marker. When he touched her, she closed her eyes, wanting to memorize the gentle play of his hand through her hair. Then he was on his knees beside her, turning her to face him. He stared at her for a moment as though he were somehow unsure of himself, as though he were seeking some kind of permission to do what he was about to do. But he didn't wait and he brought his face down quickly and kissed her, his mouth trembling upon her lips. She thrust herself against him then, pushing hard upon his chest, letting him know that she was unafraid, and that she wanted what was happening as much as he did.

She would always remember the sound of the dried autumn leaves crackling as he pressed her to the ground beneath him. And the fragrance of Calyx like springtime.

●   ●   ●

She turned when she heard the key in the lock.

"You're late." She spoke almost before he entered the room.

"Busy day." Richard had thrown his coat across a chair and was pulling at his tie. "You're not ready yet," he said, finally looking at her.

"Almost. I just have to slip on my dress." She stood and walked closer. "This is the second time this week that you've come home so late."

"Well, it's this way, Lindsey, I just don't have control over the entire U.S. Congress." He reached out and pulled on her hair. "What's this anyway? Are you keeping tabs on me?"

He wasn't angry, not even mildly annoyed. Like everything else, Richard's emotions were programmed. It was a matter of pushing the right buttons. But from past experience she knew that it was hard to make Richard Darrington angry. "No, Richard, I'm not keeping tabs," she answered. "Just amazed that you haven't figured that one out yet."

"What?" He had unbuttoned his shirt and was placing it on top of his suit jacket. In a minute the coat, pants, and shirt would be in a neat pile earmarked for the dry cleaners.

"I'm just amazed that you haven't figured out how to control Congress. Everything else works by your schedule."

"I'll ignore that last remark, Lindsey. Where is this thing tonight anyway?" He had stripped down to his shorts.

"National Gallery. Black tie." She stared at him for a moment. Then: "You want a divorce, Richard?" Now this question had real potential.

"Shit, Lindsey. Not tonight, for chrissakes. I'm dead on my feet and I have some fucking reception ahead of me, and you're standing here asking me asinine questions. Please give me a break."

She had struck pay dirt. He was angry. "I don't think it was an asinine question." She wouldn't leave it alone now.

"Okay, okay. It wasn't an asinine question."

"Well then . . ."

"What?"

"Answer me. Do you want a divorce?"

He didn't say anything for a moment, but merely stared at her. Then he walked toward her very slowly, pulling her into his arms, kissing her hard. "No, Lindsey, I don't want a divorce, now or ever," he whispered against her mouth, his blue eyes cold and clear.

"You're hurting me, Richard," she murmured, biting her lower lip.

He loosened his hold, dropping his head for a moment. When he looked at her, a softness seemed to have come into his eyes. "Lindsey..." He ran a finger down her cheek.

"No, Richard..." She pushed his hand away.

"Okay, Lindsey. I've had enough of your little games tonight. I'm not going to stand here and get into an argument with you. I don't have the time, energy, or inclination. Therefore, I would advise you to get your sweet ass dressed immediately if you intend to go with me to the National Gallery."

"What *do* you have time for, Richard?" She pressed closer to him and smiled. "Fucking your prick dry in Baltimore?"

He slapped her hard across the face. And for a crazy instant she understood what people meant when they said they saw stars. She stood dazed for a moment watching tiny bright lights dance in front of her eyes. She hadn't had time to fully accept that he had really hit her when she found that he had grabbed her into his arms and was whispering over and over that he was sorry, and to please, please forgive him. "Lindsey?" She heard him finally say her name, feeling his face against hers, his ragged breath loud against her ear.

"Let go of me." Her voice was quiet and even.

He pulled back, looking at her as if seeing her for the first time. Then his face twisted into a cold humorless smirk. "Okay, Lindsey, okay." His voice was friendly now, and she watched as he slowly finished undressing in front of her. Absently she thought that it was only the second time in their marriage that she had seen him naked like this. She stared at him for a moment, then pushed past him and walked toward the closet.

"Lindsey."

She turned. It was something about the way he had said it this time.

"I'm sorry."

"Forget it, Richard." She turned away and began pushing at the hangers in the closet.

"Lindsey, I love you. . . ."

She stopped at a dark green silk dress.

"Lindsey . . ." He spoke her name softly, and she could feel him standing beside her. "Maybe . . . maybe if . . ."

"No, Richard!" She knew what he wanted. "No, Richard, a baby won't make this better."

"Please, Lindsey." His voice broke for an instant. "Just think about it."

She turned to face him. "I have thought about it, Richard. There are just two miserable people in this relationship now. I don't want to make it three."

He pulled her into his arms then, his face coming nearer, his deep blue gaze pleading. "Please, let me make it better, baby. Please . . ." And she closed her eyes as he brought his mouth over hers.

CHAPTER TEN

Leaving the NCCB office building, John walked up Fourth Street and turned right on Michigan Avenue. It wasn't yet noon, but already heat radiated upward in steady waves from the pavement. Stopping for a moment, he ran a hand underneath his collar. Like most of the priests at Catholic University, he usually wore civies, but for his meeting with Monsignor Feeney, as on Wednesday with the Cardinal, he had worn clericals.

The traffic was heavy, and he waited patiently in front of the Theological College for the light at the corner to change. Beyond the flash and clamor of the passing cars, Gibbons Hall, like a sleeping dragon, hulked against the bright summer sky, dark grids of TV antennas spiking from its crenellated hide.

The light winked to green, and he crossed behind the cars, moving up the long stretch of concrete that fronted the Shrine of the Immaculate Conception. As he walked on toward Caldwell he reflected on this morning's meeting. Most of the Committee staff had been there to welcome him, and Monsignor Feeney had seemed genuinely pleased to have him working with them as consultant. It had gone well, and yet he had come away uneasy. There had been nothing concrete to disturb him, he admitted. It was something more nebulous—an air of unreality that had seemed to hang about the conference offices. Cardinal Camélière had assured him that he wished to avoid a schism, and John believed him. But sitting this morning in the NCCB offices, he had sensed a reckless momentum building, a rush to judgment that he wondered if even Phillip Camélière could control. For the first time he allowed himself to consider that the issues that divided the Church were not simply differences to be decided by time and careful scholarship, but ticking explosives with the capacity for great destruction. And now at last he asked himself the question that Alexandra Venée had asked. Where did he stand?

It was not so difficult to begin an answer. His personal sympathies, for whatever they were worth, were very much in keeping with what most would label the liberal line. All of the work he had been doing these past years had only reinforced his belief that the essence of all Jesus's teachings had been *Love one another*. As simple and as difficult as that.

It seemed to him that the liberal position was most in keeping with that message. Reform was necessary. But this morning in the office with Monsignor Feeney, he had begun to see the very real danger of a militant conference, an American Church united against Rome. He did not for a moment believe that the Church as a whole could ever be uprooted. His God would not let that be. But a clumsy division—that had happened once before. He did not want to be part of a revolution. There had to be a better way.

Once inside Caldwell, he headed straight for Brian's office. He needed to talk this out with him. Most everyone considered Brian to be solidly in Phillip Camélière's camp, but his guess was that Brian's feelings in this were much as his own. Whatever flaws his friend might have, he was still his own man. *Keep us straight*, Brian had joked, urging him to take the post with the Committee. But he had meant it. Brian counted on him not to follow blindly, as he himself would not.

"Monsignor Donovan is out this morning, Father Leighton." Hattie Barrett looked up brightly from her desk. "Some sort of meeting, I think. He wasn't specific."

Her smile, he noticed, lost some of its edge as she considered this. Hattie had been Brian's secretary for as long as John could remember, and usually knew better than the man himself where he would be at any given moment.

"Not a particularly pleasant meeting, I would think," she went on after a moment. "He left here growling like an old bear."

John laughed. Hattie had sounded almost glad. If Monsignor Donovan was going to start keeping secrets from her, at least he would have to pay.

"Would you like me to give him a message for you?"

"Just tell him I came by," he said, turning to the door. Then with his hand on the knob: "Nothing very urgent, Hattie, I spoke to him briefly yesterday. Just say that I'll try and catch him later."

He went to his own office and began sorting rather mechanically through his books. He wasn't really sorry now that his friend had been away from the office. It was unfair to go running to Brian, as if he were still a seminarian, to lay the burden of his conscience at his feet. It was better if he had some time to think this out and settle it in his own mind. Of course he would still talk to Brian, if for no other reason than that it would make him feel better. But there was little it would likely accomplish. As he kept repeating to anyone who would listen, he was a scholar and not a politician. In the end, he knew, he would continue to work for the Doctrine Committee. And he would pray, pray most earnestly, that whatever he might contribute would be used in a way of which he approved. What else, after all, could he do?

"Yes, Your Eminence, the Archangel is in place." Mantini spoke almost cheerfully into the receiver.

"Was there any problem executing this part of the plan?" The papal secretary of state's voice was without any particular inflection.

"No, Cardinal Flancon, there was but a small reluctance on the part of the Archangel. But in the end he agreed that it would be more convenient if he worked at the residence."

"The Archangel appears to be a very sensitive man, Archbishop Mantini. He will have to be handled with great care."

"Yes, Your Eminence, with great care."

"And Lucifer?"

"He is overjoyed at the prospect of having the Archangel where he can keep an eye on him." Mantini let out a short laugh.

"We must take great care with Lucifer as well." The secretary's voice was toneless, indicating that he had failed to see the humor in the archbishop's last observation. "He is not a man to be easily fooled, Archbishop Mantini. Everything is in a very delicate balance. The Holy Father would be most displeased if there were any costly errors."

"We have all been most vigilant about avoiding error, Your Eminence." Archbishop Mantini seasoned his voice with an unaccustomed humility, attempting to recover from his last blunder.

"That is good, Your Excellency."

"And when do we inform the Archangel of his mission, Your Eminence?" It was the old question.

"We must wait and let our young priest settle in, feel comfortable. We must not move too soon. I feel that the Leprechaun will know best when the moment is right. We will trust his judgment on this. When the Monsignor feels it is time, you must inform His Holiness."

If Mantini hated the fact that it would be Brian Donovan who would ultimately trigger *Lucifer,* he did not let it show in his voice. "Yes, Your Eminence," he said quietly.

"It is a grave and most serious thing which we are about to do, Archbishop Mantini. We must know that we are acting with right and just cause. There is no mistake, is there, Your Excellency? The Leprechaun is correct in his allegations against Lucifer?"

"Yes, Cardinal Flancon. There is no possibility of error. We have within our grasp everything we need to bring about the downfall of Lucifer and spare the Holy Mother Church."

"May God direct our hand, Archbishop Mantini."

When the papal Pro-Nuncio replaced the receiver, he

paused for a moment, staring at the white telephone. Then he turned around to face the man sitting across the room.

"It appears that Jean-Luc is a bit nervous, Monsignor Donovan."

"Nervous? About what? Everything is going according to plan. John is where we want him. I see no reason to be nervous." Donovan stood up abruptly, sensing that he somehow needed to mount a defense, and he would be at a greater advantage if he were on his feet.

"It appears that the papal secretary of state has some doubts about your suspicions concerning Cardinal Camélière."

"Were those his exact words?" Donovan took a step forward.

"Approximately, Monsignor." Mantini's voice betrayed his obvious self-satisfaction.

"For chrissakes, they're not getting cold feet now!" Donovan exploded.

"Now, now, Monsignor Donovan. Calm down. You are overreacting. It is my fault. Please, please sit down." Mantini waved his hand toward the chair that Donovan had vacated. "No, no, Rome has no intention of abandoning *Lucifer*. They just want a little reassurance, that's all."

"Reassurance?" Donovan positioned himself on the edge of his chair. "My God, hasn't Rome learned its lesson. The stench of Sindona and Calvi still pollutes the Vatican. And have they so stupidly forgotten His Eminence Cardinal Cody?" He stopped short and measured the old prelate for a moment. Then: "The evidence is there. Plain and clear. The special bank accounts. Thousands of dollars which cannot be accounted for. The secrecy. For God's sake, they would just need to watch Campesi for one afternoon to know that something's going on. He patrols that little office of his like a goddamn Gestapo chief." Donovan was on his feet again.

Mantini laughed. "I don't think I have ever seen you like this, Monsignor Donovan. I had forgotten that you Irish have tempers as bad as we Italians."

"I'm sorry." Donovan lowered his head and looked down at

his hands, examining them as though they were laboratory specimens. "'The best lack all conviction, while the worst are full of passionate intensity,'" he whispered softly.

"What words are these?" Mantini edged closer.

"Yeats. 'The Second Coming.'" Then with a jerk of frustration, he made his hands into tight angry fists and shoved them into the pockets of his pants. "I just don't understand why they cannot appreciate the simple fact that Rome has all it needs to nail Phillip Camélière. Shit, whether they like it or not, it's all they have to go on. They have no choice. If they don't move now, they may never get another chance. They might as well kiss the American Catholic Church good-bye."

For a long time Mantini said nothing. His round eyes like black marbles studied the man who stood in front of him. Slowly he angled his head to one side, as if he were considering something very important, something that was crucial to his understanding of this very dangerous game they were all playing. Then he smiled, a broad vulgar expression curling around his short white teeth.

"You know, Monsignor Donovan, I think I am just beginning to understand." His voice ran thick like heavy syrup. "I had forgotten. I had forgotten how much you really hate Phillip Camélière."

John Leighton didn't look very priestly, shuffling into the library with his cardboard box, shirt sleeves rolled up, black hair falling into his eyes. Quite a contrast to the other night, Alex thought. He didn't see her at the far end of the table till he stopped to set down the carton, and when he did, he didn't appear too happy. As if it were a shock. As if she were the last person in the world he should have expected.

"Good afternoon, John." She smiled winningly. "I was just skimming some of the books here on the table. I hope that was all right."

His face softened but he didn't actually return her smile. "Sure," he said. "It's fine. There're some more books in here." He had turned away from her, beginning to unload the carton.

Was it her imagination, or was he acting just a little strange? She shrugged it off and walked over to examine the books he had already unpacked. Kung, Shea, Rahner—she recognized the names, the new breed of Catholic theologians.

"I'm ashamed to say that I'm not very current on modern theological thought," she said, and when he didn't take the opening, she went on: "It's a good thing my editor doesn't know that. That's the one positive thing Murray sees in my being Phillip Camélière's niece. He probably assumes that I'm an expert on anything to do with the Church. The truth is I'm something of an embarrassment in that department. I'm afraid I'm not really a very good Catholic."

"There are many ways of being a good Catholic."

How very pat and preachy, she thought. Not like him at all. Standing this close, she felt acutely his unease. What had happened since Wednesday night's dinner? Whatever it was, she couldn't let it get in the way of the job she had to do. She left him to finish his unpacking and went back to her place at the other end of the table.

"I learned a lot this afternoon from my reading," she said, settling in her chair, holding up one of the books until finally he looked. "This one was totally fascinating. I had no idea that women played such a strong role in the early Church—some of the deaconesses who were mentioned seemed very much like priests."

Now at last he smiled.

That's better, Father Leighton, she thought, much better.

"I think Jesus made it plain throughout his ministry," he began, still smiling, "by his actions as well as his words, that women, like men, were to have a place in the new Church."

He stopped sorting through the books to give her his full attention. "The Mass in the beginning was very unstructured, a coming together to break bread in commemoration of the last supper Christ shared with his apostles. As you probably read in that book, the faithful celebrated Mass in their own homes. The very fact that the early Christians had no synagogues or temples was perhaps the thing which made it inevitable that the women could not be denied a role. It

would have been pretty tough, I guess, to throw them out of
their own kitchens."

They were safely on his ground now. She saw that the
tension had left his face completely. "Do I detect sympathy
for the cause of women in your voice?" she hazarded.

Her reward was another smile.

"Now that we are off the record, Alexandra... We *are* off
the record?"

She nodded.

"Well then..."

Third smile. *Jackpot.*

"I don't mind telling you my thoughts," he was saying. "I
just couldn't let you print my personal views as if they had
official weight."

But they do, she thought, or they should. You're too
modest, John Leighton. You are, after all, a theologian. But
they'd been down that road before. She knew better than to
say it, and wisely she kept her mouth shut.

"My opinion, Alexandra, is that women would make wonderful priests, and for decades now we've had a very real
shortage."

"Then why all the furor? The excommunications? It would
certainly seem that Bishop Vanderveer had practical as well
as historical justification for the ordinations. Why then is
Rome fighting it so hard?"

For a moment he hesitated. "To be fair," he began slowly,
as if easing into something he knew she would not like,
"there are the centuries of tradition. The apostles *were* all
men. And there are the faithful of many countries to consider.
Many would not easily accept women as priests."

She would not let him off the hook. "Tradition is such a
weak excuse when set against simple justice," she said.

"*Roma locuta, causa finita.*" He had looked away. "Rome
has spoken, the case is closed," he translated the Latin softly
beneath his breath. He still didn't meet her eyes, and for
long seconds he said nothing else.

"What are you thinking?"

He took a breath. "Of Rome," he said. "I was thinking of
Rome—the Vatican. Have you been there?"

"To Rome. Yes. I visited Uncle Phillip there one summer. Years ago." There was no response in his face to the lightness she had forced into her voice. She waited quietly, and finally he went on.

"But not within the inner walls. You could not have gone within the precincts of the Curia." His face remained withdrawn, and she sensed he was seeing the place as he spoke. "They are all so old in the Curia...and insular. Most in key positions are Italians, bureaucrats with no experience of pastoral work. They have not the least conception of the problems which face a parish priest. The laity they regard as a necessary evil. And women..." He made a soft harsh sound. "I guess you might say that the Curia is the ultimate men's club."

She listened carefully, watching the handsome solemn face, his lips twisting in a wry line at the last. The Curia Romana she knew well enough. Uncle Phillip had studied in Rome after his ordination and still delighted in telling tales about the papal entourage. Now, as president of the NCCB, these same Vatican bureaucrats had become his mortal enemies, and yet she had never heard her uncle describe them better than John Leighton. This was great material. John was going to be a wonderful source.

"How old are you, Alexandra?"

The question came abruptly, and totally out of the blue. "Twenty-six," she said, letting her puzzlement show in her voice.

He made no comment. Only nodded.

She started to say something to break the silence, but he spoke again.

"Practically speaking, it would be a difficult transition, having women in the priesthood, especially in combination with a change in unconditional celibacy. Catholics have no experience of either women priests or a married clergy."

It was a perfectly reasonable thing to say, but once more the tone of his voice had changed. He was putting her again at a distance.

"I'll go ahead and put together that bibliography you mentioned. In the meantime try these." He pushed several books toward her and began gathering up some of the others.

"You're leaving?"

"No... well, I'm going to my office. There are some things I need to put on computer. We'll talk later. Okay?"

He was picking up more of the books. Not looking at her.

"Yes, of course, John."

The disappointment must have sounded in her voice, because he stopped at the door. "You could make a list of questions for me...." He let it hang. Then he was gone.

She sat there stupidly for a minute staring at the door. Are you crazy, Alexandra, or did John Leighton just give you the brush-off? But she knew he had. He might be a priest, but he was acting just like a man.

"No, thank you. No dessert for me. Just coffee." Alex watched the waitress walk away with the remains of her lasagna. Italian restaurants are the worst, she thought. Why can you never stop with the antipasto?

Across the obligatory red-and-white-checked tablecloth, Frank was nodding absently in time to the piped-in music. Reflections from the low hanging fixture bounced like twin beacons in the lenses of his glasses.

"Frank, why don't you get contacts?" she asked him. "Just about anybody can wear them these days. You probably think those damn horn rims make you look the part or something, but... well, actually your eyes are gorgeous. I like to see them."

He smiled, feigning surprise. "Why, Alex, I didn't know you cared." He set down his glasses, and resting his elbows on the table, he leaned toward her, squinting, and laughed.

"What's so funny?" she said.

"You look like a very bad abstract painting."

"Thanks."

He laughed again and put back the glasses. "Maybe I will try contacts. When I get some time."

She made a sound of disbelief. "When I get some time"

was the same as "never" in Frank's vocabulary. "How's the drug story going?" she asked him. Miraculously they'd gotten through most of dinner without talking shop, but Frank's investigations were always interesting.

"I won't actually know till I hear from my contact again. *If* I hear from him." His voice was skeptical.

"Is that all you're going to say about it? Last night it sounded like you thought you had something."

"Oh, I don't know." He slumped back in the chair again. "Maybe . . . maybe." He drained the last of his wine. "There's not much more to tell you than what I could say over the phone. The guy's promising the moon but I'm just not comfortable with the setup. It'll probably all come to nothing. . . . Still, I've got this feeling."

"In your gut?" She laughed. "'Better run with it,'" she quoted. "Gregory's Ten Rules of Investigative Journalism. Number five or six, I believe."

"God, Alex. Don't you ever forget anything?"

"Just don't ask me to quote the other nine. . . . And don't you quote them." She had seen the warning sign of a smile forming beneath the mustache. "By the way, is it really true you worked for the *Enquirer* right out of high school?"

"Not that again," he groaned. "It was the *Greendale Enquirer*, my hometown paper. And I worked for them summer vacations. Carmichael's going to get himself a fat lip, if he doesn't stop spreading that rumor."

"That's what you get for planting that 'Aliens Abduct Montrose Housewife' story in the computer under his by-line." She laughed again.

The waitress arrived bearing her coffee and Frank's zabaglione. "Just a taste." She dipped a finger into his dessert.

"Get out of there, Alex." He batted at her hand playfully. "I knew that was coming. Why didn't you just order some?"

"This is all I'm taking. I said I just wanted a taste." She licked the last drop from her finger and, tearing open a couple packages of artificial sweetener, poured them into her cup. Defiantly she reached for the tiny pitcher of cream. "You know of course that I hate you," she said genially, making satisfying clouds in her coffee. "You eat like a truck driver and

never gain an ounce. And you don't exercise. Someday soon
it's going to catch up with your arteries."

"I've got faith in science." Frank smugly shoveled another overloaded spoonful into his mouth. "Just the other
day I read about some new drug waiting FDA approval.
Cleans the old arteries right out." He scraped the sides of
the glass for the last dregs of his dessert and reached for his
cigarettes.

"I guess science is going to save you from those, too."

"I'm counting on it." He took out his wallet. "My treat
tonight. You ready?" He put two twenties on the table.

She took a final sip of the coffee. "You know," she said,
"I should have ordered cappuccino." Frank just shook his
head.

Outside was cooler than it had been for a week. It was
Friday, and Adams-Morgan teemed with Bohemian energy.
The trendiest section of the District, its resident population
was a mixture of students, gays, and other nonconformists.
Everybody else turned up to slum.

"It feels wonderful tonight, but I'm afraid it's going to be a
miserable summer. D.C. gets as bad as New Orleans." She
put her arm through his as they started down Columbia
toward his apartment.

"Come on, let's cross the street." He was leading her
toward the curb.

"Oh, no you don't." She stopped solidly in her tracks.
"Annie's Attic is right on this block. And I'm going to look in
and see what's new. For as long as I want, Frank." It was a
statement and also a challenge.

"Okay."

He sounded resigned but she wasn't convinced. Still, it
maybe wouldn't hurt to relent a little. "I'll just look in the
window," she said. "If I don't see anything . . ."

But of course she did.

"Look at that pin! It's fabulous!"

"Not the big bug with the red eyes?"

"They're rubies, Frank. Or garnets. And it's not just a bug.
It's a praying mantis. It looks art nouveau."

"It looks like a bug, Alex."

"It's perfect for my decadent-jewelry collection. I'm going in, Frank." She looked up at him wide-eyed, daring him to object.

"You know, Alex, most of the time you're so normal. Why you periodically feel the need to cover yourself in snakes and spiders..."

She had to laugh. "Well, I can't explain it to you, but I've been collecting pieces like that since I was a teenager. My friend Davey's the one who named it the 'decadent-jewelry collection.'" She turned toward the entrance. "Are you coming?"

Frank's manly display of self-control didn't rule out a sigh, but he followed her in.

"You know I don't understand why you hate coming in here so much." She couldn't resist one last appeal. "You love old movies."

His look was long-suffering. "It's *not* the same thing." He wasn't going to give an inch.

The mantis was a costume piece, as she'd suspected—Annie's rarely carried the real thing. But it didn't matter. The pin was great. She didn't even bother to haggle. Just paid and put it on her collar. It looked totally wicked. Davey would die.

She glanced around for Frank and spotted him in a corner of the crowded shop. He seemed surprisingly happy, occupied in animated conversation with the owner, so she took the opportunity to browse through more of the jewelry and several racks of Annie's vintage clothes.

"Finished?" Frank had appeared at her side.

"Yes." Her eyes went inquiringly to the package in his hand.

"A radio." He opened the bag to let her look. "Old tube job from the forties. The owner here thinks he can get me the parts from some guy in Pennsylvania to make it work. It'll look great in my study."

She had a quick vision of the jumbled workroom to which he referred. Bite your tongue, she told herself, but she couldn't. "I thought you didn't like the stuff in Annie's," she said as innocently as possible.

"But this is different, Alex." He was explaining as if to an idiot. "Radios like this one revolutionized this country. This is a significant piece of American history."

Men! she thought, mentally throwing up her hands. "Why is it, Frank," she couldn't resist asking, "that anything in the decorative arts over ten years old is a piece of junk. But if it has gears, or an electrical cord hanging out of its kazoo, then it's valuable. Then it's *history*."

But he only laughed, and giving up, she followed him out the door.

She should have been suspicious as soon as they reached the apartment. It was just too neat. Although he usually did try with the living room, there was always at least some spillover from his work—newspapers spread over the dining table, stacks of files and clippings on the floor.

She flopped on the sofa, kicking off her shoes while he went over to put on a disc. "How about some Parkening?" He looked at her. "I like that dress."

Second warning. Unless it was something he hated, he never talked at all about her clothes.

"I wish you'd play for me yourself. You haven't done that in a long time."

"The Martin's out of tune." He waved a hand at the guitar case growing dusty in the corner. "And I'm out of practice. Not tonight. Listen," he said over the first strains of a Bach cantata. "Christopher Parkening sounds a lot better." He joined her on the couch. "You know you haven't said anything tonight about your assignment. You getting anywhere with the priest?"

"Father Leighton. Yes. He's preparing a bibliography for me."

"Oh, are we back to 'Father Leighton.' On the phone the other night it was 'John.'"

"Father Leighton. John," she said offhandedly, "whatever. He's been delightful. You should have heard him at the residence today talking about the Curia. They're the bureaucrats who really run the Vatican. It's the Curia that is Uncle Phillip's real nemesis, you know. Even more so than Pope Stephen. Well, anyway"—she forced herself back to the point—"John was lambasting the Curia's notorious prejudices against women. I think he agrees totally with Bishop Vanderveer that women should be allowed to enter the priesthood."

"You saw him at the residence?"

"Yes. Uncle Phillip offered him the use of his library and some office space. So it's convenient for me to do research in the library, too. I have him there to ask questions."

"Cozy."

She ignored his tone. "I think it's going to work out."

"You certainly have changed your tune about him. I remember when you thought he was something of an opportunist."

"Yes, I know. I'm really ashamed of that. I should have waited till I met him before forming a judgment."

"So you really like him now?"

"Yes, I do. I admitted that way back before I talked to Murray, remember. I wouldn't have gone out on a limb like that if I didn't think I could work with the man." She looked at him sharply. "Why all these questions?"

Frank smiled. "Jealousy?" He posed it as a question. "Maybe I don't like you spending so much time with another guy."

"Don't be silly, Frank," she said easily. "John's a priest."

"He's also a man."

She laughed. "Well, I don't think that you need worry. After all, we have a cardinal for a chaperon."

He didn't say anything more. Just reached over and kissed her. A very lingering kiss.

"Ummm," she said. "Nice." She waited for him to kiss her again but he stood up.

"You want anything from the kitchen? I'm going to have some wine."

"Okay. Sounds good. But just a little."

She was burrowed in the cushions, listening to the precise yet mellow tones of the classical guitar when Frank came back with the wine and two glasses. He sat down to the ceremony of uncorking the bottle.

"You know, Frank," she said, "this place could be great. There's so much good architectural detailing. The molding especially is beautiful."

He poured out a glass for her. "You could fix it up."

"Oh, wouldn't I just love doing it for you. You know I'm a suppressed interior designer. If only I had the time."

"What I meant was that you could hire a decorator." He drank some of the wine. "You know, to fix it up however you want. I'd like you to move in with me, Alex."

"Move in?"

"The nightly phone calls aren't getting it, Alex. If you lived here, then at least we'd get to see each other after work, no matter how late. And now that we both have flexible hours... You know the place is huge."

He kept hitting her with facts.

"You can have your own workroom. And I'd try to be neat."

He was so sincere. And he sat there looking at her, clearly expecting an answer. "Frank, I love my apartment." It was all she could think to say.

"Then don't give it up. That would be stupid anyway. It's a good investment. Just move some of your things over here, and stay whenever it's convenient."

The music ended and he walked over to the player. He put the disc into its jewel box before he turned to her. For just a moment an almost pleading note slipped into his voice. "I think we should give it a try."

She was numb. She had not been expecting this. What it was she was feeling, she honestly couldn't say. She went over and put her arms around him. "I'll think about it. Okay?"

All of a sudden he was sweeping her into his arms. Carrying her away.

"Frank. What on earth are you doing?" she squealed. "Are you crazy?"

"Pretend you're Scarlett O'Hara."

"Pretend what?" she said helplessly. But then she was laughing, all the way up the staircase to the bedroom.

He made love to her. Very sweet and easy. The evening's uncertainties faded and there was only the feel of his lips on her lips, on her breasts, brushing lightly over her belly. She heard herself moaning, "Good... so good." And then he was inside her, his big body a solid black shadow moving against

the window's filtered light. Arching upward, she moved with
him. Slow and steady. In rhythm.

When she could think again, Frank lay over her, the bristle
of his mustache tickling against her cheek, her name still
sounding in her ear.

He sat up against the headboard and lit a cigarette, but he
didn't turn on the light. And for a long time she lay silent,
watching the burning tip move from his mouth to his knee in
the dark.

"Frank..." She had started to say something, which afterward she could never remember.

The sparking stub of his cigarette flared as he crushed it
firmly out. "I love you, Alex." The soft words, never to be
spoken, came roaring out of the dark.

"I love you, too."

She was sorry before the words were even out.

CHAPTER ELEVEN

"Lindsey," Alex said, pushing the shopping bags farther to the side of the sofa, "Frank told me last night that he loved me."

Lindsey set down the two drinks she'd brought from the kitchen. "And what did you say?" She kicked aside her shoes and plopped on the sofa.

"I said I loved him, too."

"Do you?" Lindsey picked up her glass.

"Of course I do."

"So why am I not convinced?"

For a moment Alex looked almost angry. "I'm not trying to convince you, Lindsey."

"I didn't suppose you were. But I thought you might be trying to convince yourself."

Alex let out a long breath. "Does it sound like that?"

"Actually, yes. And I'm not so sure you don't love Frank, Alex. I know the other day you said there was no passion. But you might just be confusing chemistry with love. Richard and I have chemistry."

For a moment Lindsey looked away. Then: "When I met him, I thought Richard was perfect," she said. "Intelligent. Handsome. Committed. And to think by some miracle he'd chosen me. Talk about starry-eyed."

"But Richard is still all those things, Lindsey. So what's changed?"

"*I've* changed, I guess. I find I want things that the handsome, intelligent, committed Senator Darrington apparently can't give me. Things like warmth and understanding..." She stopped.

"Lindsey, I'm sorry. Is it his job?"

"That's part of it, I guess. But if he wasn't a senator, it would be something else. The job, whatever it was, would always come first. I don't know how to explain it to you, Alex—what Richard is."

"I don't understand." Alex was frowning.

"Richard has a set of roles. The up-and-coming senator. The charming sophisticate. The good friend. He runs them through like programs on a computer."

"Lindsey, you're describing a politician. Richard's got to be that way to survive. But with you..."

"No, I know what you're going to say. With me it must be different. That's what I thought for a long time. But it's not true. Richard's got a program for me, too. The loving husband."

"But, Lindsey..."

"Alex, it's impossible to explain."

"But I've seen him with you, Lindsey. I'm sure Richard loves you."

"Maybe. But enough talk about me and Richard. This was supposed to be about you and Frank, remember. Though obviously I'm the last one to give advice."

"Don't be silly. And besides, you're probably right. I'm twenty-six, Lindsey. Maybe I am supposed to be past starry-eyed. Frank said we should try moving in together, and I suppose it is the next step. We can't go on like we have been indefinitely."

"So"—Lindsey smiled now—"you going to wear that dress you bought for him tonight?"

Alex shook her head. "Frank's out of town. But I might wear the dress anyway. It's business. I'm taking Father Leighton to dinner."

•   •   •

After Alex left, Lindsey sat on the sofa, frowning into her drink. There was so much she wanted to say to Alex. But she knew she never could. As it was, she'd said more than she should have about Richard. Yet not enough to make Alex see. *You don't understand, Alex, what Richard is,* she'd told her. As if she really understood it herself.

For a long time after their marriage she'd hung on to her illusions about Richard, even while she'd watched him operate. With family and friends. With his colleagues in the Senate. Richard Darrington the perfect mirror. Hard and cold, and precisely reflective. Giving back what each of them wanted to see.

For years she'd believed herself to be the sole exception. A sort of refuge. So what if Richard's political manipulations and personal deceits disgusted her. Wasn't the fact that he let her see what he did proof positive that he loved her, trusted her? The one person for whom there need be no show. *See, Lindsey, this is what I'm forced to do. But not with you. Never with you, Lindsey.*

For a long time it had fooled her. The way he seemed to share himself. The way he seemed to understand her. Remembering all the silly little things that made her laugh. Finding all the perfect gifts for Christmases and her birthdays. The things he did for her in bed. Not proofs of love at all, but ways to control her.

Because the truth was that Richard didn't love her. Didn't even really want to know her. Not the flesh-and-blood Lindsey who cried real tears when she'd first found out about his affairs. Not the living breathing person who thought and felt, who had opinions of her own. No, Richard wanted nothing *but* the surface, the appearance of the perfect Senate wife. She was in his life in the same way as all the others. As backdrop. A thing. A piece of furniture to be moved around on the soundstage of the life of Richard Darrington.

Whoever that was.

And that was the scary part. The thing she hadn't yet figured out. Was Richard flesh and blood to himself? What was it she still loved even now? A monster or something trapped and frightened?

It was a question she had largely given up since Phillip, and yet it was always there, nagging at her. The reason why she always baited Richard now. She wanted to make him mad, force him to feel something, some emotion she could believe was real. And she needed him angry at her. She knew that, too. She was betraying him after all.

It was a gypsy moth's room—wisps and flounces of delicate lace gathered above the white iron bed and around small circular tables. Everywhere there was the illumination of flickering candles, so that one had a distinct but fleeting image of a scene from *Barry Lyndon*.

The gypsy moth spread her wings. A graceful natural motion. Her deep brown hair fanning out from her face, her eyelids fluttering open above dark irises. Carla Fiorelli ran her tongue around the pouty curve of her mouth as she yanked on the long cords that bound her arms and legs to the bed.

She raised her head and cursed him softly. Then a quick snap of her perfect white teeth. But he was too quick and he jerked his face away before she could draw blood. He laughed loudly, enjoying her anger and frustration, daring to bring his face close once more. "Tell me that you want me, Carla. Beg for it. . . ." He breathed the words against her face.

"I want . . ."

"No, not like that. You know what to say."

"Fuck me. Please fuck me now. Please . . ."

He brought his hands down to her waist, pulling her hips off the bed, so that the wings of her dark hair swung free and loose across the pillow. He made a single perfect arc of her body as he came inside of her.

After, she lit a cigarette and blew out a pale blue cloud of smoke. Then she puckered her mouth to form smoke rings, watching as they floated in ever-widening halos over her head.

"Why do you do that?" He leaned over her, his face temporarily shrouded in a puff of smoke.

"Do what?" She turned her head on the pillows toward him.

"Smoke. You know it's bad for your health."

"So's screwing . . . if you're not careful who you sleep with." She half smiled, but her dark eyes glistened mischievously.

"And what's that supposed to mean?" He sat up. "You know you're the only woman I sleep with. You're all I can handle." He garbled his last words as he bent over her and brought one of her nipples into his mouth.

"Oh, so you're not fucking your wife?" She played dumb, her fingers stroking the short hairs at the nape of his neck.

He lifted his head and looked into her face. Then he rolled onto his back away from her.

"Okay, okay. I'm sorry. Not fair. Come on. . . ." She pressed her body closer, drawing up one leg across his groin. "Come on. . . ." She moved her leg in small circles. "Please . . ."

He glanced down into her upturned face, then grabbed a lock of her dark hair, pulling it hard so that her head was angled further back and he could really see her eyes.

"You, Carla baby, are a goddamn spy. Don't think I'm not up to your little tricks, *cara mia*," he spoke into her face, purposely anglicizing the last words. "The boys say: 'Now, Carla, first you pass him the money, all sweet and business-like. Then you be nice to our man. Real nice, but all the time you keep an eye on him. And keep your ears open. Make sure our man doesn't get into any trouble. Do anything stupid. Keep him happy, Carla. Then we'll be happy. You'll be happy. Everybody'll be happy, Carla. One big happy family.'"

For a moment she didn't say anything. Then she grabbed his hand and jerked it away. "Is that what you think? You think I fuck you because I'm told to fuck you. You think that I take good care of you so that you don't get out of line. Is that what you think?" She was sitting up in bed now, the sheet pulled up to cover her breasts. "Listen, you son of a bitch, Carla Fiorelli is no whore. I don't fuck anybody unless I want

to. You understand that Mr. U.S. Senator. Mr. Big Shot
Richard Darrington!"

It was just before eight o'clock when Alex pulled up at the
curb on Connecticut Avenue. John Leighton was waiting in
front of his apartment building, just as he'd said. She reached
over and unlocked the door. "Hi," she said as he pulled open
the door and sat down. "I didn't keep you waiting?" she
asked, checking the sideview mirror as she moved out into
the flow of traffic.

"No, I'd just walked down. Thanks for picking me up. We
could have gone in my car." His voice was polite and sincere.
One thing she had learned right away about John Leighton
was that he was no phony.

"I asked you out, remember, Father Leighton. My treat all
the way. You don't have a thing about a woman doing all the
honors? But of course, you don't. Not a man ready for the
ordination of women." She laughed, making everything sound
like an inside joke just between the two of them.

"Well . . ." He stammered a bit. "I'm still fairly old-fashioned
about some things."

She had stopped for a traffic light just then, and she turned
to glance at him. He had on a light tan suit with a pale blue
shirt and darker blue tie, and he looked like something out of
Gentlemen's Quarterly, but without that slick finish that said
he had worked at it. She doubted if he even knew he was
handsome.

"I'll just bet you gave your sisters a hard time," she
teased, turning her head forward again to move on the green
signal.

He laughed softly. "No, not really. I guess I was always too
wound up in myself to really notice what my sisters did. I
regret that now."

She changed the subject. "I hope you're not one of those
meat-and-potatoes men. You know the type—won't try anything new."

"I'll have to admit my tastes are rather simple. Don't forget
I'm just a small-town Midwestern boy."

"Well, tonight you're going to have to be adventurous. And

I won't say another word. Trust me." And she turned and flashed him a smile.

"Why don't I like the way that sounded?" His voice seemed skeptical, but he had returned her smile, and she imagined that at this moment Father John Leighton was having a very good time.

Alex found a parking place a half block down from the restaurant, which was tucked neatly away on N Street, between Seventeenth and Connecticut Avenue.

"Well, what do you think?" she asked him after they'd been seated.

"It's beautiful," he said, glancing around the patio.

"It is, isn't it? Actually it reminds me a lot of New Orleans. Many of the old town houses in the French Quarter were built around courtyards. Have you ever been to New Orleans, John?"

"No, I'm sorry to say. But I'd like to go someday."

"You'd love it. It's really very special. Uncle Phillip got to serve there as an auxiliary bishop for several years."

"That must have been nice for him. Returning home."

"Yes, he loves New Orleans more than I do. But I think he's rather gotten used to the District."

"I'd imagined he was pleased when you came up to work on the *Post*."

"Yes, he was."

"You and your uncle seem close."

"Yes, sometimes I think of him more as my father than my own father. I really have to be careful. Daddy is sensitive about Uncle Phillip. And I do love Daddy so very much. I guess we just seem to close him out sometimes."

"You and Cardinal Camélière?"

"And my mother. She and Uncle Phillip are very close, too. I used to balk at all that research which claimed that there existed these strange mysterious bonds between twins. But now, when I see Mother and Uncle Phillip together, I understand what they mean."

"Do you get to see your family often?"

"I just came back from New Orleans a couple of weeks ago. For my birthday."

"Your twenty-sixth birthday."

There it was again, the reference to her age.

"Yes, my twenty-sixth. And you, do you go home very often?"

"I haven't been home in three years. Maybe after the Conference."

"Before you finish your book?"

"Yes, before the book. Mom and Dad are getting old. I don't want anything to happen. You know, my mother never ends a letter without asking me when am I coming home for a visit."

"What's home like?"

"Oh, nothing special. Certainly nothing like New Orleans. Nice town, friendly people."

"But you're not too far from Chicago, are you?"

"No. And growing up, it was a real treat going into the big city. I loved all of the wonderful chaos. But it frightened me a little, too. Made me want to protect myself. Like something was going to creep up and steal a part of me. Crazy, isn't it? But I always used to think of Chicago as this huge sucking vampire. Irresistible, but deadly." He stopped and looked at her. "Not very pleasant dinner conversation."

"On the contrary. That's just the kind of thing a reporter never finds in a press kit."

"Is that what it is, Alexandra Venée? Is it because you are a reporter that it's so easy for me to talk to you? Well, not so easy sometimes..."

She was glad he had said it, brought it up. At least he, too, conceded that he'd had a problem communicating yesterday. Why, John Leighton, why? she wondered. But she wasn't about to dig deeper. She glanced up from the menu and smiled. "Ready to order?"

"You're going to have to help me, Alex. I've never had Arabian food before."

"Actually I think it's Lebanese or Syrian cuisine. At any rate it's exquisite and, I'm afraid, terribly rich."

"Sounds wonderful."

"It is. We'll have to have some kibby, of course, and some

stuffed grape leaves. And tabouli, and tahini sauce with that fabulous unleavened bread."

"I'm afraid I don't know what you're talking about, Alex, but it sounds like an awful lot of food."

"We don't have to eat all of it. But I want you to sample everything. Here, why don't you order us some wine. I'm not very particular."

"A red okay with you? I hardly qualify as a connoisseur. Most of my wine tasting has been limited to the altar wines at Mass."

She laughed. "I'd almost forgotten about that. Where do you say Mass, John?"

"I usually say Mass at the chapel in Caldwell. But Cardinal Camélière said I could be put on the schedule at the Pastoral Center."

She didn't say anything for a moment, but thought that she'd very much like to attend a Mass said by Father John Leighton. Then: "Well, I guess we better order. Don't know about you, John, but I'm starved."

Later, as they left the restaurant and walked to find her car, she decided that it had been a very lovely evening so far. Much better than she had even hoped. John Leighton had been warm and friendly. And it seemed that whatever had brought on yesterday's bout of uneasiness had suddenly disappeared. So it was not unexpected when she drove up to the front of his apartment building that he asked her to come up for some coffee. And not surprising that she accepted.

She could hear him now, moving about, making that puttering noise men make when left to their own devices in a kitchen. He was saying something about not being able to promise her coffee up to New Orleans standards.

"I won't complain. Need some help?"

"No, won't be but a minute. Please make yourself comfortable. Turn on the TV, if you like."

She walked around the small living room, which she'd imagined served as more of a study than anything else. She didn't think Father John Leighton had many guests. In fact, her instincts told her that she was probably his first visitor.

And the apartment itself—spare, almost Spartan. Nothing about it identifying the person who lived here. Rented furnishings. She guessed that the moment she'd walked in. No pictures on the walls, no little objects collecting dust that might provide a clue to the character of the man. If there was any kind of revelation, it lay in the subject matter and quantity of the books piled in neat stacks on a desk in one corner against a wall.

She popped her head into the small, rather old-fashioned kitchen. "Sure you don't need the woman's touch?"

He turned around slightly and laughed. "I probably do. But you'll have to trust me this time. I think it'll be drinkable."

"Okay." And she moved back into the living room. Walking over to a rather longish table crouched in a corner, she reached to turn on the lamp. She was surprised that the photographs had evaded her fine reporter's eye, but it was dark in this corner, and without the lamp they wouldn't have been visible at all. A variety of frames filled with smiling faces sat somewhat decoratively arranged on the table. Simple unpretentious faces. A mother. A father. Sisters and brothers. Evidence of a loving and close Irish family. Bits and pieces of time framed and held for safekeeping. Some photographs were old, others newer. Most were candid snapshots. Unprofessional, but endearing. Others were posed studio portraits. Less appealing, but still very real and honest.

She picked up the largest photograph in the collection, held in a beautiful old silver frame. She had an immediate image of John's mother buying the frame and sending him the photograph in it. A remembrance of a very special day. It was a picture of a very young John Leighton with his parents. His dad looking so proud, his mother with so much love clearly written upon her pretty face. And there was John between the two of them, in the stiff Roman collar of a Catholic priest, just a trace of a smile about his lips, his eyes grave and intense. For a moment she stood and stared at the photograph, a small but important fragment of John Leighton's life, and tried to see beyond the simple black-and-white image. But there was just the half smile that said he didn't want to have his picture taken, and the eyes, serious but giving away no secrets.

"What's going on out there?" he called from the kitchen.

"Oh, nothing."

"I'm just about finished."

"Take your time." And she reached for another photograph. It was a group picture—one of those pictures that happens when people are very young and somehow know they'll never quite be the same as they are on this day, and someone says "We gotta have a picture." Six boys and four girls squatted or stood posed in front of some kind of concession stand, the type that used to be found at amusement parks or on beaches. It must have been a summer outing. A couple of the boys had on what appeared to be swimming trunks. The girls were dressed in shorts and cotton blouses. John was at one end of the line that stood in the background, his body thin as only the bodies of teenage boys can be thin. His dark hair tumbled into his eyes, and he had his arm around one of the girls. A small blonde who wore a rather hurt expression on her face despite the fact that she was smiling. It was something about the way they stood next to each other, the way his hand rested on her shoulder, that told her the girl was not one of John Leighton's sisters.

"Well, for better or worse, it's ready." He came in balancing a tray with a pot of coffee, cups, and saucers. "Alex..." He turned and saw her standing in the corner, still holding the picture in her hand.

"I was just looking at some of these," she stammered almost guiltily, like a disobedient child caught red-handed.

He set the tray down and walked over to where she was standing and took the photograph from her. "Brigit," was all he said as he looked down at the picture. It seemed that he was trying to explain with that single name some mystery about his life that she had stumbled upon. Then he settled the picture back among the others and walked toward where he had laid the tray. "Ready for some coffee?" His voice sounded perfectly natural.

"Love some." And she followed him to the sofa where he'd sat and begun to pour out a cup of coffee.

"Black as sin, right?" He passed her the cup.

"You remembered." She laughed, taking it from his hand. "Actually I do like cream and sugar sometimes."

"That's right. Café au lait. New Orleans style."

"Umm, this is good, John Leighton."

"Thank you. Making coffee is about the extent of my culinary skills."

"Do you like it here? Living alone?" She slid off her shoes and drew up her legs, nestling into the sofa.

"Yes, I have to admit I can get a lot more work done."

"And you like your privacy." She watched his profile over the rim of her cup.

He turned and stared at her. She saw something close to amazement in his eyes, surprise at her having discovered some secret he'd thought he'd somehow managed to keep hidden. "Yes," he said resignedly, as though knowing that his clumsy efforts at camouflage had only fooled himself.

"I think that John Leighton is a very private person. Does that bother you?"

"What? My being private?" He looked up from the black liquid he was sloshing around his cup.

"No, that I said it."

He didn't answer her at first but seemed to be studying her face. Slowly, carefully, like an artist preparing to do a portrait. She could see that his eyes were very clear and unprotected in the soft yellow light coming from the lamps.

"No, that doesn't bother me, Alex. But it's hard for me to"—he seemed to be searching for the right words—"to be private with you." He stretched out his arm and placed his half-empty cup on the coffee table.

"John . . ." He turned abruptly at the sound of her voice.

"Yes, Alexandra." He said her name like he somehow enjoyed the way it fitted between his tongue and teeth.

"Do priests . . . ever feel lonely?" She hesitated, desperately trying to recall if she had ever had the impression that her Uncle Phillip was lonely. But she couldn't remember thinking so.

"Yes, Alex." He ran his fingers through his dark hair. "We're human. Isn't that the right answer?"

"Is it? For you, I mean."

"Yes." The word seemed to close off his breathing. She heard him inhale deeply, and watched him begin to loosen his tie. Then he suddenly smiled, his eyes brighter, happier. And reaching out, he took her hand, clasping it lightly in his own. "Well, maybe not so lonely anymore."

She could feel the warmth of his palm, the slight pressure of his fingers around her wrist, and she didn't want him to ever let go of her. "John... John..." she repeated his name.

"We're friends, aren't we, Alex?"

"Yes, John, we're friends."

He brought her hand to his face and stroked it lightly across his cheek. She felt his almost too-warm skin, and the fresh beginnings of his beard brush against the back of her hand.

Then he released his hold and was standing, striding across the room toward his desk, going through a stack of books. "Here it is," he said finally as he walked back to the sofa. "I want you to have this, Alex. Keep it. I have another copy. Maybe it will help you to understand how it is with priests. How it is for anyone who has made Jesus the focus of his life. How the loneliness can never last when you know He is always close... waiting to come in."

And she reached out and took from his hand a small paperbound book. Karl Rahner's *The Love of Jesus and the Love of Neighbor*.

John sat up in bed, the force of his orgasm like a bullet searing through his chest. For a few minutes he merely sat, very still, not moving, not even thinking, just breathing very deeply. Letting the waves of aftershock wash over him. Then he got up and walked to the window and looked down into the street. There was still some life below, along the sidewalks, and in the broad stretch of road that was Connecticut Avenue. He always wondered where these faceless strangers who walked about, or drove around in cars, were going at this late hour.

He needed some time to get adjusted to it. It had never happened before... not quite like this. Oh, he had had the dream . . . the dream of Brigit. It was almost something he had gotten used to, like a tooth that was slightly out of line with the others. And he had dreamed of Alexandra before, at least twice that he could remember. But the dream had always started with Brigit, then Alex's face, Alex's body slipped under him, and Brigit faded away until the next time he had the dream.

But tonight the dream had been different. It had begun, and it had ended with Alexandra Venée.

CHAPTER TWELVE

Bright Maryland sunshine beat against the louvered windows, but inside, the office was hushed and dim. Eyes closed, head tipped back, his arms supported loosely in the big wooden frame, Phillip sat alert and quiet in the chair behind his desk.

Angelique. He had been completely certain of her reentrance into his life since Thursday when the second package had arrived, and it disturbed him that he had not yet dealt with the reality of that fact. Deliberately he settled his shoulders more comfortably against the thick leather upholstery, determined to deal with it now.

Angelique. Deviant angel. Now more than ever a secret to be kept hidden.

Angelique. There had been no word of her since the pact made with her uncle. A total and lasting silence had been part of their bargain, and the man had kept his word, disappearing completely with her as he had promised. So why now after all these years should there come these ominous silent messages? Had the money at last run out? Then why not just ask for more? Why was there the need for mystery?

Emile Robichaux had been a simple man, open and direct. These anonymous packages would never be his way. Angelique, and Angelique alone, must be responsible. And Angelique, unless she was greatly changed, had but little understanding of money. What else, after twenty-six years, could she want?

An image of her face, the dark eyes at once childlike and ageless, filled his mind. And despite his promise to himself that he would think only of now, of what he must do in the present, his thoughts slipped backward into memory.

For three or four Sundays in a row her uncle had brought her for Mass and catechism, waiting till the class was over to take her back to the cabin in the swamp. But on that Sunday he so well remembered, Emile had come to him before the Mass to explain that he must leave early today and his niece must miss her lessons. But that was not necessary, he had told the man, his heart pounding in his throat. Angelique's religious instruction was important. He himself would see her safely home.

He could not be sure any longer what he had really intended that day. For a long time, for years, he could convince himself that his motives when he spoke to Emile had been pure. Even now he remembered with some certainty his firm resolve that that first strange episode with her should be forgotten, even unconfessed, as a thing that had never happened.

She'd sat quietly in the pew, staring up at him with those haunting, questioning eyes, as the other children filed out. And he'd realized quite suddenly that except for the catechism class, there had been not a word between them.

"Angelique." He went over to look down at her. "Are you hungry?"

She nodded, the eyes still locked upon his face.

He had the lunch the rectory cook had made for him. It was plenty enough for two. "We'll have a picnic then," he told her, smiling his priest's smile, "on the bayou."

The sky was the bleached blue of summer with high white clouds like tenting gone to tatters in the wind and sun. They moved noisily on the sluggish rolling water, pushed grudgingly ahead by the ancient skiff's tiny outboard motor. Except in answer to his requests for direction, Angelique said nothing. It was the same as in his class, where her responses came only to direct questions. He didn't understand her. She was undoubtedly strange, but he did not think she was stupid, although he was told that the teacher in the one-room public school despaired of her and continued to ignore her frequent absences. Perhaps now was a good time to speak to her about the importance of her education.

"Angelique," he shouted above the angry whine of the motor.

She turned from where she had been gazing outward beyond the prow to look at him. Still she said nothing.

"Angelique," he began, "you must meet the school bus when it comes to pick you up every morning. School is important, Angelique."

"I want to eat now," she said, turning her face away. He barely caught her next words, so direct and unexpected. "I know an island." She was pointing ahead to a narrow channel.

The simple gesture was somehow compelling. He cut the engine, which throttled down to a strangled put-puttering, and nosed toward the opening. The skiff arced perfectly across the river to the channel, passing through hollow cypress stumps like rotting gateposts.

Behind them the bright sky and openness, hot sun and the dead-fish smell of the river. Within, a choking green tunnel—a leafy rib cage of black willows braced above the hyacinth-infested water. He cut off the motor and tilted it forward, out of danger. Water thick and oily ran from the propeller, clotting in swollen beads on the upturned blades. A large dark insect skimmered in over the lilies, buzzing in pale mockery of the dead engine, and for a moment he watched it hover in the blue-gas haze that lingered like a departing soul over the hot casing. Then, turning forward, he lifted the oar, cutting in slow motion through the bobbing hyacinth carpet, the fibrous root stems sucking against each stroke of the paddle. And at the very point of the prow, Angelique balanced dangerously, faintly Egyptian in her gauzy dress, her finger still pointing ahead into the dappled silence.

The island was a high rise of land in the middle of the

widening channel, large enough for a modest grove of cypress. At the sight of it Angelique was all animation—laughing in delight, helping him to pull the small boat ashore, leading him to a moss-draped oak that had somehow survived the centuries of sediment and high water. They sat in its shade sharing a thermos of milk and thick ham sandwiches. It was cooler in the shadows, and they settled against the rough bark of the oak, the soft breezes stirring in the surrounding trees. The sky was visible as it had not been from the willow-lined channel; irregular blue patches stretched flat between the black tracery of branches. And yet it was not peaceful. Insects buzzed and hummed in the surrounding scrub. Against their fuzzy rhythms, a songbird piped too brightly. This waxing and waning of sound, the incessant shifting of shadow and light, he found strangely disturbing, as if some huge and unsuspected beast moved restlessly just beneath the fabric of familiar life.

He watched Angelique devour her food with a teenager's appetite. Her air of strangeness was gone now, and despite the unsettling atmosphere, he could almost continue to believe that their first weird encounter had never been. Quite obviously she had said nothing to her uncle, to anyone.

"You are the god of the bayou?"

The question had taken him so completely aback that for long moments he said nothing, only looked at the intent face as she watched him, poised in the act of eating the last of the sandwiches. It was not only her words that had startled him, but that she had spoken at all.

Then he laughed, imagining foolishly that he comprehended her confusion. "I don't think you understand, Angelique." He smiled down at her. "I'm a priest. God's representative, not God himself."

She sat up straight, frowning as if his words were not quite intelligible. "My mother used to tell me about the gods," she said, "before she went away."

"The *gods*?"

"She said the spirits of the gods are everywhere. In the earth and the trees. In the river and bayou." She looked out toward the water, her fingers grazing lightly the rough bole of the oak. "She used to dance with them." She said it as a simple statement of fact, not as a challenge.

"I saw you in the pirogue." Her gaze was again fastened on his face. "You drew blood from the river. I knew then that you were ridden by the spirit, the god of the waters."

"Angelique..." It was in his mind to protest. She had fashioned a dark myth out of something as simple as a fish bite on the finger. Had she heard nothing at all these last weeks in his class? Had his careful words of Christ and the Father made no dent in whatever primitive beliefs her mother might have left her? "Angelique," he said, "listen."

But she had jumped to her feet, and as he shifted on his knees toward her, she began to whirl about him singing.

"Angelique," he called to her, trying to make his voice firm, angry. "Angelique." The name had become a litany against her weird singsong chant. He reached up to stop her. "You'll make yourself sick, Angelique," he cried. But she only whirled faster.

Finally he caught hold of the drifting fabric of her skirt, the cloth twisting around in his hand till she spiraled in upon him, falling, knocking him completely to the ground. Laughing. She was laughing. Her dark hair hanging above his face, the black eyes flat and shining.

Again it was as in the water. She seemed elemental, a bridge into mystery. She fell full length upon him, her parted lips soft against his throat, her breasts pinioning him to the ground. And even as he fought to resist now, the plans were forming in his mind. He would speak to her uncle, arrange to return her every Sunday to the cabin. She was moving over him wildly. Kissing him. She smelled of mayonnaise and the warm brown earth. He rolled over and looked into her face. The black eyes pulled him down....

"Uncle Phillip?"

"Oh, come in, Alex." He blinked to see her standing tentatively at the doorway.

"I just wanted to say hello before I got to work in the library. I can come back later if you're busy."

"Never too busy for you, Alex. Come in," he repeated,

motioning. "And turn on the lights. I just had some things to think over."

She hit the switch and walked over to pull one of the more comfortable chairs up to his desk.

"So how's the work going?" he asked her.

"Great. This is one epic scrape you've gotten yourself into, Cardinal Camélière."

He laughed.

"I talked to Mother last night," she said.

"Did she tell you she's going to be able to fly in early enough next Thursday to make my Mass?"

"Yes, but Daddy's not coming. He's got some important meeting. Bank business, I think Mother said."

He read the disappointment in her eyes. "It *is* a weekday, Alex."

"Oh, I know." She brightened. "Mother said that you wanted us both to stay with you at the residence through the weekend. And she told me about *60 Minutes*, too. When did that happen?"

"They called Friday after you left. I guess all this talk about schism has piqued their interest. And I guess they thought my thirtieth anniversary was a good tie-in." He smiled.

"Are they going to be at the Mass and the reception?"

"No, just the Mass. They plan on interviewing me right after."

She frowned. "I'm not sure I like all this, Uncle Phillip. It makes me realize how really close this whole thing with the Vatican is getting. I keep remembering what you told me that night on the plane about Pope Stephen. You said he would do whatever he had to to save the old Church."

"Alex. What can he do? If he tosses me out with the bad apples, he tosses out most of the American Church. This country's bishops stand with me. It was the Church I was concerned for when I said that, not myself."

"Are you sure?"

"Alex." He held out his arms to her.

She got up and came to sit in his lap.

"Still not too old for this?"

"Never, Uncle Phillip."

Later, watching her leave, he thought how beautiful and good she was, how much he truly loved her. Alexandra was one of his achievements, no doubt his best, and at least where she was concerned, he need never fear his motives.

He considered his youthful innocence, his desire to be cleansed by his church. Had he ever truly believed that he could resist the lure and the challenge of clerical politics at the highest levels? He honestly did not know. That Phillip Camélière who had spent the long night of his twenty-second birthday before the altar, bargaining with his God to save him—that Phillip Camélière was a boy he had lost touch with long decades ago. He had given up trying to remember that boy and his motives. Given up trying to justify what he had become.

And he was not immoral. He played by rules. In his world there were only two mortal sins. And these he would never commit. He would never willingly hurt the people he loved. And he would never seek to deny responsibility for even the least of his acts. Always he had sought, no matter the cost, what he deemed best for those that he cared for. And it was his pride that win or lose he could stand the consequences of his decisions. His methods, if they were known, might be condemned, but better a concrete good than an abstract one.

And Alex was happy. And Margaret. Even Lindsey.

He remembered why he was sitting here. Angelique was a threat. To him. To them. To everything he had built. Some decision was required. But what? Hire a detective? Begin some sort of investigation? He didn't like it. A third party would have to know more than he wanted to tell.

For the fleetest of moments he felt an unfocused anger, but he fought it down. Anger. Frustration. They were useless. He hated inaction, but in some circumstances it was better just to wait.

In his favorite Bergman film, Death played at chess with the Knight. In the end Death had won, but in prolonging the game, the Knight had gained time for the three that he loved to escape. Sooner or later Angelique would show herself. He'd know how to meet her then.

Angelique. The name seeped like poison into his mind.
Angelique. Angel of judgment. His nemesis.

"Hello, John." Brian looked up smiling from his desk.
"Sorry I missed you the other day."

"No problem." John settled himself in the familiar chair. "I
had just dropped by for a second to talk. I'd been to the
NCCB offices that morning and walked over here to get some
books from my office."

"What was your impression of Feeney?"

Trust Brian to go straight to the heart. "The monsignor was
very cordial," he answered. "He seemed genuinely pleased
that I had agreed to do the work." Then realizing this was not
the kind of detail to interest Brian, he went on quickly, "They
were all very busy over there, but Monsignor Feeney seemed
to have things well in hand."

"So what's troubling you, John?" Brian was watching him
intently.

For a moment he hesitated. Now that he was here, he
wondered if he had the words to explain his fears about
where the Conference was headed. Brian might be a moral
theoretician, but facts were his bread and butter. And he
wasn't at all sure he could put into words what had disturbed
him.

"I'm afraid that things might be snowballing out of control,
Brian," he said at last. "If the Doctrine Committee staff is any
gauge of the overall sentiment of this Conference, I think the
desire for a 'home-team victory' is beginning to take prece-
dence over a concern for what's best for the Church." He took
a breath. "In spite of Cardinal Camélière's very best intentions, I think there could be the real danger of a break with
Rome."

Waiting for Brian to make some comment, he began to
wish he had kept his apprehensions to himself. He knew
deep down that what he wanted from his old friend was some
sort of impossible blanket assurance that everything would be
all right. It was childish and unfair.

Brian's response when it came held a surprising amount of
bitterness. "The Curia's absolute determination to block the

reforms begun at Vatican II has created this mess. They have only themselves to blame for engineering a situation tailor-made for a Phillip Camélière."

Whatever reaction John had expected, it was not quite this implied criticism of the Cardinal. He felt himself on suddenly unfamiliar ground. "But the Cardinal is trying to avoid a schism, he's told me as much." He felt suddenly foolish, trying to explain to Brian whatever it was that Phillip Camélière was trying to do.

"That's what he's told everyone, John." The Gaelic twinkle had resurfaced. "Don't worry." Brian reached for his pipe and leaned back easily in his chair. "There'll be a way to get the reforms we want without destroying everything. We'll all have our parts to play in keeping things together."

He had listened very carefully to everything Brian Donovan had said, and suddenly it seemed that he was meant to read some deeper message between the lines. At what was Brian hinting?

"By the way, John, how *is* your work going?"

He has been trying to form his own question when the words broke in. Brian had the pipe lit now, and with his red cheeks looked as cheery as Saint Nicholas.

He gave up. What had he really intended to ask Brian anyway? "The work's actually going very well," he said.

"And the Cardinal's residence is working out as a base of operations?"

"Yes. The library is excellent. I have just about everything I need. The commute from my apartment is long, though."

"But I thought the Cardinal told me he had offered you rooms."

"Yes, he has. But I'm still a bit uncomfortable."

"We talked about that before, John." Brian's voice was impatient. "About your concern with compromising your position. As I told you then, you can't please everybody. The objectivity of your work will just have to speak for itself. You've a lot of material to cover in just a few months. You should make it as easy on yourself as possible."

"I know you're right. And when I get into the actual writing stage, I plan to take some things over there."

"The food alone should be an inducement. And Tony Campesi. He's there if you need anything."

"Monsignor Campesi has his own work. Besides..."

"Besides what?" Characteristically, Brian had jumped on his hesitation.

"I don't know." He allowed a sigh. "He's been nice enough, but I get the feeling that Tony Campesi would be a lot happier if I wasn't there. I guess that's part of the reason why I haven't been too eager to move in."

"Good grief, John. I should have known it was some foolishness like that. You're too damn sensitive for your own good. Why should you give a damn what that cassocked faggot thinks?" His laugh was harsh. "You look shocked. Oh, I know, it's not as obvious as all that, but it's no real secret. Just don't pay him any attention. He's jealous. Doesn't want any competition for the Cardinal's attention."

"Competition? Me?"

Brian's laugh turned merry. "I've really got you going now, John. But don't misunderstand. There's nothing physical going on there. Our cardinal's not bent in that direction." He was suddenly serious. "Just be sure to remember that Campesi's entirely devoted to Phillip Camélière. In *his* mind you're a dangerous outsider."

"Dangerous?"

"What about the niece?" Brian changed the subject.

He felt himself immediately on guard and hated it. "What *about* Ms. Venée?" He forced himself to meet the watchful blue eyes.

Brian shrugged. "I just wondered how she reacted to the news that you would agree to help her with coverage of the Conference. You *have* agreed to help her?"

"Yes. I'm working with her now actually." He smiled, making the words sound natural. He stood up then, looking at his watch. "I've got to run," he said. "The whole morning's almost gone. I'll keep in touch, Brian. We'll talk again soon."

He knew he wasn't very good at this. He turned to give a last weak smile as he reached the door. Through the drifting haze of pipe smoke Brian's blue eyes watched him speculatively.

• • •

Alex lay stretched out on the formal leather sofa in the library, legs crossed casually, head resting on one of the massive tucked arms. One shoe dangled precariously from a foot projecting out into space, the other sat abandoned where she had let it fall to the carpet. She had read for hours at the table, transcribing and making new notes on the portable computer she had brought with her from the apartment. Officially she was resting now, but she still read, placing pieces of paper torn from her writing tablet between the pages where she wanted to take more notes.

She put down what she'd been reading and thought of the Rahner book that John had given her on Saturday night. She kept coming back to it in her mind. She'd read a good bit of it yesterday, curled up on her sofa at the apartment, remembering her own early religious feelings.

When she was very young, she had had a personal relationship with Jesus. He had seemed very near, a more exalted form of her imaginary friend Bunky. She had talked to him all the time. It was not so different from Rahner's concept, but on a child's level.

She thought of John's eyes, dark green and luminous, as he had handed her the book. Had he achieved Rahner's ideal? Was that the message of his gift? Yet, of one thing she was sure. She had not imagined his attraction to her. It was there. And she was attracted to him. Obviously he'd sensed that.

And he'd been the one to reach out, to make the gesture. She closed her eyes, seeing him as he'd looked then, holding her hand to his face. So open and vulnerable. She struggled against the memory of her reaction, forcing herself to recall the physical details instead. His pulling away from her . . . rising . . . making her a present of the book.

Sitting up, she massaged the muscles of her neck. She had invited John to dinner Saturday, hoping to put him more at ease. She wondered now if the whole thing hadn't been a mistake. She leaned over and shook out her hair. No matter what, she wasn't going to let any of this keep her from getting her job done.

She shuffled into her shoes and went back to her seat at the table. She switched on the portable computer and began transcribing her handwritten notes. After a few minutes she stopped. Where *was* John? He hadn't been around this morning or in the dining room for lunch. She needed to talk about the questions she was compiling and when he would have the time to meet with her.

She reached for a book and turned to one of the pages she had marked. There was some material she wanted to include in this part of her notes. She started typing, but she couldn't seem to keep her mind from drifting. It was stupid, she thought staring angrily at the screen, for her to just sit here and wonder. She was going to have to leave shortly, and she really needed to talk to him about setting up a meeting. He was probably only a few steps away. She'd just march right down the hall and—

"Hi, Alex. Penny for your thoughts."

She glanced up sharply to see John at the door. She was so surprised that she didn't say anything.

"I won't disturb you," he said, looking a little puzzled by her lack of response. "I just got here and I thought I'd stop in and see how you were getting on." His voice was winding down and she saw him shift the weight on his feet. He was preparing to go.

"Good . . . that's good." It hadn't made much sense and she'd said it too loudly, but he had stopped. He was waiting. "It's perfect that you came now," she went on quickly. "I was just wondering where you were. If you're going to be here tomorrow, I'd like to start going over my list of questions."

He came a little farther into the room. "Tomorrow. Sure. What time?"

"How about right after lunch?"

"After lunch is good." He was backpedaling as he said it, but he stopped. "I almost forgot. Here's the bibliography I promised you." He set a computer-printed page on the desk. "You getting anything out of the books I gave you?"

"Oh, yes. I read all of yesterday."

He was nodding. Hesitating. She had a quick intuition that he wanted to ask her if she'd looked at the Rahner book, but perversely she didn't want to let him know she had.

The silence stretched. "Tomorrow," he said. "About one o'clock." Then he was gone.

For a moment she just sat blankly, watching the empty door.

Alex walked holding Frank's hand, her spare cotton dress whipped up by the hot dry wind blowing down over the small hill. It was early evening, but the red summer sun was reluctant to sink below the horizon. She stopped just outside the shade of a tree and turned to look up at him. Raising her hand to shield her face, she searched for his eyes hidden behind the dark sunglasses.

"And now I have a whole list of books to track down and go through." She laughed, shaking her head in mock exasperation.

"I thought I saw a stack of rather sanctimonious-looking books in the living room when I picked you up." Frank pushed the glasses down farther on the bridge of his nose.

"Those are just to tide me over. The books on the bibliography are supposed to take me to the theological heart of the matter—in layman's terms of course."

"I'd say that Father John Leighton is keeping you pretty busy." There was a slightly sour edge to his voice that she hadn't missed.

"He's my ticket to National, Frank."

"Poor guy, doesn't even know when he's being used."

"Frank, that's not fair." She was surprised at his accusation.

"Come on, girl reporter. We've been over this ground before. You like John Leighton, don't you?"

"Yes . . . but what does that have to do—"

"Remember what I said before—when the issue of Phillip's being your uncle came up?"

"Yes," she answered quietly.

"Well, it's almost the same thing here. You're not *using* Father Leighton. Just taking advantage of a fortunate situation."

"He doesn't really seem to mind helping me. Most of the time anyway."

"Good. Then that's settled. Enough talk about John Leighton."

She smiled and tugged on his arm, pulling him back toward the theater. *Enough talk about John Leighton.* The

words repeated themselves inside of her. Exactly; she agreed
wholeheartedly. There had been enough talk about John
Leighton. And yet there was that uncomfortable stab of
conscience that insisted that she should have told Frank
about taking him to dinner Saturday night. But why the stab
of conscience? Why *should* she tell him? But why shouldn't
she?

"You haven't forgotten about Uncle Phillip's reception Thursday evening?" She stopped walking and waited for his answer.

"No, Alex. I never forget a date with you."

"I don't suppose I can talk you into going to the Mass."

"Really, Alex, you can bully an agnostic only so far."

"Okay, okay. I'll settle for the reception. This isn't so bad, is
it?" she asked, tossing her head back, indicating the outdoor
pavilion. But seeing his face wrinkle into a frown, she didn't
wait for an answer. "Come on, Frank, don't be such a prick? I
know it's not your thing. Don't watch the dancing. Close your
eyes and just listen to the music. You do like Debussy, don't
you?"

"I like Debussy all right. But I like making love to you
better. Why don't we just cut out right now."

"Really, Frank. When I asked if you were too tired, you
said you were just fine."

"I didn't say anything about being tired, baby. Just horny.
I've been without you for two days. Two days too many."

"I know it's been rough, Frank." She tried her most
patronizing voice. "But until tonight . . . use your imagination.
Sex is all up here anyway." And she tapped her finger against
her temple. "You should be suitably inspired by the time we
get back to my apartment. *Afternoon of a Faun* is incredibly
sensual."

"You're a little tease, you know that, Alex Venée." His
mustache curled up over his lip in a smile.

"But you love me anyway."

"As a matter of fact . . ."

"Frank . . ."

"You brought it up, Alex. So what's it going to be? Are you
going to move in or not?"

She could have kicked herself. Opening her big mouth. If

there was a subject she didn't want to discuss... "Frank, I told you that I love my apartment."

"And I told you that you didn't have to give it up."

Alex, you dummy, she told herself, he's got a mind like a steel trap. You're going to have to do better than this, old girl. "I know, I know. But you know how it goes. First, it's my toothbrush and robe. Then my clothes for the week. Before you know it, I'll have my plants and the pictures off my walls at your place. Come to think of it, that wouldn't be such a bad idea. You know, Frank, whether I move in or not, you really ought to go ahead and fix up the place. Do it, for you."

"I've told you before, Alex, I don't give a crap about how the place looks. I would only care if we were sharing it. Alex, goddammit, stop talking interior design, and start talking *us*." He had yanked off his sunglasses and stuffed them into his coat pocket.

"Frank, keep your voice down. You're drawing a crowd. Remember, you're supposed to be a civilized man, enjoying a bit of culture at Wolf Trap."

"Fuck, Alex. I damn well know that half of the men were dragged here by their wives or girlfriends. The other half... You know all about the other half."

"Frank! I can't believe you said that. Liberal, tolerant, live-and-let-live Frank."

"I'm only giving the facts, Alex. And you're still steering clear of the subject. If I didn't know you so well, Alexandra Venée, I would have to say that you're purposely evading the issue. Now, why might I think that, Alex?"

"Stop being a reporter, Frank. The simple truth is that I have a lot on my mind right now. The Conference and all. I just told you about all the books I've got to plow through. I've got to deliver, Frank, or I won't have a chance of getting on National."

"I think I've created a monster."

"Frank, please give me a little time. I promise I won't forget."

"And you haven't forgotten about the other thing, have you?"

"What other thing, Frank?"

"That I love you."

She looked at him for a moment. His rumpled style, his nonchalant manner, his almost deliberate carelessness—all were just part of a facade. There was a beautiful sensitive man underneath that I-don't-give-a-damn attitude. She had somehow always known this. And it didn't make things any easier. "No, Frank," she answered him softly, "I haven't forgotten."

CHAPTER THIRTEEN

"Where's Alexandra?"

John looked up from his notes and saw Phillip Camélière standing just within the arch of the library's opened doors. "Your Eminence." He half rose from his chair, but eased back down as he saw the Cardinal enter the room and make an impatient wave with his hand.

"Please continue your work, John. I didn't mean to interrupt. I only thought that I would stop by and see how you and my niece were progressing. Isn't Alex coming in today?"

"She was going to stop by one of the public libraries this morning. But she had some questions she wanted to run through with me, and said she'd meet me here around one o'clock. I'm afraid I gave her a rather lengthy list of books to track down."

"We don't have what she needs here?"

"I think I would like her to read some fairly general works first." He stalled, instantly aware that what he'd said might sound too patronizing. "To give her an overview of some of the areas we're going to explore."

"You'll find that my niece is a quick study, John Leighton."

"Yes, Your Eminence, she is. I didn't mean . . ."

"I understand what you meant, John. I was only trying to warn you."

"Warn me, Your Eminence?"

"Alex likes ideas, John. Even those with which she may disagree. She's a tenacious seeker of... wisdom." The Cardinal seemed to have searched awhile for the last word, but the half grin on his face said that he was pleased with his efforts. "Just don't let her get the best of you. She'll pick your theological brain dry."

"I'm rather enjoying it. It's an interesting odyssey for both of us, Your Eminence."

"Odyssey, is it? I like that. But John..." His voice was almost hesitant, yet the gray eyes were smiling warmly. "I know it's difficult for you, and I don't mean to press, but I do wish you'd try to call me Phillip."

"I—I apologize. I don't mean to seem..." He didn't have the word for it. "It *is* difficult for me." He finally decided that there was nothing else he could say.

"Please, John, I understand. Those years in the seminary—Mundelein, wasn't it?—have a way of bringing one to one's knees. Excuse the pun." His laugh was short and brittle. "You're not to blame. They tried to do it to all of us—instill in us that blind deference to authority. Though I'll readily admit I was one of the system's abysmal failures. You see I have always found traditional Christian humility more than a bit rankling." He smiled. Then: "Always choose the lowest place and to be less than everyone else. Thomas à Kempis. *The Imitation of Christ*. A particularly troublesome piece of advice, don't you think."

"I..." John heard himself stammer.

"Please, John, forgive me. I just want us to be friends. And it seems so artificial to stand on ceremony." His hand stroked the cover of a book he'd pulled from one of the bookcases, petting it as one might a cat. "I suspect that I'm in a thoughtful mood today. A peculiar and incurable malady of old men."

John was tempted to correct him, saying that he was certainly not an old man by almost any standard, but glanced down instead, despising himself for his sudden ineptitude, wanting only to retreat once again into the pages of his notes. But he looked up quickly when the Cardinal spoke.

"Years ago, more years than I like to remember, a young

acquaintance of mine developed an obsession for the works of
Hermann Hesse. Simon was a rather passionate young man,
who I believe fancied himself something of a mystic. Yet
despite his fervor and rather nagging insistence, I was never
convinced to read any of Hesse's works.

"After I entered the seminary we lost track of each other. It
was several years before I heard anything about him again,
and it was to learn that he had died. A horrible automobile
accident. The tragedy struck me especially hard at the time,
and I was utterly confused by my reaction. Simon and I were
never really very close. I couldn't explain my sorrow then. I
can't explain it now. But it seemed that I had to do something
with this excess of inexplicable grief I felt. So I read all of the
novels of Hermann Hesse."

He held up the book he had been clutching. "*Steppenwolf.*"
He spoke softly and the thin text fell open within his hands,
cracking like an egg to a certain page. He began to read with
a gentle deliberateness. "'For all who got to love him, saw
always only the one side in him. Many loved him as a refined
and clever and interesting man, and were horrified and
disappointed when they had come upon the wolf in him.'"

The Cardinal stopped, looking up. "When I first discovered
him...my own wolf," he explained, "dark and shaggy, crouched
deep inside, I was immensely terrified. Not because he was
there; I was soon to make peace with that. But rather because
I had been so stupid and blind, my heart so poor, as not to
have seen him before.

"Yet the wolf was there in me as he is in every man. And
though on occasion I do battle with the beast, for the most
part we have become friends. Still, I must hide him from
others, from those men who yet fear the wolf inside of
themselves. Hide my beast from those who fail to see that
salvation may lie within our wolfish flesh...." His words
trailed off.

He replaced the book, and when he turned, his face
seemed less friendly, his clear gray eyes glassy, the overhead
lights reflecting like small moons in them. "You must learn to
exhibit a more dangerous curiosity about yourself, John

Leighton." The words appeared out of context. Then, "Have you read Kazantzakis' *The Last Temptation of Christ*?"

"No, but I've always meant to."

"I have a copy here." The Cardinal searched the rows of books. "I've read the novel more than once over the years," he said, handing him the book, "but I've never been able to make peace with the story's ending."

"Excuse me, Your Eminence."

"Yes, Tony." The Cardinal whirled around at the sound of his secretary's voice.

"It's Ms. Venée on the phone. She seems to have had some car trouble. And she wanted me to inform you, Father Leighton, that she is going to be rather late."

"Where is my niece, Tony?"

"She said that she was near the intersection of Columbia Road and Fourteenth Street. She was waiting for a tow truck to come for her automobile and deliver it to a garage somewhere in Georgetown. She said that she would take a taxi here as soon as she got the car settled."

"That's absurd. Alex doesn't have to take a taxi. Isn't there someone we could send to pick her up, Tony?"

"I would be glad to pick up Ms. Venée, Cardinal Camélière." He made the offer before Monsignor Campesi could reply.

"That's most kind of you, John. You sure you don't mind?"

"No, of course not, Your Eminence."

"Good. Tony, tell my niece that Father Leighton will pick her up. To stay put. He'll look for her at the corner of Columbia and Fourteenth."

John backed his Mazda out of the parking space. Circling around, he drove down the long driveway that snaked away from the residence and connected with the service road that ran in front of the Pastoral Center. He took a deep breath, trying to clear his brain, wanting to leave behind the conversation with Phillip Camélière.

Conversation? He corrected himself. He'd said practically nothing. Yet it seemed to him that Phillip Camélière had not *wanted* him to say anything. And he could not shake the feeling that the whole episode had in some way been orchestrated.

He pressed down slightly on the accelerator, and shook his head. Leave it alone, John, he told himself, and took some ease in Phillip's own admission that he had merely been in a philosophical mood. He opened the storage compartment in the console and fished for a tape. One push of his finger and Carly Simon's voice came sliding out.

At the end of the road, he made a left turn onto a tree-lined residential street and began to drum the flat of his palm against the steering wheel, keeping time to the music. After a while the rhythmic beating of his hand slowed, and the music gradually faded from his mind. His only distraction lay in the twisting Michigan Avenue traffic ahead of him. But eventually even the traffic ceased to be a focus. He had switched to automatic pilot, and his only thoughts were thoughts of Alexandra Venée.

God, he was too old to indulge in...what? Flights of sexual fantasy. Was that it? Some kind of middle-age crisis. Celibate priest wanting a twenty-six-year-old girl. No, he knew the answer instinctively, this was something different. Something that seemed to rest on firmer ground.

Of one thing he was certain—he liked Alexandra Venée. And it was perfectly reasonable that he should like her. Alex was a bright, inquisitive, charming young woman. No harm in liking Alex, he decided. No harm at all.

But then there were the dreams. And the waking thoughts apart from the dreams. Logical and controlled John Leighton didn't understand any of it. For the first time in his life he felt like a stranger in his own skin. A fresh set of responses prickling through the old flesh.

And what of Alex? What did she feel? She liked him. He would allow himself that. But he was no more than stuffy old Father Leighton to her. Yet he somehow knew that wasn't right. And he saw again how she had looked at him Saturday night when he reached to stroke her hand across his face.

He changed lanes effortlessly and smiled, remembering her as she was yesterday, sitting in the library, torturing the keys of her portable computer. He could still see her honey-blond hair swinging over her face as she glanced down now and again to examine her handwritten notes. He pressed his back into the seat, stretching his long legs, feeling just the beginnings of arousal. He shut his eyes for an instant and whispered a prayer that God might help him free his mind of her. And in the next second, to the same God, he prayed that He, in His loving understanding, might allow him her image just a few moments longer.

Carla lay staring at the dim halo of the window, sensing rather than seeing the stirring of the lacy curtains in the labored breath from the window unit. No candles today. And Paolo dragging on her body like dead weight.

But he was moving faster now, almost finished. She remembered to moan. The sound had the hoped-for effect. He hung over her, pumping harder and harder. . . .She closed her eyes.

"You gonna make it with him tomorrow when he picks up the money?" Paolo rolled off of her and flicked on the lamp. "How's he like to do it? The senator?" He reached for his drink.

She bit her lip and got up. Started pulling on her robe.

"You mad at me now, Carla?" She turned to see him smiling at her crookedly. It made him look that much more like Vincent.

"Yes," was all she said.

"Look, Carla, I know you're no whore. Johnny's my brother, but that don't mean I have to agree with him. I always thought you were good for Vinnie. Johnny's just old-fashioned. He never liked it that you were a model. He thinks all models got to be hooking on the side."

"That's bullshit."

"Sure, sure. But you know Johnny." He gulped at the drink.

"Yeah, I know Johnny."

"Don't say it like that, Carla. You know you're still family to Johnny. You never made near this kinda money modeling."

She looked at him, hating him. For looking like Vincent. For being so completely stupid.

"You still blame Johnny for Vincent's death, don't you, Carla?"

"Does Johnny know you're here?"

Paolo shook his head. "You know he wouldn't like this, Carla, me cheatin' on Rosa. Johnny's a family man. He thinks Leo's delivering the money. Same as usual."

"Where's it go after Darrington takes it?" She said it bluntly. Not giving him time to think.

"You wouldn't believe me if I told you, Carla." He surprised her by breaking into a grin. "But I can tell you, Johnny didn't like it much, not at first. Said it was mixin'...well, mixin' things that shouldn't be mixed with business."

"I don't understand."

"Can't tell you, *cara*, except for this." He waved his drink at the briefcase in the corner. "That money might go out dirty to Darrington. But it comes back pure as a convent virgin." He laughed.

"What about Darrington?" She tried a switch. "What's Johnny got on him?"

"Ask Rico Gambini." He laughed. Then: "You gotta stop with all these questions, Carla." Suddenly he wasn't smiling anymore. "Johnny'll tell you what he wants you to know."

He woke up screaming for a mirror, his hands flying to his face. But there were no mirrors in Hanoi prison. And no web of scarred tissue beneath his fingers. Not yet. It was only stubble he felt. Coarse and heavy. Grown already since yesterday's shave with the rusty length of scrap iron that had to serve as a razor.

He settled back heavily on the thin bamboo mat that covered the hard wooden platform. The dream had wakened him every morning now since they'd separated him from the others. Since the threats to his face had begun.

And it was these threats to his face that got to him. Not the things they'd already done. Hell, he could take the pain, could stand it much better than the everyday filth and dirt. And so far he'd held up just fine. Hadn't given them anything, really. Except for the fake bio he'd made up, and even the strongest ones like Benchley eventually gave them that.

But now they knew who he was.

They'd been waiting for the bowls of rotten rice, he and Benchley, when the guards had dragged him off to Major Fong. He remembered the ceiling fan turning above him as the major sat smiling into some file from behind his desk. They knew now he'd been lying to them, the major said. He was not just a dupe like the other Americans they'd captured, but the son of a rich American capitalist. One of the ruling class who made war against the people of Vietnam. He was a criminal of the very worst sort. He would have to be made to pay.

He protested that the Geneva Convention protected prisoners of war.

Fong had still smiled above the red points of his collar, all exquisite Oriental politeness, like the stereotypical commander in some bad combat movie. No war had been declared by the American Congress, he was reminded. The People's Tribunal was not therefore bound by any convention. But, of course, if a prisoner showed the proper contrition, confessed to his crimes against the Vietnamese people, then there could be clemency. Perhaps even an early release. He could go home unharmed to his rich capitalist's life.

His refusal to sign a confession brought a sharp gesture for the guards. He was taken away. Not to the old cell, but to some other part of the prison. He was never with his friends after that. They kept him isolated, and stepped up the torture. Then when it didn't work, there was the new threat. The cigarettes extinguished only inches from his face. The knife, raw and cold against his nostrils. He remembered the hot shame of his tears at the intensity of his fear. An irrational panic at the thought of some deformity that would destroy him.

Despite the heat he shivered now, staring at the four ugly walls. The cracks like running sores. The tiny lizards, pulsing grayish green against the damp concrete. His gaze traveled upward to the tiny morning-lit square of the window. The bars cast their hopeless shadow on the floor. . . .

This was all wrong. With a stab of relief he remembered. He wasn't really here. Not anymore. He was home now. Had been home for years. It had all worked out, thanks to his father's connections. He was a U.S. senator now, just as he'd planned. But the fear. The cell . . .

By sheer force of will Richard opened his eyes. The den was in total darkness now except for the cathode glow from the TV. And despite the cool air from the overhead vent, his shirt was a thin clammy layer between the leather couch and his back. He looked at his watch. Where in the hell was Lindsey?

He made himself sit up, the hardwood floor a solid reality against his stocking feet. But not a perfect reality. Not without threat. Just a tradeoff, really, with Johnny Lambruci in place of Major Fong. The dream was over; the nightmare remained.

"So would you agree that the continuing decline in the number of priests is one of the major factors pushing the American bishops toward open defiance of the Vatican?"

Alex looked up. They had come directly to the library after his sidewalk rescue of her and her tottering stack of books. He sat across from her now, his elbows on the table, chin resting on his steepled fingers.

"Yes, I guess I'd have to agree with that," he answered. "It's true that the shortage of priests in this country is becoming critical. There's an urgent lack of vocations. And with priests who are unhappy leaving the Church, the bishops can no longer afford to ignore the demands for reform."

She typed as John spoke. The tape recorder would have been nice, but informal was better. "Off the record" made all the difference. He was waiting for another question now, and she glanced unnecessarily at her notes. She knew very well what was next on her list.

"Many authorities seem to regard the rule of celibacy as the primary cause for the priest shortage." She read it out verbatim. "Do you feel that a change to optional celibacy would attract new priests and help to keep some of the older ones?" She was annoyingly aware of a need to avoid his eyes as she waited for his answer.

"Knock, knock," Frank said as he entered, and came toward her with a crooked smile.

She jumped up. "You got my message?"

"Yes, finally. I called my machine late this afternoon. What's wrong with the car? Hi, Father," he added.

"I'm sorry," she said quickly. "No manners." It sounded lame. What was wrong with her? She felt like she was moving through Jell-O, her responses all out of sync. John had risen. He and Frank were already shaking hands. "Father John Leighton," she said belatedly, "this is Frank Gregory."

"A pleasure, Father."

"'John'—please."

"It's the battery, probably," she said into the pause that followed, answering Frank's long-ago question. "At least I hope that's all it is. That car is usually so reliable."

"When's the last time it was serviced, Alex?" The words were familiar ritual, but Frank was watching her again with that same weird half smile.

"I meant to bring it in last month. I just ran out of time. What time is it?" She changed the subject.

"It's late," Frank said, looking at his watch. "Past eight. I got hung up. I thought you might have gotten tired waiting. Did you eat here?"

"No." The time had surprised her. "No," she said again. "We've been working. Going over some questions. I'm sorry, John." She turned to him. "Were you planning on staying the night? Did I make you miss supper?"

He laughed. "Madame Elise would have tracked me down long ago if that were the case. No," he said more seriously, "I'm still going home every night. I'd planned on getting something to eat on my way there."

"Well, come with us." It was out before she had time to think, and besides, it was only common politeness. He shouldn't have to eat alone.

"Oh, no, I don't think so. . . ."

"Yes. Come on, Father . . . John," Frank corrected himself, "it's Alex's treat tonight. If you come, she can put it on her expense account." He smiled. "Never pass up a free meal from a reporter."

She looked at Frank. She had half expected that he would be annoyed by her impulsive invitation. But he'd turned on the Gregory charm instead. Why was that? She turned back to John.

He had clearly been hesitating, but he smiled now. "Okay," he said. "Sounds good. Where do we eat?"

They decided on pizza, calling their order ahead to Murphy's.

At a red light Frank kissed her. "What was that for?" she said, wondering what John following behind in his car would be thinking. Ashamed that she wondered at all.

"Can't I just want to kiss you?"

"Light's green."

He turned away and accelerated forward.

"To answer your question," she said to his profile, "you certainly can 'just want to kiss me.' But if I had to guess, I'd say there was just a hint of soften-her-up premeditation in that kiss, Frank. What is it you haven't told me yet?"

He looked sideways at her, and for the first time tonight his smile didn't seem to harbor hidden feelings. "Can't keep anything from you anymore, can I?"

The words startled her, and ridiculously they made her feel guilty. "Just don't you try it, Frank." She made herself laugh.

"Okay, I confess." He smiled. "I have to make a call before nine-thirty. It's possible I'll have to leave you. Would your Father Leighton, do you think, take you home?"

Was that why he'd seemed almost eager for John to join them? And what did he mean, "your Father Leighton"?

"Alex?"

"Oh," she said stupidly, coming back to attention. "Yes. I'm sure he won't mind. Where do you have to go?"

"Just something I might have to follow up right away. You know. The usual thing. Some guy finally decides to tell you something; you got to get there before he changes his mind."

As he talked, she wondered. Certainly the convenience of having John there to take her home might have played a part, but then she could just as easily have gotten a cab. It wasn't like Frank to want a third party "horning in," especially if they might have only a few hours together. She remembered his half-joking words the other night at his apartment. Could he really suspect there might be something to be "jealous" about? Was he applying his professional methods to her, wanting to observe them together, she and "her" John Leighton?

"You aren't angry, are you, Alex? That I might have to desert you tonight."

"Of course not. You know I understand your job."

"You seem so quiet."

He was slowing for the light, but it changed immediately to green. She found John in the sideview mirror and checked that he made the turn with them before she answered.

"I'm just tired, Frank." She sighed, patting his knee. "I've been at it since early this morning."

She smiled reassuringly, but she didn't feel comfortable. She was being paranoid and stupid, and it was because she really did feel guilty. She admitted it now. As if she *were* betraying Frank. As if she suspected that her own motives in inviting John were not what they seemed. Had she wanted to throw John and Frank together just to see what would happen?

Inside the restaurant was better. The amiable gloom was so familiar that a sense of normality returned. Murphy's was Frank's discovery, a bar that served a quick, good pizza from a cramped backroom kitchen, and just happened to have his favorite imported beer. An irresistible combination, especially on nights when they ate late or were in a hurry. She felt herself relax. Maybe she *was* just tired. Tired and hungry.

Frank stopped at the bar, greeting Murphy and letting Josephine in the kitchen know they were there. Then he wriggled in beside her in the booth. "So how'd it go today?" He looked from her face to where John sat across the age-scarred table. "You two looked like you were really into it when I arrived."

How long had Frank been listening to them? she asked herself. Not that it mattered. She hadn't been doing or saying anything to be ashamed of. "We *were* really into it," she said quickly. "And I'm sure John was glad that you came when you did. I had no idea how late it was getting."

"I didn't mind," John said. "It didn't seem that long at all."

"You have to take a harder line than that with a reporter, John." Frank was smiling. "Alex is tough. Or hadn't you noticed?"

"Oh, I noticed, all right." John smiled back. "I'd say she had me pretty much where she wanted me."

Frank was looking at her with a sort of smirk now, though he had to know it was a perfectly innocent answer.

"Play fair, Frank," she said to him. "I don't go around giving warnings to your sources. Besides, you don't have to worry about John. He's quite capable of taking care of himself."

"What do you say, John? Do you think that's true?"

"I think"—John paused—"that our pizzas are ready." He pointed to where the pans sat steaming on the counter. "Shall I?" He made a move to rise.

"No. I'll go." Frank slid out of the booth.

"Here," she said, handing Frank some money. "My treat. Remember?"

He was back in a minute with the pizzas, and a moment later with a pitcher of dark beer.

"Try some of this, John." Frank poured out a mug and pushed it across the table.

"Pizza looks great," John said, laying a large wedge in his plate. He stopped to sip at the beer. "It's Guinness!"

Alex, reaching for her own mug, looked up. Frank had broken out into a broad grin.

"That's why I come here," he said with a connoisseur's enthusiasm. "Josephine's pizza's good, of course, but this is one of the few places you can get Guinness on tap. You like it?"

"My first taste of alcohol was Guinness," John said. "My

dad's always loved it. Leighton is an English name, but
there's plenty of Irish in our family."

"I learned to drink it in Belfast when I was there on
assignment." Frank took another slice of pizza. "I taught Alex
to drink it," he said, gathering in the strings of cheese.
"Didn't I?" He turned to her.

She looked at him sweetly and nodded. Like little boys,
she thought. They find some secret password and suddenly
they're members of a club.

"Damn!" Frank looked suddenly at his watch. "It's getting
late already. Better make that call. Excuse me a minute," he
said, getting up. "Remember your diet, Alex." He grinned
down at her with a significant glance at her plate. "Keep an
eye on her, John."

She watched Frank dial and begin talking. Then she looked
across at John.

"I like your friend," he said predictably.

Wonderful. She smiled, shoving a piece of pizza in her
mouth.

"Alex." Frank was coming back to the table. "Got to leave,
baby. Sorry. Can you drop her home?" He turned to John.

"Sure. I'll be glad to."

"Thanks," Frank said. For a moment he just stared at her,
then he bent down to give her a kiss. "If I can get away early
enough, I'll come by. If not, I'll call you." Another quick
kiss, and he grabbed up a piece of pizza. "'Night, John,"
he said.

She followed him with her eyes till he was out the door.
When she turned back, she saw that John was watching
her.

"I hope you didn't mind Frank putting you on the spot like
that?" She took a sip from her beer.

"You mean all that about you being so tough." He was
smiling.

"Yes, Frank just likes to tease."

"You don't have to apologize, Alex. I told you, I like him.
. . . Do you want this?" He was indicating the last piece of
pizza.

She shook her head. "No, you have it. I had more than

enough. Frank's precious Guinness has filled me up." And she laughed.

They drove to her apartment in silence broken only by her directions. For the moment she felt at peace, more relaxed than she had for days. Washington, so beautiful in the summer dark, flickered like tourists' slides past the windshield.

As they reached her block, a car was pulling out from the curb directly in front of the apartment. "Fate," she said. "No excuses. Now you'll have to come up and see where I live. I'll make us a pitcher of iced tea. You must be as thirsty as I am. It's the anchovies."

"I have Mass tomorrow at seven . . . but it's an offer I can't refuse." He grinned.

For once she found her keys quickly in the jumble of the oversize handbag she carried on workdays. She unlocked the door and walked to switch on the lamps, and was aware of John gazing around for a moment before closing the door behind him.

"This looks like you, Alex."

"I hope that's a compliment."

"It *is* a compliment," he said. "I like it very much."

She smiled. "Well, feel free to look around while I make the tea." She headed toward the kitchen. "I only hope it's as impressive as your coffee."

When she returned, she found him sunk into the sofa.

"This thing is sinfully comfortable," he said.

She laughed, handing him a glass of tea and dropping down next to him. "I adore this sofa," she said, leaning back lazily.

"This tea is very good," he said. "I like it with lots of lemon." He took another swallow and settled back again. "Have you read any of this?"

He picked up a book from the side table. It was the Rahner.

"Yes," she admitted, setting down her glass. "I read it Sunday. I liked it."

"Not exactly a rave review." He sounded as if she had disappointed him.

"I thought it was . . . beautiful," she said slowly, hoping to find the right words. "I liked very much that he made it all seem so natural. Loving God, loving your neighbor—Rahner makes it all the same thing. . . ."

"But?"

She smiled, staring at her crossed hands in her lap. So he had heard the *but.* "It's not very flesh and blood, is it?" she asked, looking up at him.

Her words had been some kind of trigger. He said nothing now, sitting rigid beside her, but she could read the longing in his face. Deliberately she took his hand as on Saturday he had taken hers, and she placed it against her cheek, slipping it palm downward, a cradle against her lips. Through it all she watched him, her glance never leaving his face, and it was pain she saw in his eyes as her mouth moved against his hand. A shudder seemed to pass through his fingers, registering its aftershock upon her lips. She saw him close his eyes against her, but he did not draw away. His hand moved from her face, turning her, pulling her against his chest.

For a moment she rested there, not daring to move or think, listening to the racing of his heart. Then his mouth opened over hers. Infinitely gentle, exploring. She lay across his knees, his hands in her hair, her arms around his neck, pressing now, both of them pressing closer.

"Alex," he breathed once, his breath warm against her mouth. And again his lips were on hers, his kisses more urgent now, his hand moving over her back, caressing the side of her breast through the cool silk of her blouse.

She moaned, conscious of nothing but her wanting. . . .

Harsh insistent ringing. The phone.

John pushed back from her almost violently. She caught herself from falling as he rose, her hand skidding against the bare edge of the coffee table. He was shuffling blindly backward for the door. Her eyes caught his, holding him in the room as she reached to stop the phone.

"Hello . . . Alex?" Frank's voice.

She stood at one end of a dark tunnel connecting her still to John. She could barely make out Frank's words over the roaring in her ears. "Hello." She forced it out.

"Alex? Are you okay? Did I catch you in the tub again?"

"No . . . I'm fine." She spoke evenly now, clutching the cool plastic tight against her palm.

"I'm sorry, baby." Frank's voice barely penetrated. "But I'm really tied up with this guy. We'll talk tomorrow, okay? Have sexy dreams about me. . . . Alex?" She realized he was waiting for some reply.

"I will," she said desperately, wanting to hang up, to concentrate on that other more tenuous connection. But John had torn his glance away. She watched helplessly as he turned toward the door.

She closed her eyes. "Love you, baby . . ." Frank's voice whispered in her ear. The metallic sound of the door lock mimicked the muffled click of the phone.

CHAPTER FOURTEEN

Alex knelt in the last row, close to the door and escape, but for now she was glad she had come. It was so peaceful in the chapel, and she had had no peace through undoubtedly the worst night of her life. She looked up, her eyes drawn to the cross suspended above the altar.

Again she tried to pray, but her thoughts would not be stilled. Even here in the pre-Mass hush of the chapel she could not prevent the relentless replaying of the scene with John last night in her apartment. Over and over again she saw that look on his face. So stricken and defeated.

The replay went on in her head, a loop endlessly repeating. Again she was in his arms, and at that moment it felt safe and right. She had wanted it to go on forever.

She was crying again now. Embarrassed, she put on her sunglasses, dabbing at her cheeks with the Kleenex she held clutched in her hand. But the tears wouldn't stop.

The chimes rang. She stood with the others as John and the lector emerged from the sacristy. As the lector gave the dedication she watched John, tall and serene in his gold chasuble. Only his pallor, nearly as white as the linen alb against his dark hair, hinted that perhaps he, too, had been unable to sleep.

She sat, rose, knelt in a kind of dazed numbness. Shrinking against the hard wooden backrest of the pew at the readings, afraid that he might see her, filled with the humiliation of her fear, hearing nothing of the words. Later she knelt, hiding behind her oversized glasses, and watched as he prayed over the Eucharistic gifts, listening to the sweet piercing chiming of the bells as the bread and wine became the body and blood of Christ.

For the first time it came clearly home to her that John Leighton was a *priest*. Consecrated. Separate. Strangely, as many times as she had seen Uncle Phillip celebrate the Mass, she never thought of him in just that way. Perhaps it was their closeness that would not allow her to see beyond it to his relationship with God.

After the Lord's Prayer, the woman in the pew ahead of her turned smiling to clasp her hand in the sign of peace. On the altar John broke the bread, placing a small part of the wafer in the chalice. She forced herself to see. John Leighton was a priest.

People stood and began walking to the rail for Communion. Folding up the kneeler, she escaped out of the chapel door, through the glass-block breezeway into blinding morning light. Stumbling down the green sloping lawn, she made her way to the front of the Pastoral Center, where she had arranged for a cab to be waiting. But she had left the Mass early and it was not yet there. She stood on the sidewalk, feeling exposed and naked.

She knew she couldn't work today at the residence, couldn't bear to face him. But she didn't want to go home. The apartment was too alive yet with memories and the wreckage of her sleepless night. Then she remembered. It was Wednesday. Tomorrow was Uncle Phillip's Anniversary Mass and reception. Her mother would be here in the morning. Desperately she tried to pull her thoughts together while her mind screamed that she could not do it, could not get through the rest of today, much less tomorrow's celebrations.

She fought her way to calmness and began to plan a schedule for the next hours, checking off in her mind each step that she must take. From here she would go to the garage. If her car wasn't ready, she must rent one. Back to the apartment to pack some clothes. Then lunch and a movie.

No matter what, she could always lose herself in a movie. Then dinner somewhere till it was late and safe to return to the residence.

The schedule was a start, something concrete to hold on to. A to B to C without the need for further thought or worry. She was not yet ready to face the problem of how she would get through her phone call tonight with Frank, or how she would deal with tomorrow, but she knew she must get some distance, regain some sense of proportion. What she needed most, she thought, was to be able to laugh at herself, to feel either foolish or very simply disgusted.

But she did not yet know that her misery was too real, did not understand what she could no longer afford to ignore. There was nowhere at all she could go. Nowhere to hide. Nowhere to escape the simple truth that she had fallen in love with John Leighton.

Richard hated summers in Washington. But there was little use in griping so early in the game. The way things were going, Congress wouldn't break until the second week of August. And it wasn't even July. He glanced down at his schedule. The rest of the week was going to be hell, and tomorrow's committee hearing was going to be a maximum fucker. And there was the important roll call in the afternoon he couldn't miss. If he made it to Phillip's reception before nine, it would be a minor miracle. The Mass was out. He would have his hands full all morning trying to marshal the votes he needed to get that finance proposal out of committee. Senator Rabinhorst was a shrewd son of a bitch. From the old school. Honey-tongued and hard-nosed. He would need to get with Andy sometime this afternoon and see if he'd gotten the inside track from Robbie. Nothing like gossip among staffers to keep tabs on the competition. He didn't like nasty little surprises when he went into the hearing room. God, he'd like to break the Jew's back on this one.

He pressed the button on the intercom. "Sally, tell Andy to see me before he meets with the staff this afternoon. I think he had something scheduled for around three."

"Yes, Senator Darrington. . . . Senator Darrington, I was

about to buzz. You have a call on your private line. Would you like me to ring through?"

"Someone I should talk to?"

"She wouldn't give a name, but since she came through on the private line..."

"Okay, Sally. Hold everything else."

He pushed down the flashing white button and picked up the receiver. "Yes," he said into the phone.

"This is quite an experience, Richard. I sometimes forget how really important you are."

"I hope this is something that couldn't wait. You know the rules. Calling here is off limits."

"I know. But there's been a change of plans."

"What kind of change?"

"I can't keep our appointment. At least not as planned. Something's come up."

"That's unfortunate.... So when? Where?"

"Now. The garden at the Hirshhorn."

He heard the click and watched as the white light on his phone went dead.

He walked out of the private entrance of the Russell Office Building and began to move alongside of the Capitol on Constitution Avenue. He shifted the empty briefcase to his left hand and ran his right hand through his hair. The air was unbreathable, hot and sticky, and he slipped a finger around the collar of his shirt to loosen his tie. A concession to comfort he rarely made. But everything he was doing at this moment was more than out of character. It was insane.

On Third Street he took a left and walked in a straight line until he made a right on Jefferson. He slowed his pace a bit and stared outward into the Mall. He watched with vague interest a jogger crossing the grassy landscape, estimating the man's body fat at about ten percent. He looked away and crossed Seventh. Turning right, he entered the sculpture garden.

He paused and looked around. It was a few moments before he saw her—the blond wig was an unanticipated touch. But her slender smooth body under the white knit dress he would have recognized anywhere. She had turned slightly, so that he now saw her straight on. She was wearing oversized sunglasses, the kind with reflective black lenses, which gave her face a rather anonymous blank look.

When she spotted him, she slid the glasses down the bridge of her nose, exposing her dark eyes for an instant, so that her face at last came to life. She almost smiled, but checked herself, then immediately walked past him without stopping.

He saw that she was waiting for him in the Mall, standing out in the open, her hip slung slightly forward. She held her briefcase tightly in one hand, tilting her head back toward the sun as though she were trying to get a tan. Then she checked her watch.

He was in no hurry as he began to move toward her. She was going to be late, he thought with a kind of perverse satisfaction, for whatever it was that had caused her to move up their appointment. He stopped an arm's length away from her, setting his briefcase in front of him. He looked straight ahead and watched a lone photographer taking pictures in the distance.

"So why are we here?" He finally spoke, not looking at her.

"I have somewhere to go this afternoon. I couldn't meet you at the apartment."

"This is not part of the deal."

"I know. But it was their idea that I meet you like this."

He looked at her then, trying to see her eyes through the dark glasses. "Tell them I don't like their breaking the rules."

"They said you wouldn't. It won't happen again."

"You have all of it in the briefcase?"

"What do they have on you, Senator Richard Darrington?"

He turned sharply to see her bright red mouth smiling at him for the first time. "Do you have it, Carla?" he repeated, ignoring her question.

"Not talking, baby. It must be something big, real big." The red smile again. Then: "Want to fuck, Richard? Want to fuck me here, right out in the open? You'd like that, wouldn't you, Richard?"

He remained for an instant watching the Mall's pedestrian traffic, listening to her soft teasing laughter. Then he reached forward and picked up his briefcase. When he turned back, her face was closer to his than he'd imagined, and it seemed that he could taste the strong sweet scent of her perfume all the way down his throat. He swallowed hard, wanting to rip off the dark glasses that covered her face like a mask. Instead he leaned over and set his case near her feet and slipped his hand tightly around her wrist, prying the handle of her briefcase from her fingers. "I have what I came for, Carla."

"Do you, my darling?" she whispered into his face. Then in the same low voice: "Where do you take the money, Richard?"

He stepped back and massaged the fine leather of the briefcase handle with his fingers, and thought that it was a surprising question she had asked. But his voice didn't betray him as he answered coolly, "You are just full of questions today, Carla."

"Ask you no questions, and you'll tell me no lies."

He laughed then. "The glasses will have to go, but I rather like the blond wig. It makes you look like a whore."

He saw her bite her lower lip and wished again that he could have seen her eyes. He supposed he might have gone too far, but one never knew with Carla. He watched her as she bent and picked up the empty briefcase. Then she turned abruptly and walked away. And for the first time since their relationship began, Richard really thought about Carla Fiorelli.

She had been the most beautiful woman at the party. Thin, but not too thin, tall but not too tall. He had heard it said many times, about other women, yet never had he actually analyzed what the description meant. But seeing her moving effortlessly through the crowd, the smooth muscles of her body working beneath the pale blue satin of her gown as if on cue—he understood. This woman had a dancer's body.

She had come alone to the party and seemed to want to stay that way. Sipping on the same glass of champagne held so loosely in her fingers that he half expected it to slip and fall to the floor. She stared boldly at everything but with no real interest in anything, tossing her thick brown-black hair across her shoulders with a flick of her hand. He had watched her do the thing with her hair over and over, and imagined that it was more of a habit than a necessity.

They had gone to bed together that same night. And it seemed to him that nobody could ever feel as good as Carla Fiorelli. It was two months before he found out that their meeting had all been arranged. Carla was a gift from the boys.

He wondered now how tight her ties were with the organization. Vaguely he remembered hearing that she'd been the wife of a cousin in the family. But he had gotten himself killed. And the family took Carla in. They looked after their own, even if it was just a connection by marriage. But he was not sure if this story were true. And she never talked.

But today she had talked, but not about herself. He could still see her red sexy mouth as she asked what they had on him, where the money went. He would have thought that she knew about everything. But maybe not. It wasn't the family's style to tell women too much. But he had no doubt that Carla Fiorelli was valued highly for what she contributed to the overall success of the operation. After all she was very good at what she did. He could attest to that. Yet he somehow knew that she was more than a pretty piece of ass. Why he knew this, and what implications it might have... He didn't take it that far.

It was very quiet in the finely appointed residence of His Eminence Phillip Cardinal Camélière. The rooms were darkened, the drapes and blinds drawn against a bloodred smear of sunset. And everywhere deep silence, almost like a roaring in the ears.

From beneath a set of double doors, a single bar of artificial light jutted onto the floor of the outer office. Making a lie of the darkness. And voices. Soft-spoken and determined. Making a lie of the silence.

Tony snapped open the briefcase and began to count the money.

"It's all there." There was the barest trace of irritation in Richard's voice.

"I must still check, Senator Darrington."

"Richard, you know that our success with this over the last months is in great measure due to Tony's expertise." Phillip put just the slightest emphasis on his last words. "And it's largely thanks to Tony's financial creativity in getting us such a rapid turnaround that I can tell you this now. We can handle more, as much probably as you can give us."

Phillip held Richard's eyes. "Of course we are going to want a higher cut each month. Say twenty percent of anything over three-quarter million."

"I'm almost certain those terms will be satisfactory, Phillip. But are you sure that more money won't cause problems?"

"I need the money, Richard."

"Because of the schism?"

Phillip smiled. "There's going to be a costly transition period." He stood up. "Tony, do you think that I might have a word with Senator Darrington alone?"

"Of course, Your Eminence. I need to start in on this anyway." Tony shut the briefcase and lifted it off the desk. "If there won't be anything else, I'll say good night."

"Good night, Tony. Early tomorrow. We have a full day." Phillip laughed, patting his secretary on the back.

Phillip watched as Tony closed the doors behind him. For an instant he stared at the dark paneling. Then he turned and moved in front of his desk, half sitting against the edge. "Is there some problem, Richard?"

Richard met Phillip's stare. "No, no problem."

"You seemed a bit worried."

"I have a stake in this, too, Phillip. I guess I'm just a little concerned about expanding this whole thing. It might attract attention."

"From whom, Richard? You know that as long as the money coming in is reported as charitable donations, no one is going to look twice."

"I wasn't thinking about the government."

"Who then?"

"Your enemies."

Phillip shook his head. "There's no real danger, Richard."

"But then you like the risk, don't you, Cardinal Camélière?"

Phillip stared at him for a moment. Then he broke into a full smile, and the laugh that followed seemed genuine. "What an interesting observation, Richard."

"It's like sex, isn't it, Phillip? Danger."

Phillip arched his brows, the lids of his eyes closing ever so slightly like a cat's.

"Why? Why the priesthood, Phillip?"

"I had a calling."

He seemed perfectly sincere, and Richard could almost have believed him had it not been for that smile. "This is Richard Darrington you're talking to, remember."

Phillip laughed softly, rising at last from the desk. "Let's just say it was something I had to do."

"The ultimate game, Phillip? Playing God?"

CHAPTER FIFTEEN

The strains of Mozart rose high into the dome of St. Matthew's Cathedral.

"In the Name of the Father, and of the Son, and of the Holy Spirit..." The assembled celebrants and acolytes formed a bright tableau around the white marble altar. And Phillip Camélière at center, princely in his rich vestments.

"The grace of our Lord Jesus Christ and the love of God and the fellowship of the Holy Spirit be with you all."

Phillip's eyes followed Tony as he stepped forward to introduce the day's Mass. He smiled hearing the words, familiar now, as he'd overheard Tony practicing them again and again in his office the last few days.

"As we prepare to celebrate the mystery of Christ's love"— Phillip moved forward to speak, his hands moving outward from his heart in a characteristic gesture—"let us acknowledge our failures and ask the Lord for pardon and strength."

"I confess to almighty God...." the large assembly intoned.

Phillip drew in a deep breath as the prayer ended and the choir began to sing the kyrie. How he loved the Mass. Linking, connecting him to some force that at other times lay quiet and hidden. Something very old, which existed even before the days of Christ, something born it seemed more of the old gods.

He had wanted to say a Latin Mass today, but Tony had

forced him to see the inappropriateness of it. He was, after all, a cardinal firmly grounded in the changes of Vatican II. There could be no looking back. Especially now when their hope lay in the future, in making other, greater changes.

He gazed out into the congregation and found Margaret. She had been at his first Mass. And of all the things he recalled about that day, it was the sadness in Margaret's eyes that he remembered most. He looked at her now, sitting in the first row, Alexandra at her side.

It was when he'd turned his head slightly to the left that he saw *her*. Sitting at the end of a pew, a black mantilla covering her head, the kind that Latin American women still wore inside churches. He closed his eyes for a moment, thinking that the lights were playing tricks on him. But when he opened them, she was still there. He imagined he saw her smile, but he could not be sure, for her face seemed now almost without expression, except for the eyes.

He brought his focus back to the altar as he heard the choir sing the alleluia in preparation for the Gospel. Then he watched as Bishop Estevez mounted the pulpit, and his mind drifted backward. . . .

It was decided that catechism students in all of the parishes of the diocese should go to confession at least once a month. He had purposely avoided the loosely given order, and had let the children go about living, he supposed, their rather innocent little lives without the benefit of the sacrament. However he knew the day of reckoning was fast approaching— Father Bordeleon had begun to ask questions.

On the surface the dear old priest's inquiries seemed benign enough, but underneath they carried all the force of an out-and-out inquisition. Yet he was not so naive as to misinterpret Father Bordeleon's interest. Of course, the man was concerned about the welfare of those young souls entrusted into the care of Father Phillip Camélière. But the good father's chief concern in keeping tabs on his young missionary priest was his very real desire to keep everyone happy. Several of the Cajun mothers had no doubt come to him, wanting to make sure that their sons and daughters "had made the good Confession, Father."

In the back of his mind he resented Bordeleon's intrusion, felt mildly betrayed by his parishioners going behind his back to his superior. In the end, however, he decided that it was but one or two women who had beseeched Father Bordeleon, women who had suddenly become overly scrupulous, who didn't quite know how to broach the subject of Confession with him. Still, it rankled. Before he came, Bordeleon had not been able to get most of them inside a church, much less a confessional. They were his people now.

When at last he gave in, he sat patiently listening to the timid almost frightened voices whispering their "Bless me Fathers," and the innocent litanies of small lies and petty larcenies, minor disobediences and impure thoughts. For two hours he remained very still, expectant, caged behind the small grille that separated priest from penitent. His ears straining for one particular voice, his eyes for one particular face behind the latticed screen.

But it was neither his eyes nor his ears that alerted him. He could smell her. She had the odor of wet earth, like that of the lichen that grew between the gnarled toes of the oaks. If she were not so clean, he might have looked for dirt beneath her fingernails, dark rich bayou mud packed there from digging for some root or plant. But her hands would be as white as lilies, and he looked then to see them clasped like a virgin's before lips that made not a sound.

"Angelique, do you wish to confess?"

"Confess, Père Philippe? I have no sin."

For a moment he said nothing, then his hand moved, blessing her in the name of the Father, and the Son, and the Holy Ghost. "Go in the peace and grace and love of God," he whispered into the blackness.

She had not come for forgiveness. For penance. Not even for grace. That had been his idea. She had merely come. And though he wanted to see in her coming some malicious design, he knew that wasn't true. Yet she was his torment. And he sat for a long time within the cramped confessional, the white starched collar of his priesthood biting into his neck. When he touched his forehead with the tips of his fingers, it was to wipe away the beginnings of the terrible pain that had gathered itself between his eyes....

He touched his forehead now. He noticed through the web of his fingers that Estevez was stepping down from the pulpit. He stood as he heard the beginning words of the creed and looked again to see her. Her chin was held up, and it seemed that she stared out into space, apart from everything around her. He focused hard on the outline of her body and remembered that other time long ago he'd seen her sitting like this in the pew of a church....

At first he had been startled to see her in one of the pews, sitting quietly, doing nothing. Then he remembered why she had come. Yet he made no move toward her, but rather observed her from the side for a while, her well-defined profile made fuzzy and indistinct because of the dark cloud of hair floating about her face. But he could see the protruding outline of her lower lip, pouty in a childish kind of way, but really more a woman's mouth than a girl's. He noticed that she had on only a light sweater over the straight cotton shift that was her habitual costume. And he wondered that she wasn't cold.

"Angelique?" Her name sounded high-pitched in the empty church.

She turned quickly, her dark eyes fixing him with that now familiar look, that look that said she had to somehow make her presence real in his eyes. But there was nothing theatrical or in any way premeditated in what she did. As always, there was that contradiction in her, that precise awareness she seemed to have, that unexplained, yet certain omniscience. Yet there was that in her which said that she knew nothing, knew nothing at all.

"Angelique..." He repeated her name as though she hadn't heard him.

"I've come to help."

"Oh, yes, I'd forgotten." It was not entirely a lie. "The Nativity. I said we'd put it out this afternoon. Did you...?"

"Here." And she twisted around, pulling up a large gunnysack that rested on the kneeler and dumped its contents into the aisle.

"Good." He spoke without any particular enthusiasm, glancing down at the tangle of gray moss, like a ball of old woman's hair pulled from a brush. "I'll get everything." He tore his eyes from the bounty she had collected. "The wing on the angel was broken off, but Picou repaired it. It's all in the sacristy." He spoke as he walked back toward the small L-shaped room behind the sanctuary. "The angel seems all in one piece now," he called to her. "Picou left her to air so that the glue could dry." He moved out, carrying the small statue. "I rather like this old set." He spoke, smiling at her from behind the communion rail. "I'm glad St. Gabriel decided to buy a new Nativity and give us this one. I'm afraid of what Tante Louise and Mrs. Didier would have wanted to order." He laughed. "I really don't like the new things. There's no . . . feeling in the faces." He was standing in front of her now, the angel still clasped within his hands.

She rose then from the pew and reached out and touched the angel's wing, tracing with a finger the fine line where it had been glued back together. "My name means 'angel,'" she said with no discernible emphasis.

"Yes, I know."

He released the angel and watched as she toyed with the figurine, caressing it as a little girl might do a doll. He left her still holding the angel as he walked back again into the sacristy. When he returned, he was carrying a very large box stuffed with old newspapers. "This is heavier than I thought," he said, squatting to set the box down. "Picou and I went through everything. Only the angel was a little the worse for wear." He felt as though he were talking to himself as he rummaged though the newspaper, digging to find the first piece of the crèche. He glanced over to where she stood and saw that she was still holding the small statue of the angel in her arms. "We decided to return everything to the box," he continued, once more working through the crushed newspapers. "Pack it all up again. Thought it would be safer until we put it out. So here we have it." He stopped and met her eyes across the short distance that separated them. "Where do you think we should arrange it, Angelique?" He wanted her to put the angel down.

She seemed to consider the question for a moment. Then she moved forward to stand in the center of the sanctuary, before the altar. "Here, right in the middle, on the steps leading up to the altar. So that everyone can see it." Her voice sounded uncommonly happy, almost joyful in the late-afternoon stillness of the small church.

"I agree, Angelique. You have found the perfect place." And without her seeming to even notice, he drew the statue of the angel from her hands and placed it in front of the altar next to the large box.

And so they worked, drawing the bundles out of the box, carefully unwrapping the small, sometimes slightly chipped plaster statues, placing them as their real-life counterparts might have been on that first Christmas. Joseph and Mary beside the crib. The cows and sheep and donkey set into clouds of gray moss. The angel, in its newly restored glory, set high upon the wooden frame of the stable.

When she reached deep into the box, pulling the paper from the last tiny statue, he stopped her. "No, Angelique, the baby Jesus does not go in now. We must wait until Midnight Mass. He will be carried in and placed in the manger then."

She smiled down into the tiny face, petting the image of the Christ Child as though he were a stray animal she had found.

"Angelique? Did you hear what I said?" He drew closer, reaching to take the small statue from her hands.

She pulled away, cradling the tiny body against her. "He is beautiful. . . ." Her voice was low and gentle. "Like our baby, *mon Philippe*, just like our baby will be. . . ."

Tony touched him lightly on the arm. The Prayers of the Faithful were over. He glanced up at the young priest, vaguely aware of the worried look that shadowed his face. Rising slowly from his chair, he walked down the sanctuary steps to accept the gifts of bread and wine. Then he moved back to the altar. He did not have to concentrate on his movements. They were fixed, a repertoire of prayers and gestures that became a part of any priest.

And when at last he'd come to the most solemn part of the Mass, he bent low over the host and prayed the words softly.

"Take this, all of you, and eat it: this is my body which will be given up for you." He spoke aloud, lifting the large white host above his head. And in that moment through the inverted V of his arms, he saw her framed like an icon, like the dark avenging angel of death.

Lindsey stood in the center of the room as though she wanted to draw from it its special and well-defined energy. The energy of the precious hours that they spent together here. She could never quite believe that she was really in the middle of the District, that other houses were just down the road, that other people were living their own private lives around the twist of the hill that kept this place secluded, kept them safe, protected from anything that could hurt them.

She glanced about her. It was such a beautiful old home. He wouldn't have had it any other way. No small apartment on the fringe of the city. Not some anonymous shell of four bare walls and a bath. But a special place, just for the two of them. She remembered the day he'd first brought her here. He was like a small boy, brimming with mischievous joy, teasing her, making her close her eyes, sweeping her into his arms and carrying her over the threshold like a new bride.

She could hardly believe her eyes that day. The vine-covered stone cottage with gables and pitched roof, and a quaint garden with a pond full of fat and happy goldfish, was just about perfect. And inside, the coziness of old antiques and overstuffed furniture, and wide warming fireplaces in almost every room. She had a name for homes such as this one, a tag left over from her girlhood. She called them Nancy Drew houses.

And he had done it all himself. Selected what he wanted right down to the last detail. It was his special gift to her. God, she had wanted to cry that day. But she didn't, somehow knowing it would have spoiled it for him.

The housekeeper had been in this morning. She could smell the lemon scent of furniture polish, and there was cold lunch and white wine chilling in the refrigerator. All that was missing was Phillip. She walked out into the garden to wait.

The soft mechanical whir of an engine caused her to look up and see his car circling around the drive. She raised her hand and waved.

"Sorry I'm late." He had walked swiftly toward her, kissing her on the cheek. "I couldn't get away from the *60 Minutes* people." He spoke against her cheek. "Mad at me?"

She laughed. "Of course not. How did it go? I'm sorry I couldn't be at the Mass."

"It went fine." He straightened, looking back toward the garden. "It's beautiful here, isn't it, Lindsey?"

"Yes, it is."

"I wish we could stay here forever," he said quietly, resting his head on top of hers.

She pulled away and looked up at him. "Now, Phillip Camélière," she joked, "you and I both know that you would go stark raving mad if you stayed here for more than a week."

He laughed. "You know me too well, Lindsey Darrington. Let's go in. I have a surprise for you."

When they walked inside, she kissed him on the cheek. "Go sit down," she ordered, moving toward the kitchen. "I won't be but a minute, I promise. There's some wine chilling. I'd love a glass. How about you?"

"Sounds good. But hurry. I've been waiting all day to give you this."

"Hey, this is your day. . . . Give me what?" she called out.

"If you would hurry, you'd find out," he answered over his shoulder.

"Quick enough?" she said, coming back into the room with two glasses and the bottle of wine. "I have a toast." She smiled, working the corkscrew.

"Lindsey . . ."

She handed him his glass and cuddled close to him on the sofa. "To Phillip, may all of your days be celebrations."

"Thank you, Lindsey." He pulled her into his arms and kissed her. "And now for my little surprise." His face was still close and she could see that his eyes were bright and happy, and that he looked suddenly very young.

"You're very beautiful." He ran his hand across her cheek. Then he got up and moved to where he'd slung his jacket across a chair. "I hope you like this. It's what you said you wanted. Why . . . I couldn't possibly know." He walked back to her. "Open it," he said, smiling.

Slowly she pulled the ribbon and tore the paper away. "Phillip . . . you remembered." She lifted from the box a small portrait taken on his ordination day.

"Well, at least the frame is nice," he teased. "I can't say much for the photograph."

"Stop it, Phillip Camélière. I won't have you talk that way. I'm rather fond of this face." She brushed his cheek with a kiss. "Now, it's my turn."

Jumping up, she walked into the bedroom. When she returned, she was carrying a small package. "I hope you like it. I didn't know what to get you. You're not an easy person to buy for."

"I know, I'm the man who has everything."

"Here," she said, pressing the gift into his hand. "I hope you like it."

"I'll love it because you gave it to me." He had begun to tear off the ribbon and paper. "Now, let's see what we have—" He stopped short and looked up at her.

"Well . . . do you like it? Say something." She worked at making her voice sound casual, fussing over the torn wrapping paper.

"Thank you, Lindsey. It's beautiful."

"The man said it's very old. But in mint condition," she said, looking down at the watch. "It's the original chain and fob and all. Open it." She sat down next to him. "There's an inscription. I—I know I shouldn't have, but . . ."

He looked down at last and snapped open the cover of the watch, angling it so that he could read the inscription. *To Phillip, with love, L.M.*

"I hope you don't mind." She heard herself talking again. "About the inscription. You wouldn't have to use it every day. Maybe just on special occasions. I know you like your wristwatch. But of course, when you did wear it, it would be concealed most of the time. And L.M. could be anyone. The *M* is for Mertons . . . my maiden name."

"Lindsey . . . shhh. This is Phillip . . . remember." And then his lips covered hers, and she could feel the gentle pressure of his tongue inside her mouth. That he was a cardinal in the Roman Catholic Church didn't matter. That she was Mrs. Richard Darrington, the wife of a United States senator, didn't matter. No, none of it mattered. Couldn't matter if they were to exist at all.

"Lindsey..." He was talking. "I want to tell you something, Lindsey. Something I should have told you months ago. Something that you deserve to know."

She pulled away from his arms and sat up straight on the sofa. Something like a sharp pain raced up her spine. He had seemed so worried lately. "Are you ill, Phillip? Tell me. Don't keep anything—"

"Lindsey, no... please. I'm fine." He held her close again. "Lindsey, I love you."

"Take a look at Mantini's face. He looks just about ready to explode."

John's eyes had strayed momentarily to the reception line, but he pulled his glance away and followed the motion of Brian's unlit pipe to a corner of the overcrowded room.

The small retinue from the papal embassy stood at the farther wall. Except for the archbishop, the Italians appeared content enough, chattering among themselves. But Mantini, a little apart from the others, glowered toward where Phillip Camélière stood holding court with the guests who streamed into the hall. His ill temper barely concealed, the Pro-Nuncio fairly quivered in his expensively tailored cassock and patent-leather pumps. He looked ready to stamp the floor.

"Look at him." Brian repeated as the Archbishop puffed viciously on his cigar. "I can tell you just what he's thinking. He's adding up the cost of this reception and comparing it to his yearly budget. That's the real reason the Curia hates the American hierarchy in a nutshell. Money. For years the Curia has been running the show carte blanche on U.S. dollars while laughing behind the backs of the kowtowing American bishops. And the whole time the old boys dreading the day when someone would stand up and call a halt to their neat little arrangement. Now someone has."

"Cardinal Camélière?" John asked simply.

"Exactly. Did you see Mantini this morning when he saw the TV cameras?" Brian chuckled. "You can bet that the Vatican won't like it one bit that Phillip is being portrayed in the American media as some kind of folk hero. But truthfully, I can hardly blame the Pro-Nuncio for his evident disgust. That Mass was a circus." Brian's voice held the bitter note he had heard before.

"You know, Brian," John said softly, "sometimes I get the impression that you don't much like the Cardinal. I thought you'd been close since the two of you were students."

"We *are* close. That's why I see him so clearly." Brian had avoided the direct answer. "You've been with him almost every day. What's *your* impression?"

"I don't really spend all that much time with him." John did some hedging of his own. "He's in his office. I'm in mine . . . or in the library."

"But you see him at meals. And you talk to him sometimes."

"Yes." He was thinking of that strange interlude in the library. "He's brilliant actually. As I'm sure you know. Very subtle and complicated. I'm never sure exactly what he's thinking. But then that could describe you lately, Brian."

Donovan ignored the comment. "But you like him?"

"Yes." He said it without hesitation. "I like him very much. He's been extremely kind to me. . . . And Brian." He met and held the older priest's flat stare. "Never once has he brought up anything regarding my position with the Committee. There's been no attempt to influence my work in even the slightest way."

Brian's short laugh made a harsh sound against the background of celebration. "Are you so sure of that, John? Maybe the fact that he's remained silent on the subject *is* an attempt to influence you in his favor. As you've pointed out, Phillip is subtle. And then, of course, there's the niece."

"Alexandra?" Perversely he could not keep his eyes from wandering again to where she stood in the reception line next to an attractive older woman. Brian's eyes had followed his. When he turned back, his old friend was still staring across the room. "What did you mean about Alex?"

"You sound defensive, John." The familiar wry glint that Brian turned toward him was suddenly irritating. "What I meant was that it need not be Phillip himself who tries to sway you. An emissary, particularly such an attractive one in the guise of a supposedly objective reporter..."

"Whose side are you on, Brian?" The bluntness of the question surprised even himself.

But Brian seemed unmoved. Casually he began the ceremony of lighting his pipe, striking the match deliberately, sucking out its flame into the cradled bowl.

Obediently John watched it all, mesmerized into the familiar pattern, his mind struggling to cope with his own unexpected outburst. It was hard to think straight. And his feelings about the other night with Alexandra were coloring his ability to be rational about anything.

"You haven't answered me, Brian. Whose side are you on?" For once he was not going to let Brian off the hook. "You're supposed to be the Cardinal's ally in this fight with Rome. And you agreed that I should help Alexandra with her assignment. Frankly, Brian, I'm confused."

His elbow resting on the arm he held folded across his stomach, Brian stood casually, his free hand supporting the pipe. A thin smile appeared around the stem still clutched in his teeth. "What I think about Phillip Camélière is irrelevant, John. It's you who'd better keep holding on to that objectivity you're always so worried about. Because I can promise you that before this is all over, you're going to be needing it. ...Now, come on." He touched a hand to John's shoulder. "The line's not getting any shorter, and I think it's time we presented ourselves to our host. After that I'd like to try some of this famous food."

Alex had been watching. And as John and Monsignor Donovan walked to a place at the end of the reception line, she made a hasty excuse, slipping from her mother's side.

"Over here, Alex." She heard herself called.

Frank *would* have to spot her as she made her escape. She hadn't wanted to see him just yet. She needed a few moments alone. Yet it was remarkably easy to give him her best smile as she walked toward him; he looked so grudgingly handsome in his rented tux. Still it was a reprieve when almost immediately Lindsey and Richard drifted over.

"Deserting your post, Alex?" Richard cast an ironic glance over his shoulder.

"And not a moment too soon. I've had it."

"Can I get you something, baby?" Frank turned to her. Then: "What about you, Lindsey?"

"I'm fine." Lindsey smiled. "I still have some champagne." She lifted her half-filled glass.

"I'd love a plain old Coke right now," Alex answered him. "I'm really thirsty. I need some food, too, I guess. I've been in such a rush today, I don't even remember eating."

Frank's laughter was disbelieving. "That must have been some rush, Alex. Stay right here. I'll be back in a minute."

"Good evening, ladies. Richard." The Vice-President had come up and was pumping Richard's hand. "That was some job you did for the party this morning, Senator, getting that finance proposal out of committee. Damn impressive. Believe me, the President appreciates it. You can be real proud of this husband of yours, Mrs. Darrington."

Lindsey's smile looked genuine, if one avoided her eyes, and she seemed grateful when the Vice-President apologized for the need to "drag Richard off." But when she turned, her expression changed. "What's wrong, Alex? You look ill."

"That bad, huh?" She tried to joke. "Truth is, I'm not feeling great. I haven't slept the last couple nights, and Mother came in so early this morning." She let it hang, gazing about for Frank. He was standing near one of the buffet tables, trapped in conversation with a Maryland reporter. In a moment he would break away and return with the food.

She was turning back to Lindsey, wondering how the evening could be any more miserable, when her eyes met John Leighton's. He was several feet across the room, talking with another priest, but he had stopped to watch her.

"Lindsey, I *am* feeling bad," she said suddenly. "Tell Frank I'm really sorry, but I have to go and lie down for just a minute."

"Do you want me to come with you? Do you need something?"

"No. No, I'll be all right. I just feel overwhelmed all of a sudden. I told you I haven't eaten, but the thought of food right now makes me nauseous. I have to get away from all this. Tell Frank I'll be back after a while."

Lindsey frowned, watching her friend walk quickly away. Something was going on. Her eyes turned to where Alex had been staring just before her abrupt decision to leave. A man, a priest, was watching Alex's retreat intently.

"What's happened to Alex?" Frank was standing there, balancing a plate in one hand, a Coke in the other.

"I'm afraid she's not feeling well, Frank. She's going to lie down for a few minutes. She told me to say she was sorry for running off. And that she'll be back."

It didn't seem to satisfy him one bit.

"Alex felt terrible about deserting you," she began again, smiling reassurance. "And don't worry, I'm sure she's okay. Mmmm. That food looks good." She tried to distract him. "Mind if I have some?"

He stared down at the plate as if it were some totally alien object. "Oh, please, take it, Lindsey." He handed the plate to her. "I'll keep the Coke. Alex always likes to drink it when she doesn't feel well."

"Are you going to look for her?" she asked. "Do you know your way around the residence?"

"I'll find Mrs. Jordan, the housekeeper. She'll know which room is Alex's. I just want to make sure she's all right."

She watched him walk away. The reception line had broken up at last, and she allowed her eyes to roam, to seek out Phillip. He was across the room talking with a group of important-looking men. She felt a smile breaking out upon her face and forced her eyes away. Today had been the most wonderful of her life. The words she had feared for so long had been said. And *he* had said them. Said them to *her*. Her eyes strayed again. Phillip was looking back. He reached into his pocket, and with the most impish of grins, he checked the time.

"Lindsey."

Her head jerked round. Richard stood there, exasperation in his voice. "Must you stand here alone like this? It's so conspicuous," he said under his breath. "You've got to mingle a little, Lindsey. I really can't stand here with you all night, and it certainly doesn't look right for you to be by yourself. Where's Alex?"

"Alex isn't feeling well. She went to lie down."

He frowned. "Look," he said with affected patience, "I have to go find Harold Godfreys. There's another committee meeting called for Monday, and I've got to make certain of where he stands. Go talk to somebody. There are plenty of Senate wives around. You like Gerrie Franklin, don't you? Hell, go talk to Phillip. He *is* your host."

"Maybe I'll do that." She gave him a noncommittal smile. His suggestion was tempting, but she knew she wouldn't do it. Moments with Phillip were too precious for the eyes of strangers, and she could never really be comfortable playing at the public lie.

Richard bent toward her, giving her a light theatrical kiss. "I'll look for Gerrie," she said, before he turned away.

In the library Alex flung herself on the leather sofa. It was all such a pain. Feeling so miserable and guilty. She couldn't continue to avoid talking in more than casual sentences to Frank forever. And she couldn't avoid John forever either. She really didn't understand why she was so afraid. It was stupid. She'd have to talk to John sometime. Get this thing settled and get back to work. .

"Alex?"

She sat bolt upright. John Leighton stood tentatively in the doorway.

"What's the matter?" He was studying her face. "Are you crying?" He came quickly toward her but stopped short of sitting down. Just stood there at arm's distance.

Hastily she brushed the tears away. She hadn't known she was crying. It made her feel worse than ever.

"I'm fine now," she said. "I wasn't feeling very well. I came in here to be alone."

"I'm sorry," he apologized. "But I do need to talk to you."

She didn't say anything. She couldn't. Sitting there like

wood, stupidly staring. His eyes seemed so truly compassionate. Why did he have to look at her like that?

"About the other night..."

She felt her eyes close, blocking out his image. She wanted
not to be here, but she couldn't get up or move away. It took
all her strength not to cry again. She just sat there listening
to him.

"It was my fault, Alex. I understand that. And I don't want
you to feel bad about...about what happened. I've tried to,
but I can't really. I don't even think it was a sin. You're such a
wonderful person. So beautiful and bright. I've never known
anybody like you." For a few moments he said nothing else,
but she still couldn't open her eyes, couldn't look at him.

"I've been so lonely, Alex. And I didn't know it. Not really.
I guess you were God's way of waking me up." His tone had
lightened. He even laughed. "'Come on, Leighton,'" he
mimicked playfully, "'there are people out there. Real people. You're getting old and stale...isolated.'"

He sat down beside her taking her hand. She had to open
her eyes now.

His face was radiant. "God wasn't taking any chances," he
said softly. "It had to be somebody spectacular." When he
smiled, the tears started again.

"It's okay, Alexandra. Really." He had not let go her hand
and he pressed it now. "We're friends, Alexandra Venée," he
said firmly, "the best of friends. We'll still see each other here
at the residence. And we'll help each other. Help each other
to do our very best work."

He stood, and still smiling, he let her hand slip away. He
stopped only once at the door to look back at her.

She sat there numb, makeup and tears drying stiffly on her
cheeks. She couldn't think. Not yet. But she had a suspicion
that when she could, she was going to be very, very angry.
Angry mainly at herself for sitting helpless and mute while
Father John Leighton so cavalierly absolved her from guilt.
As if she had simply been an unconscious pawn in a game
between him and his God.

She jumped up and began to pace. She was more than
angry, she was *furious*. She had been worried about him,

worried about what he was suffering. And all the time he had been playing little mind games, never once bothering to discover what it was *she* felt. Typical, totally typical. He might be a priest, but he was first of all a man. He'd just proven that.

Back and forth she paced past the rows of leatherbound volumes. They'd help each other do their very best work. How long had he rehearsed *that* line?

She stalked over to a large framed lithograph which lamplight made into a serviceable enough mirror. She combed her fingers through her hair and dabbed beneath her eyes with a moistened finger. She had to get back out there.

"*Here* you are."

She whirled to see Frank frowning near the door, a drink in his hand.

"Lindsey said you were feeling bad. I went up to your room . . . . What's going on, Alex?" He was looking hard at her face.

She swallowed. Dammit, she wasn't up to any kind of interrogation. "Nothing. I just came in here to lie down on the sofa. I'm ready to go back now." She started toward the door as if she'd move past and have him follow.

He caught her arm. "No. I want to talk."

"This isn't a good time."

"It's never a good time, is it, Alexandra?"

She looked up. She hated what she saw in his face. "I don't know what you mean."

"Yes, you do. And you can't keep avoiding it . . . avoiding me."

She stopped straining against his grasp. "Oh, Frank, I'm sorry. Really. It's just that the last few days have been a nightmare. All the research and reading . . . I don't have much longer to pull this thing together for Murray. National means so much to me. You know that. . . . And then my mother coming in and Uncle Phillip expecting me to be here to play hostess . . ."

She saw sympathy and hope replace the anger and hurt in his eyes. It made her feel completely awful. She took a breath and smiled up at him, brushing back the hair that had fallen across his brow. "You look damn good in that tuxedo."

Relief lit up his face. "And you look sensational in that dress." He seemed to be waiting.

"We *will* talk," she heard herself saying. "I promise."

Now he was really smiling. Happy to indulge her. "I'm sorry, too, Alex. I really have been pushing. . . . Here's your Coke." He looked ruefully at the remnants of ice cubes floating in a watery layer above the darker brown. "You sure you're ready to go back out there, baby."

"I'm ready." She took the glass. "Let's go find some food. And let's find Lindsey, too. I promised to introduce her to Mother."

CHAPTER SIXTEEN

Alex woke up in the Rose Room. She had dubbed it that the first time she'd slept here, and it was always the room she used now when she stayed overnight at the residence. It was late morning and she still lay in the big antique bed staring up at the creamy rose ceiling, just one shade paler than the petal-pink walls. She'd always found it very difficult to be depressed or miserable in this room, but she'd given it a damn good try the last couple days. Even with Frank promising not to pressure her about moving in. Even with John Leighton safely tucked away, hiding out in his apartment till the anniversary hoopla was over.

It was funny, but she hadn't been able to think of one of them without thinking of the other. But then, they were both part of the same problem. Dear up-front no-bullshit Frank, holding out that glass of diluted Coke to her, looking so handsome in his rented tuxedo. And John Leighton, so perfect and controlled in his black clericals.

If she said that she didn't love Frank, she would be lying. He was a solid reality in her life, strong and steady and reliable. In a special way, she loved Frank Gregory more than she loved anyone else in the world. Frank was a part of her, part of her becoming what she now was.

She'd told Lindsey that there was no *passion* with Frank.

But she'd known that passion wasn't exactly the right word. Or even what Lindsey called "chemistry."

No, it wasn't passion that her relationship with Frank lacked. It was *conflict*. Being with Frank was just too damn easy. She didn't have to work at it. It simply existed—comfortable like an old shoe. And she was tired of easy. Easy had been her whole life. She wanted hard. She wanted something to claw at, sink her teeth into. She needed a good fight, something to make her go the distance.

John Leighton?

She saw his image again, remembering how he'd looked as he'd smiled down at her, confessing that all of it had been his fault, that she wasn't to blame for that kiss.

Very nice, John, she thought to herself. But she wasn't willing to accept that what had happened between them was simply God's way of slapping John Leighton in the face. Not for one minute did she believe that God had had anything to do with it. Still, if John felt the need to call it something else, that was fine with her. Yet she was not so easily fooled. Why couldn't he accept his loneliness for what it was? Why couldn't he be honest with himself? Why did he have to make his needing her, wanting her, into something more than simple physical desire?

But he was a priest. That was the single answer to everything. That was the simple reality she had ignored. It had come so sharply into focus that day in the chapel when she sat alone, watching Father John Leighton celebrate the Holy Mass. She had seen it clear upon his face as he lifted the host, drank the consecrated wine from the cup. How could she have forgotten? Was she so selfish and insensitive? Was she so wrapped up in her own little world of feelings that she was oblivious to what was truly happening? In his calm priestly discipline, as he'd sat next to her in the library, taking her hand into his, could she not see that he was fighting for his very life, trying to save himself, preserve the single thing he cherished and loved above all else—his unique and privileged union with God? *Oh*, she strangled on the sound and felt at last the tears begin to fall. Dear, dear sweet man.

She remembered the kiss again. His mouth on hers, so

needy, yet so giving. That kiss had meant something to him. It was his way of reaching out. Making contact. But he had gone too far, and he understood that. *He was a priest*—that was the beginning and the end of his existence, the alpha and omega of his life. There was and could be nothing more.

And she wasn't going to destroy that. Wasn't going to become for him his *mortal sin*. Yes, he had free will, was responsible for himself. But he was also a man, a warm and loving man, who by his own admission felt lonely, isolated. No, she wasn't going to make it rough on John Leighton. Wasn't going to precipitate his fall from grace, tempt him to do something for which he would forever and always despise himself. She was going to cooperate with God's plan for him. Let him come back into the human race, but reserve that special part of his humanity, that part that had touched her that night in her apartment, for God, for God alone.

How kind and gentle he had been to her, letting her believe that she was for him an inspiration, a gift from God. And he had believed his own words. She understood that now. Understood that those words were his survival, his lifeline. They kept his step firmly planted on the path he had chosen long ago, held him on course, steady in the sacrament of his priesthood.

She wanted what he wanted. To be friends, to help each other to do their very best work. And she would help him remain where he wanted to be—in the arms of his loving God. And what of this God? She would pray to Him to give her the strength she needed, pray that He didn't ask too much of her. And that He didn't ask too much of His faithful and loyal servant, her good friend John Leighton.

"Alex?"

"I'm in here, Mother." The voice echoed out from the bathroom. "I'm getting ready to run the water."

"Well, stop for a minute and come here. I've something to show you."

Alex, looking like her teenage self, appeared almost immediately, wrapped in her battered chenille robe, her hair in heated rollers.

"Alex." Margaret picked up a flat box at the side of the chair. "I wanted to have this ready for your birthday, but we only had one copy of some of the older photographs. So I brought it with me to Washington."

"Mother, this is great." Alex had lifted out the thick photo album and began flipping through the pages.

"There are pictures of the whole family," Margaret said. "You come home so seldom now, I wanted you to have a little bit of family and tradition up here with you."

Alex sat down at her mother's feet and began flipping forward to pages filled with fading Brownie snapshots. "Oh, I love this one of you and Uncle Phillip. *Mardi Gras 1945*," she read the caption. "Where was it taken?"

"At the home of a friend of your grandmother's, I think. One of the Tollivars. The parades passed very near there, so it was perfect."

"Your costume is wonderful."

"I was supposed to be a fairy princess." Margaret bent closer, examining her eight-year-old self.

"Well, you look beautiful. And Uncle Phillip makes a very dashing pirate. Look at him hamming it up with that eye patch."

Margaret laughed. "Oh, he insisted on that. It's one of the few times I remember his having a real argument with Mother. She was sure it wouldn't be good for his eyes, covering one up like that. But he wouldn't hear of being a pirate without one. Mother should have known better than to try to dissuade Phillip. He went on wearing it for days after. He would have had a peg leg too, if he could have thought of some way to manage it."

"But here," she said, "go forward a few pages. . . . Oh yes, here it is. You haven't seen this one before. I got it from one of your father's old teammates."

"Oh, no!" Alex exclaimed. "This must be when Daddy played for Tulane. Look how thin he looks."

"He was second-string wide receiver. And for heaven sakes, don't ask him what the score of the Tulane–LSU game was the year that picture was taken."

"Wait a minute. Look at these." Alex had turned the page.

"And look at that hat. The dress is pretty, though. Oh, I love *this* page," she went on. "These must be double dates. And just look. Uncle Phillip is with someone different in every one, and there you are, always with Daddy. I think that's sweet."

Margaret smiled.

"And here's your wedding portrait. You look so lovely, Mother. I've always thought your bride's dress was the most beautiful I've ever seen."

"It's in one of the storage closets, cleaned and packed in a special box."

"That's an awfully broad hint, Margaret."

"I only meant that when you married, Alex, I'd hoped you'd wear my dress. I've always told you that. But since the subject has come up . . . You are twenty-six, darling. It does seem time you were thinking of marriage more seriously."

"You were older than I am now when you married Daddy, and see how well that's worked out."

"Your father is a very patient man, Alex. I was very foolish to have taken so long, and very lucky that he didn't give up on me. I often regret that we didn't marry sooner. . . . I would have been younger," she explained. "Maybe there could have been other children."

"Brothers and sisters would have been nice," Alex admitted. "But I have to look at it another way. If you and Daddy had done things any differently, then I wouldn't be here."

Margaret was staring thoughtfully at the wedding portrait. "That's right, isn't it, dear," she said softly. "Everything would have to be different, not just the parts I might wish to change . . ."

Alex turned, looking up into her mother's face. "Mom, are you all right?"

"I'm fine, darling," Margaret said lightly. "It must be looking at all these old pictures. But come on, you need to get ready. I have to leave for the airport in just a few hours."

For some minutes Margaret just sat listening to the soothing sound of running water coming from the bath. Then she picked up the album and opened it again to the yellowed snapshots of her childhood. There was not a single photo here that did not include her brother. Not that this was deliberate, but there were simply few photographs of herself alone.

She hardly remembered their father, a shadowy taciturn figure who had gone away, then died when they were only six or seven. She could recall his features only with the aid of these faded pictures, but her memories of their mother were sharp and clear all the way back to early childhood. Their mother was blond and beautiful, with the strength and determination to have made her own way in the world even had she not been born to wealth, and it seemed to Margaret that from Catherine had come all that she or Phillip would ever be. Her own fairness of coloring was Catherine's, as was Phillip's vitality.

In their father's absence, Phillip had become the man of the house, their mother's staunchest ally, while she herself was shy and fragile, pampered and protected by them both. The failure of her father to return from the war had made no great change within the household. The three of them had simply become closer.

As she'd grown older, happily her health improved, and it might have been expected that in their teens, she and her brother would grow apart. Most boys would have turned away from a sister, even a twin, but other boys were not Phillip. And because he was so outgoing and attractive, so good at everything in school and sports, his protectiveness toward her was respected, and even admired.

She was moderately popular and a good student. Not as bright overall as Phillip, but gifted in the fine arts and in music. Her talent at the piano delighted him, and he loved to hear her play. It was Phillip who decided that she must have the best of private teachers. Phillip who insisted to her mother that after high school she be sent to Juilliard. Swept along by his love and encouragement, she had studied for years, practicing by the hour and dreaming of a concert career. But as graduation neared she had applied not to Juilliard, but to Newcomb in New Orleans.

In her college years she blossomed, her fragile prettiness proving itself an asset. She continued to favor the romantically flowered dresses that suited her best when capri pants and twin sets were the style. It set her apart in a decade of crass conformity, which might have worked against her. But she was attractive and talented, and this eccentricity of dress seemed of a piece with her music. And, of course, she was Phillip's sister.

In the middle of her junior year, she met Alfred.

Always before she had taken care to keep her wry humor and keen intuitions to herself, saving her intimate impressions of the larger world for Phillip. She was more than happy to be admired for her music and judged a beauty. There were lots of friends, and a string of beaux always on hand for double dates with her brother. And if after a week or two they inevitably bored her, well then, there were plenty more. But from the beginning Alfred was different.

Alfred had not been introduced to her by Phillip, but had come backstage after a student recital to say how much he'd liked her music. He'd asked if she'd have coffee with him that night, but she'd had plans, yet surprised herself by adding that she was free for Saturday. It was forward and a lie, but she felt suddenly reckless. She'd break her date, or get Phillip to do it, but she was going to go out with this altogether pleasant and quietly attractive boy.

It had been a shock to learn that weekend that Alfred played for Tulane. She had never dated a football player. But of course he wasn't typical of the breed. He wasn't typical at all. Alfred was purely himself. So easy to talk to, so interesting and interested, that almost immediately she found herself sharing parts of herself formerly reserved for Phillip. After that first date, there was never a thought of seeing anyone else.

Alfred had been there when Phillip had made his announcement about the seminary. Even now she could remember every circumstance of that day—the late-afternoon sun pouring in at the open window, the incense smell of dying flowers, their mother's shocked expression mirroring her own. Catherine had never understood, really, why Phillip had had to leave them, but she had known, even before their talk alone that night.

"Be happy for me," he had said somewhat grandly. "I've

found that thing which will be my salvation." And then when she'd looked at him questioningly: "You know what I mean, Margaret. You see better than anyone how I . . . how I can make people do or be anything I want. Well, I don't want to be like that anymore, and I think that the Church can change me."

She remembered smiling, touching his cheek. "Have you considered how ultimately selfish that might be, Phillip? Perhaps we lesser mortals like to be controlled. Perhaps *we* don't want to be saved."

"Don't say that, Margaret." He had recoiled from her. "And don't include yourself with the others. I like to believe that I never tried to control you . . . or Mother. You don't really think that I have, do you?"

"No," she lied. She knew that his wish to believe was sincere, and it would be cruel to say how futile she thought it was for him to try to go against his nature. She understood that he must try, understood that he must leave them at least for a time. But understanding hadn't made it any easier.

For some minutes, she realized, she had been staring at the same page. She flipped forward now to once again find her wedding portrait. It seemed truly amazing that she could have appeared so serene. After nearly twenty-seven years, it was easy to know that things would turn out right, that she had made the correct decision. She could only pray that Alfred could by now believe that their marriage was more than the one-sided bargain it must have seemed at the beginning.

"Oh, Alfred, I do love you," she whispered. "I was only so very afraid. Thank heaven I had you to trust."

Almost twenty-seven years. It all seemed so completely normal now. So much easier than she could ever have believed. "It's all in the secrets we keep," she murmured to the lost self in the picture. "Who we spare. Who we save."

The escalating sounds of revving engines were only slightly muffled by the barrier of glass and concrete and distance. They stood with their arms locked around each other's waists in a kind of sweet comfortable middle-aged affection, the lines in their faces more noticeable, the gray in their hair more plentiful beneath the harsh unforgiving fluorescent lights.

"I miss her already," Margaret said softly, leaning against her husband.

"I know, I know," Alfred soothed, hugging his wife close, watching her reflection in the glass window of the concourse. Frail and tiny against the bulk of his body.

"I hated leaving her, Alfred. Alex just didn't seem herself." She tried not to sound too worried.

"I'm sure she's fine, Margaret."

"Alex has always had things easy. Perhaps too easy." Margaret sighed. "Maybe it was just her luck, or maybe we made it that way for her, Alfred. I don't know, but she's never seemed so . . . so distracted."

"Did she say anything specific?"

"No. You know Alexandra. Always trying to protect me." She released her hold on him and tugged playfully on his arm. "Like all of you."

He smiled down into her still-very-pretty face. "It's because we love you, darling."

"Well, don't love me so much." She returned his smile, but there was a slightly bitter edge to her words. "Sorry, that sounded awful. It's just that I hate not knowing when something's hurting Alexandra. And she's hurting, Alfred."

"That reporter?" He still had his arm about her waist.

"Frank? Maybe, but I don't think he's the whole problem. It's someone else . . . another man. I can feel it."

"Ah, woman's intuition."

"Stop teasing me. I'm right about this, Alfred."

"Well, when and if Alex needs us, she knows where we are. Come on, darling, we're at least twenty minutes from home."

His arm dropped from her waist then, and they walked at a leisurely pace, side by side down the long concourse. Despite the hour, the airport was still busy, and it was a while before they were able to get clear of traffic.

"I wonder if Alex has talked to Phillip?" Margaret asked once they were settled in the car and on their way. "She's always been able to confide in him. Maybe I should have—" She stopped and quickly her eyes searched her husband's half-shadowed profile. "I . . . I won't say anything to Phillip. But it is nice that he's right there if Alex needs him, don't you agree, honey?"

"Yes, Margaret, I think it's good that Phillip is close by if Alex should need him."

There was no bitterness in his tone, but a kind of weary resignation that hurt her more. "Alfred . . . no regrets?"

"No, my darling, no regrets."

She was very quiet for a while, lulled into peace by the steady pace of the Mercedes taking the gentle rises and curves of the elevated interstate.

"She's wonderful, isn't she, Alfred?" she said finally.

"Yes, my darling, Alex is truly special." And then turning slightly: "You know, Margaret, in my heart, Alexandra is *our* daughter."

And she took his hand from the steering wheel and pressed it hard against her lips.

CHAPTER SEVENTEEN

She knelt quietly inside the confessional. Nervous and uncomfortable, waiting for the shutter to be drawn open and the frail light to eke through the grille into the darkness. She wanted the whole ordeal to be done and over. She looked down at the simple dress she wore, and from somewhere inside of her she knew that the dress was all wrong, that she had never worn a dress like this. That this place, too, was somehow wrong, and this time. But she saw herself clearly. Saw herself as she was now, and as she had been fourteen years ago.

She let go of the stubborn contradictions and allowed her mind to flow freely. Confession, sins . . . Yes, it was sin she'd been considering. She'd better have her list ready when that small window opened. And what of her sins? Oh, she had been reprimanded often enough for being strong-willed, and there were several occasions since her last Confession when she had been especially obstinate. But had she committed a sin? She twisted a lock of her hair and frowned. She hated it when she couldn't decide if she had committed a venial or mortal sin. Or if she'd sinned at all. Sins were never black or white to her, no matter what Sister Eugene said.

She breathed deeply as she ran through her mind the litany of sins she would confess to Father Gervais. She hoped she sounded suitably sorry. She would, of course, confess to

three impure thoughts. It always seemed extremely important to Father Gervais that everyone confess that they'd
sinned against the sixth commandment. She certainly didn't
want the priest to think she was holding back. If only Father
Gervais were not such a... She couldn't find a nice word,
and surely she wouldn't want to have to confess that she'd
said something ugly about him. But still, if he would smile
once in a while, and if he didn't always seem to like the boys
better than the girls, maybe it wouldn't be so bad. The small
window slid open.

"Bless me, Father, for I have sinned—"

"No, Alexandra," the voice interrupted softly, "you have
not sinned. You are God's gift."

She looked up from the tiny knot of fingers that she'd made
of her hands. Looked up and saw not the dour empty face of
Father Gervais, but the face of John Leighton, his beautiful
forgiving mouth smiling at her through the tight web of wire
that separated them....

The harsh knocking came again. A third time on the door
of her apartment. Alex had counted the measured beats in
that half sleep that fogs the mind just before waking. A fourth
time. There was no putting it off; it wouldn't go away. She
opened her eyes and threw back the comforter, swinging her
feet onto the floor.

"Okay, okay," she mumbled, not loud enough for anyone to
hear, and padded to the front door. She looked through the
peephole. Quickly her hand fumbled at the dead bolt.
"Frank..." She stood holding the door open.

"Sorry, babe. I just couldn't wait."

"Come in, silly." She murmured against his cheek, kissing
him on the neck. "Mmm, you smell good. I thought you
hated cologne."

"Nothing's too good for my girl. And while we're on the
subject..." He thrust out his hand. "They're kinda wilted. I
had planned on coming by last night. But I got hung up, and
by the time I finished, it was too late."

"You're sweet, honey." She gave him another kiss, taking
the flowers.

"Babe, I'm sorry I woke you up. You tired?"

"A little, but stop apologizing. I needed to get up. What time is it anyway?" she called back over her shoulder on the way to the bathroom.

"Almost eleven."

"I'll be finished in here in a minute. Put the coffee on. I could use a cup."

"I'm ahead of you."

"What?" She had walked back into the living room.

"Violà! Eggs McMuffin." He made a grand gesture with the McDonald's bags. "I know it's not eggs Benedict. But—"

"It's decidedly you, Frank." She smiled, coming closer, locking her arms around his neck, opening her mouth against his.

"Hey, the eggs are getting cold. . . . And I'm not." He pried her arms from around his neck. "Let's eat and then . . . Well, we'll just let *then* take care of itself."

"Is this the same horny-all-of-the-time Frank Gregory I once knew? You know you could give a girl a complex." She bit his nose and began fishing through the bags, placing the cups of coffee on the table.

"Alex, you know I want you. I want you so bad now I can barely stand it. It's just that . . . It's that I've been doing some serious thinking." He cleared his throat.

"And?" She had turned to face him.

"Well, I think that maybe I've been putting too much pressure on you lately. I mean, asking you to move in with me. Maybe you're not saying no, maybe you're just saying 'I need time.' So I'm giving you time, Alex, all of the time you need."

She moved away from the table and stood close to him. She didn't touch him but remained looking up into his face. Then she reached up and brushed her finger against his mustache. "I love you. You do know that, don't you, Frank? That I love you."

"Alex . . ." He choked on the sound of her name, his arms moving tight around her, his mouth covering hers. "Oh God, I love you." He fought with the words. "Love you, love you so much . . ." And his lips were on hers again, deep and hungry and impatient.

"Frank . . ."

"Don't say anything, Alex. Just leave everything where it is. Nice and easy . . ." He was staring at her now.

"All right, Frank. Nice and easy. And Frank, thank you."

"Thank you, baby." Then his voice became normal. "Okay, so let's eat. I've managed to work up one hell of an appetite."

"I just bet you have," she teased. "Let me at least get mugs for the coffee, and some plates. I hate these Styrofoam things. Coffee still hot enough for you? I can warm it if you like." She had returned with two cups and breakfast plates.

"Warm enough for me. Here." He passed her a muffin. "Sit down and feast."

"By the way, that was some impression you made on my mother the other night."

"I liked her, too. We had a nice talk. She's not exactly what I thought. I had her figured for a . . ."

"Snob, Frank?" She'd finished his sentence. "No, Mother's no snob. Oh, she can put on airs with the best of them when she wants. But Mother is a real person. And don't let her frail delicate looks take you in. There's a little devil that lurks beneath all of that gentility. Dad says there's a bit of Uncle Phillip there. I guess I'm rather lucky. With mothers, *loving* is the easy part, it's *liking* that's hard. I *like* my mother."

"I can tell." He laughed. "And the feeling is mutual. You two look alike."

"Actually they tell me that I look more like my Grandmother Camélière."

"Nothing but beautiful women in the family, huh?"

"I won't refuse that compliment. Grandmother Camélière was very beautiful, and I think that my mother still is."

"And so are you." He stopped short, fixing her with his eyes. Then he looked away, glancing down into the coffee he was sloshing around. "You know the first time I saw you I couldn't believe anyone could be so beautiful and not be a . . ."

"A bitch, Frank?" She filled in the blank again.

"Alex, that's not . . ." He fumbled for the words.

"That's exactly what you meant. And I can well understand

why. I do have a certain rich-girl bitchiness about me." She smiled now. "But you discovered the real me, right?"

"Well . . . let's say I'm still working on it." He bent across the table and kissed her cheek. "So what's with Murray?"

"I've given him an outline. I think he'll like the background work I've done. I know I'll get at least some feature work out of the Conference. The hard stuff . . . Well, that remains to be seen. Anyway, I doubt if the assignment will go to one person. Frank, I'm telling you, this thing is going to get big . . . real big. And I'm worried."

"About your uncle?"

"Yes."

He got up from his chair and moved to stand behind her, massaging the muscles of her neck. "Relax, baby, your uncle can take care of himself. Hey." He glanced over to the drain board where she had placed the flowers. "Is that any way to treat roses? Got a vase?" he asked, walking toward the sink.

"In that cabinet to the left. How's the drug thing going? Catch me up." She watched him try to arrange the flowers.

"Until last night there wasn't much to tell. I had a call from my informant. I think something's about to break. I'm set up for a meeting next Sunday."

"New York again?"

"Yeah, New York again. It's kinda funny but my little guy sounded really excited. Like a kid with a big secret, busting a gut to tell me something."

"Frank . . ."

He stopped fumbling with the roses and turned at the sound of her voice.

"Frank, you will be careful, won't you?"

He laughed. "You know it, baby. Mrs. Gregory didn't raise no dumb children."

Sunlight poured in at the new bay window, glancing off the glass-paneled doors of the neat cabinets and imparting a mellow glow to the hand-waxed finish of the table. The kitchen of the remodeled apartment was so bright and welcoming that it was easier to imagine it as part of a countryside cottage than the first floor of a corner rowhouse in the crowded fringes of Adams-Morgan. And Eric had done it all, Tony knew. Window, cabinets, furniture. Even the earthenware bowl, bright blue and full of fat summer oranges, had been thrown by Eric himself on the potter's wheel next to the lathe in the basement.

"It's only morning and already you're drifting. That's sooner than usual," Eric said.

Looking up from his plate, Tony watched him drop another egg expertly into the hot boiling water. "I guess I am . . . sorry." As always, Eric's perceptiveness surprised him. Which was stupid. He should have come to expect it by now. "The eggs are wonderful," he said, taking another mouthful to prove it.

Eric turned back to the stove, pouring hollandaise from a smaller pot over his own eggs, and walked to sit down across from him at the table. "Want to talk about it?"

He didn't ask about what, or try to pretend that he wasn't being read correctly. Eric deserved better than that. But his own growing transparency worried him. He didn't think he liked anyone understanding quite so much. And yet he knew he didn't want to end this.

Eric was still watching him and waiting for an answer, his pale hair bleached white in the harsh sunshine, his breakfast as yet untouched. "Is it that new priest?" he asked. "You still worried about him?"

"Leighton? I don't know really." He listened thoughtfully to his own words, formulating the answer as much for himself as for Eric. "He hasn't proven to be as great a problem as I thought. For one thing, he's not at the residence as much as I assumed he would be. And . . . well, I guess I'm just not sure he's what I'd imagined."

"And what was that?" Eric began eating.

"I thought he was Donovan's lackey. Monsignor Brian Donovan," he explained. "You remember, I've told you about him. One of the clique."

"Yes, I remember." Eric was pouring him more coffee. "He's someone from the university," he added, filling his own cup. "And you don't trust him."

"He's chairman of the theology department, the old sophist. And I don't trust him at all. Why can't Phillip see it?" The words spilled out abruptly, surprising in their vehemence. It was a question that had plagued him and it felt good to finally say it out loud.

"Are you sure that Phillip can't see it?"

"Am I sure that Phillip can't see . . . what?" Tony tested.

"Can't see that Monsignor Donovan hates him." Eric didn't hesitate to explain.

"I've never said that . . . precisely."

"I guess you haven't." Eric seemed to be searching his memory. "I must have . . ."

"You're right, though." He suddenly didn't want to prolong the game. "I haven't said it . . . but it *is* what I think. The old bastard is eaten up with envy. He actually believes that it's he who should be wearing the red hat. You are exactly right, Eric"—he enjoyed repeating it—"I think that Donovan hates Phillip, and I worry that his envy will interfere with his effectiveness as an ally when the going gets tough at the Conference."

"And have you said this to the Cardinal?"

"I've tried to suggest to him on more than one occasion that Donovan was not totally to be trusted. Yet if Phillip has a weakness, it's his total loyalty to those he considers his friends. He and Donovan go back a long way. They were seminarians together. For Phillip it's some kind of bond. But for Donovan?" He shook his head. "I think he'd like it very well if this Conference should fail. An American Catholic Church with Phillip Camélière at its head would be the final blow to his pride.

"Still . . ." He took a breath, considering. "I know that Phillip is not completely sure of him. I've heard him compliment Donovan half seriously that he is not a man easily controlled. But I don't think that Phillip can conceive of any kind of real betrayal in someone he calls a friend. . . . No," he said, softly now, as if he spoke more to himself. "It's not anything to do with Brian Donovan, but something else completely different that's bothering Phillip."

Eric met his eyes, but did not follow with the obvious question. Eric never pressed. "Do you need more coffee?" was all that he asked.

"Yes, please." He pushed away his unfinished breakfast. The eggs were as delicious as he'd said, but he wasn't really hungry. Now that he had started, he found he wanted to talk about his fears. And who was there other than Eric to whom he could say these things? For the first time it frightened him to consider that he was not the only one who could end their relationship.

"There is something troubling Phillip," he said finally. "Something that has nothing to do with Rome or the Conference. It's been eating at him since the trip to New Orleans." He looked across at Eric. "That's when I first noticed that he seemed so distracted. I thought perhaps he was only tired, but it's gotten worse. . . ." The words died away, his thoughts carrying him onward to that strange faltering moment at the Anniversary Mass when Phillip had looked at him out of almost vacant eyes. Silently he sat staring, trying to forget that glimpse of Phillip's vulnerability, letting his mind achieve a certain blankness, like clearing the board of pieces in a stalemated chess game. Only when he felt Eric's hand on his did he let himself know how very afraid he was.

I'm here, the gentle touch seemed to say. I won't leave you. He heard it more clearly than if the words themselves had been said.

Alex watched as Clarissa brought in the iced tea and laid out two sets of flatware. She had a sudden uncomfortable premonition of who her luncheon partner would be, and so wasn't really surprised when John Leighton walked in the door. The universe was completely unfair. He was in casual slacks and the knit shirt he had worn on the day when they'd met for coffee. God, did he have to look like that today? She pasted a smile to her face. She'd be damned if she was going to let this seem awkward. "Hello, John," she answered his greeting.

His smile appeared entirely natural and he really did seem glad to see her. Not overjoyed maybe, but glad. You're a friend, Alex, she told herself. Remember.

Clarissa returned with a tray—salad for her and a small filet for John.

"Is that all you're eating?"

It was surprisingly easy to laugh. "That's it," she said lightly. "Though it was difficult convincing Madame Elise that it was all I *should* eat. I don't know who's worse actually, Madame or our cook Sarah in New Orleans. Why is it, do you suppose, that everyone is always trying to feed me?"

His smile grew broader. "My mom always explained it as a way of showing affection. I guess people tend to equate food with love."

God, she wanted to hurry. Just finish her salad and get the hell out. Heaven knew she had plenty of work to do. But the damn lettuce kept sticking in her throat. She took a huge gulp of unsweetened tea. This is ridiculous, she told herself. Say something.

"Wh—" She stopped short. He'd started talking before her first word was out. They both waited. "You first." She smiled sweetly, shoveling in a forkful of the fatal lettuce. If she was chewing, he'd have to be the one to speak.

"I was just going to ask how your writing was going. Have you given anything yet to your editor?"

"I spoke to Murray this morning, and he seems pleased with what I've done so far." She smiled. "You've been a big help, answering all my questions."

He was staring over her shoulder. She wondered at what. "How's your book going?" The question came out a little flat, but it seemed to work against whatever had held his interest.

"Okay." He set down his fork as if suddenly surprised to find it in his hand. He pushed his plate away. "It's going okay," he repeated, "though it gets a little confusing trying to work on two projects at once."

"How far have you gotten?"

"With the book?"

She nodded. He seemed completely comfortable again, talking about his work.

"I have a rough draft," he answered her. "That's as much as I can do till the Conference is over."

She realized when he stopped that she'd been staring at him while only half listening to his words. He was sipping on his tea unconcernedly now. Was he really finding this cozy little luncheon so easy?

"Do you have any idea where Uncle Phillip is?" It seemed a safe enough question.

John shook his head. "No. I guess he's really busy. Did you know that CBS is going to air the *60 Minutes* profile next week?"

"This coming Sunday? No, I didn't know," she said when he nodded. "Uncle Phillip must have forgotten to tell me. This Sunday is really soon."

"I know, but that's what I heard from Monsignor Feeney. Evidently they got it put together quickly because of the further trouble in Holland."

"I wonder what Uncle Phillip thinks about the timing?" she thought aloud. "It's still four months before the Conference."

She glanced over at John. He wasn't saying anything, and she couldn't read his expression. "John . . ." She had begun to ask him something else, but he was distracted by Clarissa.

"Oh, no." She was looking at the dessert plates that Clarissa was carrying. "Don't you dare set that down in front of me, Clarissa. I told Madame nothing but salad."

"But, Miss Alex, this was left from dinner on Friday night. Madame Elise's been saving this mousse specially for you. She's gonna be hurt if you send it back. . . . You finished with your salad?"

"Yes, take it please."

"You can take mine, too, Clarissa." John handed the girl his plate.

There was the click of the door as Clarissa left, and Alex looked up to see John's gentle grin.

"They've done it to you again, huh?" He looked from her face to the chocolate.

"Will you take it, please?" She picked it up, offering.

Their eyes met.

"Alex, I . . ." he began. "Yes, all right," he said after a moment.

She stood up. "I'll talk to you later," she said quickly. When she backed out, he was staring ahead, his hands still holding her plate.

• • •

Phillip paced about the room. It had been four days since
he'd seen her sitting in that pew at St. Matthew's. Four days,
and still nothing. He'd expected that she would have contacted
him by now. Another package. Another appearance. Yet . . .
nothing. At first there was just the slightest gnaw of doubt
that it was Angelique whom he'd seen, but not now. She had
changed very little. Older, yes. But the wild and knowing
eyes—they hadn't changed.

It was the waiting, he finally decided, waiting for Angelique
to make another move that caused this uncharacteristic agita-
tion in him. He had thought too long and too much. And he
was letting her have the upper hand in whatever game she
was playing. And he was sure Angelique was playing some
kind of game.

For a moment his mind drifted back to that first day he'd
seen her. It was a picture forever etched upon his memory.
Her suntanned body swimming inside the thin white sheet of
her dress. Her arms reaching out like tendrils, grasping,
pulling him through the thick muddied bayou water. In a
single blinding instant he'd lost his will that day, his well-
intentioned vows. And as his mouth had sucked against the
curve of her open lips, he'd opened his eyes and seen for the
first time his wolf of the steppes within the liquid-dark
shadows of her eyes.

But no thought of Angelique now came without a thought
of Emile. What of Emile? he asked himself for the thou-
sandth time. Something had surely gone wrong. Was he ill?
Or worse, dead? It was certain that Emile was in some way
incapacitated, or Angelique would not have been able to
come into his life again. Emile had always been able to
control her better than anyone. And it had seemed that she
had resigned herself to the baby's death, to never seeing
her Père Philippe again. It was a quiet, passive child that
Emile had taken away with him across the Louisiana border
into Texas.

But the Angelique he'd glimpsed in St. Matthew's, the
Angelique who had sent "the little gifts," was not that silent
almost listless young girl he'd helped to escape to a new life.

Not the small brown angel who had cuddled against Emile's cheap but clean white shirt as they settled into the seat of the Greyhound bus that day. No, it was the wild bayou Gypsy who had returned to him, haunted him now.

Why? Why had she returned? He could guess. He closed his eyes against the thought, and remembered. . . .

He and Emile had spent almost every evening together right after she had delivered. Emile in a straight-back chair, the cane seat sagging even beneath his bone-thin body. He in the only upholstered chair in the house. From there he could glimpse Angelique curled on her cot in the corner, like a little girl of five or six instead of sixteen, legs drawn up, one hand cradled under her loose hair.

Every once in a while he would turn deliberately to watch her sleeping. At least he always believed she slept. Yet there were times when he sensed that she was awake, only feigning sleep, listening.

It seemed strange at first that Emile had not taken him off into the bayou and shot him. For certainly the man knew the truth. Yet Emile did nothing, said nothing. And there exploded in him at the time an almost joyous adolescent gratitude that he had somehow gotten away with it.

But after this childish sense of thanksgiving passed, there came long nights when he shivered in his bed, cold with naked uncompromising fear. At first he had no name for this heavy hollow feeling that gave him no peace. But soon it found a name. And he knew it for guilt.

But nothing ever came of his terrible bouts of remorse, and he calmed down after a while, coming in the end back to himself, sleeping a dreamless sleep till morning.

He supposed Emile had had his own reasons for keeping quiet. Perhaps he felt a proper portion of his own guilt. Yet he suspected that the older man probably understood that there was in truth nothing he could have done to have prevented what had happened. It was Angelique's universe. She had been in control from the beginning. And neither Emile's Cajun good sense, nor his own priestly intellect had had a chance against her.

There was no guilt, he'd decided at last. All of them had

been victims. Yet he had wanted from the beginning to
somehow make everything right for the girl and her uncle.
He'd at least played the part of the "good priest" through it
all, and surely the money had brought comfort. And the
child. The child was freed, forever untouched by this thing
that had happened.

Emile had not hesitated to take the money. "*Merci*, Père
Philippe," was all he'd said. Anything more would have
seemed hypocritical, and they'd both understood that. He'd
seen them board the bus that day, and watched until it
disappeared into the distance, but its dirty choking fumes
seemed to remain in his throat for days after.

He moved now to look out the window of his study. How
long ago it all seemed. And yet how near. There was really
nothing else for him to do but wait. If she did not contact him
today, there was always tomorrow. She had not finished with
him yet.

The hairbrush, like a small bristly animal in her hand,
burrowed in rhythmic strokes through her hair. Like most of
her clothes and the other things she had with her, the brush
was bright and new, and Angelique enjoyed watching its
motion reflected in the motel mirror.

She laid the brush down and picked up her ribbons. Blue
today, the Virgin's color. It was something she'd never forgotten, perhaps because she'd always liked the statues of Mary
best. Mary with the baby Jesus. She watched herself tying
the ribbons, thin and shiny with long streamers, and she
thought again about the church.

She had never seen a church like St. Matthew's before.
Big. Beautiful. Filled with statues and bright pictures, alive
with light and color. She sat like a statue herself now, staring
into the mirror, remembering the snowy-white figure of Mary
on its special altar. Reaching out. Mary's arms like her own
arms. Empty . . .

She had been sick when they'd moved to east Texas. The
only time she'd been sick in her life. She couldn't remember
it really—the moving. Exchanging one swamp for another,

where her uncle would fish and trap as always. Leaving one cabin for a second as isolated as the first.

What she remembered was her mother and the things her mother had taught her—how to call the spirits, and how to make the little bag of hair and cloth that, filled with certain things and worn between the breasts, would get a baby.

And still she dreamed of Philippe. Of how she had first found him alone in his small boat upon the bayou. The hazy Sunday afternoons on the island when they'd lain together. Her waiting, as the moon had grown small and fat again, and still she had not bled.

She had told no one but Philippe about the baby, but eventually Uncle Emile had known, crying to her that she had been wicked, wicked like her mother, despite his prayers and the catechism class. But she didn't tell, no matter how many times he begged. Even at the end, she never told him whose seed she'd drawn to make the baby.

Her uncle had forbidden her to go to the settlement. No one, he said, must know her shame. But Sunday afternoons Philippe had still come to her, bringing her clothes and little presents, looking at her with secrets in his eyes. And she would sit quietly as he spoke with her uncle, dreaming in the meaningless flow of his words, dreaming of the time when the child would come and Philippe would stay, and be with her forever.

She remembered the moon, nine times full, its face filling the window of the room where she lay panting in her labor on the cot. Philippe had already come with the midwife, and she could hear the soothing tones of his voice blending with her uncle's in the space beyond. When it was over, he came to her. She watched his face in the bright silver light, bending close to see the child at her breast. *Michelle* . . . She had whispered the name. Michelle for the mother who had not returned. She had drifted into happy sleep then. Her Philippe would never leave her now.

But in the morning Philippe was gone. And the baby, her little girl, Michelle. *Dead*, said Uncle Emile. *Taken away to be buried in the night*. She remembered the screaming. Remembered something of the swamp before Philippe found her, his hands about her wrists, holding her from escape, forcing her to listen. *God's mercy . . . Everything for the best.*

She had not forgiven him. Never in the long years, which were only a short space in her mind. A space where nothing much had happened to wash away the sharp memories of happiness and betrayal. She loved Philippe, and she hated him.

And then it changed.

Uncle Emile had become sick. Very sick. She understood it when he told her. People in the stories on the television were sick like that sometimes. He had pains, bad pains around his heart, and he had to go to the doctor every month in Sabine. That part was good because she got to go into town more often, and she liked to buy clothes and ribbons. She supposed she knew he was going to die, but it was still a surprise to find out he had a secret.

It was a late afternoon, hot and still. She came in carrying the smell of the swamp with the plants and pieces of bark in her basket. Uncle Emile sat alone in the dark kitchen drinking a beer at the table. "Angie," he said to her, "sit down with me here, *chère*. I have something I need to tell you."

She sat down across from him, tracing her finger in the deep scratches left by the knife he used to prepare the game.

"The doctor, he told me I will die, Angie. Not today. Maybe not tomorrow." He shrugged. "But someday not so long from now. There is a lot I have to tell you. You listening to me, Angelique?"

She lifted her head. His voice seemed different, though no louder than before. He never raised his voice to her, not even when he called her "wicked." Yet she understood that she must pay attention.

"I try to do my best for you, you know, *chère*." It was always what he told her. "I will fix it so you will be all right. There is the money, Angie . . . a lot of money that is still here for you. I will show you, *chère*. When I am gone, you will need to have it."

She listened now more closely.

"Real soon we will move nearer into town," he said. "You

cannot be out here all alone. It was easy, you know, for me to keep you here. But now I think, I keep you here too long."

She watched the dirty-looking foam rise slowly in his glass as he poured out more of the beer.

"A long time now it is, Angie, since you had a real bad spell. Time, I think, that things should change for you." He looked up at her again. "You can learn to drive the car, *chère*. I will find a little house, with ground in back for you to have a garden. The money will be in town for you, in the bank, Angie. And you can learn to make the checks for what you want."

She sat silently and imagined Uncle Emile dying. So he was leaving her, too. Still it would be nice, she thought, to live near the town. To have the stores so close.

"Something else I must tell you, Angie." He had stopped, his fingers making clear marks where they touched the glass. "This part, it is hard, *chère*. It is something I keep from you. A secret."

This was the real surprise. Uncle Emile with something dark and hidden. She waited.

"I have thought a lot about this, Angie. Since the doctor, he told me I will die."

He took a drink of beer and stared at her. His eyes made her think of a turtle's eyes, old and dark, buried in folds of skin.

"I try to think, should I tell you, or let it die with me. But it is not right. And it is all so long ago now. I think, what could it hurt for Angelique to know?"

She was very quiet, matching his stare. If she waited and watched, he would tell her.

"It is about that baby you had, *chère*. Remember?"

She looked away from him, his question seemed so stupid. But she nodded.

"That baby, she is not dead, Angie. Père Philippe, he took her. Gave her to some people in New Orleans that wanted a child real bad. Père Philippe said it was the best thing, *chère*. For you. And for that baby, too."

She had turned to him sharply, but he was staring down into the flat surface of his beer. *Not dead. Not dead.* She felt hands, then, her own hands, gripping her shoulders while her body rocked back and forth against the hard spindles of the chair. She struggled to understand. Philippe? Why had Philippe taken her Michelle away? Why had he left her?

"Angie, Angie, do not do that." Her uncle was on his knees by her chair, shaking her. "*Bon Dieu*, Angelique, do not look like that at me. I am a simple man, *chère*. I try my best with you when your mama left. Try to do what I thought was right. What else could I do, Angie? You never said who was the father of that baby."

His words had stopped and he looked up at her, waiting. But she made herself quiet now. She said nothing.

He sighed. "I know what I think, but it is maybe too wicked. I turn my face away from such a thing." He let go of her and again slumped in his chair. "When you ran away, I go to Père Philippe. He say it is too late, that the baby is already in New Orleans, that we do the right thing for that baby. He said he know where he can find you. And when he come back with you, we make plans. And Père Philippe, he is the one gave me the money to take you off. Someplace new, he said. Someplace you can forget that baby . . . be happy.

"I thought it was the right thing, Angie." He stared at her again, turtle eyes pleading. "It went to good people. Père Philippe, he promised me that. . . . Try to understand, Angie. It was not some doll. What would you have done, *chère*, with that baby? In my heart, I still believe it is the right thing."

He wasn't looking at her now. He had drunk the last of his beer and he went on talking. "*Mais oui, chère*, the only thing I could do. But it is not good, I think, to take such a secret into the grave. So I tell you now, Angelique. To make my peace with God. And with you."

He got up slowly from the table and came around to stand behind her. Still he did not look into her face, but bent down from above to kiss her forehead. She sat unmoving while he disappeared into his bedroom, returning with a rumpled pillowcase.

"It is here, Angie, like I told you." And he poured it out—more money than she had ever seen.

In the weeks that followed she learned to drive, but they had no time to move into the town.

The day his pains returned, she sat curled before the television as Emile lumbered through the tiny house. Her eyes set on the screen, she listened to his tired footsteps shuffling over the loose boards in the narrow hallway. His hands fumbling from drawer to drawer, ugly knotted fingers scrabbling through pencils and stray matchbooks for the plastic bottle she had buried in the swamp.

At the last he sat heavily in his own tattered chair, his face the gray white of tree moss, his hand working like a claw against his chest. "Angie," he begged, "my medicine. The little brown bottle from the doctor. You have seen it, *chère*? Do you know where it is, Angelique?"

She didn't answer, even when he said her name again, her eyes drifting back to the television. The sound from the set was very low, and she listened . . . listened for the shuddering breaths that slowed. And stopped.

She still stared into the mirror, seeing herself again now. To her own eyes, her face seemed much as it always had. She was the same. But the Philippe she had seen in the huge church was different from the man she had known. Not the Philippe she had lain with on the island, but the man in the pictures she had cut from the newspapers. It was this strange Philippe, she knew, who had stolen her Michelle and sent her away. She hated him and feared him, but she would fight him in whatever way she could. Make him give her back her baby.

She tried to see ahead but her thoughts had begun to scatter. She was suddenly hungry and the new red leather wallet was empty. Walking to the bed, she pulled the wrinkled pillowcase from under the thin motel mattress and shook its contents out upon the bed. Cardinal Camélière's face stared up from the clippings that lay tumbled among the dirty green stacks of bills. And from beneath the thick wads of money the barrel of Emile's well-cared-for .22 gleamed dully.

CHAPTER EIGHTEEN

He had read the book straight through, and now he rose from his chair and walked to the window, pulling aside the drapes. It had rained all day and the glow of the streetlights oozed ghostly images across the wide avenue.

John Leighton walked back to his chair, still warm with the heat from his body after so many hours. He sat and reached for the book—*The Last Temptation of Christ*. That day in the library when Phillip Camélière had said that he'd never made peace with the story's ending, John had not understood what the Cardinal had meant. But tonight, after having read the novel, he had no choice but to accept that Phillip believed that Christ had wrongly chosen death on the cross over the simple joys of a life on earth.

He reopened the book now, leafing through to one certain passage he'd marked. To words that wouldn't leave him alone.

He was twenty years old, his cheeks were covered with thick curly fuzz and his blood boiled so furiously he could no longer sleep at night. . . .

So there he stood, a red rose in his hand, gazing at the village girls as they danced under a large, newly foliaged poplar. . . . Suddenly he heard crackling laughter behind him. . . . He turned. Descending upon him with her red sandals, unplaited hair and complete armor of ankle bands, bracelets and earrings was Magdalene....The young man's mind shook violently. "It's her I want, her I want!" he cried, and he held out his hand to give her the rose. But as he did so, ten claws nailed themselves into his head....

He pressed the book against his chest, his heart, a thick heavy muscle lumbering inside of him. Dear Jesus, how difficult it must have been for you, he spoke softly to himself. And then quietly he began to mourn the man who never was, the Jewish carpenter of Nazareth, the gentle and loving husband, the kind and compassionate father, the grizzled and wise grandfather.

And, too, he mourned himself. Oh, how it hurt to travel this higher road, away from the flesh. And if that path were difficult for Christ, how much harder for him. But unlike Phillip Camélière, he could not question the story's ending. Jesus had resisted his last temptation, had relinquished the great and small joys of men. Everything according to his Father's plan.

And he...? He had chosen to do the same. Yet in a single instant Alexandra's face came to him, a blinding flash of light against the dark disquiet of his soul.

Six days. Six days since he'd last seen Alexandra Venée. Six days since they'd shared lunch together at the residence. He didn't think he'd ever be able to eat steak again. Strange how he remembered every detail of that meal with her. The precise way he had cut the small charred filet, the pink blood running from its hot center onto the white plate.

And then later vomiting every bite he had eaten.

He congratulated himself, however, on how well he had been able to sit calmly with her, making small talk. He had never been good at that sort of thing. Playacting. Donovan had once said he would make a terrible spy.

He looked at his watch. It was almost time for *60 Minutes*. He walked over and turned on the TV, setting up the video recorder.

The first story was a piece on adoption; the second on a controversial trial in South Carolina involving a black district attorney. It appeared they were leaving the Camélière story for last. He settled back and waited.

"Phillip Camélière started his life as a priest in much the same manner as any priest. However, any other similarities must end there." It was Wren Kelloch's familiar voice, and instantly he hit the volume button on the remote control.

"A New Orleans–born-and-bred aristocrat, Phillip Olivier Camélière came from an old family, with old money. Quite a lot of money, it is rumored. But being born with a silver spoon in your mouth doesn't necessarily guarantee success. Yet in all respects Phillip Camélière was a natural. Someone who could have aspired to become just about anything he wanted. Yet this only son of a wealthy, socially prominent New Orleans family opted for a Roman collar and cassock at the age of twenty-two, instead of a seat on the board of the company he'd inherited from his father."

He watched as a flood of photographs fed the screen, shots of Phillip Camélière going all the way back to his childhood, up to that day he received the all-important red biretta.

And then the photographs stopped, and Kelloch was facing the Cardinal himself. "And how does it feel to have thirty years as a priest behind you?"

"I try not to think of what's behind, Wren." Phillip sat comfortably in simple black clericals in one of the nondescript offices of the Pastoral center. "It's the future which interests me."

"And that future, Your Eminence, does it include the possibility of your heading an American Catholic Church?" Kelloch wasn't wasting any time.

"We *have* an American Catholic Church, Wren. It is a member in good standing of that family which is the Holy Mother Church."

"Cardinal Camélière, I meant your heading a *separate* American Church, one that has parted company with Rome because of the Vatican's hard-line stand on certain key moral issues."

"I had no idea that I had so much influence." Phillip laughed. He hadn't answered her question.

"Are you saying *absolutely* that you are not behind a movement to sever the American Catholic Church from Rome?"

"The essence of Catholicism is unity, Wren, a oneness of thought, a certain and abiding orthodoxy."

"No schism, Cardinal Camélière?"

"No schism, Wren. Sorry to disappoint you. It would have made a great story." He favored her with one of his smiles.

"But you don't deny that there are fundamental issues which divide many of the American bishops from Rome?"

"I won't deny that there are differences. But differences of opinion among members in any institution are expected from time to time. And are, may I add, healthy. It shows that we are all alive and kicking. Heaven help us if we lose our wills to disagree."

"But won't statements on those areas of disagreement be drafted at the Bishops Conference in November? Statements which will be in total opposition to Vatican policy?"

"There will no doubt be significant focus at the Conference on those areas of disagreement, Wren. They relate, after all, to very human issues, very human needs. But, as always, the effort will be to work within the boundaries set by papal teaching."

"And if the statements exceed those so-called boundaries?"

"We are a reasonable people, we American bishops, Wren, as are our brothers in Rome. The essential mandate will be: 'Church unity first, last, and always.'"

Then the inevitable question. "Within the last three weeks there seems to be movement among the Dutch dissidents to form a separatist church. Vanderveer has made it clear that the women priests are here to stay. And he seems fully prepared to accept that Rome will never lift the excommunications if they do. My question is simple. Since many of the American bishops favor ordination of women, won't it be difficult for them not to come out in support of Vanderveer at the Conference?"

"Our hearts are with Vanderveer and the Dutch people. But our allegiance is with Rome."

"Cardinal Camélière, I don't mean to be rude, but it appears that most of your statements are blatantly contradictory to the positions which insiders say you will take at the conference."

Phillip wasn't angry. The smile said that. "Wren, I have answered as I see things now. In November . . . who shall know? We are all in the capable hands of God."

John looked down at his watch. Camélière's last comment had seemed like a parting shot, but there should be at least five more minutes before the program was over. When he looked up again, it was Alexandra Venée's face he saw.

"How does it feel to have an uncle who is a cardinal in the Roman Catholic Church, and one who is celebrating thirty years as a priest?" Kelloch was asking her.

"Wonderful," Alex said, smiling at her uncle. "Mother and I are very proud of him."

"Mrs. Venée, you and Cardinal Camélière are twins?" The camera focused on Margaret Venée.

"Yes. But I'm afraid we're not the least bit alike." Margaret's voice was affectionate.

"Indeed, we are not. My sister was blessed with all of the talent and beauty." The Cardinal laughed.

"Actually if I might interrupt here . . ." It was Alex's voice. "I think both of them are pretty terrific. But, of course, I'm prejudiced."

"Speaking of prejudice . . ." Kelloch sounded suddenly less friendly. "Isn't it true, Alex, that you're going to cover the Bishops Conference for the *Washington Post*? Any conflict of interest there?"

Alex's smile was not unlike her uncle's. "None at all. I can't do anything about the fact that I'm Phillip Camélière's niece. But rest assured that my Uncle Phillip will have no immunity."

Cardinal Camélière made a comment, causing Kelloch to follow with another question for Alex. But John was no longer listening, for Alex's glowing image had suddenly eclipsed everything. And strangely, it seemed to him that she had never appeared more alive than she did right now on the television screen.

And in an instant the passage from *The Last Temptation* came into his mind.

"Suddenly he heard crackling laughter behind him . . . . He turned. Descending upon him . . . was Magdalene . . . . The young man's mind shook violently. 'It's her I want, her I want!' he cried . . . ."

Like a clear crystal bell, Jesus's words rang out over and over again inside his head. John got up and went to the door.

Frank had never liked Sundays; they always seemed dead. Even when, as a kid, he had something fun to do. Even now, when his schedule was so erratic that the days fit no distinguishable pattern, he could always sense Sunday coming, a dry flatness at the end of the week.

He pulled back the edge of the red curtain and peered through decades of street dust and greasy exhaust. He glanced again at his watch. Jano was late. Might as well get himself another beer. He slid out from behind the table, noting that it was not as empty tonight as the other two times he'd been here.

"Another Guinness." He pulled a couple of bills from his wallet and turned back toward his table with the drink. It was impossible at this angle to see into his booth, but instinct told him there was someone there.

It wasn't Jano who was waiting for him, but the woman he'd noticed when he'd first come in. He had wondered then what she was doing here alone among all these old men.

"Hello, Frank," she said, surprising him completely. "I'm Carla."

To give himself credit, he recovered immediately. *Carla* not Carl. This was the actual contact. He slid into the seat across from her. "Hello, Carla." He extended his hand.

She watched him without smiling, making him wait a fraction longer than was polite before accepting his handshake. She was assessing him and didn't bother to hide it. That was all right. He was trying like hell to read her, too.

She released his hand and leaned back against the worn

padding of the booth, still watching him. She was really a very beautiful woman, sensual rather than overtly sexy. And yet there was something about her that put him off.

She picked up a small glass of brandy, which she held without drinking. Beyond the first simple greeting, she had still said nothing. Apparently she was waiting for him to talk, which was okay, too. There were some things he thought needed saying.

"I'm surprised to be dealing with you directly," he began. "Your friend Jano led me to believe that I wasn't going to meet you. I hope this means that you have something concrete for me."

Leaning forward, she set down her glass, brushing her hair back from her face before she spoke. "What exactly has Jano told you?"

"That you have inside information on one of the Lambrucis' laundry operations.... And that it might be something special."

She shrugged. "Johnny and Paolo seem to think it is."

"May I ask how you know this?"

Now she took up the glass again and began turning it lightly in her fingers. "I know because the money comes to me in D.C. from here in New York, and I deliver it to a middleman."

"Who is?"

"A United States senator." The answer came quick and even.

He was careful to show no reaction. She seemed to want to play it low-key. He took a minute to offer her a cigarette before he spoke. "You going to give me his name?" he asked easily.

Now at last she smiled, ignoring the cigarette. He took one himself.

"Let's talk some more first."

He watched her sweep the dark fall of hair backward again. Even with the too-knowing eyes, she was soft looking for what he guessed she must be.

"Are you going to write about this?" she asked, looking at him.

"I thought that was what this was all about."

"I just want to be sure we have an understanding of what happens after I tell you." It was her longest sentence so far.

"Good," he said, "that's how it should be. We need to understand each other. And I'll tell you just what I told Jano, Carla. I can't print what I can't back up. So tell me, what does this senator do with this money? And how much are we talking about?"

"A lot," she said. "I get a call two, three days before the money comes through. When it's delivered, I make my connection then or a day later. So I'm handing over one, most times two, briefcases a month. It might be all they can handle."

"Who? All that *who* can handle?"

"That part I don't know yet."

"That's too bad. It's important to know who's at the other end of the money."

She frowned. "Why, isn't a senator enough?"

"Is he the one you want to get?" He stubbed out the cigarette.

"I want to get all the motherfuckers."

He let out a quiet laugh. "I'd like to get them all, too, Carla. But it's easier said than done. And there's something real important you have to consider."

She looked at him now and waited.

"This is dangerous, Carla. You've got to be damn sure—"

She cut him off. "I'm sure."

He lit another cigarette, and this time she took one when he offered. "Okay, then," he said, leaning forward. "What we've got so far is a senator playing middleman for the Lambrucis. Passing the money to some third party who is doing the actual laundering. Right?"

"Right."

"And you are, before you leave tonight, going to tell me who this senator is."

She nodded.

"Okay. So you're going to continue passing the money?"

She nodded again.

"All right. Then I'll try to come up with something from my end, using some of my contacts. Agreed?" He pushed away his empty glass. "What about future meetings? You live in the District, right?"

"Yeah, the District."

He thought for a minute. Then: "From now on we'll make contact there. I'll give you several numbers where you can reach me." He picked up a book of matches from the table and scribbled inside the cover. "I'll need to know when you set the date and place for the next drop. We'll have to work out a code."

She was nodding again.

"And, Carla, pay attention to everything. You never know what will be the tip-off. Got it?"

"Don't worry so much."

"Okay," he said. "Now what about the name of that senator?"

She hesitated for only a moment, then turned to open the large flat purse on the seat at her side. He watched, not sure what to expect, as she slid from the cramped space of the seat and walked around to stand beside him, slipping a thin manila envelope across the table.

He didn't watch her all the way to the door, turning almost immediately to the envelope. Inside were five telephoto shots, thirty-five-millimeter blowups. Very clear.

His second thought was that in the blond wig she looked like a whore.

Hard and cold was the message his brain sent down to his fist. And the sound, he'd heard that. Harsh and solid against the door.

She stood there, one hand resting at her side, the other clutching at the opening of a robe.

"John? John, what's—"

"Alex?" He hadn't wanted to make her name a question. But then she was saying "yes, yes," over and over again, and he felt her arms go tight around him, and her mouth open warm under his. And he forgot everything but the dream.

And as in the dream she was beneath him, and his mouth was kissing her breast. His hands moving against the scented skin of her underarms, running across the tight sunken landscape of her abdomen. His lips between her thighs, feeling the trembling of her body against his mouth.

Alex ... *Alex* ... He cried out her name in his mind a thousand times. His body driving hard into her, knowing that for all of his life he would never have enough of her. And then the dream fled before his mind. And he knew that what was happening was real.

And his voice real. The words breaking from his throat: "Alex, I love you. ..."

CHAPTER NINETEEN

From the perspective of his flattened pillow, the bunched and twisted sheets appeared craggy and pocked like a moonscape in the watery gray light. It must still be raining, John decided as he sat up. He hadn't really slept since returning to his apartment sometime this morning after three. Now it was almost eight and his head was splitting.

He looked at the clock: 7:43. Still too early to call Alex. She'd been sleeping when he left her, was probably still asleep now. He looked at the clock again, but still the numbers hadn't changed. For the last half hour he had been checking the time and telling himself that he should wait, that it would be better if Alex were completely awake when he spoke to her. But maybe waiting to be sure she was awake was really just an excuse to put off making the call. Maybe he wasn't so eager to call her at all. Maybe...

He got up and walked to look out. It *was* still raining. Not the powerful slanting sheets that had broken last night against the hard black glass of his window, but a steady drizzle that muffled the morning sun. He stood touching the cool glass, looking down at the traffic that swished past in the street below like small fast ships on a river. There was a really simple reason why he might not want to call Alexandra right now, he thought. He didn't know what to say.

A memory that had been teasing all night around the edges

of his mind came suddenly into focus. He was thirteen years old, in eighth grade, and Father Jameson had asked him at morning Mass to come after school to the rectory.

"The Bishop is coming next month for Confirmations," the pastor had said to him, smiling. "Altar boys will be needed for the special Mass, and at the ceremony. Here's the list of boys, John. I'm putting you in charge." The warm brown eyes had looked down on him with total trust. "I know, John, I can always count on you."

He was feeling now something of what he had felt that day in Father Jameson's office. That's why the memory had struggled all night to free itself from his unconscious. He had felt an undeniable happiness then, and the simple pride of being chosen. But he had felt fear, too. The terrible fear that he might make some mistake, somehow prove wanting, a disappointment.

He had left her last night. And that had been the wrong thing. Against the rules. He saw that clearly now. It would make it seem as if he thought that what had happened between them was . . . what? A one-night stand. That was what people said, wasn't it? No, she wouldn't, couldn't think that. Surely Alex understood.

He pulled away and sat on the edge of the bed. From this new angle, the window was a huge flat swatch of impenetrable gray. A nothingness. What *should* Alex understand? he asked himself bleakly. What was it that he himself understood about all of this? That although last night with her had been the most intensely happy of his life, it was something that could not be repeated? *One-night-stand.* Wasn't that all that she would hear?

He let his hand rest for a moment on the cradled receiver. Was that really what he was going to tell her? That it couldn't happen again? The clock squatting next to the phone rolled the minute as he watched: 8:07. It was still too early.

When he'd finished his shower and shaved, it was well after nine. Staring at his cereal took almost till ten. He poured the whole soggy mess into the sink and listened for a minute to the whine of the disposal. Then he went back to the bedroom phone. Her machine answered the third ring.

I'm unable to answer your call now. It was Alex's strangely uninflected voice. *But if you'll leave your name and number at the tone . . .*

He hung up, entirely certain now of his need to speak with her. He paced once to the window before walking back to pick up the receiver. And dialed.

"Hello."

The voice surprised him. He hadn't expected the Cardinal to answer the phone himself. "Good morning, Your Eminence. It's John."

"Good morning, John. How are you?"

"Fine, Your Eminence. I . . . I was calling to let Madame Elise know I wouldn't be there for lunch. I'm not coming in at all today. . . . Probably not for a few days . . . actually."

"Alex won't be in either. She called early this morning, John. She's headed up to the Cape for the Fourth. Some of our friends have a summer home there. Beautiful old place. Very secluded, but most everyone between Ballston and Highland Light knows how to find Gulls' Gate. . . . Well," he said, after a pause, "I'll let Madame Elise know not to expect you. I suppose we'll be seeing you in a few days?"

"Yes. Of course. I just expect to be doing some writing this week at home." He hadn't lied as he said it, but his mind was already racing over what the Cardinal had just told him. "Good-bye, Your Eminence. Thank you."

The phone went dead.

For a moment Phillip stood listening to the low metallic burr of the dial tone, smiling crookedly to himself. Then slowly, as if with great care, he laid the receiver in its cradle. Why had he done that? Given John what he'd wanted.

Leighton had been so pitifully obvious. As had Alexandra. Neither of them had been able to fool him these past few weeks. And now today—John's little fishing expedition. And Alex, calling this morning at seven to tell him her plans, her voice sounding vague and wounded despite its careful steadiness. He hadn't liked that. And he didn't like it that she seemed to be running away.

He closed his eyes against the remembered sound of her voice, leaning back heavily into the thick padding of his chair.

God, he didn't want her to be hurt. Not his good, beautiful Alex. He never, ever wanted that. But the world was often cruel, and not even he could protect her from all its terrors and hurts. Fight, Alex. Fight, my darling, he thought fiercely. Take what you want, and accept the price.

In the end it was the only way.

The cooling water sucked at her feet, depositing spidery traceries of sand around her ankles, staining the edges of her carelessly cuffed jeans. Alex moved back a bit, but not really far enough to keep from getting wet. She wrapped her arms about herself to ward off the almost sharp wind now blowing in over the tide, ruffling the sea grasses on the distant dunes into tufts of unruly hair. She was surprised that she even noticed the chill, although the breeze was blowing colder than was usual for this time of year on the Cape.

A thin line of horizon was quickly funneling the last of the day's color into the dull gray basin of the sea, and she wondered at the speed with which the light changed. How hard Monet must have had to work against time, she thought, matching brush strokes to light.

Monet? She had thought of Monet. And thinking that she'd thought of Monet, she laughed aloud. Well, Alex, you're not completely lost, she said to herself. There must still be a part of Alexandra Venée that could function independently of thoughts of John Leighton. But it was only a temporary reprieve.

What about last night? That was the hard part, that was the damnable hard part. She didn't know about last night. They hadn't talked after they'd made love. There had been just the long empty silence between them. The silence that had seemed to stretch out beyond anything that they might try to say to each other.

She remembered staring at him for a long time as he lay next to her, watching the rise and fall of his chest, feeling his arm hooked about her almost too tightly. His face appeared empty, like a blank expanse of canvas. And insanely she'd begun to fear that he'd lost all power to do anything with that face. Lost any real connection to that thing that defined him as John Leighton.

Yet in an instant she'd understood that he hadn't really lost contact with himself. Rather it was some great act of will that had put that blankness into his face. And this, she remembered, had frightened her more.

Finally he'd closed his eyes and slept. And when at last she'd felt him move from the bed, she watched his shadow dress and move silently out of the room. The click of the door closing in on itself had been her final cue. She'd shut her eyes, and cried.

She could almost be angry with him. Coming to her, standing like a pitiful pilgrim at her door. Begging with those green eyes of his to please understand, understand all of what was going to happen. Understand and not question. She sighed deeply, and for a time she watched the tide circle impatiently around the invasion of her two naked feet. Oh, but I tried, John Leighton, she thought.

She felt again the sheltering masculine weight of his body on top of hers, the sharp urgent thrust of him inside of her. His mouth kissing her again and again as though he would never stop. And then there had been those few words, those words that had torn out of his throat, terrible and beautiful all at once. *Alex, I love you.*

And with that single utterance, he had pushed her off the neat straight-as-an-arrow path of her life. "Well, Alex, old girl, here's the struggle you've been asking for," she reminded herself.

But this was not what she wanted. *This,* she couldn't handle. And from somewhere came the promise that God never gave mortals more than they could bear. You goofed, God, she thought, this is way more than one Alexandra Venée can handle. If only he had not said he loved her. She was prepared to accept that he could need her physically, want to make love to her. But to *love* her. . .

She turned for one last look at the darkening horizon where the moon had now turned its pale face toward the empty beach. There was no trace of the bright day that had been. *I love you too, John,* she had answered him last night.

It was, after all, what she'd felt then. And damn it all, it was what she felt now, believed she'd feel for the rest of her life.

She walked away from the shoreline, her feet making shifting potholes in the sand as she trudged up the slope to the beach house. Maybe, just maybe, she'd get lucky and a few days here on the Cape would help.

Pulling the hose from the wall bracket, she washed off her feet and moved down the small .walkway to the house. She had her plans for the evening carefully laid out. Start a fire first; it was surely cool enough for that, and she'd seen some wood in the small closet off the kitchen. Then a big green salad, a glass of wine, some Mozart on the compact-disc player, and a good book. She'd even decided what book she was going to read: *Rebecca*. The Du Maurier novel was one of her favorites, and being in the old house on the Cape somehow always reminded her of Rebecca de Winter's ill-fated bungalow, although there was not the least thing mysterious or maudlin about Gulls' Gate. For an instant, she wished she'd rented the Hitchcock movie.

The fire had been easy to start, and now she sat curled on a warm rug, sipping wine, turning the pages of her book, going back to Manderley again.

It was but a slight noise, the shuffle of leather soles on sand that caused her to look up. At first she glimpsed just the broken reflection of the firelit room upon the panes of the door that led out to the shore. Then the image changed, and it was his dark outline she saw standing solid behind the small glittering rectangles of glass. In faded jeans and a knit shirt, he looked much as he did that day they'd had coffee together, that first time she'd decided that she liked John Leighton, liked John Leighton very much indeed.

CHAPTER TWENTY

"Get up, sleepyhead." The voice seemed to come from a great distance, but the soft marshmallowy swat of the pillow against his head was close, very close. "You've already missed breakfast, and you're well on your way to missing lunch." Again the downy crush of pillow. "John Leighton, do you hear me?" This time the voice was clearer, and very, very familiar. He sat up.

If he'd expected to see a serious or strained Alexandra Venée, he was wrong. Instead she stood over him smiling, her hair pulled back in a ponytail, dressed in old jeans and a man's long-sleeved shirt. He decided she looked about sixteen.

Last night they had made love again. And after, like the first time, there had been the silence. The silence that had eventually melted into sleep. He remembered bending and kissing her hair before he drifted off, and a dull sleepy promise to himself that in the morning they would talk. But this *was* morning, and Alex stood over him like a once-lost-now-found childhood friend. And all of his good intentions faded in the brightness of her smile.

"Well?" she asked.

"Well, what?"

"Are you going to get up?"

"That depends."

"Depends on what?"

"Depends on if you're coming back to bed."

She looked at him, her eyes narrowing, trying it seemed to fully comprehend what he'd just said. He could well understand her problem; he was having a bit of a time believing that he'd said it himself.

"I am not. And if you think I'm going to let you waste this entire day, you've got a lot to learn, John Leighton. Especially not today. It's the opening of blueberry season, my man, blueberry season in these here parts."

"Blueberry season!" He'd almost shouted it.

"Shh," and she clamped her hand over his mouth. "You're aiming for the whole world to know. Blueberries are mighty special treasures, John Leighton, and the time of pickin', and the places of pickin', are just about the best kept secrets on the Cape."

"Alex, I wouldn't know a blueberry from a . . . a . . ."

"Boysenberry? Nothing to know. Get dressed. And don't wear anything nice. The scruffier the better. And wear long sleeves. I'll provide the hats and boots."

"Long sleeves? This is summer, Alex."

"It's sweat a little, or be eaten alive by the mosquitoes and ticks. We're headed for the swamps, tenderfoot. And unless you're immune to bug bites and poison ivy, I suggest you put on a long-sleeve shirt and button up all the way to the neck."

She had moved into the kitchen, and he could hear the lively clinks of dishes. He could certainly use a cup of coffee. *Blueberries?* Well, John, this certainly wasn't how you figured to start off the day. He had pulled on his jeans and was buttoning his shirt when she came back into the bedroom.

"Here, it's black and strong. You look like you could use it." She was smiling sheepishly as she handed over the cup.

"You read my mind." He took a large swill.

"You hungry? I've packed a lunch for later."

"I can wait. You've certainly been busy this morning, Alex Venée."

"When the berries are ready to harvest, there's no time to waste." She was walking back toward the front of the house. "I hope these boots fit." He could hear her rummaging around in a closet.

"Oh, yes, I'd forgotten; boots too."

"Stop complaining and try on these." She had returned, and was handing him a pair of olive-green rubber boots, the kind he'd seen fishermen wear. "And this too." She tossed a battered old straw hat into his lap.

He'd just managed the boots, and had given the straw a jaunty tug over one eye as he stood up. "Well, how do I look?"

"You'll do. Grab those pails, and pray for your very life, John Leighton, that my favorite bogs have not been discovered."

Her favorite bogs had not been discovered, and now they sat upon an old quilt on drier, higher ground, eating the picnic lunch she'd packed, two large pails of blueberries glistening like black marbles in the veiled sunlight of late afternoon.

"Here, try one?" She had dipped one of the blueberries in her wine and was offering it to him.

"Mmm, good. Another."

She laughed, handing him another berry.

"Delicious. I'm afraid you're spoiling me, Alex Venée."

"I'd like to try." And this time there was no laughter, and he had to look up.

"Alex . . ." He could hear the strain in his voice.

She dropped her head, and he could see how the fading sunlight rippled in dark golden threads through her hair.

"Alex."

She looked up. Her face was expectant, now that he'd made her name sound stronger, firmer.

"We have to talk, Alexandra." The words finally came out.

She didn't say anything at first, and he thought he saw a faint shadow of doubt pass across her eyes. Then as quickly she was smiling softly. "Please, John. Not now . . . not here . . ."

He reached out and cupped her face with his hands. "Okay, Alex," he whispered. Then he kissed her gently on the lips. "Here," and he reached back and handed her one of the berries from the pail.

"We didn't do so badly." She looked over his shoulder at the two buckets brimming with berries.

"Not so bad at all, considering what a tenderfoot you had for a partner."

"Yes, but look who got hurt. I can't believe I—"

"Let me see that." He took her hand into his and examined the small cut. "Not really very deep. I think you're going to live, Alex." And bending, he kissed the scratch. "Mom used to do that when I was little. I guess moms everywhere do that. I don't know how it worked, but my cuts always seemed to feel better after that."

She moved her hand from his and ran it through his dark hair. "It surely does." Then: "You and your mom were close?"

"Yes," he said, leaning back now so that he was almost reclining on the quilt. "I could talk to her better than to my father. God knows I loved Dad. It's just that I always felt he was uncomfortable with . . . with talking about ideas."

"And friends? What about friends?"

"There were ten of us in all." He had now stretched out completely, his hands propped behind his head. "Six boys. Four girls. 'The Brain Gang.' That's the name the other kids hung on us. I guess we were all pretty smart. Billy Nielson was the unofficial leader. There wasn't anything old Bill wouldn't try. At least once. I guess that's how he got himself killed." He stopped for a moment.

"Then there was Clark Johnson, and his younger brother Ray. They acted more like twins than older and younger brother. We used to laugh when Clark would start a sentence, and Ray would finish it.

"Mario Calabruzzio was the clown in the group. But we all had a healthy respect for his Italian temper. Every Saturday he would pull one of his scams. Steal some of his Grandma Lucia's cookies and bring them to us. I think Grandma Lucia suspected who the thief was, because he never got caught.

"The smartest of the group was Laurence Wilbert. He and Ray were the same age. But he was in our class. One of his teachers had talked the principal into letting him skip the fourth grade. Only one grade . . . Larry could have skipped grammar school entirely. I think he's some kind of physicist working for one of the big independent research teams in California."

"And John Leighton?"

He frowned. "I guess I was the quietest. Shy, actually. Even in the Brain Gang I was always an outsider. Old Bill used to get frustrated with me sometimes. 'My friend, you think too much,' he would say. 'You gotta go with your feelings sometimes.'" He looked up then, staring at her for a long moment, watching the sunlight still work on her hair.

"You said there were six boys and four girls." She broke the silence.

He leaned back again. "Calabruzzio was all for letting the girls into the group. I never knew a guy who thought and talked more about girls than Mario Calabruzzio. Clark said it was because he was Italian. Bill said it was because he was horny." He laughed. "Well, at any rate, Mario convinced us that it was more than a good idea to let the dames, as he called them, into the group. So Carole Beecher, Mary Faye O'Malley, Diandra Matthews, and Brigit Callahan became members of the Brain Gang."

"Brigit Callahan. She was the one with you in the picture."

"Yes."

"Your girlfriend?"

"I guess you could call her that. I was pretty dumb about those kinds of things back then. But I seemed to have had this feeling, though, that I was kind of...responsible for Brigit."

"And what happened to Brigit?"

"I don't know really. She moved away right after graduation. We lost track of each other."

"Do you ever hear from any of the others?"

"I get a letter from Ray once in a while. He fills me in on what he knows about the others...which isn't much. Except for his brother Clark. Clark is a petroleum engineer for one of the big oil companies. He lived in Saudi for quite a few years. He's back now. Living in Houston. Ray says he has four girls. Unbelievable."

"The four girls?"

"That, yes, and how we all grew up. It's strange, but when you're young, you never really think about growing up. Oh, you say things like 'when I grow up I'll do such and such,' but growing up is no more than an abstract idea. And you think that life is some kind of wonderful mystery and that the magic will go on forever. But it doesn't, and one day you find that you've turned into a man, and you don't feel the same at all. *Life* feels different... and there's no mystery really, and somehow the magic went away before you could do anything about it, if you ever could."

He continued to lie back quietly for a moment, then he sat up suddenly and pulled her tightly into his arms. "When I'm with you, Alex"—he breathed the words softly against her hair—"I feel the *magic* again. And God could not be so cruel as to punish me for that, could He?"

Then his mouth found hers, and he kissed her long and deep.

CHAPTER TWENTY-ONE

"Are you glad now we drove to Provincetown, John?"

She watched him pull his eyes away from the black water that lapped gently at the pilings of the wharfside restaurant.

"Very glad, Alex." He smiled at her over the candle flickering redly inside its lantern-shaped globe. It made of his face a pleasant mask of light and shadow, and something about the way he grinned at her stirred memories of long-ago Halloweens. She smiled back at him.

"What are you thinking?" he asked her.

She laughed and sipped on her wine. "Nothing really. Just remembering things about my childhood... Who was your best friend?" It came out abruptly. "One of the boys in the Brain Gang?"

He picked up his glass. "I'm not sure I had a *best* friend," he said. "It's hard to single out any one of them from the others."

"What about in high school?"

"We all stayed pretty much together, except for Larry. His father got transferred to Indianapolis in his junior year. Nothing really changed much after eighth grade, I guess, except that I decided definitely on the seminary. That's when they all started calling me J.C. My middle name is Christian." He laughed. "And *Father* Leighton. They called me that, too. I hated it."

"Why did you hate it so much, John? It sounds like an affectionate kind of teasing."

"It was. They weren't being mean. But it let me know they thought of me as different. And I just wanted to be one of them."

"What about the seminary? You must have been 'just one of the guys' there. Or maybe not." She smiled. "I guess you'd stand out anywhere."

He laughed and shook his head. "I did have a couple of good friends at Mundelein. A guy from Chicago I really liked. But they try to discourage close friendships in the seminary."

"So no real *best* friend then?"

"In a way, Alex." His words were careful. "Jesus was always my best friend. He's always been there for me. I've always felt his love, and I guess I wanted everyone else to feel it, too. I think that's why I became a priest."

"I understand, John," was all she said. Then: "I love what you bought me." She took out the little carved gull from the box near her glass on the table. "It's perfect," she said. "But I wish you would have let me buy you something today. There were so many shops."

"And you went in every one."

"You said you liked them."

"I did. I enjoyed watching your face. You're like a child, you know."

"I know. I'm silly about shopping. So, why didn't you let me buy you something?"

"Not necessary. I've got my shell."

"You're really going to keep that big conch you picked up on the beach?"

"Sure. I can listen to the sea."

She smiled. "Then let's just sit out here for a while and finish the wine. It's so nice and peaceful, and you won't need your shell to hear the sound of the ocean."

There was the waxy scent of the melting candles just beneath the salt-laden breeze coming in through the open doors. Not enough wind to blow out the flames, but enough to stir and cool the air. She lay soft and golden beneath him, her hair spread like wheaten sea grasses against the pillows. He smiled, and she smiled back.

She forced her eyes closed, losing the sensation of tears stinging behind her lids. Losing all sensation now. Except of his touch. Feeling him stretched long and hard above her.

She heard her own name whispered against her ear, and felt the soft hair of his chest brushing her nipples as he moved to come inside of her. *So good, it was all so good.* From the beginning this was what she had wanted. To stand defenseless. Without armor.

"John," she cried, letting his hungry thrusts tear her open, strip her naked. "John . . ."

"I'm not the first, John." Her words finally broke into the silence.

"No, Alex. Not the first."

"Brigit?"

"Yes."

She just lay quietly, knowing he would talk about it if he wanted.

"In my mind," he began slowly, "Brigit was more like a sister than a girlfriend. That was my first mistake. I should have realized from the very beginning that Brigit didn't think of me as a brother.

"Right from the start, I somehow felt responsible for her. To be truthful, I understand now that she played upon my own need to be really close to someone. But I soon understood that what Brigit wanted, I could never give her. But because I was weak when it came to Brigit . . ."

"You made love to her."

"Yes. But my real sin was that I let her go on thinking that things might turn out the way she wanted. That I would always be there for her. On her terms. I was weak and stupid."

"But, John, you were only a boy."

"I should have known better. I should have found the courage to be cruel." He looked away for a moment. "Alex," he began again softly, "I lied yesterday when I said I never heard from Brigit after her family moved. She wrote letter after letter to the seminary. But I didn't write back. I couldn't, Alex."

"But you must have loved her... in some kind of way."

"Yes, of course, I loved her. I've only told you about the bad things. Brigit was beautiful and intelligent. And fun to be with. We had good times together. She just refused to hear that I was going to become a priest." He closed his eyes, and for a moment she thought he wasn't going to say any more. Then: "I have to go back tomorrow, Alex."

She turned her head and stared into the shadows beyond the circle made by the candlelight. "Go back, John? I'm not sure I understand."

"I mean that we have to go back to being what we were before, Alexandra. Friends."

She stood up and walked across the room, reaching for the robe she had flung upon a chair. "I see," she said. "But, John, before you leave, there's something I have to ask you, something I have to understand. If you knew that this is the way it would have to be, why did you come to my apartment that first night? Why did you follow me here?"

"You know the answer to that, Alex."

"What? That you love me?" The words had sounded harder than she'd meant. "That's great, John. So now what are we supposed to do with all of this love?"

"God, Alex, surely you understand that it's possible to love someone without being with them."

"That's very philosophical, Father Leighton, but hardly practical. I don't see that you've done so well these past few days."

"Please, Alexandra. You must understand. I'm not perfect. But I've got to try. Go back to where I was before."

"Back to your God?"

"No, Alex. I never left Him. Back to my church. I made a commitment. I have to play by the rules."

"And so I'm the one with no choice. I have to play by the rules, too."

"Alex?" He had said it evenly, and yet she'd heard the pain.

From across the room she turned. "I love you, John." The words were her only answer.

CHAPTER TWENTY-TWO

The District this morning seemed like a stage set, John decided as the car driven by a silent Brian Donovan turned down Massachusetts Avenue toward the papal embassy. Another hot but perfect day, the sky overhead stretching blank and blue and faceless.

Brian's strange call had not wakened him—he hadn't slept at all after returning from the Cape. But it was not until several seconds into their conversation that he had begun to understand at least some of what his friend was telling him. His first thought after Donovan's abrupt "I'll pick you up in twenty minutes" was that there must have been a lot he'd missed.

But he knew he hadn't missed anything now. In the car Brian added nothing to what he had remembered. They were going to a meeting at the embassy. That was all.

He supposed the meeting this morning with the Pro-Nuncio must have something to do with the Conference. Perhaps some compromise was being worked out at the highest levels. Though why he, John Leighton, should be included, he couldn't guess. And he didn't really want to think about it anyway. He had no desire to think at all.

But from time to time stray images assaulted him—the way Alex had looked at him when she'd said she loved him, her hair spread out across the pillow, the darker color of his naked skin against hers. He slammed his eyes shut and fought the waves of feeling that left him shaken and almost physically sick.

It was a relief when Brian pulled the car into the curve of the embassy driveway.

The heavy door was opened by a silent nun, who faded in the shadows of the hall. "Come on, John." Donovan motioned him forward.

He stopped, suddenly alert. Odd, he thought, that Brian should know the way. "Wait a minute," he said, hanging back from the paneled door where Brian stood poised to knock. "I don't . . ."

"It will all be clear very soon, John." Brian's smile seemed less predatory now, his tone almost compassionate. He turned back and knocked on the door.

"*Avanti!*" Archbishop Mantini rose from behind his desk as they entered. "*Buon giorno*, Monsignor Donovan. Father Leighton." He moved toward them, his hand extended to Brian. "So the day is here at last, Monsignor," Archbishop Mantini was saying. "*Lucifer* truly begins."

The words meant nothing. He couldn't read the expression on Brian's face.

The Pro-Nuncio turned to him now. "Come with me, Father Leighton." The tiny black eyes were piglike in their intensity. "There is someone waiting to see you."

There was no doubt now that the morning's unreality was having its effect. The seconds seemed to stretch. In slow motion he moved with the archbishop toward a wall with paired doors. And the old riddle came to him, the story in which one portal led to paradise, one to certain death. But he was not asked to choose. "Through here," the Pro-Nuncio said with a palm against his back.

What he expected he didn't know. Logic had been left behind. It was almost fear he felt as he moved alone into the darkened room and heard the door closing behind him.

A figure, tall and aristocratically thin, stood silhouetted against a curtained window, the head lifting as he entered. "Good morning, Father Leighton."

The English was perfect but the accent decidedly French.

It was his first clue, and as his eyes adjusted to the dimness, he recognized the man as one he'd seen many times in photographs—Cardinal Jean-Luc Flancon.

"Your. . . Eminence." He struggled to overcome his amazement, commanding his legs to move.

But he got no farther. For the Papal Secretary was moving away, the motion of his hand revealing the figure seated behind him.

And now his mind stopped its futile spinning, and he did move, pulled forward, drawn to the perfect certitude that seemed the essential quality of the face before him. He knew that he was smiling foolishly as he dropped to his knees before the extended hand.

"Your Holiness."

He said it as a fact. And bending forward, he kissed the ring of Peter.

Brian Donovan sat warily on the edge of the small apartment sofa, listening for sounds of movement from the kitchen. He hadn't really wanted the coffee. It was just an excuse to give John some simple task on which to focus. He hoped it worked. He hadn't liked the look of John one bit since he'd come out of Mantini's inner office. He'd expected shock, of course. You didn't send a priest like John Leighton into a secret meeting with His Holiness Pope Stephen XI and not expect some psychological fallout. But after all, that was the effect they'd intended. They had counted on John's shock. That . . . and his essential innocence.

He got up and paced to the window, peering through the blinds to the busy street below. Well, he thought wryly to himself, John Leighton had come up with a few surprises for them, too.

He, for one, certainly hadn't foreseen where recommending John for the *Nightline* spot would lead. The TV appearance had been engineered partially for Mantini's benefit, a convincing showcase of his protégé's ability to perform under pressure. It had definitely not been his intention that the media exposure should serve as a springboard for John's greater independence. No, he thought, absorbed in how the summer sun glinted hot white points off the chrome of passing automobiles, he hadn't for a moment imagined a publisher's offer of a time-consuming book project, or the move to an off-campus apartment.

The reassuring clatter of china from the kitchen signaled John's imminent return. Donovan watched the traffic light at the corner shift from green to red. Then, letting go the cool metal slats, he allowed the blinds to snap into position and walked the short distance back to the sofa.

What, he wondered, forcing himself to relax back against the stiff foam cushions, had been John's answer to Stephen? John had said nothing since coming back into the archbishop's outer office. Not that Mantini had waited for anything John had to say, brushing impatiently past him to get back to Stephen. He alone had been left to witness the look on John's face, and judge that it was best to get him away quickly. He had thought that John might talk to him in the car, but he had remained almost stubbornly silent on the drive back here to his apartment.

"Where have you been the last few days?" He said it as naturally as possible, half joking, half accusing, as John entered with the coffee. "I know you're on sabbatical, Father Leighton, but I am still technically your superior, and it's unlike you to go off without letting me know. You had me damn worried, John."

He let a trace of sincere reproach enter his tone. "His Holiness insisted on speaking with you personally, and this little visit had to be timed perfectly in order to keep it secret. If I'd had the least idea you might pull a disappearing act, I could have given you some reason why I needed to have you here. As it was, I had to go on blind faith that you'd be back in time. I never did let on to our dear Pro-Nuncio that you were missing. The old bastard would have—"

"How long have you known about all this?" John's voice cut in, clear and firm, yet with an infinite weariness. He had set down the tray with the pot and one cup on the coffee table, but had not sat down. His face remained blank, unreadable.

"How long have I known?" Donovan made himself ignore the implications of the lone cup, the fact that John still stood rigidly before him. "I've known from the beginning," he answered, reaching for the pot. "I started *Lucifer*."

"*Lucifer?*" Curiosity had leached some of the hardness from John's tone.

"Lucifer is the code word for our operation. The name was Flancon's idea."

John seemed determined not to show any reaction, but he sat down now. "But you said *you* started it?"

He took his time pouring the coffee, adding just the right amount of sugar and milk. "I was the one who first learned that there might be something wrong with the archdiocesan accounts. A tip from a friend at the bank." He looked up now. "It wasn't an easy decision, John . . . going to Rome. I wrestled with it for months. But when I'd finally weighed all of the implications, I felt that I had no real choice but to inform His Holiness through the proper channels. I contacted the Pontiff and Flancon through Archbishop Mantini. Actually, it was the four of us together who came up with *Lucifer*."

"But why me, Brian? You said once I'd never make a spy. Why choose me?"

"But that *is* why, John. Because it's what everyone believes about you. That you'd never make a spy. It's the reason you're absolutely perfect as our Archangel."

"And that's why I was asked to serve with the Doctrine Committee. It's the real reason why you wanted me to work at the residence." The weariness was in John's voice again. "Why didn't you tell me any of this sooner?"

"It just seemed easier. We wanted to have you well in place before you had to deal with the complexities of the situation. Think how much harder it would have been if you'd known beforehand, John. This way you won't have to *be* a spy for very long. At least not knowingly. And you've been spared a lot of unnecessary worry by not knowing. You'll have to admit it's all worked perfectly so far. You're there almost every day now at the residence. You can move in completely with no suspicion . . . You look confused."

"I guess I'm just surprised that you would betray the Cardinal, Brian. I thought you were on his side. That you were convinced of the need for reform."

"I am, John. But that isn't it at all. This has nothing to do with which side of the moral issues I'm on. Didn't His Holiness explain? It's not reform that Phillip wants. It's power. Power at any cost. He's planning a schism. He wants to destroy the Church."

"I understand that His Holiness believes that. It's what you've both told him apparently—you and Archbishop Mantini. But the Cardinal's never given any indication to me that a schism is what he wants at all. He—"

"I see." It was Donovan's turn to interrupt. "So Phillip confides everything to you now, does he?"

"Of course not. It's just that—"

"Be assured, John. Phillip Camélière *is* planning a schism. He wants the break with Rome. The red hat isn't enough for him. He intends to be the American Pope." He caught the flare of impatience in his voice and fought to soften it. "You think you know him, John. You don't. He's out of control, a danger to himself and to those very ideals that mean so much to you."

"Ideals, Brian? Is that really what this is all about?"

"You know, John," Donovan began again, answering not the question but the accusation he'd heard behind it. "I thought you of all people would be able to see through him. I thought I could count on you not to be blinded by the surface brilliance but to see through to what Phillip really is."

"Maybe I do." The voice, which was hardly above a whisper, was as harsh as the eyes that sought his. "Maybe it's you who are blind, Brian," John continued quietly. "At least I'm beginning to understand what I should have seen a long time ago. Your friendship with the Cardinal is a sham. You've never liked him at all. You hate that he's who and what he is. You're actually enjoying this. You'd happily destroy him because you're—"

"Jealous?" He supplied the word. "Perhaps I'll admit to that, if you'll start to concede your own blindness where Phillip's concerned. You're taken in by him, John. You've got to get over that. If Phillip is allowed to go on, he will destroy not only himself but the Church as well."

The energy seemed gone from John now. He sat slumped

forward in the chair, elbows on his knees, his head resting in his hands. "Maybe, Brian. But these charges against him are so vague. Especially this whole thing with the archdiocesan funds. You don't seem to have anything really substantial."

Inwardly Donovan smiled. John was not arguing now, but asking questions. "That's where you come in, John," he answered carefully. "That's why there has to be an Archangel. What do you think would happen to the American Church if the Cardinal has his way at the Conference, and *then* it comes out that he is no better than a common criminal. That would be the ultimate tragedy. That's why we've got to get at the truth before the Conference."

"And if I do get information which proves that he really is doing something illegal, exactly how will it be used?"

"To ensure Phillip's last-minute resignation from the presidency of the NCCB, for one thing. And then a forced retirement as Archbishop of the diocese for another."

"And if the Cardinal refuses to step down?"

"In that case there will be no choice but public exposure. No one will want an American Catholic Church with a corrupt leader at its head. Either way Phillip will be neutralized and the separatist movement thrown into disarray. Rome will be able to buy some time to salvage the situation. Of course, the Vatican wishes to avoid a public scandal, if at all possible. But in the end, we will do whatever it takes to destroy Phillip."

He had allowed himself to be too blunt. John was out of the chair again, pacing, his body banded in shifting bars of light and dark by the sunlight shafting through the blinds.

"You're disgusting." The voice, when he spoke, hardly sounded like John's at all.

"Is that what you said to Stephen?" His own voice was showing an edge of anger now.

"No, of course not." John had stopped moving and was facing him again.

"*Of course not*." He flung back the words. "I'll not be your scapegoat, John. It's Phillip who has betrayed you. Lied to you. And what of His Holiness?" He coated the words in irony. "Are his hands not dirty, too? Or is it only me that you find disgusting?" In that single moment, watching John's face, he was sorry. "What answer *did* you give His Holiness?" He said it quickly.

"I told him that I needed time to consider before I gave you my answer."

"Don't think too long, John." He granted a smile. "If you refuse him, His Holiness must find someone else." He got to his feet. "It's Friday. Why don't you take the weekend to decide. It will have to be early Monday, though. I have to be at the residence at eleven o'clock. Phillip is calling together his inner circle."

Frank heard Alex's clipped even voice through the line. The slight artificial edge of the recorded message bothered him more than it should have. She wasn't back, he grumbled to himself, slamming down the receiver for the fourth time in the last hour and a half. He leaned back against his chair and looked out through the window of his office, focusing on the tangle of computer wires snaking around the desks like umbilical cords. He had never felt more isolated in his life.

Damn, why did he have to learn from Murray that Alex had gone out of town for the holiday? He'd hoped they would do something together for the Fourth. Where in the fuck was she anyway? He had almost called her uncle, but ended up convincing himself that that wouldn't have been too cool. Jesus, what right had he to check up on Alex? And there lay the rub. Just what in the hell were they to each other anyway? He had thought he was beginning to get a handle on that one. But then she had backed off when he'd asked her to move in, and he wasn't so sure of anything anymore. Yet there was one constant in this whole mess, though it wasn't giving him any comfort at this moment. Loving Alex made him feel like the loneliest kid on the block.

He pulled open one of the bottom drawers and took out a manila envelope. The edges of the flap were curled and stained, and he slipped out the now familiar eight-by-tens. As he looked at the black-and-whites it was still hard to believe that it was Richard Darrington in the pictures with Carla Fiorelli.

After Carla had left that night in the bar, he had sat for a long time just staring at the bloated glossies lying on the table. His first thought was that the pictures seemed somehow obscene, like shots taken for some sleaze porn magazine. His second thought had been a question. Why would a man like Richard Darrington get down and dirty with the Lambrucis?

He stuffed the photographs back into the envelope and tossed it on top of his desk. His butt was sore from sitting so long while he tried to sniff out something that would give him a clue. But digging was the nature of good investigative reporting, and he wasn't about to forget the two most sacred truths of the trade: one, there is no perfect crime, and two, everyone has something to hide.

And coming up with info on the senator was easy. Politicians could hardly avoid high profiles. If there was a problem, it was that there was too much ink on Darrington. Too much paper could easily hide a nasty little glitch in a man's life.

The *Social Register* didn't tell him anything that he didn't already know. Darrington was from an old Boston family with lots of old money. The only thing that was slightly out of sync about the very social Harvard Law School graduate was his marriage to one Lindsey Mertons. Decidedly not the type that Daddy and Mummy would have picked.

The court records were clean. There wasn't so much as a traffic ticket in the files. His public disclosures looked good, too. The report from the Federal Election Commission revealed plenty of support from big-money interests, but nothing out of line. And Darrington's voting record was fairly typical of a senator who thought of himself as a middle-of-the-road conservative.

He lit up another cigarette and exhaled, watching the smoke settle like a flimsy gray cloud in front of his face. Nothing caused a tightening in his gut. Made him tingle or scratch. He jerked forward and stabbed out the butt in the overflowing ashtray. Gotta quit, he reminded himself as he shifted through the debris on his desk, looking for the report from his contact at the Pentagon.

First Lieutenant Richard Darrington had returned home from 'Nam something of a war hero. His record read like the

script of a Chuck Norris movie. Taken captive by the Cong
during one of the major offensive pushes, Darrington spent
five months in the Hanoi Hilton. Then, during a transfer
from the prison to a POW camp nearer the front lines, he had
escaped.

The escape story made very good copy. But he still didn't
like it. Didn't like it one fucking bit. Why in hell had
Darrington been taken back into the jungles? POWs as a
matter of course had never been moved *out* of the Hanoi
Hilton. Unless... Unless the whole escape thing had been a
setup.

He lay the folder down and rummaged around for his
cigarettes. He had nothing. Nothing that could give him a
clue as to why one of this country's wealthiest, most powerful
men had become a middleman in a Lambruci laundry operation. Richard certainly didn't need the Mob's money, their
kind of influence. So he was left with but one irrefutable fact:
The boys had something on the senator, something really
nasty. Something that would deny Darrington what he valued
most—political power. And his nimble reporter's mind kept
coming back to that time First Lieutenant Richard Darrington
had spent with the Cong in Vietnam.

He lifted up an old newspaper clipping that showed a
movie-star handsome Richard Darrington with his bride on
their wedding day. Lindsey was smiling happily, her hand
raised to push back her veil. If anything had changed between the two of them since that day, he had no feel for it.
But what came across from that single picture taken eight
years ago was undeniable and clear. At that moment, standing
on the steps of the cathedral where they had become man
and wife, Richard and Lindsey Darrington were very much in
love.

The clipping floated from his fingers onto the desk. This was
part of the business, too. The part he didn't like. The part
where the innocent bystanders got hurt. There was no question in his mind that Lindsey was completely ignorant of what
her husband was doing. She had victim written all over her.
Fuck, he cursed to himself. He liked Lindsey Darrington.
She deserved better.

He leaned back in his chair and wished that Carla would call. Another drop, and hopefully Richard Darrington would lead him straight to the final link in the chain. Somehow he knew that Richard wouldn't hold on to the money for very long. He would want to make the transfer as quickly as possible, the same day probably. And then it would be a simple matter of tailing him.

So if the most essential question was *why* Richard was doing what he was doing, the second most important was to *whom* was Darrington giving the money. It was a complex puzzle, and in his gut he knew that when all of the pieces came together, it would make a very ugly picture, a very ugly picture indeed.

CHAPTER TWENTY-THREE

John stood alone in the sacristy slowly removing his vestments—red this morning for the feast day of a martyred saint. He was in no hurry to leave. After yet another sleepless night, he had been more than usually glad for the peace that the celebration of the Mass had brought him.

For a moment he thought he could smell the warm buttery odor of the altar candles even here in the sacristy, and he imagined their faint scent intensifying in plumes of smoke as one by one, they were snuffed out by the lector. Then he realized he was simply standing, staring aimlessly. Carefully he finished putting his vestments away, and picking up his wallet, he hesitated a moment at the door before turning back to walk into the chapel.

The lector was indeed gone now, the candles extinguished. The chapel stood completely empty. John genuflected before the altar and went down the steps to sit in the first pew. It was a better place to think than his apartment, which seemed too charged now with all that had happened in the weeks since he'd first moved in. Here, he thought, he might be more at peace within himself, more able to find his way to some reasoned decision about what he was going to do. Tomorrow Brian was expecting his answer. Correction, he told himself: Rome was expecting his answer.

Was he really going to spy for the Vatican? Betray Phillip

Camélière? His own heart and mind said no. But it was his
Pope, Stephen himself, who had asked it.

It all seemed so impossible. Could it really have happened
as he remembered? Had he actually sat with His Holiness
Stephen XI, face-to-face, in the papal embassy this Friday
morning past? It was ludicrous—a "hypothetical" straight out
of one of the moral theology classes he taught. The kind of
question every first-year seminarian loves.

"What if, say . . . the Pope—yeah, let's make it the Pope." In
spite of himself he smiled, hearing the words so clearly,
seeing in his mind the appreciative smirks on the faces of the
other students. "Yeah, let's say the Pope came to you, Father
Leighton." The imaginary voice settled into a spurious sincerity, confident now of an attentive audience. "And let's say he
asked you to do something—something not absolutely evil
exactly, but something *you* didn't think was right." A slight
pause for effect. Then quickly, the voice rising for the question, homing in for the kill. "Well, Father Leighton . . . should
you do it?"

How many times had he answered that question, or others
very like it? It had seemed easy then, pointing out the pitfalls
of moral absolutism, the fact that "following orders" had little
to do with the making of moral judgments, no matter how
exalted the authority. But now, without warning, he was faced
with exactly this question. His Pope had asked him to do this
thing, to be his right hand in the destruction of Cardinal
Phillip Camélière. For the good, he'd said, of Holy Mother
Church. Was it not intellectual pride of the worst sort to
place his own moral judgment before that of his Pope. But in
the end hadn't he always told his students that no one stood
between the soul and God. There was only individual conscience. It was what he told himself now. He would have to
decide on the moral issues alone.

Perhaps the Cardinal was as guilty as Brian had said. Did
that change things? Lessen the sin of betrayal? But if Phillip
Camélière planned a schism, didn't he, John Leighton, have
the absolute responsibility to do everything in his power to
stop him? And if the Cardinal was involved in criminal acts,

wasn't it right and necessary that he be brought to some kind of justice?

Perhaps it was irrelevant, but he wished he could feel that Brian's motives in all this were pure. But he knew they weren't. And he suspected that Mantini, too, was not really after justice. Justice was simply the window dressing. And the Vatican's motives? Stephen at least had seemed sincere in believing that all this was necessary to save the Church.

For a minute he just sat, unconscious of the hard wooden pew, fighting to clear his mind. How had he gotten to this point? he wondered, amazed at his own desperate unhappiness. All he wanted, this minute, this second, was the one thing he could never have again. A time apart with Alex. Being with her. Loving her. Their short time together on the Cape seemed like part of some other lifetime, not days, but centuries ago.

And then suddenly it struck him. A fact so obvious that it was surely a deliberate trick of his unconscious that he had overlooked it. Alex and the Cardinal. The two could not be separated. Whatever... whoever hurt her uncle, would hurt Alex, too.

He thought of their last night together. What he had seen in Alex's eyes was unknowable... a mystery. An echo of Brigit's eyes from long ago. He'd hurt Alex so much already, yet in some way she was beyond him. It was himself that he would hurt by hurting her. Pushing himself farther and farther from any chance of healing.

He knelt now, looking toward the tabernacle, trying to feel the presence of his God. It had been true what he'd told Alex. Jesus had always been his friend—he felt that love now. But muted. He tried to pray. But the words would not come. And for the first time since the long-ago years of his childhood, he cried.

Alex dumped the last of the clothes on the bed and lifted the folder from the bottom of her suitcase. Her story on the Dutch dissidents. It was what Murray had decided she should tackle before she left for the Cape. A background feature to the fast-breaking story that was making headlines.

She tossed the folder on the bed next to the rumpled heap of clothes without opening it. She had no desire to see what she had written. She could scarcely remember writing a word. The last four days had been like sleepwalking. Except for one sharp prick of reality—John Leighton was out of her life. Out of her life for good.

The day had dawned hazy and sluggish, and she would have still been sleeping had she not heard the steady splashing of the water against the bathroom walls. She had met him in the short passageway between the bedroom and the bath, a towel wrapped about his waist, the shower water beading brightly on his smooth skin. They hadn't spoken and she'd imagined that he was upset that he'd awakened her. He'd wanted to leave without having to say good-bye. Just disappear into the early-morning fog, leave behind everything that had happened, go back to being a priest.

She remembered how warm his wet skin had felt beneath her hands as she'd reached and wiped away the water from his shoulders. How thick and silky his damp hair felt when she'd slid her fingers up the nape of his neck. And when she'd moved against his chest, how the sharp angles of his body pressed into her as his towel fell away. She'd felt his heart pumping heavily against her face as she kissed first one dark nipple then the other. And when she moved her mouth down the flat of his stomach, along the fine line of black hair that grew from his navel downward, she'd felt his fingers grip her shoulders. *Please, Alex, no . . .*

She had stopped, and looked up into his face. And then she moved away, back into the bedroom, back to the safety of the covers, where she'd lain until she heard the door closing softly in after him.

That had been Thursday morning, and now it was Sunday evening. She had gotten through those days. Now she had but a lifetime of days to get through without John Leighton. She gazed down at the pile of discarded clothes and picked up the long T-shirt she'd slept in that last night they were together. She could almost detect his own clean smell just beneath the fresh cotton scent. And for a moment she buried her head in the soft yielding folds and felt the warm welling of tears behind her eyes.

"Stop it, Alex, stop it," she cried half aloud. And then almost immediately she softened, knowing that the soap-opera theatrics were necessary if she were to go on from here. Fuck the stiff upper lip. That'll come later, she told herself. What she wanted now was to cry.

The solid knock at her door was familiar.

"Just a moment," she called out as she ran her fingers under her eyes, and then quickly through her hair.

"Hello, Frank," she said quietly as she stood holding open the door.

"May I come in, Alexandra?" His voice sounded tired and he looked like he hadn't slept for days.

"Of course, silly." She lightened her tone and pulled him by the arm into the apartment.

"Alexandra . . ."

"Okay, okay, I'm an inconsiderate bitch. You don't have to tell me. It's just that Murray laid this story on me at the last minute, and I wanted to get away to get some kind of perspective." She was rambling and she knew it. But he wasn't stopping her. "Frank . . ."

"Yes, Alexandra."

He wasn't going to make this easy. "Frank, I don't know what else to say. Except that I was kind of hassled when I left Monday morning, and I didn't want to talk to anybody."

"You called Murray."

"I couldn't just run out on my job, Frank. You of all people should understand that. I wanted Murray to know that I was getting away to work on the piece."

"And your Uncle Phillip?"

"God, Frank, somebody had to know where I was going." And as soon as the words were out she regretted them.

"I see." He had turned away from her a bit and began staring down at the hardwood floor as if looking for something he'd lost. He pushed once against the bridge of his glasses.

"Frank, please sit down." She took a step toward him. "I'll fix us some coffee."

"I don't want any coffee, Alexandra." He stared up at her.

"Frank, please..." She could hear the panic rising in her voice. He hardly ever called her Alexandra. Except when they made love. And now this. She moved away and slumped down into the sofa. "What do you want, Frank?" she said finally, looking over at him, seeing for the second time how really thin and drawn his face was.

"The truth, Alexandra."

"Okay, Frank. The truth." She had never wanted to hurt Frank. It wasn't something she'd planned. God, she loved him. But she had hurt him. Hurt him terribly. And the worst part was that she was going to hurt him even more, and she hated herself for it.

"I'm in love with John Leighton." She stopped after these first words, half expecting him to say something. But he didn't and she went on. "I don't know how or why it happened, but it just did. I guess it had something to do with being together so much, both of us focusing on the same project. I... I don't know."

She waited again for him to say something, but he only remained standing very still, like a giant cardboard cutout of himself, his familiar hazel eyes a mystery behind the wide bright lenses.

"Sunday night, after the *60 Minutes* thing on Uncle Phillip." She fumbled for words to soften what she was about to say. "I heard a knock on the door. It must have been almost nine o'clock. I was already in bed. I thought for a moment that it was..." Her voice failed her. Then: "It was John Leighton. John Leighton standing at the door of my apartment..." She glanced down at her hands lying limply in her lap. "He... he came in." She looked up. "We made love."

She thought she heard him say something, but she knew it was just the sharp intake of his breath.

"I... I was so confused," she began again, her eyes once more fixed on her hands. "I had to get away. I needed to think. So I left for the Cape. You know the place."

This time she did hear him, but it was just a single word, a *yes* to what she'd last said. "I brought along the material I needed to work on the assignment Murray and I had discussed. I was going to get settled in, try to get some things straightened out in my mind, and then I was going to call you, Frank. I promise I was going to call." She could hear the foolish pleading in her voice and stopped.

"It was almost eight o'clock that first night, Monday night, and I was just relaxing, stretched out on the floor reading. I had made a fire. It was actually kind of chilly that night. Then I thought I heard a noise outside, and when I looked up..."

"How long did he stay?" They were his first real words in a long time, and she thought how controlled his voice sounded.

"He left Thursday morning."

"Thursday morning..." He repeated her words as if trying to get the chronology straight in his mind. "Okay, Alexandra, let me see if I've got this all down pat." He had moved from where he'd been standing and began pacing in front of the sofa where she was sitting. "You are in love with a Roman Catholic priest. And you've just come back from a little holiday on Cape Cod, where the two of you have been screwing your brains out. Now, did I get that right?"

She felt her throat tighten, and the sting of fresh tears threaten. "No... no, Frank, you don't have it right at all." She had trouble getting the words out.

"Come on, Alexandra. Speak up, I can't hear you."

"No, Frank, you don't have a fucking thing right!" This time she was screaming.

Her anger had brought him closer, and now he stood directly in front of her, looking down into her face. His eyes were still hidden behind the shining ovals of his glasses. "I'm sorry, Alexandra, I shouldn't have said what I said. Poor choice of words. *Indelicate.*"

He seemed to be mocking, and she saw his lips stretch into a thin tight smile beneath his mustache. "But you know, baby, I feel like I don't know who in the hell you are anymore. You tell me you love me, and maybe you're ready to move in with me. And I'm easy. I wait. Give you time. Now all of a sudden you tell me you're in love with John Leighton." He paused for a moment, the strained smile still fixed on his face. "Alexandra, level with me," he began again, "do I have something wrong here? Am I being played for some kind of asshole? Because if I am, I really would like to know."

"Frank, I told you I didn't plan any of this. It just happened. And . . . and I know you won't believe this, but I do love you, Frank. It's just . . ."

"That you love John Leighton more."

"It's over between John and me."

"Over between you? That was quick. What happened, did he suddenly remember that he was a priest? But hey, I don't understand the problem there. Priests fuck around all the time, Alexandra, or didn't you know that?"

"That's not true, Frank. And besides John's not like that. It . . . it wasn't that way with us." Her voice died.

"Oh, he has to be in love before he fucks someone. Noble son of a bitch."

"Stop it, Frank! Stop it, please. . . ." And she was on her feet, crying real tears.

He waited for a moment, staring into her face, which was now only inches away from his. Then: "All right, so it's over between you and Leighton. So where does that leave us?"

"I'd . . . I'd hoped we could at least still be friends." She knew how lame that sounded, but she said it anyway, said it because she wanted it to be true.

"That's a terrific idea, Alexandra." He almost laughed, tearing his glasses away finally. "We'll be good buddies. I like that. Are we going to be fucking friends, Alexandra?"

She didn't answer him right away, but searched his face, wanting to see his eyes, see them naked without the barrier of the lenses. "I hate you right now, Frank Gregory." And she was surprised at how easy the words came.

"Good, Alexandra, good." He laughed for real now, using one of the stems of his glasses as a pointer. "Now we're getting somewhere. No more bullshit."

"I never meant to hurt you, Frank." She dropped back into the sofa.

He shook his head and turned away. "I would be a fucking fool to try to compete with a priest." He looked back at her over his shoulder. "You ever think, Alexandra, that just maybe you love this guy because he *is* a priest?"

"I don't know what you mean, Frank?"

"Sure you do, Alexandra. That you love John Leighton because he reminds you of your Uncle Phillip."

She couldn't recall afterward walking up to him, but the sharp sting of her hand as it cracked against his face she would always remember.

Rico Gambini had the biggest penis Carla Fiorelli had ever seen. But he didn't know what to do with it. In and out. But that suited her just fine. Let him get his rocks off, and then really go to work on him.

He rolled off her like a dead man.

"Well?" she asked, propped on one elbow, looking down into his dark, sweaty face. She thought some women might find Gambini attractive. She thought he looked like an ape.

"Well, what?" he asked, massaging the thick hair on his chest.

"Did you like it?" She favored him with a smile.

"That's a stupid question, baby. You've got the tightest pussy in the world. How you manage that?"

She was still smiling down at him. "I'm no whore, Rico. I don't fuck just anybody."

He looked up at her, laughing now, his hand working lower toward the hair at his groin. "I didn't know you liked me, Carla. Not in a million years would I have bet I could have made it with Carla Fiorelli."

She relaxed back down. "Well, that shows how wrong you were." She reached and pulled her hair from behind her shoulders. "You know I get tired of fucking who Johnny says I should fuck."

"The senator?"

"Yeah, the senator." She turned and stared at him.

"That son of a bitch."

"What's Johnny got on him anyway?" She looked away from him now, running her fingers backward through her hair. "It must be good."

"It's good all right, baby. And Johnny Lambruci has me to thank."

"You? I didn't know you knew Darrington."

"Oh, I know the senator. Better than most. I was with him in 'Nam."

"Vietnam?"

"Yeah, we were together in Hanoi."

"Together?"

"In prison. Except the senator got special treatment."

"I thought . . ."

"Oh, I know what you're gonna say. That I got good treatment, too. You damn right I cooperated with those slanty-eyed bastards. It was that or my balls. But pretty boy got primo treatment. He knew more."

"But I thought he was some kind of war hero."

"War hero, my fucking ass. That escape of his was fixed. Comes home smelling like a rose. Gets hisself elected to the Senate." He scratched himself. "I'm lookin' at this newspaper, and right on the front page is pretty boy's face. He's cozying up to the President. Fucker. I liked to shit in my pants. So I tell Johnny what I know."

She brought her hands up to her breasts. Her nipples felt sore. Gambini liked to bite. She sat up and reached for her robe.

"Where you going?"

"To the john." She looked over her shoulder. "I need a shower."

"Not yet, baby." He was smiling his thick-lipped smile. "I'm gettin' a hard-on again."

CHAPTER TWENTY-FOUR

Brian Donovan sat waiting in the comfortable chair behind the desk in his office, sucking angrily on his unlit pipe. It was still early. John wasn't late; it wasn't John he was angry with. It was himself. Since their conversation Friday in John's apartment, he had been like this. Just a bit on edge, uneasy... he couldn't really describe it.

From the early decision to enlist John in *Lucifer*, he had savored the intricacies of bringing the younger priest along. Plotting, hinting, cajoling. He had anticipated with particular relish the moment when John would understand, when he would be initiated at last into their secret. Not that he hadn't anticipated John's reaction. He had fully expected the younger man's irritation at being manipulated, his distaste for the methods employed. Even the anger that would be directed at him, Donovan, personally.

What he hadn't expected was his own reaction to John's necessary disillusionment. He had thought it would be a kind of satisfaction, a feeling almost of vindication. But it didn't feel like that at all. *You're disgusting*. He heard the words again. He was tempted to agree for his own reasons with the assessment. "Old fool," he said to himself beneath his breath. "You should be worried about what his answer will be." But he wasn't really.

He had finally lit the pipe and was glancing toward the clock again when John came unannounced into the room.

"Good morning, John."

There was no return of his greeting. John just sat down heavily in the chair across from him. "You'll have your answer in a minute, Brian," he said curtly, responding to the question that hadn't been asked. "But first there are some things I have to know."

"All right." Donovan made his own voice normal. Leaned back. Drew casually on the pipe.

"I want to know exactly what evidence you have, if any, that the Cardinal is really doing something illegal. What you've given me so far isn't very much."

He sat forward. "There isn't a lot. I'll admit that. If we knew exactly what was going on, we wouldn't need you." He kept his voice neutral. "We do have a report, a leak from an officer at the bank that handles the archdiocesan accounts. There's just too much activity there. Too much money. Multiple accounts, huge transfers of funds, massive withdrawals and deposits."

"But surely if there were something irregular, the government—"

"Not necessarily, John. As long as the money is being represented as ordinary church funds, there's no tax liability. And therefore no interest from the IRS."

"What is it that the Cardinal's supposed to be doing with all this money?"

"Phillip's not stealing, if that's what you mean. It's more complicated than that."

He heard the sigh before John spoke again.

"You've still given me nothing specific, Brian."

"We did trace a recent stock buy that was strange."

"Strange. In what way?"

Donovan held back a smile. John was not bothering to hide his interest. "The archdiocese paid almost ten times what the stock was worth on the market," he said. "It had to be deliberate. Campesi's too smart to make a mistake like that."

"That does seem odd, but it doesn't sound illegal. Nothing you've told me about so far really has."

He allowed his own sigh now. Letting John hear it. "John, if you're not going to help us with this, just tell me. His Holiness will have to know immediately."

"Just one more question, Brian." John was refusing to be hurried. As if, at least in this, he would have his way. "What exactly would I be looking for?" he asked.

"Ledgers, computer discs, any kind of records." he answered quickly, allowing the smile to show now. "We've got to have some sort of solid evidence of illegality to make *Lucifer* work. I'm sure you'll find what we need in Campesi's office. . . . You *are* going to do it?"

"I'm not convinced, Brian." Again John would not be pushed. "As I told you on Friday, you've got a damn weak case. You want me to betray a trust, act to destroy someone who has been nothing but kind to me, on the basis of unsubstantiated accusations. I can understand why the Vatican might wish to believe the worst of Phillip Camélière. But I, for one, don't believe that the Cardinal wants a schism—"

"John . . ."

"Let me finish, Brian." The green eyes were frighteningly intense. "What the Cardinal wants, what I always thought you wanted, is reform. What the Vatican refuses to understand is that American Catholics will never go back to the old ways now. Without reform, the Church in this country will tear itself apart. Rome needs Phillip Camélière to hold the American Church together."

"I see," Donovan answered flatly. "And so you're willing to ignore what Phillip is doing? It's okay that this savior of the American Catholic Church may be no better than a criminal?"

"That's not what I'm saying at all, Brian. It's just that—"

"I've got to have your answer, John. Now."

"All right then. Yes. The answer is, yes, I'm going to spy for you. I'm going to do it because I don't want anyone else to do it. At least I know I'll be giving Phillip Camélière the benefit of the doubt. I still believe that he may be innocent of these charges that you and Mantini are making. And if he is . . . I want a chance to prove it."

"You still insist on taking Phillip's side, don't you, John." He found it was impossible to keep the hurt entirely from his voice. "He has certainly dazzled you. But you're not the first. And I'm truly sorry that you're going to have your pleasant illusions dashed. Because rest assured, you are going to discover that he's guilty. Guilty on both counts. There is something very illegal going on with archdiocesan funds. And he does want a schism. He won't keep the Church in this country together as any favor to Rome. He wants it for himself.

"And as for reforms, you needn't be worried, John. The Holy Father has promised that our concerns will be addressed. Rome just needs more time."

"More time, Brian? They've had two thousand years."

He laughed in spite of himself. "Why, John, I believe you're getting cynical. But that's good. Cynicism is an ally you're going to need. . . . Are you going to the residence now?"

"Yes. You'll be happy to know I've packed up a few things. I'll be living there, more or less."

"Perfect. I'll be there today, too, as I told you on Friday. For Phillip's meeting. I wish you could join us. But stick close. I may just have a little something for you before I leave there today."

John didn't answer, just nodded as he rose. For a second he hesitated in the doorway, as if there was something he might yet do to change all of what had just passed between them. But he did not turn back, and in a moment he went on, the door shutting blankly behind him.

Brian Donovan reached for the phone. There was still the call to Mantini to make.

Alex woke up on her sofa. The sunlight slanting in through the half-opened curtains made it obvious that it was well into morning. She reached to flick off the table lamp that still burned brightly from last night's attempt at reading. The novel, a mystery, lay opened spine upward on the floor. From the number of pages turned, she'd apparently made it through several chapters. But she couldn't remember any of it.

The phone rang.

She sat up, switching off the answering machine.

"Hello."

"Good, you're back," Murray said by way of greeting. "Gonna have that story for me like you promised? The Dutch-dissident thing?"

"Oh . . . yeah . . . sure, Murray," she mumbled. "It's pretty much finished. At least the background part. I still need to get some expert opinion as to how the whole thing might go."

"I thought you had your expert . . . that theologian. Father Leighton."

"Yes, I'm going to see him today. In a little while, in fact. I'll have the piece for you day after tomorrow."

"Great. We're going to be doing expanded coverage on this whole Rome versus America thing, and I'm going to want to use your piece as soon as possible. Uh-oh, there goes my other line. Talk to you later, Alex." He hung up.

No help for it now, she was awake.

She'd really made a mess of it. One hell of a mess. And not only for herself. Frank's face came back to her now in total focus—the way he'd looked at her last night. So hurt. More hurt, really, than angry. She felt terrible inside. It was the first time she could remember that she did not like herself. The first time that being Alexander Venée didn't feel good.

But she knew she wouldn't change things. Set back the clock. No matter what the cost, to herself, to anyone, she wouldn't give back a minute of the time she'd spent with John. If that was wrong, so be it. She was being honest.

And Frank had been wrong. What she felt for John was real. And it certainly had nothing to do with Uncle Phillip— that had been Frank's anger talking.

Why did he have to be a priest? That was the question that kept coming back. If John were not a priest . . . And yet, it was those very qualities that made him a good priest that drew her to him. Wasn't that typical? A woman couldn't win for losing.

My, my, just look what she'd accomplished. She'd gone from feeling sorry for Frank to feeling sorry for herself. Not very admirable at all, Alex. Well, she might as well admit it, self-pity might be disgusting from the outside, but inside it felt damn good. And besides, who else was going to give her any sympathy?

Uncle Phillip? She would see him today at the residence. She had realized immediately that it had to have been her uncle who had told John where to find her on the Cape. Why, she wondered, had he done that? It made her uncomfortable to think that Uncle Phillip might know about her and John. And yet he must. He knew her better than anyone else.

She forced herself up from the sofa and headed toward the bathroom. She reached to start the water in the tub, then straightened, turning toward the mirror. She hadn't taken off her makeup last night, and smudged mascara made the circles under her eyes seem even worse. She looked terrible. Maybe a long hot soak and some breakfast would help.

She was going to see John. That was the thought she had been avoiding, though the truth was that she wanted to see him badly. It was *all* she wanted. She wondered if all of this were as hard for him as it was for her. Would it make her happier if he were as miserable as she was? If she loved him, as she said, shouldn't she want him *not* to be unhappy?

"I want him to be miserable, dammit," she said to the face in the mirror. "Really miserable." She was laughing, but the tears had started again.

The telephone ringing woke him up. A shattering, bell-jangling ring, not the anemic electronic burr that passed for ringing in phones now. The old black standard had been here when he'd bought the place, still sleek and shiny beneath its coat of dust, packed in with some other old stuff in a cardboard box in the attic. He'd brought it down and plugged it into the bedroom jack by the table, never once considering trading it in for one of the newer models. It rang again.

Frank dragged the receiver from its cradle, glancing at the clock: 10:00. Not really so bad. He'd gotten to bed not too long after dawn. "Yeah." He hadn't meant to bark it out like that.

There was a moment of silence on the line. Then: "This is Marilyn."

He smiled. It was Carla. She'd come up with Marilyn

because of the blond wig. He sat up straight, propping both pillows behind his back. He reached for his cigarettes and matches. "You at a booth?"

"Sure."

"It's okay, then. We can talk. I just had this line swept. It's clean."

"I found out what Johnny's got on the senator."

No bullshit dancing around. Not since he'd passed muster in Brooklyn. "And what's that?"

"Darrington was no war hero. He cooperated with the Cong."

"Says who?"

"Rico Gambini. Friend of Paolo's from way back. It was Rico tipped Johnny to this 'Nam thing."

"How'd he know?"

"He was there. In the same prison as Richard. Knew him by sight. But it wasn't till he saw Darrington's picture in the paper that he knew he had something. That's when he told Johnny. It got him back working for the family."

"Rico was out?"

"Yeah, Johnny's real patriotic."

"You did great, Carla."

"I'm going to be seeing him Friday."

"Darrington?"

"Uh-huh. Money's coming in. He's picking it up around two."

"I'll be there. And you be careful. . . . You are being careful? Not ready to pull out?"

"Me? No. I want to nail the bastards."

"So do I, Carla, and we're close. Check in later when you can, and I'll tell you what I find out Friday. Okay?"

"You can count on it." She hung up.

For a moment he just sat there on the bed, listening to the receiver's dry whine. Then he reached over and laid it gently in its cradle. He wasn't sure why, but he was worried about Carla. There was something, some undertone in her voice, he didn't like. Something single-minded and reckless. He'd heard it before, could recognize it even if he didn't always understand it. Sometimes the hate just got so big it made you careless. He hoped that wouldn't happen to Carla Fiorelli.

For a long time Alex stood at the library door, content just to watch John read. He appeared much as he had on the Cape, dressed in light casual slacks, a cotton shirt with sleeves rolled up for comfort. He looked so manly, she decided, as he sat absorbed in his work, his head bent over his book, black hair half threatening to fall into his eyes.

He brushed it back even as she thought it, glancing up at last to see her in the door. She felt her own mouth form a smile, but John's face registered only shock at seeing her. She had considered a call to let him know she was coming, but it had seemed wrong, somehow impersonal, that their first contact since the Cape should have to be by phone. Now she regretted that she had not warned him.

"Hello, John." She tried to make it natural.

"Hello, Alex." He looked down.

This was worse than anything she had imagined. He was making her feel she shouldn't be here. He'd said, after all, that at least they would be friends.

She forced herself to move into the room.

"I need to ask you some questions, John, for an article on the Dutch dissidents."

He was buried in the book again.

"Of course, if you don't have time . . ."

The words had been soft, but they'd held a sting. He looked up again, the pain in his eyes making her instantly sorry. She remembered her earlier foolish thought, that she had wanted him to be miserable. That was not at all what she wanted. "John . . ." She began to walk toward him.

He stood up. Moved away. Stopped to stand before one of the bookshelves with his back to her.

For a minute she turned her own head away, fighting back the tears. Then violently she wiped her hand across her eyes and reached to pull back a chair. She sat down at the table.

At the squeak of her chair on the hardwood floor, he turned around.

"What did you want to ask me, Alex?" He walked back to take his own seat.

She tried to make her voice as matter-of-fact as his. "I'm writing an article, as I said, on the Dutch dissidents. It has to be turned in tomorrow. I've done all the background stuff already. What I need to ask you are some technical questions."

"Like?"

"How exactly is Rome going to handle this whole thing in Holland? Will the Pope be appointing new bishops to replace the ones who are siding with Vanderveer? And what will happen to the churches—I mean the actual buildings themselves. Who gets them?"

He was looking at her almost blankly now, and she wondered for a moment if she had not imagined the pain. "I'm not an expert on this, Alex," he answered her. "Nobody is. This kind of thing hasn't happened for centuries."

"But you can give me your opinions."

"Yes. I could give you at least an educated guess. But I think your uncle would probably be the better one to ask."

"You're probably right, John. But I don't really want to ask Uncle Phillip. This whole thing with my reporting on the Conference is so sensitive, especially since the *60 Minutes* spot. Uncle Phillip and I—well, we have a kind of pact not to talk too much about any of this. . . . What were you working on when I came in?" She wanted to get him talking about himself if she could, try to get some idea of what he was really feeling.

He indicated the papers piled near his notebook. "These are mostly letters from the bishops on the Doctrine Committee. I'm trying to answer some of the questions they've raised. It's not really all that interesting." He was looking down at the letters again, as if what he'd just said had been a lie.

She felt numb. This just wasn't what she had expected, not this cold attempt to cut her off so completely. She did not understand, and again she wondered if something might have changed since he'd left her on Thursday. Or was it just that now, in the time away from her, he had begun to blame her in some way for what had happened?

What she wanted was to shake him, force him to tell her why he was acting like this. Surely he must understand how much this was hurting her. She looked across at him. He had apparently returned completely to his reading, and yet she sensed his lack of concentration.

Did he think she was going to just accept this? She might not choose to confront him now, but she wasn't going to let him force her to leave. She wasn't going anywhere till *she* was good and ready. Till she couldn't stand another minute in this room.

She reached down in her briefcase for her notebook. "John," she said, smiling sweetly till he looked up, "I'd really like you to help me with this."

"I'm sorry, Alex. Of course." He made a pretense of straightening his papers. Anything now to avoid looking at her directly. "What again," he asked, in the soft tones of resignation, "was your first question about the Dutch?"

No one smoked. Camélière hated cigarette smoke. But they talked casually among themselves, sipping at the coffee that Madame Elise had brought in. It was a cheery group. Everyone knew everyone else, felt he knew where everyone else stood. It was, after all, a common cause that bound them.

"I think we're ready to begin." It was Tony Campesi's voice. "Monsignor Feeney will start us off."

"Thank you, Tony. I'm not a statistician, but Bob Hendley coached me before I came in today." Feeney's opening remark brought a chuckle from the group, and the mention of Bob Hendley's name clued them in quickly as to the exact nature of today's meeting.

"I'm going to pass out copies of the poll we had Hendley's group take," Feeney continued. "I think you'll find that they did a very thorough job. And I know you'll all be more than pleased with the results. This recent poll emphatically reaffirms one of the most important conclusions drawn by the Greeley team in their 1984 report. American Catholics are convinced that they are not sinning when they defy Papal authority on matters of sexual ethics."

Feeney handed out sets of legal-sized papers, each stapled into a neat booklet. "Cardinal Camélière"—he turned and nodded at the Cardinal—"has already reviewed the report and has expressed his satisfaction."

Camélière smiled but made no comment.

"Just ignore pages one through three for now. They deal with the scientific methods that were used to make sure that the results of the poll were valid."

There was a shuffle of turning pages. Then Feeney went on. "There were a great many ways to approach this poll. But the Hendley group felt that the two most important characteristics were geography and age. Sex, education, marital status, racial background, socioeconomic factors, are of course also important, but to a slightly lesser degree. And for our purposes here today, we are going to simply look at the bottom line, if you will." Feeney smiled, obviously feeling that he had gotten it right.

"Any questions before we begin?"

"Then we are to understand, Monsignor Feeney, that the statistics presented here are as inclusive as was possible?" It was Bishop Estevez's subtly accented voice.

"Exactly, Your Excellency. It's solid, sound research." Feeney smiled again. "Any more questions?" A pause, then: "As you can see from the sheets you have, a variety of questions on the significant issues were posed—all issues with which we know Americans differ from Papal policy. What we found was that American Catholics have become increasingly rebellious. The present crisis therefore is not simply a matter of issues, but one of authority." There was a decidedly political edge in his voice.

"To begin, on the issues of divorce and birth control, there was the widest margin of disagreement. We expected this. After all, these two issues have been around the longest, the most visible." He waited for the group to locate the stats on their sheets.

"We find that ninety-seven percent of American Catholics believe that divorced Catholics should be able to remarry. Ninety-six percent believe that the use of artificial means of contraception is absolutely morally defensible. Further, as you can see, American Catholics believe that sexual pleasure can properly be the primary goal of sexual intercourse, and not simply secondary to procreation."

There was a loud chuckle.

"Yes, Monsignor Donovan?"

"Did we need a poll to ascertain that, Monsignor Feeney?"

Feeney looked miffed, but found his winning smile. "No, Monsignor Donovan. But it's always nice to have hard evidence."

"Is that a pun, Monsignor Feeney?"

"What? I—I'm afraid I don't—"

"Continue, Monsignor Feeney." Camélière spoke half laughing, looking at Brian Donovan, who sat in one of the wingbacks, his open briefcase on an ottoman in front of him.

"Yes, Your Eminence." Feeney's voice had lost some of its punch. "On the issues of optional celibacy and ordination of women, a significant majority of American Catholics disagree with the Vatican line. Seventy-five percent were in support of a married clergy. Sixty-one percent in favor of a female priesthood." Feeney looked up. "Everyone with me so far?"

"What about homosexuality?" Auxiliary Bishop McKeever was leafing ahead several pages.

"That's next, Bishop McKeever. If everyone would turn to page thirteen." Another pause. "This is perhaps the most complicated issue. But the evidence is clear, seventy-eight percent of the Catholics polled accepted the concept of constitutional homosexuality, the condition of being born homosexual, as a normal sexual variation. Yet, when asked if they thought that homosexual acts were morally wrong, over sixty percent still believed that the physical expression of homosexuality was sinful."

"It seems that some of our American Catholics are not aware of their faulty logic." It was Donovan who had interrupted Feeney again. "Would God create homosexuals and not allow them to *be* homosexual?"

"As I stated, Monsignor, it's a complicated issue."

"Yes, Monsignor Feeney, a most complicated issue." Donovan drew out his words, his gaze finding Tony Campesi across the room. The young secretary met the mocking blue stare head on.

"Concerning the issue of premarital sex." Feeney took up his monologue once more. "Fifty-five percent of those polled believed it to be always nonsinful. Actually we rather expected that statistic to be somewhat higher. But of course, there has been much over the recent years which has taken the thrust out of the so-called sexual revolution." Feeney smiled, unaware that he had again made a double entendre.

Donovan graciously let this one slip by, but could not avoid flashing Camélière a broad grin.

"And on the issue of abortion?" Bishop McKeever pressed.

"Turn to page fifteen, Your Excellency. It seems that on this issue, Roman Catholics do not differ greatly from the population at large. Approximately forty-five percent of those polled approve of abortion on demand."

"Are the results of this poll going to be used at the Conference? I certainly think that what we have here could bolster support for our side. Definitely take some of the fight out of Kirkpatrick." Auxiliary Bishop Lester's rather coarse voice was heard for the first time.

"Yes, Bishop Lester, I think that this poll can be a useful tool for us." Feeney smiled through his words.

"Good. This added to the work which Leighton is doing should give us just what we need. Is Father Leighton working out as well as we'd hoped? Will he deliver?" Bishop Lester turned in his chair, directing his question this time at Brian Donovan.

"Yes, John Leighton is a superior theologian, with an unimpeachable reputation. He'll deliver, as you so succinctly put it, Bishop Lester."

"It seems that the primary focus of the poll was on key moral issues? What about the Dutch problem, Monsignor Feeney? Did the poll address more pragmatic matters?" Bishop McKeever asked.

"Yes, Your Excellency. The situation in the Netherlands along with several other related issues are covered on the last three pages." Another shuffle of paper.

"It appears that sixty-four percent of the American Catholics polled support the Dutch dissidents. And further, when those same Catholics were asked if they would favor a separatist American Church with only symbolic ties to Rome, the response was the same, another solid sixty-four percent."

"Have you had any recent communications with Bishop Vanderveer, Your Eminence?" Bishop Estevez directed the question to Camélière.

"Yes, Eduardo, as you know, I am in almost constant contact with Bishop Vanderveer. He is very anxious for us to show some kind of visible support."

"But we must not be premature, Your Eminence," Bishop Lester broke in. "The Conference is still more than three months away. Surely Vanderveer understands our situation here. We cannot, as they say, play our cards too soon."

"Bishop Vanderveer is quite aware of our situation here," the Cardinal answered. "I pleaded for patience on his part, and assured him that our goals are not at variance. And that with God's help we shall all reap what we have sown."

Donovan shifted forward in his chair, quietly rearranging the contents of his briefcase. He glanced up, now that his papers seemed to be in order, and asked, "Since it certainly appears that most American Catholics favor a split with Rome, Monsignor Feeney, whom would these same Catholics desire as the head of a new American Catholic Church? I've not read ahead, but I assume you asked that question."

"Indeed we did, Monsignor Donovan." Feeney spoke smugly, his bright smile of self-satisfaction reappearing on his face. "If everyone would please flip to the last page. It appears that Cardinal Camélière made quite the favorable impression on *60 Minutes*." He glanced slightly over his shoulder so that Camélière could receive the benefit of that beaming smile. "The overwhelming choice of a leader for the new American Catholic Church would be His Eminence, our own Cardinal Phillip Camélière." Feeney waved the report he was holding with a kind of flourish.

"*Your Holiness . . .*" It was Bishop Lester who in the end showed the poor taste to draw Feeney's last comment to its obvious conclusion.

Donovan focused his gaze on Camélière. The Cardinal seemed to have forced a kind of smile upon his lips, and his hands were drawn together in a tight closed web upon his desk. He didn't comment.

"An appropriate if premature deduction, Bishop Lester." Donovan's voice cut into the strained silence. "Monsignor Feeney, are we just about finished here? I'm afraid I have another engagement."

"Yes, Monsignor Donovan, I'm finished. Everyone please . . ." Feeney laughed almost self-consciously this time, the smile now overworked. "I know I don't have to remind you that this is"—he waved the poll over his head—"confidential. Like everything else. Okay? Cardinal Camélière . . ."

"Thank you, Monsignor Feeney. Well done. And thank you all for coming this morning. I appreciate your efforts, and I know, as always, I am in your prayers. I shall need them. Tony?"

"There is nothing more, Your Eminence."

The small group chatted among themselves a bit longer, filing out slowly. Donovan snapped shut his briefcase, made a departing comment to Phillip, and walked from the inner office down the hall toward the library.

"Am I disturbing something?" Donovan stepped inside the library doors, his eyes moving first to John, then Alex.

"No, no, Monsignor Donovan. We were just finishing up here." John's voice rushed ahead: "Alex had some questions she wanted to ask me about the Dutch situation. That was about it, wasn't it, Alex?"

"Yes, John, I believe that's it. Hello, Monsignor Donovan. Please come in, sit down. I just have to pick up a couple of things here. Meeting over?"

"Just adjourned." Donovan moved in closer and watched as John stole a quick glimpse at Alex, then as quickly turned away, rearranging a perfectly ordered stack of books on the library table.

"Thank you, John, you've been a great help. I think I have just about all that I need." Alex was swinging her purse over her shoulder. "Monsignor Donovan, it was a pleasure seeing you again. Oh, Monsignor Donovan, is my uncle still in his office?"

"Yes, Alex, I believe so. It was good to see you again." And he watched as she went through the library doors. In the moment before he turned back around, he thought he heard John suck in a deep breath. "Well, John." He made his voice friendly. "It seems that you and Phillip Camélière's niece have a nice arrangement."

"Arrangement?" John had forced the word up an octave.

"You seem to work very well together, John."

"Oh." The single syllable was quieter. Then: "Alex is very good at what she does. I really haven't helped her that much."

"I see." Donovan held on to the words a bit longer than was necessary. "At any rate, I wanted to catch you before you got snowed under. Here," he said, handing over a small cassette he'd taken out of the tape recorder that lay at the bottom of his briefcase. "The little gift I promised. I think you shall find it quite interesting, John." And with his last words he snapped the case shut, flashing his former pupil his inimitable Donovan smile.

"May I come in?" Alex peeped from around one of the doors leading into her uncle's office. "Tony said it would be okay."

"Alex, my darling, Tony said you had come in this morning." Phillip rose from behind his desk and walked over to his niece, taking her into his arms for a long hug. "Have a nice trip?" He held her at arm's length, eyeing her closely.

"It . . . it was nice. I got a lot of work done."

"You must have worked day and night, Alexandra. You look like you haven't slept in a week." He gave her another hug and a kiss, then walked back to his desk. "Sit down. Talk to me. I've missed you, Alex."

"Well, the Cape was as wonderful as always. Not as warm as I thought it would be. I guess no matter where I go in the summer, I expect the weather to be as hot and humid as it is in New Orleans. I actually lit a fire the first night."

"It's a special place, isn't it? Remember last February when I got away for a few days early in the month? Well, I don't think I ever told you, but it snowed, Alex. Just a few flurries, nothing much to speak of. I don't think I shall ever forget. . . ." his voice drifted off.

"Uncle Phillip?"

"I'm sorry, Alex. Just reminiscing. Now tell me about this story that's kept you up night and day."

"It's a page-two feature on the Dutch dissidents. John helped me out with some questions this morning. He said there's never been a situation quite like this before. So there are no real precedents. The best he could do on some of the questions was an educated guess. Not a chance that you'd give me a hint as to what the NCCB is going to do?"

Phillip laughed. "You know, my darling, I love you more than anyone. But you're not going to get a single shred of information out of me. Work on John Leighton some more. His educated guesswork is probably better than anything I could tell you."

Alex glanced down at the notebook she'd placed in her lap. "Uncle Phillip," she said, looking up from the leather folder, "why did you tell John where I was?"

"I'm sorry, Alex. Did I do something I shouldn't have? Should I have not mentioned it?" Phillip stood abruptly and walked to where Alex was sitting. With one hand, he clasped her chin and tilted her face up so that he could look into her eyes. "Is there a problem, my darling?"

She cupped his hand against her cheek for a moment. Then she brought his palm to her mouth and kissed it. "No, Uncle Phillip, there's no problem. Not anymore."

The room was in almost total darkness, and lying here, bolstered by the two large pillows against the solid rosewood headboard, he could still hear beneath the whirring of the recorder, the old familiar sounds of night.

It was very different here from his Connecticut Avenue apartment, different, too, from his rooms in Curley Hall, where even amidst the relative peace of the campus, one could not be unaware of the larger city beyond. But here on the borderline between the District and Montgomery County, the sounds were almost rural, conjuring boyhood memories of his second-story bedroom, where the small sounds of night would drift upward to keep him company or softly blend with his dreams.

It was always his father who made the rounds from bedroom to bedroom each night, looking in to see that all was well, announcing in his best no-nonsense voice that it was "a schoolday tomorrow" and time for "lights out." After he had called his "Good night, Papa" and heard his father's heavy tread retreating down the stairs, he would lie secure in the old oaken sleigh bed and say his prayers. Then, eyes closed, he would listen to the pillow-muffled giggles coming from his sisters' room next door. In a while their laughter would stop, and as if it were a signal, he would crawl from his bed and, retrieving his flashlight, would creep back under the covers to enjoy his newest book.

It was his major disobedience, this flaunting of the schoolnight curfew. His father had been not strict but firm—rules being a necessity in a family of seven children. A simple request that he be allowed to read for an extra hour each night would almost surely have been granted. Secretly he must have known this, but found it more fun to huddle beneath the covers each night, Will's long unused BB gun propping the blankets into a kind of tent.

He could still see the intricate patterns of his faded Indian blanket made bright again in the flashlight's yellow glow. Still hear the sharp click of the flashlight's metal switch plate when some stray sound alerted him. Still feel the delicious fear of the plunging into darkness, waiting, all senses alert, for the telltale footsteps that would mean discovery.

But tonight was not like that at all.

He punched stop, then play, listened for a moment, and hit fast forward once more. He had played the tape through completely one time already, now he was letting it play again, speeding through Monsignor Feeney's recitation of statistics, searching. He hit stop, then play again. . . . *should give us just what we need . . .*

This was it. Bishop Lester's voice. He turned the sound up just a little.

Is Father Leighton working out as we'd hoped? Will he deliver?

*Yes, John Leighton is a superior theologian, with an unim-
peachable reputation.* The answering voice was unmistakably
Brian Donovan's. *He'll deliver, as you so succinctly put it,
Bishop Lester.*

What about the Dutch prob—

He leaned over abruptly to hit stop, cutting McKeever off.
In the deeper silence a pond frog sounded its double-noted
song from somewhere below his window. He leaned back
heavily against the pillows. Not really thinking now. Watching
the dappled walls, shadow boughs moving like crippled hands
in the moon's uncertain light.

Unimpeachable reputation—he didn't need the recorder to
hear it again. The words were very clear now inside his head.
It was what they were all counting on obviously, his
"unimpeachable reputation," each side in its own way, and for
its own purposes. He had never thought of personal honor as
a commodity. Apparently these men thought of it as little
else.

Why me, Brian? he had asked naively. *You said once I
would never make a spy.*

But that is why, John, had been the answer given with
conscious irony.

He shifted his gaze to the ceiling, but the shadows crawled
there, too. He closed his eyes, thinking of his brave answer
to Brian this morning. That he was going to do it, that he
would spy for the Vatican because he felt that Phillip Camélière
might yet be innocent, and he, John Leighton, wanted to be
the one to prove it. That had been his way out of the whole
moral dilemma—allowing himself to believe in the Cardinal's
probable innocence.

God, how idiotic he must have sounded to Brian. How
many times in the last weeks had he stood up for the
Cardinal, insisting that the man did not want a schism. And
all the time he had been so stupidly wrong about the Cardinal's motives. Phillip Camélière had very simply lied to him.
Or if it were not a direct lie, certainly the words had been
meant to mislead. *Surely, you don't think I want a schism,
John?* It had been said with such a look of hurtful reproach

that obediently he had read into the words and gestures exactly what His Eminence had intended.

He rubbed his fingers hard against his closed lids, trying to blot out just how incredibly foolish it all made him feel. So much had changed for him since he'd heard the tape. Absently he reached over and restarted the tape from the beginning, as if, listening to it for a third time, he might hear something different.

He could no longer pretend this was some brave crusade to prove Phillip Camélière innocent, at least not of the crime of plotting schism. But of those other crimes—Brian's suspicions about the archdiocesan funds? He'd have to find out.

Lucifer was horribly real for him now. He would have to go through with this plan to discover if the Cardinal was really doing something illegal. He could not go back on his word to Brian. And again he considered. Was it possible that the destruction of Phillip Camélière, by whatever methods, was morally defensible as a means to preserve the Church?

That was the question that bothered him most. And he could not forget that hurting Phillip Camélière meant hurting Alexandra. And God knew she'd been hurt enough already. He had seen it again in her face today in the library. He needed her so badly, as a friend if not as a lover. He had thought, perhaps foolishly, that after the Cape they could be friends still. Until this. Until *Lucifer*.

It was some seconds before he realized that the noise he heard was knocking. Guiltily he remembered where he was and that the tape was playing. His hand jerked to hit the stop switch as he swung his legs over the side of the bed.

"I'm coming." He walked into the sitting room to answer the door.

"I hope I didn't wake you." It was Tony Campesi. "But I thought I heard the television, and I supposed you must still be up. I just wanted to check, make sure you had everything you needed." The dark eyes moved from his face to look over his shoulder.

He realized he'd been standing there, clutching the knob with the door only half-open. He stepped backward, forcing himself to smile. "Everything's fine," he said.

Tony Campesi came forward, staring at him again with his self-amused smile. "I'm glad you're getting settled," he said. "I was a little surprised when His Eminence told me today that you'd decided to move in. You had seemed so reluctant. . . ." He didn't exactly finish.

"I guess it just took me a while to see that it was the most practical solution."

"Yes, I'm sure it's that . . . practical. Well, good night. I hope you sleep well, John." His eyes drifted again toward the bedroom. Then turning, he moved back into the hallway. "See you at breakfast," he called.

"Good night . . . Tony." He felt the clutch of guilt like a physical sickness, even as the cassocked figure moved dimly down the hall. It was impossible that the monsignor could have heard any of the recording playing in the bedroom as he'd stood waiting to knock. And he'd stopped the tape himself before opening up the door. And yet throughout their conversation he'd seemed to hear its clear accusing voice. Even now it echoed in the room.

CHAPTER TWENTY-FIVE

"This looks fine, Alex."

Murray sat scanning the pages in front of him, swivel chair sprung forward, the ever-present cigarette shoved neglectfully into one corner of his mouth. A too-wide tie, a refugee office-party present from two Christmases ago, rode half-mast below the open collar of his shirt. His elbows, bare beneath rolled-up cuffs, stood guard against the clutter on his desk, one on each side of the neat computer-printed sheets she'd handed him.

"Just fine," he repeated.

Sitting across from him, she took a breath and smiled. "So what's next?"

He looked up. "I want a general piece, the kind of stuff we talked about."

"I understand." She nodded.

"Good. Then you follow up with an in-depth series on the issues. One, possibly two, per article. You know what I mean. Birth control. Premarital sex . . . Celibacy."

"Hmmm." She sat thinking out loud, already seeing the angles. "It might be a good idea, Murray, to combine those last two," she said. "I'd like to show how the Church's attitude toward sex outside of marriage clouds the celibacy issue."

"How's that?"

"Well, most people don't realize that a vow of celibacy is technically a promise not to enter the married state. It's not a renunciation of sex, at least not directly."

"Does that make a difference?"

"Yes, a big one. Because the point people miss, the really important thing, is that the Church still does not sanction sex outside of marriage. Not for a priest. Not for anyone. It's not because a priest has taken a vow of celibacy that he is denied sex, but because, as a celibate, he is unmarried. Do you see the distinction?"

"Yes." Murray drew out the word. "But it sounds like hair splitting to me."

"Maybe. But the Church's blanket prohibition on sex outside of marriage has other consequences, too . . . especially for homosexuals. If you accept that sex outside of marriage is always wrong, then homosexual acts must be sinful per se, since they always take place outside the sacrament of matrimony."

Across the desk Murray was stubbing out his cigarette. "I've got to hand it to you, Alex. You really know your stuff. I'm glad to have you on National."

"It's permanent then?"

"As permanent as you want it."

"Thanks, Murray." She hid her relief in reaching down for her briefcase. "I'll have that first piece in a couple of days." She stood. "It's done, basically. I just have to call up my notes and do a little editing. Then I'll get going on the others. How do you want them? One a week?"

"Yeah. One a week would be great." He tapped another cigarette from the pack. "We'll work out the actual scheduling later."

She gave him her best smile as she shut the door behind her to walk the short distance to her desk.

Well, it was official now. She was permanently assigned to the National desk. When they'd talked last week, Beverly had hinted that she'd probably be clearing her stuff out of the Style section before too long, but she hadn't been so sure. Thank goodness Murray had liked the Dutch article. She'd been a little surprised at how good it was herself when she'd read it through this morning. At least one part of her mind must be functioning on something like automatic. Though to give credit where it was due, John had given her good material yesterday, despite his initial reluctance.

What had that scene in the library been all about anyway? She'd been so busy working yesterday afternoon that she had absolutely refused to think about it. And then last night, when she'd finished with the final draft, she'd actually been too exhausted not to sleep.

Well, she really didn't want to think about it now either. What was the point? Better to sit here and savor this morning's success. She was practically assured of at least a share in the Conference coverage, although now that she'd already won the permanent assignment to National, it was not quite so important.

She sat staring for a moment at the gray blankness of her monitor, her hand hovering over the on switch, debating whether or not to leave a message. It would seem strange, almost ungrateful, not to tell Frank about getting on National. She missed so much having him share her success.

Grow up, Alex, she told herself. Can't it be enough if just you know it? She let her hand fall. She couldn't make the first contact with Frank. He might misinterpret, might think, even if he were willing to forgive her, that she was offering more than she could.

If she had to share her success with someone, she could always tell Uncle Phillip . . . or Lindsey, or her parents. Both Lindsey and her mother had phoned and left messages, but so far she'd avoided calling either one of them, afraid of what they might pick up in her voice. Well, she'd gotten herself under control now. She'd make it a point to call them both back tonight.

She looked at her watch. It was getting close to lunchtime, and she'd promised herself that today she was going to eat properly. Go someplace nice and have something really terrific. Great. She was hungry. But what after that? She wasn't ready to start work on her next assignment, not after the long hours she'd put in last night. And she definitely was not going

to go home and stare at the four walls. If she did, she'd have
to start thinking again. And that would be a disaster.

For a moment she thought of calling Lindsey now. But she
knew she didn't really want to see her. Not yet. There was no
one she wanted to see or talk to. Nothing she wanted to do.
There was just this desperate need to have time pass, to have
a space between herself and the things that had happened.

The tiny work cubicle was suddenly a cell. She felt wild.
Claustrophobic. The way she had felt for the last two days in
her apartment. She had to get out now. Right away. She
fished in the bottom drawer for her purse and pulled its strap
across her shoulder. Reaching for her briefcase, she began
walking toward the elevator. When she started feeling like
this, there was only one thing to do. It was shallow and
ridiculous, but she was going to celebrate her permanent
assignment to the National desk by shopping for something
completely frivolous. She'd remembered the advertisements
from last night's paper, and felt better already. They were
having a sale at Woodies.

Lindsey breathed deeply, feeling his body constrict tightly,
then slump as solid dead weight against her. His cry of *Oh
yes, baby* still reverberating in her mind. She reached up and
stroked his back, feeling him wince. He was always so
sensitive after he came. She could barely touch him. Moving
her hips just slightly, she became aware once more of how big
he was, and how long he could stay hard after he'd climaxed.
His penis throbbed gently now, like a small heart inside of
her. She sighed again, and this time he looked down into her
face.

"It hasn't been this good in a long time, Lindsey."

"No, Richard."

And he rolled over, staring up at the ceiling.

"What's the matter?" she asked softly.

"Everything's right . . . when it's this way with us." He
reached up and hooked his hand around her neck, massaging
his thumb against the line of her jaw.

She looked at him for a moment, thinking that he would

never lose his boyish handsomeness. Then she moved closer and kissed him.

"Lindsey..." he breathed between her lips. "You're making me hard again, baby. Feel." And he moved her hand.

She gave him a playful squeeze and laughed. "Good, because I've been thinking..."

"Uh-oh, this could be dangerous," he said, rising up on one elbow.

"Maybe." She was teasing him and enjoying it.

"Is this some kind of game we're playing? Am I supposed to guess what's in that devious mind of yours?"

"I like that! I haven't a manipulative bone in my body."

"I'm of the firm opinion that all women are schemers, Lindsey Darrington. Not to be trusted.... But about your body..." He bent his head and took one of her nipples into his mouth.

"Stop it!" she giggled. "I intended this to be a serious discussion."

"Your own fault." He laughed, finally lifting his head. "Don't you know, Lindsey Darrington, that playing games is a deadly serious business."

"Okay, okay, you win. It's just that I was thinking that maybe you're right."

"Yes?" He was now propped again on his elbow, looking at her intently.

"About our having a baby."

She watched the light drain from his eyes and his face lose its open expression. "Richard?" There was a slight edge in her voice. Perhaps she'd miscalculated. Then...

"Lindsey..." He stretched out her name. "Are you sure?"

"I'm sure, Richard. So sure that I..."

"What?" He was still cautious.

"So sure that I didn't take any precautions this morning."

"No..."

"No diaphragm, Richard." She returned his stare and saw the blue eyes at last come back to life, the all-American boy smile once again stretch across his mouth. Then his face grew serious once more, and he was bending toward her, taking her into his arms, holding her tightly. He didn't say anything;

he didn't even kiss her. And for a moment she listened to his breathing against her ear, deep and deliberate, like someone who's run a long race and finally won. Then quietly he pulled away. "I love you, Lindsey. You do know that, don't you?"

"Yes, Richard, I know."

He had showered and dressed in record time. And she had sent him off with a kiss, and a promise that she was going to go to the luncheon at the Willard for the Senate wives. Now she walked slowly into the bathroom, her pale green kimono hanging off one of her shoulders. She moved in front of the sink and looked into the mirror.

She washed her hands and splashed cold water over her face. Then she let her kimono drop to the bathroom floor, and bending over the tub, she turned on the faucets. More hot than cold. Next, she moved to the toilet and urinated. When she'd finished wiping herself, she very carefully inserted her fingers into her vagina and dislodged the diaphragm.

The long soak was what she'd needed. And now, as she sat behind the wheel of the car, she congratulated herself on how far she had come. And in the same mental breath she thanked her husband, Richard Darrington. After all he had been her best teacher.

She turned the car onto the parkway now and thought how very much she still liked the old Jaguar sedan. It had been her first little victory over Richard. A small one, but one that she cherished. A senator's wife driving a foreign job in D.C. was taboo. Richard had been suitably furious, but in the end she'd won. As she was going to win this one, too. Of course the stakes this time were much higher.

It was just a little after noon when she drove up the circular drive. He was already there, waiting for her. She slammed the car door and walked inside.

"Been waiting long?" she called.

Phillip smiled. "Not long."

She almost ran toward him, and in a moment she was in his arms kissing him. "Oh, Phillip, I do love you."

He laughed against her hair. "My, but you sound determined."

"I'm sorry. It's just that loving someone has never felt so good before."

"I'm glad you're so happy, Lindsey. I'm happy, too."

It was a sweet time together. His mouth, his hands, giving her joy in a thousand different ways. His wanting to please her, make her happy. And it was an easy time, too. As if there were no tomorrows. Only today. This moment that would go on forever. His body sliding up and down over hers. His words of passion whispered over and over again. His palms pressing against her face before he came, willing her to look at him, look into his eyes. See his love.

She lay now in the cradle of his arms smiling. Thinking that she had done well. That no matter what happened from here on out, she would be okay. It was not having anything really tangible that had always frightened her. But now there was hope, a real chance that she would have Phillip, at least a part of Phillip, with her forever.

She was still smiling when she finally drifted off to sleep.

John stood in the hot July sun watching Brian Donovan walk down the steps of Caldwell Hall toward him. Even from the short distance, and even with the dark glasses that shielded the quick Irish blue eyes, he could see that Donovan's face was fixed in a friendly smile.

"I hope my call didn't catch you at an inconvenient time, John." Donovan, hands stuffed casually inside the pockets of his khaki pants, was speaking almost before he reached him. "I'm glad you could come." Brian wrapped an arm around his shoulder. It was a familiar gesture, automatic.

"No problem, Brian." His words came out clipped. Yet he hadn't really meant them to sound that way. Despite how he felt on the inside.

"Good. Let's walk a bit. It's not too warm," Brian continued, tilting his face up toward the bright cloudless sky.

John followed Brian down Ward Road, first circling behind the shrine, then toward Michigan.

"I rather like the lull of the summer." Brian spoke again, stopping near the side of the cathedral, looking out over the slope of dull black pavement in front of the shrine. "But it won't be too long though before we have a full house again." He laughed a little, his gaze seeming to have now settled on the Gothic facsimile of Theological College across the street. "Do you miss teaching, John? The students?"

John turned at the question and saw that Brian had refocused his attention. The eyes behind the smoky lenses were fixed squarely on him. "Yes, I miss teaching . . . the students." A simple, direct answer. He couldn't seem to manage anything else. Hell, that was just the half of it, he reminded himself. The real truth was that he didn't much like his old theology teacher. He turned away and gazed out over the cluster of seminaries that the students had christened the "Little Vatican" and thought idly that Rome probably wouldn't find much humor in the Yankee joke.

Abruptly Donovan turned and began walking down Harewood Road. The Irishman seemed hell-bent on some destination. But when he'd reached the Hartke Theatre, Brian stopped and waited for him to catch up. "Well?"

He had arrived in time to hear the half-asked question, the irritation in the voice. But he ignored the inquiry and walked past Donovan, moving toward Curley Hall. "Well what, Brian?" He finally spoke, keeping his back turned to him, his eyes intent on the roof line of his old residence. "*You* called this little meeting."

"For God's sake, John, give me a break here."

He turned at the pain he imagined he heard in Brian's voice, and saw that his old professor had at last stripped his eyes bare of the sunglasses, his face wiped clean of the earlier cheerful smile.

"Sorry." It was his first concession, and he watched as Donovan closed the distance between them, fumbling all the while to find a place in his shirt pocket for the sunglasses.

When Brian spoke again, his words seemed without conviction. "His Holiness is most pleased that you have agreed to help us."

His Holiness. Brian had pulled that card from the bottom of the deck. He bit his lower lip and waited for Brian to speak again.

"I . . ." Donovan started, and stopped. Then: "What did you think of the tape?" He'd finally gotten it out.

John knew he smiled before he answered. "The tape . . .

Ah yes, the tape. I knew we would finally get around to that. The *tape* is what this little get-together is all about, isn't it, Brian?"

"John, I know this is hard for you. Please believe me, I understand."

"Do you?" His words were brittle.

Donovan glanced down.

For a moment John only concentrated on the crown of Donovan's silvered head, noticing how the thick curling waves spread away from the side part. Then very deliberately he moved to stand directly in front of him, so that their bodies were almost touching. He was conscious of the accelerated noise of his own breathing in the instant before he spoke. "Look at me, Brian Donovan. Goddamn you, look at me!"

Donovan looked up.

"Good. That's better." He let out the breath he'd been holding. "So you want to know about the tape." He could feel the blood heat in his throat. "Well, I'll tell you how it is, Brian. I'll tell you, but I—" He pulled up short, shocked that Donovan's eyes were no longer the clear bright blue he'd always remembered. They suddenly seemed the eyes of a blind man. And for the first time the eternal Brian Donovan seemed old, very very old. And he wanted to shake the image of those eyes from his mind more than anything else.

"You win, you son of a bitch. You win." His words finally came out.

"John..."

"You were right." He had regained something of his composure. "And I was wrong about Camélière. Does that make you feel better?"

"No, John. I hate it that you are...hurting."

John had heard the sadness in the last word, but he refused to accept it. "Stop it." He forced himself not to scream. "If you really cared a goddamn about me, you would not have—" He stopped and shook his head. "No, no, there's no point in going over all of this again." He spread his arms in a halting motion and drew in a deep breath. "Yes," he exhaled. "I concede that His Eminence Phillip Cardinal Camélière is

behind a movement to bring about a schism between the
American Catholic Church and Rome." He recited the phrase
like a small boy in catechism class.

"And now?" Donovan asked.

"And now," he said, "all that remains is to discover if Phillip
Camélière is the crook you suspect him to be."

Donovan appeared embarrassed, but when he spoke it
seemed that he had recovered some of his easy self-assurance.
"I will do anything I can to help you, John. If you need any
money. There . . . there is never a problem with money, you
know that."

"I don't know that I'll need anything." He cut him off, not
wanting to hear any more.

"You know your way around a computer pretty well, John."
Donovan was speaking again and had begun to pace around a
bit as if hatching some new strategy. "If you can get a hold of
Campesi's discs, you could make copies and he would never
know. I feel certain that he has recorded everything. Saved it
all. He's extremely efficient, as you've probably already noticed.
Methodical to a fault. Get the discs, and we get Camélière."

He'd heard the almost vulgar excitement in Donovan's
voice, and he turned his back on it, moving to the small hill
overlooking O'Boyle Hall. He watched the sun fire off of the
grainy texture of the concrete steps that formed a long spine
up and down the slope. He could hear that Donovan was still
talking, but he made no real attempt to listen. Instead he
continued to stare out and away from the university grounds,
thinking rather calmly that the whole of his world had
seemed different today.

For so long he had pulled these comfortable university
surroundings around him like a nourishing membrane, had
worn them like a warm second skin. Being a part of Catholic
U had been something he'd never really given much thought
to after a while. It existed simply as a part of him, and much
like that essentialness he called "self," he had never analyzed
its close fit.

He now watched the sunlight beam off of the roof line of
Marist College in the distance, and thought the light too
clear, the solid edges of the building too well defined. Like

everything else, this image seemed too real, too precise. He was suddenly incredibly exhausted.

He shut his eyes tight, feeling the pain build in subtle layers behind his lids. And for a moment he believed that there was suddenly too much air in his lungs and that they would burst.

"John?" Donovan's voice. "John, are you all right?" A touch on his shoulder. The touch now only remotely familiar.

He opened his eyes and turned. "Yes, Brian. I'm all right." It was a forgivable lie. "I was just thinking. Thinking of something I'd lost." And with the crushing weight of truth, he understood what thing it was he'd lost. He understood it for his innocence.

She was far behind, neglecting the scrapbook for days now. Sifting the newspaper and magazine clippings out of the large manila envelope, Angelique watched as the scraps of paper, large and small, fluttered like confetti onto the puckered bedspread of the hotel double.

After, she sat quietly staring at the kaleidoscope of faces. The same face, *his* face, mirrored again and again in the pictures. Still thin and handsome after all these years. She touched her brow. All these years? How many years had it been? Twenty? Twenty-five? She'd somehow lost track. She hadn't meant to do that. But then, time meant nothing to her.

The small paper sack was neatly tucked away inside her purse. She reached into its zippered compartment and pulled out the bag, opening it. *Pentel Roll'n Glue*, the label said. *Roll'n Glue*. New things everywhere. Everywhere new things. She tossed the plastic bottle aside and opened the scrapbook, leafing slowly through the many sheets already fixed with his smiling face. Then an empty page. She'd paste this one in first. She picked up the photo from *People* magazine. Big and bright and glossy. It was her favorite out of the new pictures she'd collected. She looked down and studied the photograph. *Catholic Cardinal* 60 Minutes *Star*, the caption beneath the picture read.

She closed her eyes and remembered. It was strange seeing him move after all of these years. Move and breathe.

Talk and smile. Really make a smile. It was so different from just looking at the pictures. And as she had looked at the image on the screen that Sunday it seemed that there had been no years in between. That Père Philippe looked out at her from the television set as he had looked at her when they'd sat together by the bayou. She could feel him reach out and touch her, smooth her hair back from her eyes, press his warm mouth against her mouth, stroke the narrow channel of space between her breasts.

And then that woman who asked him questions said something that had pulled her back into the present. And she saw on the screen not his face but a young woman's face, oval-shaped and beautiful. Golden-skinned and golden-haired. Like a bright angel, she thought, if angels had bodies, if angels had hair. She imagined that they had.

And as is the case sometimes with people like Angelique, rational thought filtered through the perpetual fog inside her brain, and real time ticked inside her head. For a single instant she understood that her Michelle could no longer be a baby. That she must be all grown up now. Sweet and beautiful as this young woman who glowed across the television screen.

Angelique reached out and gently touched the colored picture from the magazine with her finger. Then very slowly she began to press against the image, press until the sharp edge of her nail sliced cleanly through the neck of Phillip Camélière.

Twenty-three minutes after one. John's passage from his room was silent, marked only by his shadow, which moved ahead of him on the carpeted stairway. Faint and wavery in the soft glow from the lamp on the upper landing, it flowed ahead of him from step to step like a spreading stain, seeping into deeper darkness as he reached the final stair.

Since his meeting this morning with Brian, he had tried to form some plan, some definite course of action. He had been concerned with it all day. Thinking. Considering alternatives. But the hours had passed, and his thoughts wound only in the same tired circles without coherence or conclusion. He still had no plan. And no time. He had to act.

As today on the campus, his senses now seemed simultaneously both heightened and detached. His surroundings poignant, unreal. He stood, still on the last step, looking, listening. The hall clock ticked loudly in the woolly darkness. The fanlight above the entrance, lit brilliantly by the outdoor lamps, cast its bright pattern over the foyer floor. He felt nothing. No apprehension. No fear. Stocking feet soundless on the cold marble, he brushed against the shadowed walls, moving through the long hallway.

Inside the offices, the reception desk crouched like a square sentinel on its clawed feet. He paused a moment at the threshold, waiting for his eyes to adjust to the room's greater dimness. Then he walked on down to the first office along the narrow hall. He tried the knob. But Tony's door was locked.

He tried it again with no result, standing there shoeless in the darkness. The unlighted corridor, the unmovable door, seemed very real now. Concrete. He wondered why he felt such unreasoning disappointment. What had he actually expected? He knew very well that Tony always locked the office when he left. In his pocket was the credit card he had taken from his wallet. He tried slipping it in between the doorjamb and the lock. He had seen it done a hundred times on television, but fumbling inexpertly in the dimness, he knew now he could never make it work.

His hand fell at his side. He felt completely ridiculous. He could no more break into Tony Campesi's office than fly. He sank back against the wall, shaking his head. After all his mental gymnastics, after his final tortured decision, his great moral dilemma was going to be solved for him by a single locked door. He almost laughed aloud, but checked himself. He couldn't allow himself to simply walk away. He had agreed to this thing. Given his word. He had to find some way to do it.

He was discovering in himself something he had never before suspected. A pride that would not let him so easily admit failure to Brian... to his Pope. Before this he had always set his own goals, been the only real monitor of his own successes. He had not guessed that within him such a pride existed, such a deep unwillingness to fail. He heard the Cardinal's voice. *You must learn to exhibit a more dangerous curiosity about yourself, John.* The voice seemed mocking now, smug. Brian Donovan was not the only one who had played upon him, used him. Well, he thought, the Cardinal should be well pleased. His pupil, John Leighton, was learning, finding out more about himself than either of them might ever want to know. He stood straighter in the blackness, brushing his hand softly against the smooth plane of the door. He wanted to get in now. *Had* to get into that office.

He remembered the first time, the one time he had nearly been in there. Even then, before he'd known about any of this, he had sensed Tony's nervousness. He closed his eyes, picturing it as he'd glimpsed it from the doorway—the dark leather chair, the computer screen filled with glowing figures, the rows of files . . . the door. *The door!* Of course. There was another door at the back of the room. It might very well open from the Cardinal's office.

He began moving back down the hallway, excited now, entirely focused on solving the puzzle.

In a moment he was there, in front of the Cardinal's door, surprised to see that his hand trembled as it touched the knob. He brushed aside the suspicion that he might be enjoying this. Forced himself to be calm, breathe slowly. The door opened inward at his touch. He closed it behind him, fighting down the impulse to turn on the light. At the far corner of the office there was indeed another door. He turned the knob. Pushed into the room beyond.

Why hadn't he thought of a flashlight? It was really black in here. Though, despite the dark, he recognized Campesi's office. For a moment he considered flicking on the brass desk lamp. But even a small light was too risky. With the thick carpeting, he would never hear approaching footsteps, and the telltale glow might be seen from under the door. He walked to the window to open the blinds. It was bright outside. He caught a glimpse of moon above the trees.

He sat down at the desk and tried the drawers. *All locked.* The computer drives? *Empty.* He sat for a moment staring, beginning again to feel foolish, then walked to the filing cabinets. *Locked*. So much for his great inspiration. He felt deflated now. Frustrated. He would just have to get the keys. But exactly how was he supposed to do that? Tony probably always kept them with him.

He went back to the desk to think. If he had not been leaning, half sitting against its edge, staring idly at the bottom of the door, he would have missed the first flickering of the light. Someone in the reception area had switched on the overhead fluorescents! For a moment he strained to hear, but there was nothing except the pounding of blood in his ears. He jumped up and closed the blinds, hesitating at the connecting door. Who was it? The Cardinal or Tony? To which office?

A key scraped in Tony's lock. He went quickly through into the Cardinal's office, hoping that the soft metallic click would be concealed by Tony's own entry. His hand still on the knob he pressed against the door, his ear to the cool wood, listening.

There was a protesting squeak as Tony sat in his chair. The sound of a drawer sliding open. Was the secretary going to do some work? If that were so, he might be trapped here for hours. He had a swift vision of himself still crouched here, listening, when the Cardinal arrived to begin his day. For long minutes there was nothing. Then to his great relief, he heard the drawer being closed again, the creak of the chair as Tony shifted his weight. Seconds later the outer door was closed firmly and locked. Instinctively he faced toward the double doors of the Cardinal's office, imagining Tony moving down the narrow corridor, padding past him....

The knob was turning! For a split second he watched it in fascination, till pure reflex took over, and he was dropping to the floor, shrinking back into the corner, screened from the doorway by a console and the wide dark leaves of a plant.

The lights flickered on. He held his breath, stealing a glance beneath the table's carved legs. Jeans. Top-Siders. Still it had to be Tony. He must have gone out tonight and was just now coming back in. It was probably routine that he checked the place before he went to bed. For what seemed a very long time, the legs didn't move at all, but at last Tony turned, switching off the light. There was the jangling of keys... some softly murmured comment. Then the door closing. The click.

He forced himself to wait, Ten whole minutes by the desk clock. Then he walked to the door. It was entirely possible that he was now locked in. But no, the door could always be opened from the inside. He was safe. And only now, with the danger past, did he finally feel the fear. His knees actually wobbled as he made his way to the Cardinal's chair. Just what *would* he have said if Tony Campesi had actually found him, cringing in his stocking feet behind the potted palm?

The desk clock glowed in the darkness: 1:42. Less than twenty minutes since he'd left his room. It seemed like forever. God, how he wanted to get out of here. Not just out of this office, but out of *here*. Out of this whole mess. But he couldn't now. He'd made his choice. And he was relatively safe at this moment. He'd better use this time to best advantage.

Quickly he removed his shirt and, rolling it up, stuffed it tightly against the bottom of the door. At the desk he switched on the lamp and pulled at the file drawer. It slid open easily, and he picked out several folders. Correspondence. Copies of letters to contributors. He rifled through it all quickly, being careful to replace it back in order, though it was obvious that there was little here of significance. Nothing like what Brian would want. He went through the other drawers, but there were no records. It all had to be in Tony's office.

And then it struck him. There had been a ring of keys in the center drawer. He pulled it open. They were there, beside one single key, shining up at him in the lamplight—the duplicates probably of the keys he had heard jingling in Tony's hand.

He sat resting for a moment, his head against his arms, which lay folded on the desk. He had been up now for almost twenty straight hours. He was exhausted. It was suddenly hard to move. But for the first time he was beginning to believe that he could do it. That *Lucifer* would actually happen.

But he was also beginning to see things, feel things he did not like. He had changed these past weeks. He hardly knew himself. The old John Leighton had been isolated, naive, in many ways immature. He could see that now so clearly. He didn't want to be that person anymore. Didn't want to go back. Even if he could.

But he didn't like this new self either. This strange John Leighton who could betray a man in his own house. Who cared so much that he might fail in others' eyes. The old John Leighton had found it easy to be good. But then he had never been tested.

He thought of Alex—she was never far from his thoughts— and he considered again just how badly she might be hurt by what he was doing. What would Alex think if she could see him now? What would she feel? Hatred? Contempt? She would never forgive him for destroying her uncle.

Yet if Brian had told the truth—if the information he gathered was to be used simply to force the Cardinal's resignation—then Alex need never know what either of them had done. Neither Phillip Camélière nor John Leighton.

But if Brian were lying. If the Cardinal was to be given no chance. If the plan was to go immediately public . . .

He got up and switched off the light and, retrieving his shirt, went back through to the connecting office and opened the blinds. He sat again in Campesi's chair, his fingers sorting through the ring of keys. There weren't many that could fit a desk, and on his second try the center drawer opened.

He could open the side drawers now. In the top one, computer discs stood upright in their envelopes. He brought up the screen, tried the first of the discs in the slot. The pale green glow spilled onto his clothes like neon. Figures. Columns and rows of figures.

He studied the data. ACCTS. It was a record of cash flow over the last several months. Money "in"—considerable funds from an unspecified source. The mysterious funds that Brian Donovan had talked about? He couldn't tell. Money "out"—he cross-referenced the debits against REAL/EST and STOCKS. Despite Campesi's reputation as a financial whiz kid, it certainly appeared on the surface that he was taking a beating now.

Somebody, somewhere was making a killing off of Campesi's blunders. If they were blunders.

He found some blank discs and copied the files. He'd examine them more closely later, where it was safer.

As he reached to shut down the system, the golden lettering on Campesi's appointment book caught his eye. Bright and shiny and expensive. Exactly the sort of thing he'd expect the Cardinal's secretary to use. He accessed the ACCTS file again. Why not see what sort of appointments coincided with the dates when Campesi logged in the money?

As his eyes moved from the neatly penned pages to the screen and back again, there seemed to evolve a very simple synchronicity. On every single date that the file was credited with an extremely large sum, Senator Richard Darrington's name appeared in Tony Campesi's appointment book. Coincidence? Maybe. At any rate, he'd put off calling Brian. Better wait and see first if there'd be a new credit entry made for Friday. Senator Richard Darrington was written in for three o'clock.

CHAPTER TWENTY-SIX

The Adams-Morgan sunshine was hot. Too hot, Alex told herself, to stand here indefinitely holding this huge package. She took a deep breath and banged on the door. It took a long while for Frank to answer. More time to bake in the sun and worry about her reception.

"Happy birthday!" She gasped it out before he'd completely opened the door.

"Good God, Alex, what time is it?" he grumbled. But he took the gift from her hands and turned for her to follow him inside.

"It's almost nine, Frank." She started to make some little joke about getting older and not needing as much sleep. But the words didn't come, and she just waited.

He had turned toward her again, standing at the far end of the sofa in the terry robe that had been last year's gift. She thought that he seemed taller, or somehow different than she'd remembered, as if it had been three years instead of only three days since she'd last seen him.

"I was shopping the other day and I remembered your birthday," she said to break the silence. "Aren't you going to open it?"

The question was trite enough, but it worked. He stopped staring, and sat down to fight with the yellow ribbons.

"Wait," she said, getting up, heading automatically for the

kitchen. She caught herself. Turned back. "I'll go get the scissors," she said, explaining.

The hand pulling on the handle of the junk drawer shook, and she fumbled around in the mess, angry at herself now for coming. What exactly was she doing here?

Frank had his glasses on and had started a cigarette when she returned with the scissors. The box was still unopened in his lap. She sat down next to him and snipped the ribbons.

"It's something you've been needing," she began, watching him tear ferociously at the wrappings. "The shoulder strap on your old one is just about to go." She wished she could shut up, but now the words just kept coming. "If it's not right . . ."

He was holding the big leather and canvas satchel up to the light so he could really see it. His lips quirked slightly beneath the mustache. She took a breath. Smiled back. He liked it.

"The man said it would hold more than one camera, with separate pouches for four lenses and enough space for film and notebooks. Even a change of clothes." She still couldn't let herself be quiet.

He got up. "It's great, Alex. You want some coffee?"

She nodded. "Yes. Thank you, coffee would be nice."

She watched him stub out the cigarette and disappear toward the kitchen. Why had she said yes to the coffee? She'd made her peace offering, and it had been accepted. Staying longer was dangerous.

She stood up and walked to the CD player. The disc in the machine was Beethoven's *Hammersklavier.* One of her favorites. Was that the reason he'd been playing it? Conceited thought. She picked up its empty jewel box, thinking she'd replace it. Play something else. But suddenly it seemed presumptuous. Too proprietary. Like her excursion to the kitchen for the scissors.

She heard him returning, and walked back to sit on the sofa.

"Instant," he said, as if she might think he had suddenly gotten a coffeemaker. "You did want it black?"

"Yes," she said, waiting for him to sit down, too. "Aren't you going to have any?"

"No. I haven't brushed my teeth yet." He made a twisted smile. "I'll just have another smoke." He reached for the pack in his pocket.

"I got the permanent assignment to National." She sipped on her coffee, trying to ignore the fact that he was still standing.

"It's not really a surprise, Alex. Is it?"

"What do you mean?"

"Don't you usually get what you want?"

The words were mild, his face blank as he looked down at her. If she wanted to launch a defense, he was not giving her the slightest handhold.

"Yes," she answered softly, gazing down again into her cup. "Usually."

For a minute he didn't move, didn't say anything, and she wondered if it had made him angry that she was trying to play his game. Did he really *want* a fight?

She heard him sigh. "Alex . . ."

"I've gotta go." She stood up as he started to talk. "I have to run some errands before I head over to Lindsey's. She's invited me to lunch."

"How *is* Lindsey?"

The tone of his voice made her look up at him. "She's fine," was her automatic response. Then: "I don't know exactly, Frank. She sounded a little strange on the phone. Almost too happy, if that makes any sense."

"No, Alex, it doesn't. How does a person sound when they're too happy?"

His tone now was suddenly belligerent. She was thoroughly sorry she'd gotten into this, but he had appeared really interested. "I can't explain it." She kept her voice even. "It's just that Lindsey has been kind of down the last few times we've been together, and now, when nothing at all in her life has seemed to change, she sounds positively euphoric."

He shrugged. "Let's hope she can stay that way."

She wondered what that comment meant. "Well, I guess I'd better—"

"Why did you come, Alex?" He was pushing the glasses up the bridge of his nose. The better to see her.

"I don't really know." She tried honesty. "It's true about my shopping and remembering your birthday. It's hard for me to ignore your birthday, Frank. And the other day, at the paper, when Murray told me I could stay on the National desk—the first thing I wanted to do was tell you." She hoped she wasn't going to cry. She felt the first hot tears threatening at the corner of her eyes and blinked them back.

"I know you're angry at me, Frank. And I don't blame you. I made a real mess of things. I've admitted it. But you've got to know I wouldn't intentionally hurt you. We've been friends so long. Does the fact that we can't be lovers anymore have to make us enemies? I miss you."

He shook his head. "You're a piece of work, Alexandra. . . . And stop crying, dammit!" He turned away.

"Frank—"

"We can be friends, Alex," he interrupted her. "But there's still one thing I've got to say."

She stared at his back, willing herself to hear whatever it was without anger.

"Obviously"—he laughed at the word and turned again to face her—"you have decided that the two of us do not have a chance. Well, that's fine, Alex, though I think you might have found a better way than last week's little interlude at Cape Cod to let me know it."

He stopped, but she kept silent. He hadn't finished.

"Well, Alexandra, maybe you were right. He seemed calmer now, his words almost gentle. "Maybe we never had a chance. But one thing I do know. You and Leighton don't have a chance either. Not a snowball's chance in hell, lady. Dammit, Alex, the man is a Catholic priest."

"I know that, Frank," she said as simply as she could. "I told you Sunday that it was over."

"But you don't believe it. Do you?" He didn't wait for an answer. "It's like I said before. You usually get what you want, don't you, Ms. Venée? You just can't accept the fact that this time could be any different. If I wasn't so busy feeling sorry for myself, I could feel sorry for you, Alexandra."

She didn't say anything. Just let him watch her till she closed the door.

• • •

"She'd just come in from shopping." Margaret's tone was almost exasperated. "You know, Phillip, Alexandra always goes shopping when she's upset. You know what she purchased, Phillip? Three pairs of high-heel shoes. Joan and David's. I couldn't even bring myself to ask her the cost. But, Phillip, you know I don't care about the price of things. It's Alex that I care about."

"I know, my darling. . . . Who are Joan and David, Margaret?"

"Oh, Phillip, really. It's a shoe company. What I can't understand is why she hasn't said anything to you. She tells you everything." He heard his sister's deep sigh through the line. "Are you sure you're not keeping anything from me, Phillip?"

"I promise, Margaret. And really, Alex doesn't confide everything to me."

"Well, practically everything. I think this little rift between her and that reporter must be bothering her more than she wants to admit."

"Alex told you that she and Frank Gregory were having problems?"

"You didn't know?"

"She didn't come out directly and tell me, Margaret, but I suspected as much."

"There, I knew it. Alex *is* upset about something. So upset, she's not even talking to you, Phillip. Do you think that she's in love with this Frank Gregory?"

"Maybe. But I don't think Alex knows what she wants, Margaret. She's just going through one of those crisis periods. She'll be fine. Let her be, Margaret."

"And this trip to the Cape." Margaret went on as though she hadn't heard a word he'd said. "What was that all about? All alone in that beach house."

Not all alone, Margaret, he thought. With John Leighton. "She went there to work on a story, Margaret. Really, my darling, if you're that worried about Alex, why don't you just come up again for a visit. Alex would love it. You know I would."

"Oh, Phillip, I just can't go running up there every time I

get a notion that something is wrong with Alex. I'll have to let her find her own way. Let her be, as you said." Another sigh through the line. "Besides, Alfred needs me right now. He's been so busy lately. I'm worried about him. Damn, Phillip, I'm worried about all of you. You do know that I worry about you, Phillip." Her last words were finally gentle, slightly tentative, spoken more like the young Margaret Camélière.

And for a long time after she'd hung up, he thought about what she'd said. That last sentence. That last comment about worrying about him. How different it was now. Always when they had been young, it had been he who had worried. Not Margaret.

Almost from the very beginning, it seemed that Margaret had found her strength in him. Expecting him to be what she believed she could not be—the best for the both of them. He was the outgoing one, the self-assured one with all of the answers, all of the charm.

But she had had her own charm, too. A natural sweetness that translated into a kind of aching vulnerability that caught him off guard. He had wanted to protect her from the very first. It had been easy to look into her wide, almost frightened blue eyes and say "Yes, Margaret, everything is going to be all right," or "Yes, Margaret," he would do this or that thing. Always she had made him want to make everything perfect for her. Yet at the time he believed it wasn't something that she did consciously—depending on him. Rather he'd accepted it simply as a very endearing part of who she was. And he had done nothing to change that. In truth, he had encouraged her reliance on him. It formed the core of their special relationship.

But now he guessed that in her own way she had manipulated him. With her gentleness, her helplessness. Her *Oh Phillip, I can't do this without you*. She was, in truth, stronger than either of them ever believed. But then they had both seemed to have needed what the other had to give. She needed to depend on him. He had wanted her to.

He remembered the day when she had first begun to slip away. It was a hot and sticky August afternoon. *Thick* was the word that always came to his mind when he thought of New Orleans summers. He had come into her room and found her curled up with a book.

"Margaret? What's the matter? You not feeling well?"

"I—I'm okay, Phillip. Just feeling kind of lazy." She looked down at the open book in her lap, avoiding his eyes. Self-conscious.

"You're not going with us to the camp?"

"To Pass Christian?"

"Of course, Margaret, what other camp do we have? Hey." He sat on the edge of the bed and pulled the book away. "Something *is* wrong. Margaret . . . No secrets. Ever."

"It's just that I . . . I wouldn't be able to go swimming. And it isn't any fun if you can't swim. You know that, Phillip." She took his hand and began to stroke it with her thumb, concentrating on the motion.

"Can't go swimming? Who says you can't go swimming?"

"Mother."

"Mother? What's the matter? Does she think you're coming down with one of your strep throats? Open your mouth. Let me see." And he bent forward over her, trying to pry open her jaw.

"Stop it, Phillip!" Her voice was louder than he had ever heard it. And she jerked her face away.

"Margaret . . ." He dropped his hand. "Margaret, I—I'm sorry. I didn't mean . . ."

"Oh, Phillip, I'm sorry." She was looking at him now and he could see something very close to pain in her large blue eyes. "It's not your fault. You didn't do anything. It's just that . . ." And she glanced away again.

"It's just what, Margaret?" And the way he said it had forced her to look at him.

"I can't go with you because Mother says that it wouldn't be good for me to get wet." She stopped as though she expected him to say something. But he didn't. "I . . . I think that it's supposed to be bad if a girl goes swimming while she is having her period."

He thought that she would have turned from him then. But she smiled instead.

"I really don't feel bad at all, Phillip." She was talking again, still smiling. "Actually I feel . . . kind of good. Like I'm all grown up. A woman, or something. I've been really kind of worried. I'm almost fifteen. Most of the girls started last year. I guess I'm just a little slower than everyone else. . . ." Her words drifted off, and this time she did look away, so that now he saw only her profile.

He stared at her. Her thick blond hair fell away from her face and rested silky across her thin shoulders. Almost too much hair, he thought, for her delicate face. An especially pretty face, though, particularly when she smiled.

She turned a little, as if sensing that he was watching her, and he saw that the blue eyes suddenly seemed more open, somehow more confident. As though they were unafraid, unafraid of anything or anyone. And the nose that had caused her long hours of agony in front of the mirror seemed to have finally lost its despised little-girl pugness. He sighed inwardly, thinking how much he was going to miss that turned-up nose. Lost forever now.

But her mouth seemed the most changed. It had grown much fuller, and he decided immediately that it was more of a woman's mouth now than a girl's. And then and there, beyond all reason, he felt a hollow little ache deep inside his fifteen-year-old boyhood heart.

He took a deep breath now and offered a silent thanksgiving. Margaret had made it. Made it without him. Despite everything that had happened. Their mother's death. His leaving her behind to become a priest. She had made it. He smiled to himself as he thought about Alfred. Alfred had guessed from the first the depth of Margaret's strength. Something that neither of them had known. But then it was not, after all, in the nature of the game for the players to know the outcome.

Alexandra looked around the Capitol Hill town house. It had always been beautiful, but it seemed that Lindsey had recently added some fresh touches, done a bit of redecorating. The windows were bare of the heavy draperies, and now French-striped balloon shades were rolled up midway to let in the late-morning light. Bright splashes of sunlight pooled across the polished hardwood floor and over onto a scatter of colorful dhurries. There were freshly cut long-stemmed flowers in a crystal vase on the coffee table where Lindsey was placing a large silver tray.

"Like it?" she asked.

"Yes, it looks lovely, Lindsey. It's just that I'm . . ."

"Surprised? Please, Alex, don't feel embarrassed. I know I have always said I hated this place. But . . ." She stopped as though she wanted to say something more but thought better of it. "Well, let's just say that I've decided to make the most of it. I'm afraid that we're here for the duration. Richard will probably be a senator until the day he dies. So . . . I thought I'd fix up the place. You know I didn't even repaint when we moved in. God, I hated those funeral-parlor green walls in here. And those draperies. They belonged in Versailles. This place is at least cheery now."

"I love it, Lindsey. . . . And you seem so much happier."

Lindsey appeared to consider these words a moment. Then: "Yes, Alexandra, I am happier."

"Am I to assume that things are better between you and Richard?"

Lindsey was pouring coffee into one of the cups. "Black, or café au lait, Alex? I've warmed some milk."

"Black's fine. After that lunch, Lindsey, I don't think I'd better consume another calorie. I didn't know you were such a good cook."

"Full of surprises, huh? Actually I'm just good at following a recipe." Lindsey passed her a cup.

She sipped at the coffee. "Mmm, delicious."

Lindsey poured herself a cup and leaned back into the soft cushions. "Yes, Richard and I are getting along better. In fact"—she paused, and her green eyes were almost wicked— "we've decided to start a family." She finished with a smile.

"Lindsey! I'm so happy for you. That's the best news I've heard in a long time. Even better than my getting on National."

"Alexandra, you made it! Why didn't you tell me?"

"I just found out. It seems that Murray likes what I'm doing with the Conference thing, and he's made it permanent."

"That's wonderful, Alex. I know it's what you've been wanting. But I knew all along it would happen. It seems that the two of us are finally getting it together." She sat forward and rearranged the coffee server on the tray.

"But about the baby. That's just marvelous, Lindsey. How... how did it happen?"

"Nothing in particular. Things just kind of smoothed over between Richard and me, that's all." She was fidgeting with the coffee service again. "And you? You and Frank?"

"We're still friends. . . . I think."

"Still friends? What happened, Alex?"

"I really can't blame Frank. I . . . I guess he just got tired of waiting for me to make up my mind." It wasn't a complete lie.

"About moving in?"

"Yes . . ." Alex hesitated, then rushed on. "I didn't mean to hurt him, Lindsey. It's just that things are going so good for me now. With the paper and all. I just need to be on my own for a while. I . . ." And she turned away, feeling the hot sting of tears starting in her eyes. Tears over Frank. Tears because she wasn't able to get the whole truth out.

"Oh, Alex, I'm so sorry. Can't you make him understand. I know Frank cares about you. Hell, the man's in love with you."

She brought her head up and stared at Lindsey. "That's the problem, Lindsey. He's in love with me."

Lindsey reached forward and poured more coffee into her cup. "Yes, I know. Most of them get kind of crazy when they fall in love. They get frightened. Start wanting to own things. Own you."

She didn't say anything, but took a napkin from the table and wiped her eyes. Then she began to twist one of the edges into a tight little cord.

"Listen, Alex, do what you have to do. I mean go with the newspaper thing. Call your own shots. Make your own time, your own space. If Frank loves you, the kind of love that really counts, he'll wait."

"I don't expect him to wait, Lindsey. I don't even know if

want him to." She had abandoned the napkin and began concentrating on the new floral chintz that covered the love seat.

"Alexandra?"

She looked up.

"Alexandra, you don't love Frank, do you?"

"Of course, I love Frank, Lindsey." The answer was reflexive.

"But there's no passion?"

"Right, Lindsey, no passion. Whatever the hell that means."

"It means the kind of thing that gets you right here. Grabs you so hard that you can't breathe. The kind of thing big liberated girls laugh at. Say will never happen to them."

"Yeah, the kind of thing that makes you miserable."

Lindsey laughed. "Remember when we talked before. And I warned you that mad passion wasn't what it was cracked up to be."

"Yes."

"Well, Alex, I was wrong. Maybe passion isn't something you work out of your system. Like a cold virus. Just maybe passion is what love is all about. The real honest-to-God kind of love." Lindsey smiled. "I can't believe I'm lecturing you, Alexandra Venée, the most intelligent woman I know. It's just that I've learned some things along the way, Alex. And I want you to be happy."

"I know, Lindsey."

"We get caught up in all the labels sometimes. Love, passion, sex. But I think that the kind of passion that you're talking about, Alex, has everything in the world to do with love. And if it's not Frank, then find that passion you want with someone else. You owe it to yourself. You deserve the best, Alex."

"Frank *is* the best, Lindsey. I don't think I deserve him."

"Don't say that, Alex. And I'm not saying that Frank's not a great guy. He is. It's just that if you're not in love with him, it doesn't matter how great of a guy he is." Lindsey stopped for a moment and put her cup down. "And for chrissakes, don't play it too safe. You'll never find love that way. You've got to go after what you want, Alex. Go after what makes you happy."

"And if what makes me happy hurts too much?"

"That's the price, Alex. Sometimes the hurting is the price."

Alex looked hard at Lindsey. The green eyes held a kind of exuberance she'd never seen before. A kind of wonderful recklessness that only very young eyes can have.

"Thank you, Uncle Phillip." Alex accepted the snifter of brandy. "Mmm...this *is* nice." She looked around her uncle's study. His favorite room in the residence. Hers too, she decided. "I've missed it being just the two of us." She smiled, patting the sofa so that he'd come and sit next to her. "Give me a hug."

"Alex, you're still such a child." He chuckled against her ear as he brought his arms around her, then sat down on the sofa.

"I don't know why it is, but when I'm around you, Uncle Phillip, I enjoy being that little girl you seem to remember so well."

He stared at her, his gray eyes luminous in the soft lamplight coming across his shoulders. "I'm glad, Alex." he placed his hand over hers and squeezed it. "And so my girl is permanently on the National desk for the *Washington Post*."

"Proud of me?"

"You know I am, darling."

"Well, it's this furor between Rome and you American bishops which made it all possible."

"Gifts come in strange packages." She heard what she thought was almost a bitter laugh. Then a smile. "So what has the new National reporter been up to lately to earn her keep?"

"My latest article is on homosexuality. A real tough one. If I have a handle on the American position, it seems to reflect what Father Charles Curran has been saying for the last several years."

"Charlie Curran is a very humane theologian."

She nodded. "I'm enjoying putting together these articles, Uncle Phillip. There're certainly no easy answers."

"When I spoke to Margaret this morning, she was positive-

ly delirious over her daughter's new status. I could barely
hold a conversation with her. Of course, she commented that
she guessed they'd never get you back to New Orleans now.
What's Alfred have to say?"

"Oh, he's overjoyed. But you know Daddy, Uncle Phillip,
he always gets kind of quiet when things get a bit exuberant."

"Funny, I've never seen his mellow side." His wicked smile
curled about his mouth.

"Uncle Phillip . . ."

"Just teasing."

"Speaking of Mother. I've been meaning to show you this.
Mother gave it to me when she was here." She walked to the
desk and picked up the album resting beneath her purse.
"She said she wanted me to have a little bit of family and
tradition up here. There are some absolutely wonderful pictures of the two of you." She sat down on the sofa again, and
the book fell open somewhere near the end.

"Oh, Alex, wait. . . . I remember this. Almost like yesterday. Your seventh birthday." Phillip brought the album closer
so that the light could fall at just the right angle. "Your Alice's
Adventures in Wonderland Party."

"Look, Mother even saved this." She pointed to a party
invitation on the facing page. "'You're cordially invited to go
down the rabbit hole and join Alexandra Venée on the occasion of her seventh birthday at a mad tea-party.' Whose idea
was this, Uncle Phillip?"

"I think it was mine. But Margaret came up with all of the
special touches. Like getting the puppet show. Here you are
with the whole group." He pointed to a picture of her
standing with the March Hare, the Hatter, and the Dormouse. "Remember how you squealed when you touched the
Dormouse because his fur felt so real. Just look at you, Alex,
with your long blond hair tied back with that blue ribbon.
You were a perfect Alice."

"I think I look horribly prissy, Uncle Phillip."

"You do not. You were wonderful, Alexandra. . . . Still are."
He turned to her and smiled, his face kind and gentle, his
eyes full of that same unconditional love she'd always seen
here.

"This is my favorite photograph from the party, Uncle Phillip," she said finally, pointing to a picture of him with his arms around her and her mother.

"Doesn't your mother look pretty?" he said, studying the image of the three of them.

"Where was Daddy?"

"If I recall, Alfred didn't want to have his photograph taken."

"Daddy still hates the camera." She ran her fingers over the photograph. "I just love this picture. You can see how really proud Mother was of you, Uncle Phillip. So distinguished in your black clericals. Just look at that expression on her face."

He smiled, glancing down again at the picture. "Yes, she was." And he, too, passed his fingers over the photograph as if trying to grasp the moment in his hand. Then he looked up and gave her a quick kiss. "You and your mother are still my two favorite girls, darling."

She smiled.

"How are things with you and John Leighton?"

She looked up quickly then down again. There was no mistaking it. She'd heard it in his voice. The clear, calm understanding. So completely without judgment. She had never fooled him. Had never meant to. They had both understood that. And for a long time all she could do was focus on his hand resting across her arm. And then, without warning, the mask slipped away, and she wept.

She was conscious that he held her in his arms. Ran his hand in gentle circles across her shoulders, whispered soothing words against her ear. And then she felt him chuckle, and she looked up into his face.

"It's all so unfair, my darling. Not God's law, but man's. Yet I think that soon the letter of the law shall finally give way to the spirit. As Christ had always intended. And then, my love, you may have your John Leighton, and he still his Church."

She continued to stare at him, watching the intelligent light in his eyes grow brighter and brighter. Then she asked, "There is to be a schism, Uncle Phillip, isn't there?"

He didn't answer, but then she hadn't expected him to.

Hadn't in truth wanted him to. And in the next instant she reached out and snuggled back into his arms, feeling a strange new comfort in the secrets they'd shared.

Alex was at the residence now, John knew. Picking up her spoon, eating the chocolate mousse that Madame Elise knew to be her favorite. Laughing at some comment her uncle had made. Her skin flushed from the wine she'd drunk with her dinner. Her eyes golden in the candlelight that illuminated the room.

And he... He had made his lame excuses to the Cardinal, had sneaked out of the residence like a thief in the night. And now he paid dearly for his cowardice. Paid for it in the sharpness of his memories. Paid in the raw unrelenting ache that bubbled at the center of his chest.

From the first it had been a struggle. His vows, his celibacy, his damnable chastity a wall standing between them. A wall erected by his Church. And surely, too, he must believe, a wall constructed by his God. Yet if that wall had shown cracks and chinks on more than one occasion, it had in the end held.

But now, if he went any further with this thing, it would be the Archangel who guarded and fortified the wall. For if John Leighton the priest had found making love to Alexandra Venée unconscionable, John Leighton, Vatican spy, would find it inconceivable.

And yet he was not going to be able to avoid Alex completely and still do the job he had to do. But tonight he had run away, taken refuge in his apartment. And he could hardly maintain an effective surveillance of Phillip Camélière from here on Connecticut Avenue.

He should have called Brian today about the discs from Tony's office that he'd copied. But he hadn't. He figured his reluctance to tell Donovan had something to do with his will to maintain control, his desire to see the whole picture for himself. To find guilt, if there was any guilt to be found.

Alex stood for a moment outside the apartment building looking up, listening. Lamplight shone dimly from behind partially drawn drapes, half-pulled shades. And she had a vague awareness of the whirring of window units. Ninth floor, on the end, to the left. His apartment. She took in a deep breath and walked inside the building.

She stood for a moment in front of his door, thinking about what she was going to say. She had to get it straight if they were still going to work together. She'd made a commitment to Murray. No matter what, she couldn't let this thing with him screw up her career. She lifted her hand and knocked.

"John . . ." He didn't let her finish. Just moved aside so she could come in.

He had the two lamps on either side of the sofa lit, and there were several pillows thrown against the cushions. She hadn't noticed pillows the last time. She looked around. Prints on the walls. Nothing remarkable. But before the walls had been bone bare. She smelled coffee perking.

"Sit down, Alex. Like a cup of coffee?"

"Yes, that would be nice. I hope I'm not disturbing you." She saw that he had been working on his computer.

"No, not at all. I needed a break anyway. Be just a minute." And she watched him as he walked into the kitchen.

She sat on the sofa. God, what was she doing here? Was she crazy? Instinctively her eyes went to the photographs on the table. Like quiet ghosts, she thought, living alone with John Leighton in his apartment.

"Here we are." He was carrying a tray into the room.

"Thanks." She took the cup from his hand, forcing a smile. At first she thought he was going to sit next to her on the sofa, but he walked to the window instead.

"I hate keeping the windows closed. I like fresh air. But it's so hot in the summer, you have to keep the air-conditioning going full-time." She heard him laugh quietly, saw that he'd turned to look over at her. "Sometimes I just forget the heat, shut off the unit, and throw open all the windows. If I'm lucky, I'll catch a cool breeze. Especially at night. It seems that the wind's been waiting all day for things to just settle down."

His voice sounded husky, vaguely sad. Mourning over the

necessity of closed windows, the loss of fresh air. She sat her cup down and walked over to stand next to him. "John . . ."

He turned and looked at her, his hands braced against the windowsill.

"John," she repeated, moving closer. The draft from the air conditioner surged out between them.

"John . . ." And this time his body straightened so that it became a solid barrier between her and the cold air.

There was the slightly bitter taste of after-shave around his lips as she brought her mouth to his. And in the exact instant before, she'd watched as he'd closed his eyes, heard his breath catch, like silk brushing against thorns.

Her arms went around his shoulders, pressing him against her. She could feel him already hard and solid through the thick denim of his jeans. She moved her fingers down.

"No, Alex!" He pulled away. "No, Alex, I can't. . . ."

She looked up into his eyes, watching something like pain and bewilderment pass across his face. Then he turned away.

"Damn you, John Leighton! Damn you and your precious little vow!"

He wasn't angry, she could see that. His eyes were only very kind and gentle.

"I'm so sorry, Alex. So sorry that I've hurt you. I didn't mean to, Alex. I really didn't mean to." He stopped and brushed the back of his hand against her cheek. Then he turned and gazed once again out of the window. "By all of the laws, by all of the laws of God and man," he said softly, "I am committed, Alex. Committed now in ways you'd never understand."

She stared at him just a few moments longer, before she walked out into the hot July night.

CHAPTER TWENTY-SEVEN

"You were certainly greedy," Phillip teased, pulling gently at a strand of red hair that trailed over Lindsey's breast.

"Mmm..." She smiled up at him from the crook of his arm and, turning on her side, rested her face against his chest. "I love the feel of this." She pushed her fingers through the graying hairs beside her cheek. "It's comforting somehow...."

His hand ran lightly along her back, from the base of her spine to her neck. "I love the feel of this. And the way you always smell, Lindsey."

She lifted her head to smile at him again. "That's just the Calyx."

He raised her wrist to his nose. Planted a kiss. Ran his mouth down to the inside of her elbow.

"Phillip, stop. You know how much that tickles. Phillip! Stop!" She was laughing and struggling, but his hand was locked upon her wrist.

"It's you *and* the Calyx." He let her go.

"Monster!" she said, still laughing.

"I didn't plan it."

"Didn't plan what?" She didn't understand this shift.

"Seducing you. I had no idea of just how much I wanted you, Lindsey." He sounded as if the thought still surprised him. "But finding you that day..."

"Is something wrong, Phillip?" His voice had become suddenly too serious.

He laughed. "No. Nothing... Have you seen Alex?"

"Yes," she said slowly, knowing that the question was a distraction. "I saw her yesterday. She came to the town house for lunch."

"How did she seem?"

She sighed, lying back down against the pillows. "Well," she said, hedging, "Alex is a little upset, I think, about how things... about how things with Frank Gregory are going. You did know that they broke up?"

"Yes. I knew about that."

"Well, I don't know what else I can tell you. It's all girl talk. Alex will be okay."

Phillip nodded as if he understood. She pulled herself up. "I'm going to the kitchen to get something started. I saw some fresh salad things in the refrigerator."

"Don't put on that robe."

"Phillip." She turned toward him, pushing back her hair from her breasts. "Don't be silly. I'm not going to make lunch naked. I'd feel ridiculous."

He was watching her with that half smile. She put the kimono on slowly. Her turn to tease him now.

"Why don't you come over here."

"Now who's greedy? Uh-uh," she said as he reached out a hand toward her, "I'm going to fix us some lunch." She backed away as he lunged forward, and darted out, laughing.

In the kitchen she stood in front of the open refrigerator, thinking of what Phillip had just said about that first day together. It wasn't anything specific he'd said; she'd just picked up on something in his voice. Something was bothering him. He was worried.

She heard him coming and opened the crisper drawers, pulling out the things for salad.

"Are you sure you want to do that, Lindsey? We could order something. Maybe Chinese?"

"No. I've suddenly become domestic. Ask Alex. Besides, I've always liked making meals here." She pulled out more things from the pantry. "And it won't take long. Most of this stuff is already washed. The housekeeper is very efficient."

"Your hair is beautiful with the sunlight coming in like that from the window. . . . There's something I want to tell you, Lindsey."

She was halving the tomatoes now. Very carefully. She forced herself not to look up.

"I'm having this house transferred to your name. That way, if anything should happen, it will be totally yours. There are some papers. . . ."

She put down the knife. Turned completely to face him. She wanted to see his eyes. "Phillip, please don't talk like that. What is it that's going to happen? You're not saying that you want to end this . . . ?"

"Good God, no." He came over to her, held her against him. "Lindsey, you're trembling." He held her tighter. "Lindsey, poor Lindsey. Why would you ever think that? This house . . . you. It's the best part of my life."

"Oh, for me too, Phillip. I love this house. And I love that it's our secret." She huddled against his chest, relieved. "I'm horribly selfish, Phillip, I'd never want to share this place with anyone. Except . . ."

"Except?" he prompted. Pulling back, trying to see her face. "You're being mysterious, Lindsey. What were you going to say?"

She shook her head. Looked down. "Nothing."

He kissed her ear. Released her. "Well, whenever you're ready to tell me . . . Now, just how hungry are you, Lindsey?" His tone was playful. "Sure I couldn't talk you into letting this lettuce wilt?" He drew her closer again, his thumb moving on her nipple beneath the thin silk.

"No, Phillip." She pulled away, trying her best to say it seriously. "But then, that's why we have these miracles of modern science." Laughing, she turned, and shoved the bowl into the refrigerator.

The curtains were drawn, the office dark except for the glow of the desk lamp. Phillip leaned forward into the circle of light. Slowly he massaged the knotted muscles above his shoulders, trying to ease the tension from his neck. The whole afternoon had been filled with endless politicking, with round after round of calling. No matter how well things were going, it seemed that everyone, even his closest allies, still needed his personal and constant reassurance.

But he should be counting his blessings, not complaining, he told himself. At this point, only a few months before the opening of the Conference, things could hardly look better. The careful laying of the groundwork and favorable media exposure were paying off. Support for his own position had been growing, his opponents steadily losing ground.

So why did he feel this sudden void? Why now? With everything he'd planned for so long almost within his grasp, why did the reality of it seem to be slipping away?

He leaned back into the darkness. Rome was too quiet. That was one thing that nagged at him. The Pope had been strangely silent since the Dutch excommunications. What was he waiting for? The fools in the Curia might have once underestimated Cesare Sersone. He never had. As he did not underestimate Flancon.

He forced himself up from the chair. He needed to get more sleep. Try to rest this weekend. At least he could look forward to seeing Lindsey on Tuesday. No matter what his schedule was like, he was going to make the time to see her as he'd promised her. Only a short time ago, a couple of months at most, he might have asked himself if he had not let Lindsey become too important. But not now. Loving Lindsey was a strength, not a weakness. Like his love for Margaret. And Alex. Loving Lindsey was salvation.

He slid open the top drawer and picked up his keys. Tony would fuss if he failed again to lock up properly. He switched off the lamp and walked to the door. Outside he hesitated. A light shone at the far end of the corridor. John Leighton was working late in his office.

"Trying to show me up, Father Leighton?" He leaned in at the open doorway, smiling at the priest's startled expression. "Sorry, I didn't mean to surprise you, John. I just wondered if you were going to make it a matter of policy to work later than 'His Eminence.'"

"I always work late." John tried a smile at last. "I like the quiet."

"Which I've disturbed."

"Oh, I didn't mean . . ."

Phillip held up his hand. "I know you didn't. But you know, John, I am a bit disappointed in you."

John didn't say anything. Just waited with the strangest expression.

"I know I've brought this up before, but I thought for sure when you decided to move in with us, that you'd loosen up a bit. Relax. But if anything, you're more formal than ever."

"I'm sorry."

"Stop apologizing, John. I didn't come to criticize. I wanted to let you know what a fine job I think you're doing for the Conference. Everybody's pleased as hell. And if Brian Donovan would quit reminding everyone that it was he who recommended you, I would certainly try to claim you as my protégé." He laughed. "Don't look like that, John. I'm perfectly aware that that would be a mixed blessing. And your reputation is safe. No one sees your work as anything other than impartial scholarship. It is fair, and it is brilliant."

"Thank you."

The unspoken "Your Eminence" was clear in the silence.

He heard himself sigh. Why did it always seem that John Leighton was fighting him? "What are you working on now?" he said.

John seemed at last to relax. "My book. My editor called a couple weeks ago to see how things were going. It made me feel a bit guilty that I hadn't done anything with it for so long."

"Well, I'd better let you get back to it, then. See you at breakfast, John."

"Good night . . ."

Your Eminence. That silent echo again.

He turned away and started toward his rooms. He thought a moment of stopping at the kitchen—he hadn't really eaten much tonight—but decided that he still wasn't hungry. He walked on past the elevator to the long staircase at the entryway, his shadow trailing behind him as he moved slowly upward. As if it, too, were reluctant.

What was wrong with him lately? It was not fear he felt. Not weakness. But darkness gathering. A sense of the inevitable. Like a predator who senses in the sudden hush that he is now the prey. The lion yet strong in tooth and claw, who welcomes in its heart . . . the hunter.

His sitting room was empty. Exactly as he'd last seen it, except for the lamp the housekeeper had left burning. He went on into the bedroom.

No light here but moonlight.

The French doors stood open, the white drapes shivering hotly in the muggy July air. He walked out onto the terrace. Leaned out against the rail.

"Angelique?" he whispered, watching the shadows.

When he turned back, he saw it, like stardust in the light pools on the floor. *Coup poudre.* The soul-stealing powder. He had tracked it through his bedroom from the door. And upon his bed so neatly turned down not hours ago by Mrs. Jordan, a black form limp and twisted. A dark blot upon his pillow. Black feathers. Red blood.

CHAPTER TWENTY-EIGHT

Raindrops big as quarters splashed one, two, three, making beaded circles on the dusty windshield. The impact was loud enough to give the illusion, if he'd been moving, of small rocks thrown up from the tires of passing cars. Four, five, six. Wet trails ran down like cracks. Frank made a move to turn on the wipers. But as quickly as it had begun, the rain stopped. The black cloud overhead having changed its mind with the wind that was blowing west and south. It would pour instead in Virginia.

His hand jerked forward again, and for the third time in less than half an hour he turned off the radio. Not a single DJ in the District today was playing anything he liked. The Oldies but Goodies were all pure crap from the late seventies, the kind of mindless rock he hadn't even listened to then, and his favorite classical station had on an opera. But he shouldn't complain. At least the overcast had made it bearable to sit here in the car without the air conditioner running, and he'd found a parking space right off, with a perfect view of Carla Fiorelli's building.

He tore off his glasses, and tossing them next to the camera on the passenger seat, he leaned forward with his elbow against the steering wheel to massage the bridge of his nose. The rearview mirror sat at an odd angle, knocked aside in his earlier search for a spare pack of cigarettes. When he looked up, his own eyes stared back at him.

His image careened sideways as he righted the mirror. And picking up his glasses, he satisfied himself that Richard's car still sat unoccupied a half block up on the other side of the street. He punched in the lighter and tapped out another cigarette. It always made him edgy when he got down this close to half a pack. He sat still, not breathing, puffing out his cheeks, as he waited for the metallic pop of the lighter. He pulled in a huge dose of smoke before allowing his next thought. He'd been eager enough to see this thing through when Carla had contacted him on Monday, so why now was he suddenly reluctant for the big moment of truth? What was making him so damn fidgety?

Maybe it was all the coffee this morning, he reasoned. He'd poured half a pot down his throat, waiting till it was time to get here. He punched on the radio again, but the opera was still playing. Something mournful and Italian. He twisted the dial and half listened as he ran through the stations, stopping on a soft-drink commercial that sounded better than the programmed music. He looked at the clock. It had been more than thirty minutes since Richard had entered Carla Fiorelli's apartment.

He shifted in the seat, lighting another cigarette from the butt in his hand, and found himself still worrying over the few that were left in the pack. He blew out a blue ring of smoke, watching it break like a ghost against the windshield. This wasn't adrenaline or coffee that was nagging at him. This was something else. He'd never admit exactly to a belief in ESP, but a good reporter, like a good detective, lived and died by his hunches. By gut instinct. It was the same feeling he always got when fate was about to deal him one from the bottom of the deck.

He made an abortive attempt at a laugh that sounded sour. This was exactly the way he'd felt about his relationship with Alex for weeks before her little revelation about John Leighton. And if he'd been willing to face it, he'd have read the handwriting on the wall in the undercurrent he had sensed that time they'd all gone for pizza at Murphy's. Funny.

Despite everything, he had almost liked John Leighton that night.

Why was he doing this again? Thinking of Alex? He couldn't seem to help it. The truth was that he still loved her. Still hoped...

Oh shit! A half block away, Richard's car was backing away from the curb. He ducked down and cursed again as ashes from his cigarette fell into his lap. He had let his mind wander, and now he'd missed getting pictures of Richard with the briefcase leaving Carla's apartment. He waited, slumped down in the seat till he heard the Lincoln go past, then he sprang up, starting the ignition.

Richard turned on to New Hampshire, moving north, and he followed at a distance. They would soon be into the heavier traffic at Dupont Circle, and it was going to be a little tricky, hanging back out of sight, anticipating where he would have to exit. He patted his pocket, feeling for the cigarettes, but decided he'd better go easy. Carla had felt certain that Richard always delivered the money on the same day he picked it up. But there was no knowing if he planned to go there directly, or even if there would be only the one stop.

Watching the distant silhouette of Richard's head behind the wheel of the Continental, he began at last to feel some anticipation about his destination. And yet there was still that tiny niggling fear, the little tug at the corner of his brain, which warned that he wasn't going to like it.

A large delivery van cut in front, blocking his view of the Lincoln completely. When he worked himself around it, he couldn't at first catch sight of the big sedan, and he wondered if Richard had exited back onto New Hampshire from the circle. He pulled out as far as he could to the left, looking ahead. No, there he was, four cars up in the right lane, his signal light blinking. He was turning at Connecticut Avenue.

Only one of the three intervening cars was exiting, so he slowed, letting Richard take more of a lead. Exactly where was the senator headed? Adams-Morgan? Chevy Chase? But before the Taft Bridge, Richard surprised him by turning onto

Columbia. The acid level in his stomach shot up another notch. What did he know that he wasn't letting himself in on? Just where in fucking hell was Richard Darrington going?

It wasn't until he saw the gold and blue dome of the Immaculate Conception Shrine, super real and glowing in the clearing sky above the neighborhood of run-down brownstones, that he finally understood. And even then he couldn't let himself admit to any kind of certainty.

When they were nearly to Maryland, he dropped back still farther in the thinning traffic and parked on a residential street. He was on automatic as he picked up and checked the camera, got out, and locked the car doors. For a moment before he started to walk, he gazed up into the sky. But the National Shrine was farther away now, the dome hidden.

The Lincoln wasn't parked in the drive fronting the Pastoral Center. Nor had he expected it would be. He looked around once, but there seemed no one about to observe him, and he began walking up the long private driveway. Still out of sight from the house, he left the narrow road to slip into the woods, coming up to a front view of the residence through the last line of trees.

Richard's car was sitting some twenty yards away near the entrance. He crouched down behind a row of bushes. It had rained here earlier, and the air held a strange mixture of clean and rotting smells. He pressed his hand for balance against the rough bark of a tree. Maybe this wasn't what he suspected. Maybe he was jumping to unjustified conclusions. Senator Darrington's friendship with the Cardinal was no secret. The most simple explanation was that the Cardinal was only the first, and the most innocent, of Richard Darrington's appointments.

He looked at his watch. If he were going to follow the senator to his next stop, he had better go now and get back to his own car. The odds certainly favored that decision. In fact, it was stupid to wait here another minute unless he truly believed that Phillip Camélière was taking part in an operation to launder funds for the Mafia.

A drop of water, surprisingly cool, slipped from the leaves to fall on his face. He pressed his head hard against the damp bark, thinking, trying to give himself the permission to go back the way he had come.

Five minutes had passed when he looked again at his watch. It had seemed like seconds. As if there'd been some merciful short-circuiting of the mental processes by which he normally measured time. He rose a bit, still out of sight behind the shrubs, the cramps in his legs seconding the evidence of his watch. He turned to look, thinking that he'd heard something. And now the door was opening. He drew back and instinctively lifted his camera.

Richard was coming out, followed by the Cardinal. He watched them move toward him through the viewfinder. They were talking, laughing over some private joke as he snapped the pictures. Richard still had a briefcase. He swung it lightly as he walked down the steps toward the car. At the edge of the porch the Cardinal paused, waiting, it seemed, till his guest reached the driver's door.

He zoomed in on the single figure, white Roman collar stark above the perfectly cut black suit, and suddenly a sharper sense of where he was and what he was doing returned, and the woods behind seemed suddenly very quiet. He paused with his finger above the release button, as if even the sound of the shutter's tiny motor might shatter the man in the eyepiece to splinters of glass.

"Thanks again, Richard." Phillip Camélière's voice came to him, remote but distinct. "And don't forget what I said . . . we can handle more."

He pressed down on the shutter button, turned the lens on the other.

Richard was still waiting by the car, his face turned toward the Cardinal. "I know," he said, "the transition is going to be expensive. . . . You going to be here all of next week. Just in case . . ." He patted the leather briefcase.

"I plan to be. There are things here I don't like to leave just now." The viewfinder was focused on the Cardinal again. A close shot of his face. There was a self-conscious irony in the smile that Frank doubted Richard Darrington could see.

He panned back to take in the scene. Richard had unlocked the back door and was tossing the case onto the seat. The senator waved and got behind the wheel.

At that instant something made him look up.

In a second-floor window, partially obscured by curtains, another silent witness stood watching the Lincoln disappear. Through the close-range lens he could see that it was John Leighton, with a look on his face that must exactly match his own.

Frank sat naked in the darkened room and pulled hard on his cigarette. It was all he'd done since he'd returned home. Sit and smoke. And think. His thoughts hadn't amounted to much, though, if you judged thinking in terms of the number of ideas you came up with. He'd had only two, but they were both real winners. Enough to make any investigative reporter get a hard-on. Richard Darrington was funneling Mafia money to His Eminence Phillip Cardinal Camélière and Father John Leighton was wise to it.

His first conclusion was based on fact. The second on instinct.

He stubbed out his cigarette and lit another. It had been that tight gripping in his belly, like a bad case of diarrhea, that had caused him to glance up from where he crouched in the bushes and see John Leighton looking down from the second-story window. He could have drawn a straight line from where the priest stood behind the curtain to where he squatted behind the shrubbery. Point A to point B. A simple 180-degree shot. "Plain" geometry. He and Leighton were joined, connected, linked.

And the expression on the man's face had really decided it for him.

He had only actually talked to John Leighton that one time. At Murphy's with Alex. So he hadn't really much to go on. Any idiot could have picked up on the fact that the man was extremely intelligent. And likable. He figured him right away for the sensitive type, with the kind of looks women wet their pants over. And of course he knew that the CU theologian had been recruited by Camélière to work with the Doctrine Committee for the Bishops Conference in November. There was also some kind of book contract. And . . . Alex was in love with him.

Nothing earthshaking in any of it, except maybe that last part. And that only to him. Yet despite all of the missing pieces, he was sure that John Leighton was not directly involved in what was going down between Darrington and Camélière. It simply didn't wash. The priest was the odd man out.

But Leighton *was* involved. Involved on some level. That look on his face had said that. But involved how? He crushed out his cigarette and reached for his pack. Empty. He twisted the package between his fingers. He'd already raided his emergency stash. He looked at the clock. It was just after five. Time for a quick shower before he went out for cigarettes and a bite to eat. He hadn't eaten all day and this morning's ration of black coffee had rusted out his stomach.

He swung his legs over the edge of the bed and looked at the phone. He wondered if Leighton were still at the residence. Alex had mentioned something about his staying there overnight sometimes. With any luck he'd catch him.

"Hello." *Bingo.* He hadn't expected that John Leighton himself would answer.

"John. Frank Gregory here. Alex's friend." Damn, he hadn't wanted to say that.

"Hello, Frank. How are you?" Too polite to say "What the fuck do you want?"

"Listen, John, I hope I'm not disturbing you, but . . ." He paused a moment, working on the next words. "I know this is short notice, but I'd like to meet you for a cup of coffee. Right now if you can make it. I think we need to talk."

"So, Father Leighton, just what is it you know about Phillip Camélière washing drug money for the Mafia?"

"Mafia? So that's where it's coming from." John had reacted, spoken before he'd had time to think. But then that was exactly what Frank Gregory had intended. Gregory was, after all, the professional here. He slumped back against the padded vinyl of the booth, thinking that he'd never had a chance from the moment he'd agreed on the phone to this meeting. The reporter had implied only that it was about a mutual concern, and he'd jumped to the conclusion that that meant Alex. He'd no idea what she had or hadn't said to Gregory about what had happened between the two of them, or if indeed she'd said anything at all. He'd met with Gregory because he'd thought perhaps he owed him this meeting, man to man. He certainly hadn't expected the litany of leading questions about his work at the residence. And then the last question, aimed straight for the jugular.

"You *do* know something?"

He looked up. It had taken him a second to realize that Gregory. . . that Frank was talking to him again. Asking more questions. "I'm sorry, what did you just say?"

He had the feeling that the reporter had been observing him closely, but now Frank crushed his cigarette into the remains of his ham sandwich and glanced away.

"I'd like to know just what *you* know about this whole operation, and in particular this afternoon's meeting between Camélière and Darrington." Frank was looking through the diner window at the traffic moving along Connecticut Avenue as he spoke.

John stared at the man's profile. He was beginning to think straighter now. At least straight enough to know he was thoroughly confused.

"I was there today," Frank explained, as if reading his thoughts. "In the woods near the front of the residence. I saw that chummy good-bye scene. I saw you, too."

"Me?"

"Yes, in the window."

"And that's why you decided to call me?"

"Yes."

"Why? I mean, it might have just been chance that I was watching at that moment. Maybe I was just curious. Or worse, part of whatever you think is going on. On their side."

Frank did smile now. He shook his head. "I was watching your face through the zoom lens on my camera."

"So you got pictures?"

"Yeah. But they don't prove a thing. That's why I need to know what you've got."

"I'm not sure that I should tell you anything," he said.

"But you've already told me something. By your reaction a minute ago." Frank didn't appear to be having any trouble confronting him now. And his voice seemed only impatient. "Look, Father Leighton . . . John, it's apparent that we both have information about this thing. I think we could help each other."

"Maybe." John took a breath. "You said that the Cardinal and Senator Darrington are washing drug money. I want to know how you know that?" It had occurred to him suddenly to start asking his own questions. He needed time to get his bearings. He looked at Frank directly and thought he saw a trace of a smile beneath the mustache.

"Fair enough," Frank spoke without hesitation. "In a nutshell, I have an informant. Someone who can prove that Senator Richard Darrington is acting as middleman in a major laundering operation. What I don't have is solid evidence to support my theory that the drug money is being washed through Camélière's diocesan accounts. *I* don't have the evidence, but I think—at least I'm hoping—that you *do* have it, Father Leighton."

They were back to "Father Leighton" now. And Frank was watching him again with full attention.

He made himself stare back. "What if I do?"

"Then I would think that you'd want to do what's right. *Will* do what is right. You know, John, this is all going to have to come out. . . . No matter who gets hurt."

The hazel eyes behind the glasses didn't really change. But he suddenly understood that Frank Gregory knew everything about him and Alex, and that what he mostly felt for Father John Leighton was contempt. But there was something else that Frank Gregory knew. Whatever pain John Leighton might have caused Alexandra Veneé would be nothing compared to what was coming. And in this they would be equally guilty.

He looked away. "What do you want to know?" It was all he could think to say.

"Like I said, I need proof of the Cardinal's involvement with Richard Darrington in this laundering scheme. Something tangible like ledgers or bank statements."

"I might be able to help. But first I'd want to know... I mean what exactly do you have on the senator—what real evidence? You did say that you had something, Frank." He couldn't seem to complete a sentence. It was simply hedging, a last-ditch reluctance to make any of this too final. But Frank seemed to understand.

"No problem. Come over to my place. I'll show you some pictures."

"All right."

Frank pulled out a book of matches. "Here"—he scribbled on the inside cover—"my address. It's in Adams-Morgan. Not too far from here. Pretty close to where you live, actually. My car's in the lot. You can follow me."

He watched as Frank stood up, feeling like he should say something more, but not knowing what.

The reporter seemed to hesitate, then leaned down, his fingers splayed out on the faded pattern of the tablecloth. "Just tell me one thing for now. Who exactly are you working for?"

The answer seemed so grandiose that John almost smiled but didn't. "The Pope." He said it as simply as he could. "I'm working for the Pope."

Alex stopped at the light and glanced down at the keys dangling from the ignition. Frank's front-door key was still on the ring, jangling against her own apartment key and the trunk key to her car. She should have returned his key, but she just hadn't thought about it.

Maybe he'd be home by the time she got there, and she wouldn't have to use the key. Damn him, why couldn't he keep up with his own shit. But she couldn't refuse Bob when he'd asked her if she wouldn't mind dropping off something at Frank's.

It's like I needed this yesterday, asshole, had been Bob's scrawled note to Frank.

"Sorry, Alex, didn't have time to put it into another envelope." The editor had stumbled over an apology when she'd glanced down to read it.

"That's okay, Bob. I think he's an asshole, too." And she had laughed.

She wasn't laughing now. She didn't want to see Frank, but the thought of going inside his apartment when he wasn't home was even less appealing.

She pulled up alongside the curb and got out of the car. Well, he wasn't home. His car was nowhere in sight. She walked up the steps and worked the key into the lock. Hell, for all she knew, something might have happened to that bomb he drove, and he might be inside right now screwing his brains out. Somehow the thought of Frank making love to someone else disturbed her more than she liked to admit. She halted just inside and called out, "Frank, you home? It's Alex." Nothing. She closed the door behind her.

It was strange, but as soon as she walked into the living room and saw his clothes lying in a heap on the floor next to a nest of fast-food wrappings, she suddenly realized she'd missed him. Frank's messiness had somehow always made him more endearing, and she reached down and picked up his jacket, hanging it over the back of a chair.

She glanced around. There wasn't a single ashtray that wasn't overflowing. She checked herself. She wasn't going to empty Frank's ashtrays. But, dear God, she didn't have the heart to be merciless. She walked over to the potted plant she'd given him a couple of months ago and brought it into the kitchen. Maybe a little water would pull it through.

The kitchen was a disaster. She shoved over a stack of greasy dishes and sandwiched the pot under the faucet. She watched the running water bubble through the dirt until it ran out of the drain holes. Then she moved back into the living room.

Enough of the Susie Homemaker bit, and she walked over to his desk and rested Bob's envelope against the computer. For an instant she had an idea that she would leave him a message on the screen, but decided that that wasn't such a good idea. There was no predicting when he'd come home, and she didn't want to leave the computer on. Better just leave a handwritten note. If she could find some paper...

She was shuffling some folders around when she noticed she'd pushed a large manila envelope off the edge of the desk. "Damn, you're messy, Frank," she cursed him softly. As she bent to pick it up, several large black-and-white glossies slipped out and fell to the floor.

For a moment she just stared at the photographs, not really taking in what she was seeing. Then slowly she reached down, her mind finally jolted by the sharp bloated images spread out like a poker hand beneath her fingers. She didn't recognize the blonde. But the wig was obvious. However, the man in the photo... There was no mistaking who he was.

She didn't know how long she remained there, stooped over the photographs, but the sound of a key in the lock caused her to look up. And in the next moment she was staring at Frank.

"Alex, what...?" He didn't finish. His eyes had found the blowups she held in her hands.

"Frank..."

"Give me those, Alex." He bolted across the room, grabbing the photos, shoving them back into the envelope.

"Frank, that was Richard Darrington in those photographs. What in the hell...?"

"What in the hell is right, Alex. What in the hell are you doing here? And what in the hell are you doing going through my things?"

"Frank, I... I wasn't going through your things. Bob gave me something to drop off. I was looking for paper to leave you a note. The envelope fell to the floor—" She stopped. "Fuck you, Frank Gregory." And she was running from the room.

"Alex, wait! Please. I'm sorry. I shouldn't have said what I said. Please, Alex..."

"Save it, Frank. I don't give a crap about whatever the fuck is going on. I'm out of here." She went for the door. The hard knock stopped her.

"Come in. It's open."

She never could recall the exact emotions she'd felt in that next instant when the door slowly pushed inward and she saw John Leighton in his prim black clericals standing just outside.

Alex hadn't said a single word since Frank had told her what he suspected about Richard Darrington. She had just remained standing quietly as he'd revealed everything from beginning to end, giving her back the photographs, as if only they, and not his words, could actually make his story real. Then the last—how he'd followed Richard to the residence and hid in the bushes.

And then it had been Leighton's turn. The priest spoke in measured tones. His voice as precise as a recording as he talked about *Lucifer.*

"It was really quite easy," Leighton was saying now. "Monsignor Campesi had left his appointment book out on his desk. And when I compared the dates of Senator Darrington's appointments with the credits to the accounts on the disc, they matched."

John Leighton stopped and his face seemed to alter. The muscles of his jaw constricted and just the barest trace of a frown passed between his dark brows.

"I should have reported what I found to Monsignor Donovan." His voice was still matter-of-fact. "But I wanted to wait and see if a new entry would appear in the accounts after Senator Darrington's visit today. Now. . ."

"You know, Alex, a bishop can do whatever he wants with diocesan funds." Frank spoke for the first time since Leighton had begun talking. "According to John, not even the Pope can tell a bishop what to do with the money."

Alex looked down for a moment, examining the worn patches in the carpet. There was the sound of a soft but distinctly indrawn breath. Then a low laugh.

"You know, Frank, if nothing else, I had you pegged for the best investigative reporter there was. But I can see I was wrong. You're off, Frank. Way off base. What you've got here"—she waved the photographs she'd been holding—"is nothing. A big fat zero. In the vernacular of the law boys, baby, what you've got is circumstantial evidence."

"Alex, you know goddamn well that what I have here is good, and with John's discs..." He stopped, and looked at her hard. "You don't want to believe this because you can't accept—"

"That my uncle is laundering Mafia money. You bet your sweet ass I don't accept it."

"Alex, I..."

She twisted around at the miserable sound of Leighton's voice.

"Please, Father Leighton," she said, "I think I've heard all that I need to hear from you. Everything is perfectly clear."

"Alex, you're not being fair." Frank was almost angry.

"Fair! Hey, I don't see anybody around here playing fair." She threw the photographs on the desk. "But listen, Frank." She was smiling as she moved toward him. "I'll give you both a chance to play fair. Let me talk to Uncle Phillip. I know he'll be able to explain all of this. Just let me have a few days. Deal?"

He shook his head. "You know I can't promise you anything, Alex."

She was listening to his words, but her eyes were on John Leighton.

She wasn't a bad driver, but she did tend to cruise on automatic sometimes. Not tonight. Tonight she was completely alive in the nerves and muscles that connected hand and eye. Aware of the machine. The streets. Aware of her own responses.

When the images again intruded, she'd been driving the District for hours. The numerals glowed past ten on the dashboard clock. She braked for a red light and brought her head down hard against the steering wheel, as if some act more physical than driving would now be required to make the pictures stop. She had always smiled at the glibness of TV flashbacks, so cinematically perfect, pretending to be memories in someone's head. And yet tonight, scenes from earlier in Frank's apartment kept flashing on some inner screen, and she could see herself so clearly. As if somewhere outside her brain there had been a camera.

The signal turned green and the images fled, but the illusion of perfect connection with the car was gone now. Cocooned as she was inside the Toyota away from the summer heat, the city beyond the windshield appeared to her suddenly remote. Blocks slipped by. She could feel the tension in her hands on the wheel increasing. And the anger that threatened to suffocate her even in the processed air. She forced one hand off the wheel, fought with the handle to get the window down, to let the outside roar in.

She was on Rock Creek Parkway past Kennedy Center almost to the bridge when she understood where she was going. She pulled off and parked in the small semicircle near the statue. In a city full of monuments, this golden horse was her favorite, so reassuringly solid despite the wings. She stared at it a moment, wishing for a cigarette. She pushed open the door and got out. Anything to keep her from remembering...

John. There was another quick flash of John Leighton complete with sound as he'd stood explaining, watching her from across the room, trying to appear so reasonable. She shook the image away. Why couldn't she stop these scenes from running like a bad movie in her head? John Leighton had used her, used her from the beginning. *No . . . not from the beginning*. Some part of her fought back. Hadn't he said something? She forced her hands roughly through her hair. Now that she wanted to remember, she couldn't make it come back, couldn't hear the words.

Wait. He'd said—said at least twice—that he hadn't known about *Lucifer*, hadn't been told about it till after the Cape. Her knees were trembling as she leaned against the side of the car, the air drifting in off the river clinging damply in her hair.

She shook her head again. She couldn't think clearly. She wasn't sure at all of what John had said. She might be remembering it all wrong, hearing in imagination what she wanted to hear. Something, *anything*, to let herself still believe. To let herself salvage... what? Her miserable ego. What did any of that matter now? She moved away from the car. The golden horse seemed magical glowing above her in the dark... but beyond her. Still too far away.

She closed her eyes. The worst was that Frank had turned against her, too. Spying on Uncle Phillip. Trying to make something out of nothing for a story. He had betrayed her, their friendship, everything...

Betrayal.

The anger left her. And that left her defenseless. She turned away with a first shattering sob toward the black sump of the river. The words slipped out aloud and real, so she could never later deny them. "Uncle Phillip... Oh my God, Uncle Phillip... *Why?*"

CHAPTER TWENTY-NINE

"Ms. Kenison on the line, Phillip." Tony's voice came over the intercom.

The Cardinal thrust aside the reports he'd been reading and picked up the receiver. Punched the button next to the flashing light.

"Lauren, hello. This must be important for you to be up so early on a Saturday." He laughed.

"I should have called yesterday, but I had a date. Left straight from the office."

"Same old Lauren."

She laughed, and he could imagine the gray-green eyes wreathed in their little crinkles.

"So what do you have for me?"

He heard another small laugh. Then a sigh. "I hope you're going to believe this."

"Try me."

"Well, it was yesterday afternoon," she started. "During coffee break, I heard two of the nuns talking. Arguing really. They were speaking Italian, but I got the general drift. Sister Rosa was angry about something that Sister Seraphina had done. Sister Seraphina left in a huff.

"Not all that unusual—the petty bickering—but I had a sort of feeling. So I got my coffee and sat down. Asked Sister Rosa what was the matter. She just shook her head at first,

360

said Sister Seraphina was getting old. I thought that was going to be that. But then she shook her head again, and I could see her deciding to tell me. Whatever the old nun had done was so outrageous, she just had to share it with someone. And I was handy."

"Well, don't keep me in suspense, Lauren."

"Okay... here goes." He could hear her take a breath. "If you remember, the Fourth was a Friday. Most of the embassy staff was off duty. But the nuns were there.

"So, anyway"—Lauren had stopped again for a moment—"Sister Rosa said that Sister Seraphina had just been so shameless, trying to impress the visitors."

"What visitors?"

"His Holiness..."

"Pope Stephen. Here?"

"That's what Sister Rosa said. He didn't stay long. Only a couple of hours.... I know it sounds crazy, Phillip."

He felt his mind racing. The Fourth would have been a perfect time to sneak into the District unobserved. A privately owned jet... It was just possible.

"Did Sister Rosa give any reason why His Holiness might have made the visit?" he said.

"I asked her that question."

"Good girl. And..."

"She didn't know. She just said he was there in the embassy with Flancon Monday morning. They met with the archbishop and two priests."

"Two priests?"

"Uh-huh. Sister Seraphina let them in herself. One was Monsignor Donovan."

"Brian Donovan? You're sure?"

"That's what Sister said. Monsignor Donovan and a younger priest. Apparently she didn't know him.... You think it's true Phillip? That the Pope...?"

"Yes, Lauren. I think it's true. And, thanks."

"I wish it could be more, Phillip. If only I'd been there."

"You did great, Lauren. Don't worry."

"I'll keep my ears open, Phillip. If I hear anything else..."

"I know. Thanks again, Lauren." He could still hear her soft breathing as he hung up.

Monsignor Donovan and a younger priest. Brian... a traitor. Why? And John Leighton. He was in on it, too. He stabbed at the intercom. "Tony."

Tony opened the door. His face said he'd been listening in as usual on Lauren's call, but he shook his head in warning. "Your niece is here, Your Eminence. She says it's urgent."

"Alexandra." He barely had the word out before she pushed in past Tony. He turned to her as Tony closed the door.

"Alexandra, you look... What's the matter? It's not Margaret?"

"Mother's fine. I just talked to her." She halted abruptly near the end of his desk. It seemed she'd no idea of what to do next.

"Sit down, Alex."

He watched her fold herself carefully into the chair. She was still staring at him.

"What's the matter, Alex?" he asked again.

She jerked forward to the edge of the seat, and for a moment he thought she was going to get up again before she answered.

"They say you're laundering money for the Mafia."

"Who does?" It came out reflexively. This was too soon after Lauren. Too much.

"Frank Gregory and John Leighton." She answered his question. "I was in Frank's apartment... they were there together. They told me."

"What are you talking about, Alex?" He tried to backtrack. Something like a laugh came out of her. But twisted. Ugly.

"Apparently they've joined forces. John Leighton's been spying on you for the Vatican. And Frank Gregory's been investigating for the newspaper. The Pope and the *Post*." That ugly laugh again. "They claim you're in it with Richard Darrington. That he's passing the money. Frank has pictures."

"You've seen them?"

"Yes. Richard and some blond whore trading briefcases." The words were hard, defiant. But he was watching her eyes, could see the pain, the pleading.

"What else do they have, Alex?" he made himself ask.

He saw her lips compress, then her tongue licking away the dryness. Her eyes were very bright.

"Frank's evidence seems entirely circumstantial, but Father Leighton claims he has computer discs showing the flow of funds. Duplicates, he says, of Tony's. He's waiting for Rome's permission to pass them on to Frank." The words stopped abruptly. She was waiting.

"Do you believe all this, Alex?"

"I'll believe what you tell me."

"There's nothing for you to worry about, Alexandra." He had hesitated, perhaps fatally, before speaking the words. "I'll take care of it." He felt himself smiling.

He stood up, watching her, willing her to come to him, to let him comfort her as always.

She didn't move. Her eyes were enormous with transformation. A light going out.

"Alex . . ."

She looked down. Shook her head. "Not now." Her voice was as steady as his. He saw her draw in a breath. Another. She stood. "I'll talk to you . . . later." She went out.

"Tony!" He hit the intercom.

"I'm here." Tony was at the door.

"You heard Lauren's call?"

"Most of it."

"You were right about Brian . . . all along."

"I'm sorry, Phillip."

He waved his hand, dismissing it. "There's more than Brian Donovan to worry about now. Alex has just told me that Frank Gregory and John Leighton are onto our operation. Frank has pictures of Richard picking up the money. And worse, John Leighton has duplicates of your computer files."

Tony went white. "How . . . ?"

"I don't know."

"Goddamn spy. I knew it."

"It's too late now, Tony. What we've got to do now is concentrate on containing this thing. I want you to get Miller on the phone, and Jennings. And Walter from the bank. It's the weekend, but I'm sure we have their personal numbers. No, scratch that. No phone calls. Go see them at home. Remind them that our records are, of course, sacrosanct, and that anything that can be done to increase their inaccessibility is top priority.

"As for your own records, Tony. Dump them. It's John's word against ours that his duplicates aren't fakes trumped up by the Vatican to discredit me. Without access to the bank or brokerage records, there's nothing to back them up."

"What if the records are subpoenaed?"

"We've got to make sure it never gets to that point. I'd go ahead and visit Mark Goldstein, too. Get him to give you the legal picture on any possible vulnerability—oh, and track down Richard. Call him, but don't tell him anything on the phone. Just get him over here for a meeting as soon as possible."

He smiled for the first time since Tony'd entered. "And Tony, one thing. I think I can handle this. But if I'm wrong, if things get past a certain point, don't you hang on. Not if you see the game is lost." He deepened the smile, heading off any protest. "I taught you better, Tony. Remember that."

John lifted his head from his desk and stared at the anemic light forcing itself through the window. It was barely past nine o'clock and he was wishing the day were over... *gotten through*. He rubbed hard at the skin at his temples.

Control. That's what he wanted. Some kind of control over everything that was happening. Control over himself. He laughed softly. That would be novel.

He pushed himself up and walked to the window. Through the dent he made in the blinds, he could see the almost empty street below. Lazy on this Saturday morning. He let the blinds snap.

He checked his watch. Almost 9:15. Twenty-five minutes ago he had been on the phone with Brian Donovan. It was a

Chinese puzzle trying to cipher Brian's reactions to what he'd told him. Of course, he expected surprise when he said that Alex knew all about *Lucifer*. And Brian's anger was predictable as he'd told him how Frank Gregory was involved. It was when he told him about the Mafia connection in Camélière's laundering operation with Darrington that he'd gotten an unexpected reaction. Donovan had seemed genuinely startled at the audacity of Camélière's crime. Then a slow satisfaction surfaced, an undisguised joy that at last Rome had Phillip where they wanted him. But the satisfaction had evaporated immediately, and Brian seemed almost panicked at the thought that Rome might feel they'd gotten more than they had bargained for. . . .

"You're not seriously thinking of giving the discs to this Gregory, John, are you?" His voice had been irritable.

"I don't see the point in holding back, Brian. Frank needs what I have. Besides Alex has told Phillip about everything by now. I would think time is of the essence. The longer we wait, the more time we give Phillip to try and cover himself."

"Yes . . . Phillip could do that." His words had seemed more for himself. Then: "Listen, John, stall Gregory. Let me talk to Rome. God, John, your first allegiance must be with the Church." He'd made his last words almost a question.

"Call Rome, Brian. Tell them their little spy has delivered." He tortured the skin at the sides of his face again. If Brian was a mystery, he, John, was just as much a puzzle to himself. What would he do if Rome balked? Gregory really had nothing solid without the discs. *Control.* Goddammit, control was what he wanted. Why was it so hard?

And then the thing that had really been eating at him gnawed again at his insides.

He could still see Alex walking stiffly out of Frank's apartment. Her bright hair swishing against her back as she moved out of the door. Then the staccato click of her heels on the concrete steps, and after, the sound of a car engine starting and moving away.

Please, Father Leighton, I think I've heard all that I need to hear from you. Everything is perfectly clear. He heard her words again. Words that his dream Alex would never have spoken. But his dream Alex didn't exist. Only the Alex standing in Frank's apartment was real. And her words real. The same words. Always.

Everything is perfectly clear....

No! Everything was not perfectly clear. He hadn't used her as she thought. If only he could tell her that. Make her listen. Make her believe...

He made himself put his hands down. It was useless. He could never make her understand what he'd done. It was out of his hands. When it came to Alex, he had no control. No control at all.

Brian Donovan sat stiffly in Archbishop Mantini's office. He glanced at the clock. Not yet noon in the District, but already evening in Rome. He'd been sitting for over half an hour now, his triumph turning sour as he listened to Mantini on the phone.

"Capisco."

I understand. He translated Mantini's heavy Italian. Well, he understood, too. It might be a long time since his student days in Rome, but he remembered enough of the language. And it was apparent even from only half the conversation that the Vatican was hedging. Cold feet even now.

"Sì, Eminenza." The archbishop was nodding, smiling in preparation of hanging up. He had to sit on his hands to keep himself from jumping up, tearing the receiver from the sallow, sausage fingers. Fools!

"Arrivedérci, Eminenza." Too late. The receiver was in its cradle. Mantini paused, turned.

"Fools!" He said it out loud now. "Idiots!"

Mantini scowled. "Monsignor Donovan, where is your respect? His Holiness..."

"Don't start with that crap! I've given them exactly what they wanted—Phillip Caméliere's head. And now it seems they don't know what to do with it."

"It's a very delicate situation, Monsignor. Surely you understand that. The Cardinal's connection with *la mafia* is very unwelcome surprise. And your Father Leighton's unfo tunate involvement with this reporter. . . Very delicate. Very delicate, indeed."

"They do want him exposed, don't they?"

Mantini's eyes narrowed. "That was never the plan, Monsignor Donovan. Public exposure. A scandal to the Church. The idea was to force him out."

"The plan was blackmail. Why not just say it? *Riccato*."

"Blackmail, then." Mantini ignored the Italian. "Call it whatever you wish, but do not be stupid, Monsignor Donovan. You are too impatient. His Holiness needs time to consider."

Brian laughed.

The Pro-Nuncio looked almost alarmed. As if he might be locked in his office with a lunatic. "What is this laughing?"

"I'm remembering something John Leighton said. About Rome . . . and time."

Mantini shrugged, made some move with his hands. The gestures of a peasant. "Go, Monsignor Donovan. Tell your Father Leighton to wait. I will call you when there is some decision." He turned away. A dismissal.

Brian left the office without a sound, but his heels played an angry rat-a-tat-tat down the hard marble floor of the hallway. The old nun materialized to let him out.

Saturday. Nearly noon now. The traffic was heavy enough, but lighter than on weekdays. He wanted to get to his office in Caldwell Hall, to the bottle of Glenfiddich he kept in the bottom drawer. Saturday. Good. No interference from Mattie.

His anger had settled to a tight cold knot as he banged past her desk and into his office.

"Hello, Brian." Phillip looked up.

He didn't answer. Just slowed himself down. Walked to his chair and pulled out the bottle and two glasses.

"Why, Brian?" Phillip accepted the drink.

He looked down into the rich amber liquid in his own glass. Took a swallow. Savored it. "Revenge," he said finally. "What else?"

"Revenge, Brian? For what?" Phillip gave a good imitation of incomprehension. "Forgive me if I'm being stupid, but I thought we had something of a partnership. I thought you wanted . . ."

Brian set his glass down hard. "Did you think I'd never find out about the list for Rome, Phillip? That it was you who removed my name?"

"Ah, of course, Mantini. Our dear papal legate told you that."

"I would have made a good bishop, Phillip."

"Of course you would. And you can *be* a bishop. A cardinal, if that's what you want. In the new American Church, Brian. Our church. But what a waste."

"Don't play your fucking games with me, Cardinal Camélière. They don't work anymore."

"Dammit, Brian." Phillip shoved his own glass on to the desk now, working up just the right mix of anger and regret. "I thought you understood that it's not bishops and cardinals that make a church work. It's the priest in the parishes, and teachers like you, who wield the real power. That's always been the great secret, Brian. That it's not the Roman Curia or cardinals and bishops, but men like you who create the real theology, the real essence of our faith.

"That damned list . . ." Phillip shook his head. "The Church didn't need another bishop at the expense of a gifted priest who could make a real difference."

For a moment he sat just looking at Phillip Camélière. He could almost believe it was true. The sad thing was that it didn't matter. Not any longer. "Get out of here, Phillip," he said. "I need to think."

He watched the Cardinal finish his drink, then stand up to go. Wisely Phillip didn't say anything now. Didn't even smile. Careful to give no sign that he might take an old friend—or an old enemy—for granted.

He didn't say any more himself, just watched till Phillip had closed the door. Then he did smile, slowly, and with enormous satisfaction. He looked around at the crammed inadequate shelving, the drab institutional carpet. Real power? He almost laughed. But for once at least, his old desk chair had become the catbird seat. For a change it was Brian Donovan in control. Brian Donovan who controlled John

Leighton and the discs—the discs without which neither Rome nor Frank Gregory would have much of a case. And Phillip Camélière knew it.

He poured himself another scotch and leaned back into the worn leather padding. He wondered which way he'd decide to go. Whether Phillip or Rome could cut the better offer.

Richard had heard Phillip's last question. But he hadn't given any kind of answer. Instead he sat very rigid in the chair staring at his hands resting in his lap. Something like bile forced its way up into his mouth.

"Richard, I asked you a question. Do you know who might have taken those photographs of you in the Mall?"

He looked up. "Yes, Phillip. I know who had those photographs taken."

"Can you handle it?"

"Yes, I can handle it."

"Good."

"What about Frank Gregory?" It was his first question since he'd sat down in Phillip's office.

"From what Alex tells me, he hasn't got much without the discs. And I'm taking care of that. The important thing is that we contain the situation, Richard. And I think if we each hold up our end, we'll be able to get through this. What about your people?"

"There's no drop planned any time soon."

"Good. That should give us some time. Of course, our arrangement can't possibly continue now. But we'll deal with that once we get over this hump. Richard, you don't think—"

"No, Phillip, the boys had nothing to do with what's happened. Why would they? No, this is something else, something personal. . . ." His words trailed off, and he watched Phillip's eyes on him. "I said I would take care of it, Phillip."

"I know that, Richard. I trust you." And the gray eyes smiled at him.

●   ●   ●

"Stop it, Richard. You're hurting me."

"I thought you liked it when it hurt?"

"I don't like *this*." Carla tried to twist away from the sharpness of his teeth on her skin, but he was holding on to her with both hands, and the cords that bound her pulled tight. His coming today had been completely unexpected, and she was never comfortable with surprises from Richard. She was sorry now she'd let him tie her up.

He shifted upward, straddling her suddenly, the dead weight of his entry pulling on the muscles of her arms. In another moment he was on his knees, rocking, his thumbs pressing into her nipples the way she liked. He moved hard, almost violently against her, his breath rasping through the white line of his teeth.

She closed her eyes tightly, giving in, letting her shoulders fall back. Her fingers closed hard on the ropes, nails digging into her palms. She *did* like the pain. Maybe she even liked the fear, too. She eased her breath out slowly now, letting her body go limp. Making him work for it. Making him force the pleasure on her.

When it came, it ripped through her like a knife. Clean and complete, as if the something fucking her had been big and impersonal. It took a moment before she felt the drag of Richard's weight against her arms.

"Untie me, Richard."

He rolled away from her, curled like a fetus. She could see nothing but his back, the flesh stretched tight across the sharp ladder of his spine.

"Please, Richard."

He moved again, bounding in a single motion from the edge of the bed. He pulled on his briefs and walked to the bedpost.

"I hate all this shit."

He stood, staring at the curtains, the gauze and lace that canopied the bed. Impatient, she tugged against the cords, straightening her fingers, pulling, till her hands slipped free of the loops.

He watched her now, as if making some decision. Then he turned and went to pour a glass of scotch.

Bastard! She wiggled down to the bottom of the bed. Began untying her foot herself.

"I guess *your* bedroom looks like an operating room, huh, Richard?" She had decided not to let the crack about the curtains go. "Your bedroom and *Lindsey's*." The cord fell away, and she massaged her ankle. looking up to watch his profile.

He emptied the glass before he turned to her. Still he didn't speak.

She shrugged. "I'm curious. You're waiting on my doorstep when I come home today. There's been no drop. What's the matter, Richard, won't your wife give it to you? No little Richards, are there? Or would Lindsey have to get an abortion, too?"

She had gone too far. He was angry now. Coming toward her. She didn't move a muscle.

"Shut up, Carla."

"Why? Because you don't want me talking about *Lindsey*?" She emphasized the name.

"That's right." He stopped abruptly. As if even these few words had been too much. As if even to talk to her of his precious wife was some kind of desecration. Oh, his fucking his brains out behind her back was okay, but speaking her name to his whore . . .

"You think you're so goddamn high and mighty, don't you, Senator Darrington?" She wasn't facing him anymore. She'd begun to untie her other foot. "But one of these days, maybe one day soon, you're going to get yours!"

She'd expected him to turn away from her again, refill his glass from the bottle. But he pounced on the words almost as if he'd been waiting for them.

"And what does that mean, Carla?"

She looked up to see him still watching her.

"Nothing."

She knew she had made a mistake. She'd never backed off that quickly. She looked away from him, her eyes sliding instinctively toward the door. She blinked back the fear. She was being stupid. He couldn't really suspect anything. She forced herself to meet his eyes again. "Help me with this,

Richard. I'm about to break a nail." She added the normal edge of anger.

"I want to know exactly what you meant by that, Carla. *You'll get yours*. That is what you said, isn't it?"

She pulled clumsily at the cord. "I don't know." She pushed the anger up another notch. "I say stuff like that all the time. I told you it didn't mean anything." She gave up on the knot, started working to slip her heel through the loop around her ankle.

The slap took her completely off guard.

"What in the shit was that for, Richard? Are you crazy?" Now she really was mad. She tried to get up, to get off the bed, but her foot was still bound. His hands were coming for her again. She put her arms up to protect her face.

"Tell me what you meant. Tell me, Carla!"

He was screaming at her now. And she was screaming, too. Incoherent things even she didn't understand. He'd never been like this before. So abruptly out of control. She was really frightened.

She pulled away hard, and the cord was finally over her foot. She was scrambling backward, but his hands were still coming at her. Harder now. She tried to keep him from hitting her breasts.

"Tell me, Carla! Tell me about the pictures."

The pictures. For an instant she let her hands drop, and his fist connected with her face. She felt the contact, felt herself lifted upward by the force. Then a sound, like a loud crack.

The last thing she heard was her own name. Far away. *Carla*.

He bent down to where she had fallen, her face a sickening ashen color against the nest of dark hair. He leaned forward, not touching her. He couldn't see any blood, but the side of her head, which had hit the table's edge, was hidden from him. His first thought was that this was stupid. People only died like this in movies.

He put his face near her mouth. The lips were dead white, yet she still seemed to be breathing. Shallow and ragged, but he could feel the movement of the air faintly against his cheek. A kind of automatic relief swept over him. He stood up and went for the phone.

The sound of the dial tone sobered him. He put the receiver down. He wasn't thinking rationally. This was real. Carla was dead... or near dead. He had to get out.

He picked up his glass and Carla's and found his way to the kitchen. It was small and neat. It looked unused. He washed the glasses and put them in the cupboard. He couldn't find rubber gloves, so he handled them with a dishcloth.

There was a spray bottle of cleaner and a plastic garbage bag under the sink. He took them and the vacuum into the hall. As often as he'd come here to this apartment, he'd spent time mostly in the bedroom and the bath. Still he couldn't take chances. He'd have to be thorough, especially with the smooth surfaces. Get all of his fingerprints. He'd go through every room with the spray and follow with the vacuum.

First the bedroom.

The wastepaper basket with the used condom he emptied into the plastic sack, the vacuum cleaner bag would go in, too, when he was finished. He bent down, not quite dropping to his knees, and lowered his face to Carla's. No breath at all now. No one alive to identify him.

He went to the bed and bundled the linens together, throwing them into the bag. Later he'd have to dump it, and his clothes. Get rid of any fiber evidence. Her address book was on the table next to the phone. He'd take care of that. But what else? A datebook or diary?

There was nothing but makeup in the dressing table. He moved to the chest. The top drawer held lingerie. He felt along the bottom and pulled up the scented lining. Here was something... An envelope. Photos.

So he'd been right. It had been Carla who'd set it up. He couldn't worry about why she'd done that now. Or stop to consider why he'd been so stupid, meeting her like that in the open. He stood for a moment with everything blanked out. Rigid. Shaking. Angry. Incredibly angry that anything like this could be happening.

One last time he stared at Carla. He was glad the lying

cunt was dead. He stuffed the photographs back into the envelope. He had to think this through. But later. After he'd finished here.

Five-forty-five. Only fifteen minutes till the local newscast. He'd showered a second time as soon as he'd gotten home and vacuumed out the car, and it felt good to relax in the terry robe before he had to dress for tonight's reception.

He glanced briefly at his watch. Still plenty of time. He hadn't had any lunch. Maybe he should go ahead and fix himself something to eat. There was roast beef in the refrigerator, Lindsey had said, and the white bread he preferred for sandwiches. He liked it toasted really crisp and the crusts trimmed, but it never tasted as good when he had to do it himself. And Lindsey was busy getting ready.

He poured himself a large scotch and went to sit in his chair. Knocking the drink back neatly, he set the glass down on a coaster. He had to think about Carla.

There had been no pickup scheduled today, no reason for anyone to think he'd ever been there this afternoon in her apartment. The Lambrucis would be angry about the inconvenience of Carla's death, but they'd blame it on one of her other playmates. They'd be no more likely than the police to suspect the truth.

Fucked-up stupid bitch. Why had she made him so angry? He hadn't really meant to kill her. He'd needed her to tell him just how far this thing had gone. How much Frank Gregory knew. Dammit! He'd been careless. But who could have figured Carla Fiorelli to set him up like that and double-cross the Lambrucis?

Still, everything might be okay now. Better this way really. The Lambrucis need never know that anything had gone wrong with the operation. Phillip seemed to think Frank Gregory had nothing much on him beyond the photographs. And they *were* nothing. He knew that now. Just pictures of him and some blonde in sunglasses. She could be anyone, a secretary bringing him papers. And now that Carla couldn't talk...

Nearly six o'clock. He picked up the controller and turned on the set. The first segments were national. After the break they switched to local news. As he had expected, there was nothing.

Later he poured another drink and went to the bedroom to dress. He had decided not to think about it any more tonight. He tucked in his shirttail and went to the mirror to knot his tie. The small pattern of the silk looked good against the navy pinstripes of the shirt. He put on his coat and brushed his fingers through his hair. He was fine. Perfect. He glanced down again at his watch. Almost time to go. He was glad he hadn't fixed the roast-beef sandwiches, there'd be plenty to eat at the White House.

CHAPTER THIRTY

Frank groaned and turned his face into the pillow. Might as well get up, he couldn't sleep. He'd been half-awake since 6:30. And dreaming or awake, it didn't really matter. His brain would still be occupied with Alex, with Alex and this whole damn mess. He hadn't thought of anything else since Friday.

He sat up and pushed the pillow behind his back, reaching for his cigarettes on the bedside table. What he wanted was to see her. That was the worst part, this absolute hunger to see Alex. Talk to her. Explain what was unexplainable. *Shit*.

The phone rang.

"Yeah." He balanced the receiver between his shoulder and cheek. Lit a cigarette.

"Frank, this is Jano."

"What's up? I haven't been able to get in touch with Carla."

A heartbeat went by.

"Carla's dead."

"Oh, shit. How?"

"Somebody beat her up. In her apartment. Girlfriend with a key found her. It took them a while to call us."

"Where are you now?"

"I'm here. In D.C. Her mama said she couldn't do it . . . identify the body."

"God . . . I'm sorry, Jano."

"Yeah. I know. You think it was the Lambrucis? You figure they found out what she was doing?"

"I don't know. She said she was being careful. . . . What do the cops say?"

Jano's skeptical grunt came through clearly. "They don't know shit. Probably don't care. They ain't so completely stupid they don't know she's connected. Probably figure it's none of their business."

He didn't answer. He was thinking.

"Frank?" Jano's voice cut in.

"Uh-huh."

"You gonna be able to do anything? I mean . . . I don't know exactly what Carla gave you 'cept for those pictures I took, but are you gonna be able to do what she wanted?"

"I think so, Jano, but it's complicated. I guess you're going to have to trust me."

"I do, Frank. So did Carla. She liked you, y'know. . . ." The words trailed off.

"Yeah. Look, Jano. Better not call again. I'll keep in touch. Let you know what's happening through Alfie. Okay?"

"Okay, Frank."

He sat there listening for the click. Put the receiver down.

What in the fuck had happened? He'd tried to get Carla since Friday night to warn her that his investigation had been uncovered. He'd been worried when he couldn't reach her, but not that worried. He had hoped she wasn't in any immediate danger. Sure, Alex had seen the photos. And he knew she'd tell her uncle, who would tell Richard Darrington. But he'd been careful not to let on that the woman in the photos was his informant. Still, Darrington might have been smart enough to put two and two together. And if he did . . .

His cigarette hung out over the edge of the table where he'd put it. It had burned down to the filter. He picked it up now, trailing ashes, and crushed it into last night's coffee. He reached for a fresh pack and his matches. Another quick smoke, and he'd get dressed. No sense sitting here trying to find away around the guilt. Carla was dead, and that changed things. Leighton's evidence was absolutely crucial now. Unless there was something the police knew. He'd better get down to the station and see if he could corner Gus.

Gus Shapiro was the best damn policeman Frank ever met. Of course, Detective Gustave Shapiro of the Homicide Division was something of a dinosaur. Though barely thirty, Gus was from the old school of criminal investigation. Thought like the cops from the good old days. Before Miranda. Before the liberals got hold of the American system of justice and fucked it over. Yet Frank suspected that Gus was less like the old dicks than he was willing to admit. Even with the trash he found on the street, Gus played it straight.

Gus was laughing at him now. The pockmarks on his face looking more like dimples than the ravages of teenage acne. He sat with his legs crossed on top of his desk, grinding on a thick unlit cigar.

"Mother asks about you all of the time, Gregory. Wants to know why you haven't been by to supper. She's worried that you've grown too high-class for her Jewish cooking."

"Tell Zellie I'll be by before too long."

"Just the other day she was saying maybe Frank has found himself some nice gentile girl who's cooking for him, so he doesn't come by anymore."

"No girl. Just busting my butt with work. Besides, I'm going to marry Zellie. She knows that."

"I'll remind her. So let me guess why you're here, Gregory. The broad that was iced in her apartment Saturday?"

He couldn't help the smile. Gus was too smart for him. "Yeah."

Another smile. Shapiro liked to play cagey. Make him worm information out of him.

"Thought you might have something for me, Gus."

"Can't even give you an ID."

"I've got a name, Gus."

"Oh."

"Yeah. Carla Fiorelli. But of course you already knew that." Another smile. And this time Gus smiled back.

"You looking for a story, Frank? Think this is something big?"

"Like sniffing pussy, Gus. I know when I've got something good." He was keeping it light, but he knew he couldn't really fool Shapiro. "So why was she killed?"

Gus shrugged his broad shoulders. "No motive. Nothing valuable seems to be missing. So robbery's probably out."

"Drugs?"

"Always a possibility. But I don't think so. Maybe . . ."

"Yeah . . ." He'd heard it, the tiny wheels in Gus's brain grinding. His friend lumbered forward, anchoring his hammy forearms in front of him.

"Did'ya know, Miss Fiorelli was once married to one of the Lambruci clan, Gregory?"

"I'd heard something about that."

"I'll just bet you have." Gus unplugged the overworked cigar and laughed. "Maybe I should be asking the questions."

"Come on, Gus. Give me a break. So who did her in?"

"You tell me, Gregory." The cigar had gone back between his teeth.

"Somebody in the family?"

"Maybe. But that doesn't feel right. Maybe it was one of those crimes of passion. A boyfriend who goes crazy."

"What kind of physical evidence?"

"Oh, that's the good part. The place was as clean as a whistle. Like maybe the cleaning woman had been in to tidy up after the murder. Even the bed was stripped."

"No prints?"

"No prints. Not even Fiorelli's."

"What about the autopsy?"

"Just got a preliminary report. But it's what you'd expect to find when a broad's gotten the shit beaten out of her. Bruises and cuts about the face and chest. Maybe a fractured jaw. Some bruising on the forearms. Easy to explain. Dames always raise their arms to protect their faces. Especially a pretty one like this. Head wound was the probable cause of death. Hit her head against the edge of a table. So maybe we're looking at manslaughter instead of first-degree."

"No semen?"

"If she screwed her killer, he used a rubber. And that he probably flushed down the toilet. Like I said, the place was as clean as a whistle."

"So what we got here is a body with no motive and no suspect."

"You got that one right, Gregory. Oh, one more thing." The cigar had finally gone into an ashtray. "We think she might've been tied up."

"Kinky."

"Yeah, real kinky." Gus gazed out the glass window of his office, his eyes straying to a couple of detectives standing over an old lady seated at one of the desks. "Sorry, there's nothing else I can give you, Frank." His focus returned and he leaned back in his chair once more. "You know, I get stomach problems sometimes. Doc said I got an ulcer. Zellie would die if she thought it was her cooking. But I say the doc is wrong."

"How's that, Gus?" He knew what was coming. But he played dumb and waited.

"You know what I mean, Gregory. You got the same problem. You see something. Something you supposed to see. But no matter what your eyes tell you, it doesn't look right. Doesn't feel right. It's like maybe somebody's pulling a con on you. And the old stomach starts talking to you. Talking real loud. Won't give you no peace. Until you think maybe you got an ulcer. But you know that ain't right."

He stared at Gus for a moment. The small black eyes shone like agates under the fluorescent lights in the office. Then the rumpled face broke into a wide grin.

"But it's like I said before, we got nothing, Frank. This case is going nowhere fast. Dead end."

There was a rap at the door. Morgan, one of the two detectives who'd been questioning the old woman popped his head in.

"Sorry, Gus, but you said you wanted to know if the old lady made a definite ID. Well, Gus, the sweet little grandma came through. Saw him right through her picture window from across the street. We got him, Gus. Got our killer. And drop your drawers, buddy, because you're gonna shit when you hear who she's fingered."

•   •   •

"Richard Darrington."

Gus's jaw went slack and the unlit cigar almost fell from his mouth. He rescued the stogie with a quick pawlike move and closed the door behind him.

"Morgan just told you the old lady fingered Richard Darrington," he said. He watched as the detective slumped back into his chair and shuffled around for matches.

"Fuck. Gotta light, Gregory."

"Sure, Gus." And he leaned over the rubble on the desk and lit the cigar.

Shapiro pumped hard on the cigar, his eyes finally settling on him through the thick ring of smoke. "You know something, Gregory, you could really piss me off if I didn't like you so much."

"Yeah, I know. I kinda have that effect on a lot of people. So what else did the old lady have to say?"

Gus had relaxed back in his chair. "Seems she's been watching Fiorelli and Darrington for some time now. She figured Fiorelli for a hooker, and Darrington one of her customers. Had Darrington pegged for a politician all along, but couldn't put a name to the face till today. Until we showed her some photographs. Says she once saw the good senator walking around Fiorelli's living room buck-naked." He laughed. "Said Darrington had a good body."

"She saw him the day Fiorelli was killed?"

"Yeah. Can put him at Fiorelli's at the time of her death. Left carrying a garbage bag." He'd hooked the cigar back between his lips and folded his arms across his chest. "So, Gregory..."

"So what, Gus?"

"Don't jack me around, Frank." He'd jerked forward and made his hands into thick fists on top of his desk.

"So I had a contact."

"Like who was the contact, Gregory?"

He studied Gus's face for a moment. "Carla Fiorelli."

The fists came undone and Gus eased back into his seat. The flat black eyes watched him.

"She came to me, Shapiro. Had some kind of an ax to grind. Put me onto a laundering operation involving Darrington. He must have gotten wise to what she was up to."

"A Lambruci operation."

"Yeah, a Lambruci operation. Carla passed the money to Darrington, who passed it off to a third party."

"And you know who this third party is?"

"I might."

"Fuck it, Gregory."

"Okay, I know. But that doesn't mean I'm telling."

"I can get your ass on this, Gregory, and you know it."

"Yeah, I know Gus. But you won't." He risked a smile.

"Alright. So talk."

"This third party is somebody real important, Gus."

"As big as Darrington?"

"As big as Darrington."

"Another Capital Hill asshole."

"No, Gus. A Roman Catholic Church asshole."

Gus rubbed a hand across his belly.

"Getting stomach cramps, Gus."

"Yeah, and you're giving 'em to me, Gregory."

"Sorry, Gus. But listen, I know you want to nail Darrington for the Fiorelli murder. But we can get all the bastards if you hold off. All I need is a couple of days. Then I deliver some real primo evidence tying Darrington and this third party to the Lambrucis. You'll have your motive for murder then, Gus. Who knows, maybe we get the Lambrucis, too."

The cigar had gone out, but Shapiro was still working the stump between his teeth. He unplugged it. "And you get one helluva story, right, Frank?"

"Right, Gus."

Johnny Lambruci put down the receiver and turned around. He was a startlingly handsome man with unusually delicate hands. He now drew one of those hands through the graying dark hair at his temple.

"That was Morgan. It seems they've just made an ID on Carla's killer."

"Yeah. That was fast." Paolo watched his brother. Johnny always made him nervous when he fooled with his hair.

"Maybe."

"So you gonna make me guess?"

Johnny grinned, showing off perfectly even white teeth. It wasn't a particularly friendly smile. "Richard Darrington."

"That son of a bitch. Why the fuck he kill her?"

"Now, Paolo, how would I know that." He moved his hand through his hair again. "She was a cunt."

"Johnny, don't talk about the dead like that. Carla was all right."

"A good piece of ass, Paolo?"

"Johnny, I never—"

"Cut the crap, Paolo. I know you fucked Fiorelli."

Paolo looked away. He hated it when Johnny treated him like this. Like he wasn't supposed to do anything without asking him first. Like he was some dumb kid.

"Forget it, Paolo. Darrington's our concern now."

"You think maybe he's gonna talk, Johnny."

"Maybe."

"We don't want that to happen, Johnny."

"No, Paolo. We don't want that to happen." He stood behind his desk now, running his hands over the fine polished surface. "Get Gambini on the phone. Tell him I've got a job for him."

CHAPTER THIRTY-ONE

"You want coffee or something?" John still stood, looking over to where Frank Gregory sat on the edge of his sofa. The reporter's eyes looked red and swollen, like he'd had trouble sleeping, too.

"No, nothing." Frank shook his head. "But I could use an ashtray." He made a motion with the burned-down cigarette in his hand.

"Sure . . . I'm sorry. Let me find you something." He headed toward the kitchen.

"We've got to get this settled." Frank was speaking again as soon as he came back into the room. "Like I told you yesterday on the phone. I've talked to the police. The eyewitness has Darrington nailed to a murder charge, but you and I both know Camélière's got to be scrambling like hell to pull the cover on his end."

"I called my superior after I talked to you last night."

"And?"

"He said he was still waiting on Rome."

Frank made a sound. "You told him the stakes had gone up? That a woman's been murdered?"

"No, things are already so complicated. I was hoping I wouldn't have to. . . . Did the senator kill her because he found out?"

"I don't know." Frank cut him off. "Probably. Either way

she's dead. . . . Come on, John, you going to stop shitting around and give me those discs?"

It was pretty much the same question he'd been asking himself since talking to Brian last night, when he'd begun to suspect that it wasn't Rome alone now that was stalling. For a few seconds longer he returned Frank Gregory's stare.

"Just give me a little more time, Frank." It was not till he heard himself saying the words that he knew he'd made a decision. "Just give me till tonight at the latest. There are still a couple things I need to do."

The chapel of the Immaculate Conception was dark and quiet now. Everyone who'd come to the early-morning Mass had gone, and John knelt alone, his hands knotted in prayer. But he wasn't praying. He shifted his weight off his knees and waited for Brian Donovan to change out of his vestments and come out of the sacristy.

He heard the click of a cabinet door. Then Donovan's tall form walking out slowly, genuflecting before the altar. Brian spotted him almost immediately as he turned.

"John . . ." His name sounded very loud in the hush of the small chapel.

He nodded and watched Donovan move down the sanctuary steps to the pew where he was kneeling.

"John, I didn't know you were here." These words seemed less loud to him.

"I came to Mass." It was all he said, and he saw that Donovan now moved to kneel beside him. He watched his old teacher cross himself.

After a moment: "You want to talk?" Donovan had turned to look at him.

"I can't wait."

"What?"

"I'm giving the discs to Gregory. A woman is dead."

"Dead . . . I don't understand. Last night when we spoke . . ."

"I know. But everything's changed now. What Rome wants doesn't matter anymore."

"I see." And he watched Donovan slump back against the pew.

"What I don't understand is why you're not happy about all of this, Brian. I should think you'd be very pleased that Phillip is finally getting what's coming to him."

Donovan shifted his expression; his clear blue eyes seemed larger beneath the shaggy arched brows. But he didn't say anything.

"This never really had anything to do with Rome, did it, Brian? It was always something personal, wasn't it, this little war against Phillip Camélière?"

Again the leprechaun face changed; this time a slow smile spread across the fine features. "Yes, John, it was something personal."

John watched the smile fade, grow ugly. "Just one more thing, Brian. Before I give what I have to Gregory, I'm going to see the Cardinal. Call it Confession, Monsignor Donovan, but I have to talk to Phillip Camélière."

He was hurting her. But she kept quiet, letting him thrust hard and quick. She closed her eyes, until he finally convulsed, letting out a single cry.

"Oh, my God, Lindsey, I'm sorry."

And she opened her eyes and saw that he was looking down at her, still inside of her, still clutching tightly against her wrists.

"Phillip, it's okay." And she felt his hands loosen and move to her face.

"Baby, I'm so sorry. Did I hurt you?" He was easing his body off, pulling out of her.

"No, Phillip, you didn't hurt me." She turned now to look down at him lying next to her. She moved her hand across his face, wiping the sweat from his forehead, smoothing his dark hair back.

"I don't know what happened. I . . ."

"Shhh," and she kissed him softly on his mouth.

He was looking at her. "I love you so much."

"I know, Phillip."

"Do you, Lindsey?"

"Yes." And she kissed him again. This time longer. "Phillip" —she watched his eyes—"is there something wrong?"

He sat up now and pulled at the sheet, wiping his face with the edge. "No, Lindsey, nothing's wrong. Just the usual." He turned and looked back at her over his shoulder. "What did you do with your copy of the papers on the house?"

He'd changed the subject. "I still have it."

"Well, you need to get it to the bank. Put it in a safe-deposit box."

"I will. I promise."

"Well, do it tomorrow. It needs to be in a safe place where you can get to it if something happens."

"If what happens, Phillip?" He had relaxed back on the bed and she bent over, watching him.

"Nothing's going to happen, Lindsey. I just want to make sure that you have the house, that's all."

He was staring ahead. "Phillip, look at me. Tell me nothing's wrong. Tell me everything's all right."

His eyes found hers, this time gray and clear and smiling. "Everything's just fine, my darling."

And she felt his mouth close on hers, hard and hungry. And she gave in to his kiss, trying to ignore the fear that had come inside of her, trying to forgive him for the lie.

It had been hot walking from his car, but it was cool here in St. Matthew's. And quiet, but for the murmur from one small party of tourists left over from the 12:10 Mass. John looked at his watch as he passed from the lobby into the St. Francis Chapel. He was early, but he wished the Cardinal would come. He wanted to get this thing over.

Inside the chapel, he took a seat in one of the small pews. *Hic Locus Sanctus est;* he read the inscription above the altar niche. "This is a Holy Place." A fresco of the crucified Christ with St. Francis and St. Claire beneath the outstretched arms of the cross filled the arch below. Francis and Claire. Brother Sun and Sister Moon. Two of the Church's most interesting mystics. His eyes strayed again to his watch. An unconscious gesture. He didn't even see the numerals.

He knelt and tried to pray.

"Good afternoon, John."

Phillip Camélière had come out of the chamber on his left, the official burial crypt for the archbishops of the diocese. He had been there all along, John realized, watching him, perhaps. But what startled him more was seeing the Cardinal in light casual slacks and a shirt. Subconsciously he'd been expecting him in the full dress of his office.

He remembered he was still kneeling, stood, and moved out a little from the pew. "Hello, Your Eminence," he said finally.

"You wanted to speak with me, John." He didn't smile but the words were still perfectly natural.

"I suppose you've talked to Alex?"

The Cardinal had been looking for a moment toward the altar, but he turned back. There was something now beyond mere politeness in his eyes. But it wasn't anger.

"You mean, of course, since Friday?"

"Yes," he said, "since Friday night."

"If you're asking, John, whether Alexandra has shared with me what you and Frank Gregory told her, the answer is yes."

John forced himself not to look down. "I called . . . asked for this meeting, because I wanted you to know . . . wanted to tell you myself, that I'm going to turn over the discs to Frank Gregory. Today. I'm not waiting for Rome."

"I see." There had been only the briefest hesitation. "And have you let Brian Donovan in on this decision?"

The way the Cardinal said it told him he'd been right in his suspicions. Brian had been bargaining behind Rome's back. "Monsignor Donovan knows," he said. "I went to see him right after I called you this morning."

The Cardinal's response was to laugh. The sound seemed painfully loud against the hard marble. "I wish I could have been there," he said. "But I am surprised, John, that you would consider acting without Vatican approval. I thought that loyalty to Rome was why you were in on this thing in the first place. The Archangel, isn't it? The savior of the Church?"

"Rome isn't the Church." He kept his own voice even. "And anyway I'm not acting for the Church now. This is something I have to do myself. . . . Why?" The word had slipped out. He'd promised himself before he came that he wouldn't ask.

"Why?"

"Why would you do it? Get involved in something like this?"

"Theoretically?"

"All right, theoretically then." Phillip Camélière wasn't admitting to anything.

"Not for my own profit, John." The Cardinal was still watching him closely. "Nothing in it for me personally."

"I know that. I've been over the records enough times. But what difference . . . ?"

"You could call it a tithe on sin, Father Leighton. Diverting dirty money into charities and halfway houses. Surely you can appreciate the irony."

"Irony?" The word was angry. "A woman is dead."

"What woman?"

The surprise was real. So Phillip Camélière knew nothing about Carla Fiorelli.

"What woman, Father Leighton?"

"You'd better ask the senator." He clipped it short. He hadn't come for this. "I've let you know what I plan to do," he said. "I have to go now."

"All right"—the Cardinal didn't press—"but there's something I'd like to say to you first, John. Perhaps I understand why you feel you have to do this. But that doesn't change certain things.

"You've told us all to go to hell, haven't you? Me. Brian. Even Pope Stephen. Well, I can't act solely for myself, as you can. I haven't had that luxury for years. And whatever you might think of me, whatever exactly you think I might have done, I do believe in the New American Catholic Church. I can't allow anything, or anyone, to stand in the way of that.

"I'm a hard enemy, Father Leighton. A powerful enemy. And I'm going to have to fight you with everything I've got."

He smiled. Not the familiar half twist. But a strange smile that seemed to mock, not the listener, but the words.

John didn't say anything, didn't move, as the Cardinal came closer.

"Tony will have your things packed for you." He felt the Cardinal's hand resting on his shoulder. "Come get them whenever you like. . . . Good-bye, John." The hand fell away.

"Good-bye . . . Phillip."

It was the Cardinal who turned away first. He followed a moment later, pausing in the dim cathedral lobby to watch him disappearing, a tall silhouette against the fiery rectangle of the door.

Lindsey was out again somewhere in the Jaguar, Richard noted as he pulled the Lincoln into the small garage behind the town house. It was getting late, and he wondered what she had planned for their dinner. He hoped they wouldn't be going out. He'd about had it for the day. Sticking it out. Going through the motions. Committee meeting in the morning. Votes in the afternoon. Still weeks yet before the recess. But he'd hold tight to the routine, make it through.

And it was going to be all right, he thought, watching as the door lowered automatically, closing off the long rays from the sun. The accident with Carla had been the best thing really, not a mistake. Very little had surfaced in the news since Saturday—just another unsolved District murder. With Phillip taking care of things at his end, Frank Gregory would have nothing left but some meaningless photographs. He might make a guess about what had happened to Carla Fiorelli. But so what? He couldn't prove it. And the *Post* sure as hell wouldn't chance libel on his assumptions.

And the Lambrucis knew nothing. They hadn't even gotten in touch with him yet. Though he was sure they would soon, wanting to set him up with some new contact. That was the only problem. They wouldn't like it that Phillip was calling it quits on the operation. That part was going to take some explaining.

It was quiet in the house with Lindsey out. And dark. He

walked to the bedroom. Hung up his coat and tie. Unbuttoned his collar and cuffs. Lindsey's desk was a bit too small and feminine for his taste, but he didn't have the energy to walk to his study. He took the photographs out of his briefcase and threw them across the small leather desk pad. Sat down, and switched on the lamp.

He had to get rid of the damn pictures today. Tear them into little pieces and flush them down the toilet in the bathroom, like he'd flushed the pages of Carla's address book. The plastic bag with the sheets and everything he'd thrown into an anonymous dumpster, along with the clothes he'd worn that day. So the pictures were the last link, the only link to what had happened in Carla's apartment.

The lamplight glared off the glossy prints into his eyes, and as he reached up to adjust the brass shade, the starched edge of his cuff caught an envelope protruding from one of the pigeonholes. It fell on top of the photos, a long business envelope without an address. A wide flowing script, black against the stark white, spelled out *Lindsey*. He couldn't stop staring. He recognized the hand.

Inside was a legal document.

"In consideration of natural love and affection, I, Phillip Olivier Camélière, hereafter referred to as donor, do hereby give, bequeath, and donate the following described property unto Lindsey Mertons Darrington..."

He read through it quickly, his glance flying to the signature line. Phillip's name again. Why would Phillip Camélière be giving his wife a house? It didn't make sense. *In consideration of natural love and affection*. His eyes locked on the words. *In consideration of*...

"No!" He stood up abruptly, knocking over the chair. "No." His arm swept the desk. The papers and photographs littered the floor. The lamp cord came loose from its socket.

For a moment he couldn't see anything but the words, neon-lit in his mind. Then he moved automatically, stooping down in the darkness to clean up the mess he'd made. He gathered the pictures together. Folded the document back into its envelope. Righted the lamp on the desk. Carefully, as if it were something very difficult or dangerous, he plugged the cord into the socket. The light came on. He sat down, took the papers back out of the envelope. Forced himself to read the document through again, paying close attention now to the description, to the address of the property.

He stood up. He couldn't be tired anymore. Taking care of the photographs was only the first thing he had to do.

The house was a revelation. As he walked through room after room—slowly, methodically, seeing everything, touching nothing—Richard understood that the two of them had hidden from him more than their affair. The Lindsey and the Phillip who shared this place were creatures unrevealed to him. He was worse than an alien here. He was nonexistent.

On the bedside table next to a small portrait of a much-younger Phillip was a photograph he'd never seen—Lindsey in a simple green sweater, the thick waves of red hair sliding forward to frame her face. It was that red hair he'd fallen in love with first. That red hair against her milky-white shoulders.

A sudden image intruded—the first time he'd taken her to bed. She'd slipped out of her clothes so effortlessly that it took him by surprise, seeing her standing there in front of him, completely naked. Naked, except for the long bright red hair. He remembered he hadn't been able to breathe, looking at her like that, watching the fluorescent glow from the bath make a bubble of light around her body and that long red hair. . . .

"Richard!"

He turned to see her now in a white kimono, outlined in the bathroom doorway. Her eyes were wide, the irises almost yellow in the pale face. But the hair was bright, polished and gleaming from the brush and the dryer still whining in her hand.

"Richard," she said again, and this time it was almost a question.

He didn't say anything. There were no words. And he

started backing away. He heard the dryer hit the floor, hard
plastic on tile. And Lindsey was coming toward him.

"Richard, please. Wait."

Strangely she seemed to know what he intended, where he
was going, before he did. Seeing it in her eyes made it
real.

"Damn you!" he said. "Damn you both to hell."

She was moving toward the phone as he turned. Dialing
frantically.

"It won't do any good to call, Lindsey." His words were
surprisingly conversational now, even to his own ears. "One
way or another, I'm going to kill him."

*I know you're angry with me, Alex. I understand that
you're hurt. But, Alex, you've never shut me out like this
before. I need to see you, to talk to you. You know I
love y—*

She reached quickly to cut off the voice. The words were
so reasonable, so calm. She hated the words, the same
message he'd left on her phone for three days now.

Though nothing was different, she got dressed. Just jeans
and a shirt, but the first real clothes she'd had on since
Saturday. And lipstick for makeup. A slash of something
orange that looked like rust in the mirrored blank of her
face.

Once, in the garage, she stopped, her hand frozen with the
key in the lock of her car, for how long she didn't know. But
she went on. Got in. Turned over the ignition.

Something. The roar of the motor. Or something else, that
she couldn't hear or see, was making her afraid. The thought
was foolish, but compelling. The fear drove her. She was
going to the residence. She had to.

Richard was in his car now, and it made him feel better.
Driving fast in the big Lincoln down the half-deserted District streets. Driving fast with a purpose. He could feel the
precision of the big engine through the steering column with
each turn, could feel the easy acceleration through the floor
of the car right up into his groin. He pressed the button of

the radio. Some music. Some background music to match his driving tempo would make everything just about perfect.

He settled back into the thick cushion of his seat and watched the licks of black road ahead, the bright city lights throwing ghosts onto the dark tunneling expanse of concrete. The flashing yellow caution alerted him, but he had the right of way. He reached and adjusted the mirror. No one behind him. He was alone on the capital streets.

He glanced at a street sign. Fuck, he had gone too far. He should have made a left before this. He sliced onto a side street and circled the block. A red light stopped him on the corner. He looked into the mirror again. Someone was behind him. The light turned green.

He checked the digits of the clock, then his watch. It was still early. He had plenty time to do what he had to do. He pushed down the wide avenue and watched now for the turn he should have made. Just a couple of blocks more. He checked the mirror again. He still had company. He pressed down hard on the accelerator, and the twin eyes in the mirror receded.

Here, turn here. He twisted the wheel easily.

He would be calm, he told himself. Rational. Let him have his say. Let him try to work his way out of it. And he would try. Phillip was a master. He smiled to himself, thinking how he would almost enjoy watching Phillip pull out all of the stops. Oh, the man was good. But not this time. He held the trump card. He had the truth.

He checked the mirror again and frowned. Someone was still behind him. Shit, did he really expect to have the street all to himself? *Yes*. He turned at the next corner and watched the beams in the mirror follow him. He slowed, and saw the lights grow larger in the small horizontal of glass. Make quick turn at the next corner. That should do it.

He could feel his fingers knot around the wheel as he twisted the car around. His palms felt sweaty, and he reached down and rubbed one then another against the legs of his pants. He slammed his foot against the gas pedal, barreling forward down the narrow side street. He stopped, shouldering the curb, and waited. Nothing.

He checked the clock. A few minutes before nine. Still plenty of time. Wait just a few moments longer. He leaned back into the seat and listened. What was the name of that song? Something he liked. Something he hadn't heard in a very long time. "Green Dolphin Street"? Yes, that was it. Hardly anyone ever played "Green Dolphin Street" anymore. He looked up into the mirror. Empty. Everything was just fine. He'd been overreacting. He straightened up and shifted the car back into gear.

Slowly he moved out onto the street. Phillip would be at the residence by now. And it would be a nice drive. Maybe he would roll down the windows, let some air in. A warm breeze and the music . . . He checked the mirror again. He wasn't alone. He gunned the engine and watched the headlights match his speed. He slowed and waited for the car behind him.

A red light ahead. Good. He inched forward, stopped, waited for his tail to move in. The illumination from a street lamp sliced across the front of the car, throwing back light into the driver's seat. In the mirror he examined the face behind the wheel. A dark man stared back at him. A dark man with thick brows that met in the center of the forehead. A monkey's face. Where had he seen a face like that before?

The light changed to green, and he watched the monkey face break into a thick-lipped smile. A nasty, unfriendly smile. And suddenly he remembered.

He could make it. He hadn't gone too far. The Russell Building was less than a couple of miles from here. He'd just have to double back. He pressed the gas pedal hard.

A *voice*. Someone was talking. Vaguely he became conscious that the music had stopped and the radio announcer was speaking. He caught a familiar name. ". . . Fiorelli was the woman with reputed mob connections who was found dead in her Dupont Circle apartment last Saturday. Speculation is that an arrest warrant will be issued soon. . . ."

He killed the voice and reached over with one hand to open the glove compartment. He fumbled against a stack of papers, a flashlight. Then his fingers made contact with the cold reassuring metal of the barrel. In an instant the revolver rested comfortably on the seat beside him.

What it was he felt, Richard couldn't be sure. After all, feelings were not the usual commodities with which he dealt. Not his stock in trade, so to speak. He did understand on some level, however, that whatever it was he was feeling, was surprisingly tolerable. He moved away from the window in his office. His tail was still parked on the street below.

It was inconceivable, but he was having to wing it. Before the robot had always been so dependable, able to assess, readjust. Conform. But now the system was having to deal with incompatible data. And this only led him damnably back, back to the old question.

For most of his very young life he'd speculated that there might be a Richard Darrington behind the facade. A real person behind the robot. But in Vietnam he'd discovered the truth. The truth that there was in fact no Richard Darrington, just the robot.

Once in a while he questioned who it was that programmed the robot. Set the system into play. Might there indeed be a Richard Darrington, a self, outside of the machine? But such an inquiry only led to confusion, the confusion of the original question, and invariably he'd left such speculations alone.

Then Lindsey had come along, and he was forced once more to consider the possibility that he was real, that the robot was just a game he played with himself. That Richard Darrington was human after all. How else could someone like Lindsey love him?

But Lindsey didn't love him. That was clear, all too clear now. And if she didn't love him...

He looked around his office. At the pictures lining the walls. The thing that had passed for Richard Darrington had done all right. Had moved with the great and near great. Had almost achieved greatness itself. At least what was perceived as greatness.

He ran his hand over the surface of his desk. He'd never really been conscious of the wood, and now it struck him as something extraordinarily beautiful. Suddenly he wished he'd

had the instincts to have selected the desk himself. But he
hadn't. Like everything in his office, Lindsey had picked it
out. He'd hardly even been aware of desk's unique separateness.
The desk was simply a factor of his office. And like everything
else, part of a well-orchestrated whole. Suitable window
dressing for Senator Richard Darrington. But the wood . . . how
could he have missed the wood?

He opened the middle drawer and pulled out several
sheets of stationery. Ivory vellum, engraved with an official
letterhead. They would certainly guess why he'd chosen to do
what he was going to do. But he'd leave no room for doubt;
he'd put his final signature to it. He picked up his pen and
wrote a single sentence. Then carefully he folded the note
and placed it inside an envelope on his desk.

He got up then and walked over to the large painting on
the far wall. He took in the blurred edges of pale color for a
moment. Beautiful, like all of the things Lindsey had selected.
Reaching forward, he drew it back on its hinge. The safe
gleamed dully in the lamplight. Another of his secrets. He
worked the combination and pulled open the door. He stared
at the neat stack of tapes. Everything was on the tapes. Every
word he and Phillip Camélière had ever spoken. He heard
the soft clicking of the cases as his hand moved around them.
Everything . . . everything here.

He walked back to his desk and piled the tapes neatly next
to his confession. He could feel himself smile as he sat back
down into his chair.

Glinting brightly on the top of his desk, it was there where
he'd left it. Shiny in all its brand-new innocence. He'd never
fired it, except that one time to test it. Now he picked it up
and cradled its weight inside his palm. It felt very natural in
his hand. And it came to him, clear and even, that what he
was about to do was going to be a very simple, rather
economical act. After all, hadn't all of the Richard Darrington
programs been played? Wasn't it merely a matter now of
shutting down the system?

"Thank you, Tony. I'll call Lindsey. You go and be with
your friend tonight. It's been a rough couple of days."

"Is there—"

"No, Tony. I can manage. Good night. Sleep well." He watched his secretary, noticing that he looked thinner in the faded jeans and knit shirt. His eyes followed him until he disappeared out the door.

Lindsey. He had to call Lindsey. Tony had said she sounded upset. He wondered why she hadn't already gone back to the town house. God, he hoped it wasn't anything too serious. He switched off the overhead light. The soft glow from the lamp on the hall table caused his shadow to twist against the wall as he made his way up the stairs.

When he opened the door to his bedroom, he felt the cold air swell out over him. He rubbed his arms. He would open the French doors and warm things up a bit. Then he would have to go down and check the thermostat. Sometimes Mrs. Jordan overcompensated for his chronically warm nature.

He walked out onto the small balcony. The moon was almost full, and its phantom-pale face seemed a great mask mocking him. He smiled, unafraid of its mystery. Unafraid as he had been of all the mysteries that had come into his life.

The air was warm and took the unwelcome chill out of his bones. From somewhere inside the distant trees the sounds of the hot July night came floating up to him. And in a moment he was back on the bayou and pale white arms slipped around him. . . .

He shook his head and thought that there was something he had to do. *Call Lindsey.* He had to call Lindsey. He'd use the phone in his office and check on the thermostat while he was downstairs.

It was warmer on the first floor. And that surprised him—it should have been cooler. Something must be wrong.

He opened the double doors to his office. In an instant the clawing too-sweet scent hit him. Old, but not forgotten. He took in a single deep breath before he allowed the odor to recede back into memory. Then he walked over to his desk and sat. The wood felt warm against the palms of his hands, the smooth surface seeming to breathe beneath his fingers.

He reached and pressed the fluorescent desk light, picking up the receiver to dial Lindsey's number. A small shuffling noise . . .

He glanced up and saw her standing in the far corner of the room by an opened window. The moonlight made her flesh luminous, and he could see that she was holding on to something very tightly. Something sleek and shiny, glinting in her hand like the tiny silver fish she'd caught that day when they'd gone swimming in the bayou.

"Angelique?" He stood, moving out from behind the desk. "Angelique, is that you? I've been waiting for you, Angelique. I've been waiting. . . ."

When Alex heard the two shots, she'd just reached out to press the buzzer. But now she could only stand outside the door, holding her breath, waiting. Waiting for the insane echo of those two sharp cracks to finally die inside her head.

CHAPTER THIRTY-TWO

Cesare Sersone stood staring down at the bold headline of
this afternoon's *L'Osservatore Romano* which lay unopened
on the heavy desk. He had already read the accompanying
article, which had been sent to him two days ago, and had
approved its publication despite the fact that he had hated it.
Fear of the economic consequences of a separate American
Church had been all too abundantly clear in the article's tone
of cringing denunciation. And yet he could not quarrel with
the writer's premise that the Church in the United States
appeared dangerously out of control.

He turned his back on the screaming black letters and
walked across the room to the window where the long scarlet
drapes billowed inward with the hot Roman air. In the Tuscan
hills, in his native village, the breezes would be milder, the
nights already damp and cool with promise. Strange that in
his sixty-third year he should long for the winters he'd cursed
as a boy.

The phone rang, and he swung away from the too-bright
view of the Vatican gardens to answer it. It was the call for
which he'd been waiting.

"*Buon giorno,*" he said simply.

"*Buon Giorno*, Cesare." His secretary of state's beautifully

400

inflected Italian came through precise and clear from across the Atlantic. Not through the cable anymore, he reminded himself, but bounced around from satellites.

"You sound better rested since we spoke yesterday, Jean-Luc. I'm glad of that. You will need all your strength, I'm afraid, for your meeting today with... what did you call them? The clique?"

"It is what they rather self-consciously call themselves, I believe, Cesare. But you are right. I will need all my strength. We have not been misinformed. These are Camélière's handpicked men, and despite the scandal, they have inherited a very solid following. I had hoped to find the Cardinal's forces in disarray, but the exposure of *Lucifer* has given them the perfect rallying point. Even the more conservative American bishops have privately condemned this 'Vatican plot' against one of their own, and are angry enough to stand against us now."

"What about Monsignor Donovan?"

"I'm afraid it's as Archbishop Mantini reported, Cesare. The man who was once the inspiration for *Lucifer* has crossed back to the other side."

"Have you talked to the Monsignor yourself?"

"I met with him late last night at the university. He seemed quite disinclined to speak of our previous arrangement. The Cardinal's death, he pointed out, had changed things."

The near-soundless laugh was his own, an unbidden response to the irony that Phillip Camélière could prove more dangerous dead.

"Cesare?"

"I'm still here, Jean-Luc. I was just thinking how well the name of Leprechaun suits our Monsignor Donovan. He seems to have been the trickster in all of this. *Lucifer* was, after all, his idea. As was the recruitment of Father Leighton. We were foolish to trust him, Jean-Luc. But more foolish still to have focused so completely on Phillip Camélière. What we underestimated, I think, was the true strength of the American sentiment for reform."

"And that sentiment, Your Holiness, is very strong indeed."

"What are you telling me, Jean-Luc?"

"That the Conference which opens in three months is going to be a circus, with acting Archbishop Estevez in the Cardinal's cloak as ringmaster. I'm saying that unity is impossible without compromise, Holiness. There is going to be change here, with or without the approval of Rome."

"Even if change comes too soon?" The question was rhetorical. They had had much this same discussion on the eve of Jean-Luc's departure.

"Yes, Holiness"—Jean-Luc made the expected answer—"even if it comes too soon. But it will not be the first time that there have been such changes. It is only perhaps that they come so seldom that we forget."

The Pope smiled in spite of himself. What his secretary had said was true. It was good to be reminded. "I know that you are right, Jean-Luc. We must change and yet find some way to preserve the essence of what has been handed down to us. In the end we can only have faith in the promise of Our Lord that His Church will never perish." He fell silent for a moment, listening to the deep resonance of bells that played somewhere in the distant hills. He wondered if his secretary too could hear them.

"There is a very old story, Jean-Luc," he began, "in which Napoleon is supposed to have threatened Papal Secretary Consalvi, that as emperor he was quite capable of destroying the Church. 'Sire,' the Cardinal says, 'not even we priests have achieved that in eighteen centuries.' I guess it would be foolish to believe, Jean-Luc, that a mere two centuries more will have made a difference."

"Foolish indeed," Jean-Luc answered softly. Then: "What is your wish, Holiness?"

They were down to the practicalities now, and Cesare paused to gather his thoughts. What he said to the papal secretary at this moment would have consequences for many more of those centuries.

"We have discussed this many times, Jean-Luc, when what has come to pass was only supposition. You know well how I stand on the issues—where I believe we may bend, where we must, I think, stand firm. You understand as well as I what is and is not negotiable. I place unwaveringly into your hands the Church which we both love. Do your best to preserve her with honor."

He paused again, but Jean-Luc, who indeed understood, said nothing.

"May the Holy Spirit be with you."

"And with you also, Holiness."

The bells again had begun to ring.

Frank was halfway out the door of his apartment when he turned back and flung his jacket on the couch. He didn't feel like going out for something to eat, after all, he decided. And there was no use going in to the *Post*. He'd been going in a lot lately, as if he could get more work done there than he could here at home, which these days was *nada*. The real reason he went to the office was that he hoped he would run into Alex.

He walked to the kitchen and grabbed a beer out of the refrigerator. He really should eat something, but he was too aggravated to fix himself a sandwich, and he'd finished off all the frozen pizza last night.

He didn't know why he should want to run into Alex. It was no good at all seeing her. Beautiful as always. Moving busily between the file room and her cubicle. Pleasant. Even smiling occasionally. Reacting when anyone spoke to her. But she wasn't really there.

He'd only talked to her once since she'd come back from New Orleans. At least he'd tried to talk to her, following her from the newspaper offices on her way over to the parking lot. She'd stopped by the loading dock behind the building, sensing him behind her. Just stood there with her head down, waiting.

"Alex . . ."

"I don't want to talk, Frank."

"I just wanted to tell you that I'm sorry. . . . Alex?" She was still standing there in exactly the same position. He couldn't see her face. Was she crying?

As he watched, helpless, her shoulders began to shake.

She *was* crying. He stepped forward, completely miserable now. "Alex..." His hand hovered above her shoulder.

She looked up. It was laughter that twisted her face. Not hysteria. Something much calmer. But worse.

"You're sorry, Frank? What are you sorry about? That a madwoman finished what you started?"

He couldn't get out an answer, just watched while she very visibly took herself in hand.

"Forget it, Frank," she said more easily. "Look, I'm sorry, too. All right?" Her eyes moved slowly over his face. It seemed for a minute as though she really might cry, but she repeated the words instead. "Just forget it."

He'd waited there stupidly, silently, as she'd walked away. Unsure exactly what it was he was supposed to forget.

In his study now, he collapsed into his desk chair and sipped on the beer. Loving Alex had always been hard; now it was torture. Seeing her, watching her pain, was a punishment he inflicted on himself.

Still, Alex could hardly blame it on him that her uncle was dead. The Cardinal's murder, at least, had had nothing at all to do with his story, though his first thought that night when Gus had called from the residence was that Phillip Camélière had been the victim of a Lambruci hit. But when he'd arrived with John Leighton in tow, there had been Angelique Robichaux, still crouched in a corner of the Cardinal's office, murmuring something incomprehensible about a baby.

Eventually she'd been traced through her driver's license. to a town in east Texas, and from there to a bayou parish in Louisiana where Phillip Camélière had once served as assistant pastor. Though there were no official records kept at the time, some of the older residents remembered that several weeks before her uncle had taken her away, sixteen-year-old Angelique Robichaux had delivered an illegitimate baby that Father Phillip Camélière had helped place for adoption. According to the locals, Angelique had never been "right," a strange girl who might easily brood for years over an imagined wrong. It was no surprise to them, they said, that after her uncle died, she had set out to seek revenge on the priest who had "stolen" her baby.

This was the official story that had appeared in every newspaper in the country. He himself had written his own sober version for the *Post*. But the grocery-store rags had had a field day, romanticizing Angelique Robichaux into a sort of deranged Evangeline hunting for the baby they pegged as a love child of the Cardinal's. A tabloid free-for-all, with neither of the principals in any position to speak for themselves.

The Cardinal was dead, and Angelique Robichaux was beyond questioning. She had literally had to be carried into her bond hearing. Ruled incompetent, she'd been remanded to a mental hospital. Undoubtably for life.

A nice neat package, really. A dead man and a lunatic. So why couldn't he let it go? The truth was probably that he was transferring his frustration about Alex to a morbid fascination with the Cardinal's death. Making it more of a mystery than it was. Building it into . . . what?

He didn't know for sure, but instinct told him there was something there. The same kind of instinct that had warned him that following Richard Darrington was leading him to something he wouldn't like. The same kind that gave Gus Shapiro his "ulcer." Suddenly he couldn't stand for another minute the familiar clutter of his desk, his apartment, or the half-written story on prison crowding in his computer. He had to get out of here, out of the District, at least for a few days.

The beer bottle hit the wastepaper basket with a satisfying plop as he pushed out of the chair and headed up the stairs to his bedroom. What did one pack, he wondered half humorously, for midsummer in a swamp?

Tony realized he'd been staring at the television for the last half hour. Staring but not seeing. He reached for the remote and switched the channel. Something busy and silly came on the screen. A game show. He pressed the controller, running through the channels. Images jerked on and off in a kind of feverish succession. Nothing. He finally settled on an all-weather station, and pumped up the audio. A voice spilled out smooth and silky and vaguely melancholy.

He had tried not to think of Phillip these last three weeks.

But each time he tried, he failed. And each time he failed, he hurt. He got up from the sofa and walked to a window.

He didn't even know where he was. Somewhere out of the District. Somewhere in the hills of Virginia. Somewhere safe. He caught a glimpse of Harvey and Edwards. He was never really alone anymore. But that was the way things were now. The way he'd chosen them to be. *Always play to win, Tony.* Phillip's words. And if winning's out of reach? *Cut your losses.* He was cutting his losses now.

The decision hadn't been really very difficult. To turn state's evidence. After all, what else was there to do. Everything that they had done was going to come out anyway. Leighton and Gregory would make sure of that. And of course, with what Darrington had left behind, he might as well cooperate. Yes, Phillip had taught him when not to play the fool. Besides, this was the best way—do what had to be done, then pull out. And he wanted to pull out. Start a new life in a new place. Put on a new identity.

And that, too, really wasn't so hard. After all, it wasn't anything he hadn't been doing his whole life. Playing at different roles. But he was going to hate not being a priest. It had become, despite everything, his most satisfying role.

He looked at his watch, turned, and checked it with the time running across the television screen. Eric would be here in less than half an hour. He hadn't seen Eric since he'd decided to take them up on the offer of the witness protection program. He supposed the Lambrucis were some kind of threat. But in his mind, they were never more than names. At any rate, his visitors up to now had been limited to his lawyer and Father Bedford, a priest-psychologist, sent by the archdiocese to administer guidance. He had seen Bedford only once. Had told him to get the fuck out.

But today they were letting him see Eric. And he was nervous. He walked into the kitchen and opened the fridge. It was well stocked. They were at least going to see to it that their star witness didn't starve to death. He pulled out a Coke, opened it, drank straight from the can.

He looked over when he saw the door opening. It was Harvey.

"You got some company, Tony." And the agent opened the door wider.

"Thanks, Harvey."

"Anytime." He nodded, closing the door.

"Eric . . ."

"Listen, Tony, let's just get one thing straight right off. If you think you're going to get rid of me by telling me how hard this new life of yours is going to be . . ."

"Eric."

"Yes, Tony."

"Shut up."

Lindsey had taken very little from the Capitol Hill rowhouse she'd shared with Richard. Just a few personal things. Everything else had been sold or given away. She had all that she needed and wanted here. Here in the house that was hers and Phillip's.

She looked around the spacious living room. It was strange, but in the beginning she'd thought it would be too painful to live here now that he was gone. But it hadn't been. Not from the first. There'd been no pain. Just a kind of welcoming peace. A comfort.

When she'd first heard that Phillip was dead, it seemed a kind of terrible lie. How could anything exist, if there were no Phillip? She could yet hear Tony's subdued voice when she'd phoned the residence later that night, phoned because Phillip had still not returned her call. Terrified that Richard had really done something wild and foolish. But it hadn't been Richard who'd come into Phillip's office that night. It had been Angelique Robichaux.

Like someone deranged, she had run from their house then, desperately wanting to get to the residence. See for herself, prove what Tony had said was a lie. Prove that Phillip, her Phillip, was alive. But she hadn't gone there, had gone instead to the town house. And when she'd driven up, Andy Cauley, Richard's aide, was waiting for her.

Andy'd seemed much like a sleepwalker as he told her of how he'd gone back to the office to get some papers he'd forgotten. He'd thought it strange the lights were still on.

Thought perhaps the cleaning woman had gotten an early start. Instead Richard was there, fallen asleep at his desk. But that wasn't like Richard. And when he'd moved closer. . .

The days that followed were a nightmare. And though she found it easy enough to harden herself against the scandal that followed, she found she could not ignore the pain that fell so heavily on Richard's parents. She remembered standing between the two of them, staring into the empty well of Richard's grave, fighting her heart, which cried out not to be here, here in Boston, but in New Orleans with Phillip, one last time.

And then after the shock, the grief, the sense of betrayal, there had come the moment of utter calm, coming at last when she was finally able to accept that the scales had perhaps been balanced. Accepting that none of them was, after all, without guilt. They had all kept their secrets.

And yet, despite everything, there was one constant, one certainty. She would never take back loving Phillip. No guilt in loving Phillip. And now. . .

She looked down and smiled. There would not be long to wait. The months would pass soon enough.

"Oh, I'm doing okay, I guess." Lindsey settled back against the flowered chintz cushions. "I don't read the paper any more or listen to the news. I just keep myself busy with this house and getting ready for mother's visit. I think I may convince her to stay for a while. But what about you, Alex?"

Uncharacteristically pale in a dark knit dress, Alex sat across from her, poised on the edge of the sofa. She shrugged away the question, but the gesture was far from relaxed.

"I'm back at work," she said. "Murray very diplomatically suggested that I drop what I was doing to take over some special assignments. But I'm still on the National desk. Apparently it's permanent."

"That's good."

"Yes."

"Would you like some more tea?"

"No, I don't think so, Lindsey."

"Alex, we're not talking about it. Don't you think we should?"

"I don't know." Alex looked at her strangely. "Do you think so?"

"It helps...really," she said. "I don't know how I'd have gotten through all this if not for the nightly phone calls with my mother. I'd just like to know—"

"I guess you want to hear about what happened that night?"

Lindsey started to say no, that it wasn't facts that she wanted. But then maybe Alex needed to tell it. And maybe she did need to hear.

"I had—I don't know—this feeling," Alex had started. "It was late, but I knew I had to go to the residence. I don't remember the driving, but I'm sure I must have tried to get there as fast as I could. Not fast enough, though. When I got to the door, I heard the shots.

"For a minute or two I just stood there on the doorstep, and then I had to fumble in my purse for the key. When I did find it, I couldn't get it in the lock at first—my hands were shaking. And I think I must have been crying, because I remember it was hard to see. But then finally the door was open, and I was running in the dark, down the hall.

"Uncle Phillip was lying on the floor in his office. He didn't look hurt at first. Just... not right, lying there like that.

"And then I saw the woman in the corner...."

"Angelique."

"Angelique Robichaux... yes. But, of course, I didn't know that then. The window behind her was open, and the breeze from outside was blowing her hair. It was long and dark... with ribbons. Bright colors. I remember that. She looked so strange sitting there. Rocking back and forth. Singing.

"It was dim in the office, except for the desk lamp. And yet I saw it all so quickly. It seemed like I had forever to think before I got to Uncle Phillip.

"I knelt down and took his hand." Alex had been looking at her, but now her gaze slid away. "I said, 'It's me, Uncle Phillip.' He opened his eyes for a minute, smiled and said my name. I felt him squeeze my fingers, just a little. Mrs. Jordan had come in from somewhere, and she just sort of moved me aside, trying to do something to bring him back. And then Madame Elise was there, too, praying and pushing buttons on the phone. Trying to call for help. But she was speaking in French and anyway, I knew it was useless. All the blood...

"I don't remember getting up. But somehow I was standing in the corner. That woman was still there rocking. Still singing to herself, the same thing over and over about a baby. It sounded almost like a lullaby, and I leaned over her, trying to hear, because I wanted to understand why... why she would want to..."

Alex had wrapped her arms around her shoulders, moving back and forth at the edge of the sofa in a parody that seemed unconscious. Now she stopped and sat motionless.

"After a while," Alex said softly, "she saw I was there, and it was almost as if she recognized me. She stopped the rocking. Reached up and touched my hair. 'Angel,' she said. Then: 'Michelle.' Like a question. As if she thought it might be my name."

Again Alex was silent, unmoving, and Lindsey understood. This utter stillness was a defense. Alex wasn't letting herself cry.

"The emergency people came. I guess Mrs. Jordan finally called them." She was talking again. And the police were there, too. They took me into the library. Frank and John arrived after that. I think that detective called Frank, but I told Mrs. Jordan not to let them near me. I never went back to the office. I didn't even see them take Uncle Phillip away. I..."

The last words had been rushed and very soft, at the end almost fading to nothing. Perhaps now, Lindsey thought, she'll let go. But Alex just sat looking straight ahead, and after a moment she finished.

"I told the police what I've just told you."

Lindsey closed her eyes, fighting the sting of her own tears.

"But it's not everything."

She looked up. Alex was watching her closely.

"Uncle Phillip said something. When I knelt down beside him. Before he knew it was me."

"What did he say, Alex?"

"Your name. 'Lindsey,' he said. 'Lindsey?'"

The tears fell. Lindsey stood up. This wasn't the way she'd planned it. She'd wanted to tell Alex in her own time. When it was right. She walked to the window fronting the garden. The bright heads of flowers dipped in the light breeze. She liked to watch them from the window. But she couldn't cut them. Couldn't stand the smell of flowers in the house. Maybe when her mother came . . .

"There were so many times that I wanted to tell you about Phillip and me, Alex. Please believe that. But it just seemed impossible." She turned. "We made each other happy. I hope you can understand?"

"So it really is true." Alex had picked up her tea glass to study the melting ice. "I knew it must be . . . the way he said your name. I guess I just . . . I don't know why I should be surprised. Not after everything else."

Lindsey watched Alex put the glass down, hating the way her voice had hardened.

"And why shouldn't you have been sleeping with a cardinal?" Alex said now. "I slept with the priest who was stabbing him in the back."

"Alex . . ."

"Oh, yes, Lindsey. I had my secret, too. While they were busy fucking over my uncle, I slept with them both. Frank Gregory *and* John Leighton. What do you think? Quite a nasty little triangle?"

"Oh, Alex, you sound so . . ."

"Bitter? Yes, I suppose so." She opened her purse and got out cigarettes and a lighter. "I'm just so damned angry."

"Angry . . . yes." Lindsey came back now to sit in her chair. "I can understand that."

"I'm angry at myself, Lindsey, For being so stupid." The cigarette sat for a moment between her lips.

"You know, Lindsey, for the last three weeks, I've been trying to sort this all out. And the thing that keeps coming back is the night I found out from Frank and John what Uncle Phillip and Richard were doing."

"You knew?"

Alex shook her head. "Not till the very end. And then I wouldn't believe it. I asked Frank to give me some time to talk to Uncle Phillip. Give him a chance to explain. And he said no, that I knew he couldn't promise me that. I was a woman talking to a man who'd said he loved her. But he was talking to a reporter." She stopped to examine the burning tip of the cigarette in her fingers, reached for the ashtray, and crushed it out.

"That's what makes me angry, Lindsey. That there's no answer in any of this. I always thought that if you were good, if you did everything right, then it would all be okay. You'd be happy. But that's not life, is it? Frank thinks he did the right thing. And John Leighton. And even Uncle Phillip. That's what hurts the worst. That Uncle Phillip could do what he did, knowing how all of this could hurt everyone who loved him. Me. And Mother."

Everyone who loved him. The words repeated themselves in her mind. "How is your mother?" It was all she could trust herself to say.

For the first time Alex smiled. "Strong," she said. "You know, despite the scandal, they still wanted him in the crypt in St. Matthew's. Quietly, of course. But Mother said no, he was coming home."

Lindsey wanted to explain how hard it had been for her not to be with Phillip there in New Orleans. Wanted Alex to understand what had been between them. To see what was still here in this house.

"Alex," she said suddenly, "there's something you have to know. I'm pregnant. And it's Phillip's. Please be glad."

John shot up from sleep. It was the first orgasm he'd had since before Phillip died. But now he no longer dreamed. At least not any dreams he could remember. But tonight . . . He'd dreamed. Dreamed of her.

He shoved the sheet away. The cold air from the window unit reached him, dried the perspiration from his body. He sucked in a long breath. It had happened only once before, a dream like this, and that time he'd dreamed of her, too.

A dream that seemed not a dream at all. But real. *Real*. So that he could feel her, smell her, hear her cottony laugh against his ear. As though he'd given himself permission to cross over from dream reality to waking reality. *This is not a dream anymore. This is really happening*. He'd turned his head and seen a quick flash of tawny brown flesh, her shoulder. Coming against his back...

He sat up now and rubbed his hands over his face. His hair was damp, and he imagined that had he been a smoking man, he would have reached for a cigarette. Instead he turned on the bedside lamp and reached for his breviary.

He hadn't seen her since that night. And then only from a distance. The tall outline of her body solid against a frail light coming from a lamp somewhere. He remembered how she'd reached for the back of a chair as though to steady herself. And then someone coming over, and she straightened, nodded her head, walked into another room. He never saw her again.

Yet he knew she was back in Washington. Back at work. Frank had told him that much. Working on National. Keeping busy. But he hadn't asked for more. And so, like much of what had happened these last weeks, Alex had become part of the constant sadness that formed the core of what he was now.

He had done his part. *Lucifer*, the rest of it, was over. It was up to Frank, the authorities, to do what had to be done. If there was any kind of legal action, it would be way down the road. Right now, he lived with the sadness, and his work on the book.

Rome had made no move against his defiance. At least not yet. And there was, of course, little he could do but resign from the Conference, despite his allegiance to its ideals. No matter what Brian had said, there was no doubt in his mind that he was now perceived as something of a traitor by both sides.

He looked down into his hands. The breviary still held unopened. He had wanted some control. He had told himself that almost from the beginning. But in the end there had been no control. The universe had no master. It had been deuces wild. Who could have predicted that Phillip would be murdered? Murdered by a force outside of the game they were all playing.

Except the Cardinal had been playing another game. And there lay the real irony. Phillip had never been their prey. Never their victim. It was Phillip who had set up the board, named the rules. And in the end, in a singularly perverse way, Phillip had won.

He remembered the scene that night in Phillip's office, with the police moving like ants about the woman in the corner. And Frank, barking out strings of words into the phone. He remembered the technicians, so precise in their white coats, packing away their now useless equipment, parting before him as he moved forward with the sacred oil.

The light and the noise had died away behind him, so that he was again alone with Phillip, as earlier they had been in the chapel, when they had said their true good-bye.

Through this holy anointing . . . and Phillip's eyes had seemed to open. Even in death they had appeared so very clear and knowing.

John shifted in bed, slammed pillows against the headboard to meet his spine. The breviary drifted down into his lap, and he closed his eyes. So hard. So hard. For despite everything, he still wanted Alexandra. Wanted her with a hunger so fierce, so relentless, that it crushed him beyond all reason.

He had wanted to be the good priest; the whole of his life had been molded, carved, twisted to follow Christ. Sacrifice, denial, suffering . . . The defeat of the flesh in the triumph of the spirit. But he was not God. He was not a martyr. He was a man, a simple lowly human being. And he had failed.

He inhaled deeply as though gathering strength for some difficult task he'd set for himself. And then he remembered the words, words from *The Last Temptation.* . . .

Her heart swelled with distress as she recalled the games they used to play together when they were still small children, he three years old, she four. What deep, unrevealable joy they had experienced, what unspeakable sweetness! For the first time they had both sensed the deep dark fact that one was a man and the other a woman: two bodies which seemed once upon a time to have been one; but some merciless God separated them, and now the pieces had found each other again....

He drew his fingers across his face and discovered, with some small measure of pity for himself, that he wept.

CHAPTER THIRTY-THREE

Frank Gregory knew just about as much as anyone outside of Louisiana about Cajuns. He'd read *Evangeline* in high school, eaten gumbo and blackened redfish, and heard on at least two occasions Clifton Chenier play his "chanky-chank" zydeco music. He'd even seen *The Big Easy* some years back. And of course, he knew all about Louisiana's flamboyant onetime Cajun governor, Edwin Edwards. But that wasn't a whole hell of a lot. He'd known nothing about Our Lady of the Butane Tank, or that *traiteurs*, practitioners of Cajun folk medicine, were in as much demand as orthodox medical doctors.

Felice Oulliber was a *traiteur*.

He'd located Cassie Duhon, Felice Oulliber's granddaughter, almost immediately. She lived with her husband and three children in a modest brick home in Golden Meadow, Louisiana, on Bayou Lafourche. He noticed the statue of the Virgin Mary in the front yard as soon as he drove up. Then Cassie herself waiting for him at the front door. She was a smallish woman in her early thirties with smiling dark eyes and a head of the shiniest curly black hair he'd ever seen. There was just the hint of a Cajun accent when she spoke, and the tiniest bit of little-girl shyness he found extremely appealing.

She asked if he'd like a cup of coffee after he'd begged off sitting in the living room, telling her that the kitchen would do just fine. He watched her tie on an apron.

"Please, sit." And she pointed to a small aluminum and vinyl dinette set. The kind that was popular in the fifties, the kind in Ozzie and Harriet's kitchen. He pulled out a chair and watched her give a quick stir to a large pot on the stove. Then she opened a cabinet and reached in to get out cups and saucers.

"Would you like a mug instead? Alcide hates these cups. Says you can't get enough coffee in them."

"Alcide just may be right. Mug'll be fine."

"Hope you take it strong." She turned and smiled.

"The stronger and blacker the better." He smiled back.

She brought two mugs to the table and sat down.

"Now, that's coffee." He'd taken a long pull on the mug. "Smells good." He nodded toward the stove. "What're you cooking?"

"Chicken and okra gumbo. Have you ever eaten gumbo?"

"Yes. But I think it had shrimp in it."

"Seafood gumbo. My favorite, but Alcide was in the mood for chicken and okra."

She never did really lose her shyness with him. But that didn't disappoint him. He rather liked it. *Sexy.* That was the word that he'd missed earlier. He found her shyness incredibly sexy. He could feel his mouth twist beneath his mustache into a smile. For the third time? Or was it the fourth? He'd lost count, but one thing for sure, he'd been smiling a lot since he sat down at Cassie Duhon's kitchen table.

It was the usual small talk. Was this his first trip to Louisiana? No, but he'd only been to New Orleans. Was Cajun food really as popular "up north" as everyone claimed it was? Absolutely. What was Washington like? She'd never been. It was really a wonderful city despite what everyone said. She should go. A great trip for children.

"Are you doing a story about Cajuns, Mr. Gregory?" she asked finally. "Is that why you want to talk to my grandmother?"

"Please, Frank'll do. Actually no. But it might work out that way." She was staring at him with her dark penetrating eyes. *Play it straight, Gregory,* he thought. *You can't bullshit*

this woman. "I'm curious about the woman who shot Cardinal
Camélière, Cassie. I think your grandmother may be able to
help answer some questions I have."

Cassie offered him a second cup. "So you want to know
about Angelique?"

"Yes," he said. "I understand that your grandmother delivered
her baby."

"That was many years ago." It was an unsatisfactory response, but then he hadn't really expected more. He was in a
land of mystery. A place where herbs and holy water were
still used with the same good results as penicillin.

She'd read his thoughts. "Maybe..." She drew out the
word, "Just maybe *Grandmère* will help you with your questions, Mr. Frank Gregory." And her dark eyes smiled over the
rim of her mug. "I think I like you better than the others who
come and ask questions."

"Michelle Robichaux was no good." Felice Oulliber wore a
stern look on her ancient face. "Poor Emile with such a sister.
And the girl... Angelique. Like her mother... *dans la lune.
Le Bon Dieu...*" She'd lapsed into French and shook her
head.

"*Grandmère*, you must speak English so that Mr. Gregory
can understand you."

"The old church, the one we fix up for Père Philippe is no
more." She was speaking English again, picking up another
thread in her narrative. "Even St. Gabriel is gone. We go to
the big church now. But I think I like the old church better."

She made the sign of the cross. "God rest his soul. He was
good to us, our Père Philippe. I knew Angelique Robichaux
would come to no good. Better she die when she have the
baby. I blame myself." She passed a gnarled hand across her
thin lips as if to wipe away spittle.

"Please, *Grandmère*. It is not right that you talk like this."

"Always they were apart from us. The Robichaux. I think
Emile wanted to come to us, but Michelle she want no part
of us. Too good for the bayou. Ran away with some trash, left
Emile to take care of Angelique."

She fixed her dark eyes on him. "Emile did the best he

could." The words were a defense. Then her eyes seemed to glaze over. "She have the power, too. . . ." She brought her left hand into the air. "Angelique's mother."

"*Grandmère*, please." Cassie seemed embarrassed.

"What is this? This man is from the big city so he does not understand the power?" She chuckled, and reached out a weathered brown hand and patted his. "The power from God. The power to heal. Make things right that go bad. You understand the power, Mr. Gregory?"

"I think I understand, Mrs. Oulliber." And he placed his hand over hers.

"But the power also can come from the devil." She removed her hand and frowned, her thick dark brows a queer contrast to the head of steel-gray hair. "Michelle's power came from the devil." Her voice was solemn. "And she passed it in the blood to Angelique."

"Did Cardinal . . . Father Camélière try to help Angelique?" He'd worked up slowly to the question.

"Emile have nowhere else to go. He talk to me many times. But I . . ." She threw up her hands in a gesture of helplessness. "Angelique was Michelle Robichaux's daughter." The words held a kind of finality.

"Father Camélière helped Angelique with the baby?" He steered her back.

"He come to me. Say that I must help with the delivery. He know I was *traiteur*. I bring many babies into the world. I could not refuse Père Philippe." She let out a long regretful breath and stared out of the half-open door.

"I remember I put the baby in her arms, and she call for Père Philippe. And when he come, I see her smile at him and say the baby's name.

"The next day Emile told her the baby die. Too small and weak, Emile say to her. But me, I could see Angelique was not so sure. I think she believe that maybe they lie to her." She fingered the silver medal around her neck.

"It was not such an easy birth. And for days, so sick Angelique seem after the baby come. Still I can see her on the bed in Emile's house. Quiet, like the dead she was. But I see her eyes, like Michelle's eyes. I know better. I knew she was thinking inside of herself." She stopped for a moment, remembering.

He waited a moment. "And the baby's father? Did anyone know who the baby's father was?"

"The devil." She spat the word and clamped her mouth shut. She stood then, and he saw that she was smaller and thinner than he imagined. He watched her hands first go inside, then come out the pockets of the oversized dress she wore.

"I said it was a sin to talk that way about a priest," she said at last, staring down into his face. "Père Philippe was a good man. He would not do such a thing." She shook her head sadly and sat back down. "The father you say? Who knows the father."

"What happened to that baby, Mrs. Oulliber?"

She smiled for the first time, as though she were amused. "Mrs. Oulliber. You call me Mrs. Oulliber. Such a long time since someone calls me Mrs. Oulliber." Then, remembering what he'd asked: "Père Philippe took the baby away."

"Where?"

"*Pichouette* . . . a little girl." She wasn't going to be pushed. "And so pretty. Like the mother. Except the hair. I remember the hair. Blond like the belly of a baby duck."

"Where did Père Philippe take the baby, Mrs. Oulliber?"

"To New Orleans." She'd answered his question at last. "Père Philippe took the baby to New Orleans. To someone he know there."

"Where in New Orleans? Do you know who he gave the baby to? Did Père Philippe mention a name, Mrs. Oulliber?"

"Such a long time. Twenty-five, twenty-six years. My memory is not so good anymore."

"Please, Mrs. Oulliber. It's important."

She smiled and for the first time he could see that she had once been a very pretty woman.

"*Le present a ses racines dans le passé.*"

"What did she say, Cassie?"

"She said that the present has its roots in the past."

"Oh . . ." He turned back and watched the old woman. Waiting.

"A French name," she said slowly, remembering. "The family had a French name. . . ."

Alex pulled the old cotton cardigan closer around her and slumped backward in her chair to reread the last paragraph of her story. It wasn't all that great, but it would have to do if she was going to make tomorrow's edition. It was the first piece she'd be handing in since coming back, and she'd wanted it to be really good. But no matter what she wrote, it just kept coming out cynical.

She pulled herself up straight, made her few corrections, and phoned in the copy through the modem. Watching till the light went out, she reached to hang up the receiver. She shouldn't be worried, reporters were supposed to be cynics. Murray would probably love it.

With the story done, it was hard to put off thinking about Lindsey. She'd failed Lindsey, she knew, the way she seemed to fail everyone lately. Maybe when she could feel, she'd be glad about the baby. But for now at least, Lindsey's news meant only the burden of one more guilty secret. Her mind shut down. She was still sitting at the desk when she heard somebody knocking.

John Leighton stood at her door.

"Hello, Alexandra," he said. "May I come in?"

She nodded. Stepped backward to let him pass. John Leighton is here, she said to herself, but she couldn't get a reaction.

"It's cold, isn't it?" The words were hers. "Too much air conditioning." From somewhere she'd remembered he preferred open windows. She went to turn up the thermostat. Walked back into the room.

"I'd like to talk . . . If that's all right?" He was standing by the couch. Studying her.

She went over and sat on the end of the sofa. "What did you want to talk about?"

"I just have to make sure that you understand one thing, Alex." He sat down, too.

"And what's that, John?"

"What I told you that night in Frank's apartment was true.

What happened between us, what I said . . . what I did, was before I agreed to be a part of *Lucifer*. If nothing else, I have to know you believe that."

"My uncle is dead." The anger in the four words was frightening. She huddled into her sweater. Watched him watch her face. When he spoke again, it seemed he'd been reading her thoughts.

"I can't tell you why he did what he did, Alex. I met with him that afternoon, you know. That Tuesday—the day he was shot. I wanted to tell him myself that I was handing the discs over to Frank Gregory. I got the feeling that in some strange way he approved of what I was doing."

His eyes were still on her face, but she could tell he had stopped seeing her.

"He did say he was going to fight me, though." John's lip curled in a kind of smile. "Fight me with all he had for his New American Catholic Church. He told me that whatever I might think of him, he believed in that church. . . ." The words failed, but his eyes focused again on hers.

"And now, despite everything that's come out, Alex, the Church is going to change. One way or the other, there's going to be reform. And Phillip made that possible. The best of him is *not* dead."

"The best? What could you possibly know about the best?"

"Tell me."

She knew what he was doing. He was patronizing her. John Leighton the priest, her self-appointed confessor, supposed that he understood better than she did what she felt.

"Oh God, Uncle Phillip!"

She had not been conscious that she had said the words aloud. She was seeing him . . . one of her very first memories. He was coming through the door of her nursery. Smiling. Something shiny and bright, something wonderful just for her in his hand. *Here she is. Here's my special girl* . . . .

She was crying, for the first time since that night when she'd left her apartment to go to the residence. And John was holding her.

"I love you, Alex." The words were very soft, whispered against her hair. But she had heard them.

"Oh, no, Father Leighton, you don't love me. You have no idea what it means to love someone." She had pulled away from him. Stood up, trying to wipe her eyes with the hem of her sweater. "You never loved me." She was trembling with anger. "Fucking me was simply your way of taking control of your life."

He shook his head. Looked away.

"I don't think I've ever been a free man, Alex," he said finally. "There have always been rules in my life. And I was afraid to live without rules. Afraid of making my own. Perhaps that was the real reason I became a priest. The rules are so clear in the priesthood. You do this. You don't do that. I had nothing to do but obey.

"And then I met you, and all of the rules got in the way. Suddenly, for the first time in my life, I wanted to be free." He looked up.

"But I was never free, Alex, because I had taken a vow. And it wasn't the vow itself that was so important, but the fact that I had gone back on my word that made what I'd done so wrong. But loving you, Alex, loving you was never wrong."

He got up, came closer. "With everything that's happened these past two months, the rules don't seem as clear as they once were. Yet there are still some solid truths in my life." He reached out and carefully took her hand.

"I love my Church, Alex, and I love my God. And yes, despite everything, I still love being a priest. And whatever you might think, I love you, Alex."

She looked up into his face. She envied him his certainties. Well, he was a good priest, she'd never denied that. Forgiveness, that was the easy part, it was forgetting that was hard. But the hurting didn't change the love.

She reached up, her hand brushing back a lock of black hair that had fallen across his brow, and felt the fresh prick of tears start behind her eyes. There'd be a lot of tears now.

"I love you, too, John," she said.

"Why did that sound so . . . final, Alex? Didn't you hear what I said? The best of Phillip is not dead. We're going to fight for those reforms he wanted so badly. And high on the list is optional celibacy." He made a sort of smile.

Reform. She knew it wasn't going to be as easy as he made it sound. But the release of tears had left her emotions too close to the surface. Had made her vulnerable. And looking at him this moment, so boyishly hopeful, so earnest and handsome, she wanted to believe him. *Did* believe him.

Something of what she was feeling must have shown in her face, because suddenly his arms were around her again, holding her. It felt so good and so natural. The way it should have been from the beginning, but couldn't be.

"You could wait for me, Alex." He had made it a kind of joke, but his eyes said he was serious.

"If you don't keep me waiting too long, John," she said softly.

He pulled her closer. And his kiss, so hard and hungry, said to her that he wouldn't.

CHAPTER THIRTY-FOUR

It was even warmer here today in the heart of the old city than yesterday on the bayou—the shadows denser, the colors deeper. Amidst the wind-stirred greenery, the Veneé mansion gleamed hugely white in the August sunshine. Frank, in his rented car, sat parked in front. He had been sitting, staring at the house for almost fifteen minutes, wondering what the hell he was doing here.

He was still wondering the same thing all the way up the paved walkway, and again on the shaded veranda before the beveled-glass door. From inside he could hear a piano, and wondered if it were someone playing or a recording. It sounded like Chopin.

He rang the doorbell.

"Yes?" A pleasant dark face had appeared in the darker rectangle of the open doorway. This had to be Sarah.

"Hello." He took a breath and smiled. "I'm Frank Gregory. I work with Alexandra at the *Post* . . . in Washington."

A thousand-candle-watt smile lit up the black woman's face at the mention of Alex's name. Then, a slight frown. "Miss Alex ain't here, Mr. Gregory. She ain't been here since the funeral." The frown deepened.

"I know Alex is in Washington," he said. "I saw her there just a few days ago. It isn't Alex I came to see, Sarah.

It was Mrs. Veneé that I wanted to speak with. Is she home?"

"Miss Margaret's here." Sarah looked him over now a little more appraisingly. "And Mr. Alfred."

He smiled again at her afterthought. Best let this strange Yankee know another man was in the house.

Sarah seemed to come to some decision. "I'll tell Miss Margaret you here," she said, stepping back to let him in. "You can wait for her in the parlor." She led him through the foyer and disappeared toward the back of the house. After a moment the Chopin stopped.

He saw the portrait almost immediately. Alex looking terrific in an old-fashioned blue dress. Then, walking closer, he saw that the eyes, too, were blue, and he realized that he stared at a painting of—

"Alexandra's grandmother." Margaret Veneé had come up behind him.

He turned, taking the hand she offered. "Alex told me once that she looked like her Grandmother Camélière. Thank you for seeing me, Mrs. Veneé. I wasn't sure. . . ."

She smiled, withdrawing her hand as the words faded. He noted that her own eyes were as blue as her mother's.

"Come and sit down." She led him toward the most comfortable looking of the sofas. "Have you had lunch? Sarah is bringing us coffee."

"Coffee's fine," he said. "I had a sandwich in town."

"How's the weather been in Washington?" she asked conversationally as the maid entered, placing a silver service on the coffee table in front of them. "Thank you, Sarah. I'll pour. How do you like yours, Frank?" She turned back toward him.

"Black, please . . . The weather's been pretty hot." He accepted the delicate china cup. "Not as hot as here, though, not as humid."

"Hello, Mr. Gregory." Alfred Veneé had come in. "Sorry I can't stay." He moved to plant a kiss on Margaret's cheek. "Board meeting this afternoon at the bank."

Alfred had straightened up now with a hand still on his wife's shoulder, looking over her head at him directly

"Everything okay back in Washington?" It was clear that "everything" meant Alex.

"Yes." He managed to make it sound convincing. "Fine."

Alfred nodded, satisfied. "Good. Well, I'll leave you two to talk." He smiled down at his wife again and gave her shoulder a last reassuring pat.

"More coffee?" Margaret's glance had turned back from the door.

"Yes, please." Surprisingly his cup was nearly empty.

"How can I help you, Frank?" She poured his coffee.

He set the cup down on the table without drinking, delaying looking up.

"Is this about Alex, Frank? I know she's been—"

"No." He stopped her. "I mean yes, in a way it is about Alex. Or at least I thought it was." He looked up now to see her eyes still on his face.

"The truth is, Mrs. Veneé, I don't really know *why* I'm here with you. Why I'm even in Louisiana. Except that I just wasn't satisfied. . . ." He knew he was taking too long about making any kind of sense. He tried again.

"There were just some things that bothered me. Some things I felt I had to know about . . . about the woman who shot your brother."

The words did not seem to upset her as he'd feared. "I see," was all she said. Then: "Not 'satisfied' . . . as a reporter?"

"No, not exactly." He looked away again. "It's hard to explain this"—he heard his own dry laugh—"but I get these feelings sometimes; and I can't . . . I just can't seem to let things go." He stopped.

"So what did you find out, Frank? Here in Louisiana?"

He looked back at her, surprised. The eyes seemed less brilliant now, flat. But still benign. She glanced down to sip on her coffee. She was trying, he realized, to make this easy.

"Yesterday," he began, pausing for just a second to pick up his own cup, "I drove out to Bayou Lafourche to talk to Felice Oulliber. She's a *traiteur*"—he used the word he'd been given—"the midwife who delivered Angelique Robichaux's baby—"

"The child she thought that Phillip had stolen from her."
The voice that had interrupted was very low.

"Yes," he answered her. Then: "I had the craziest idea
about that baby." For better or worse he had said it.

"What idea, Frank?" She was intent again. Expectant. The
wide blue eyes were disconcerting.

"You have to understand," he said, backtracking, "I'm not
always perfectly logical when I get one of these feelings I told
you about. And, of course, the age was right. And the way
the Cardinal always treated her."

"And you thought?"

She was leading him, he realized, bringing him along in
exactly the way he sometimes led his sources and informants.
He remembered what Alex had said once about the kind of
mind that lurked beneath all that gentility.

"Felice Oulliber... the woman I saw yesterday..." He was
backpedaling again, trying to reassert some control. "She
hinted that the Cardinal—Père Philippe was what she called
him—hinted that Père Philippe himself was the father of that
baby."

He watched for some reaction, but in the next second she
was sipping again, serenely, from her cup.

"She said, too, that Père Philippe had sent the baby to New
Orleans. To a family he knew there."

He wasn't sure but he thought she might be smiling. She
was still looking down, into the coffee.

"I thought the baby was Alexandra," he said, plunging
ahead. "I thought that your brother had given his own baby
to you. To you and your husband. But then the midwife blew
that theory. The name she gave me for the family wasn't
Veneé.

"I checked it out this morning. The parents were still very
grateful to your brother. He was very sympathetic, they said,
when the baby he'd found for them died some six months
later. They told me he'd helped them then with a regular
adoption through one of the Catholic agencies."

She still wore that same expression. Was still not looking at
him.

"I shouldn't have come. It was stupid." He set down the

cup and saucer too abruptly. They rattled like old bones in the silence.

"Alfred was my only comfort when Phillip went away."

He'd been about to get up when she'd spoken. Now he sat back to listen. She had begun so quietly that he'd had to strain for the words, thinking at first that she'd meant now, now when her brother was dead.

He was wrong.

"We were in this room when Phillip made the announcement," she continued, "Alfred, Mother and I. It was the day after our twenty-second birthday, and the sun was pouring in that window." Her glance was turned inward now as if she were seeing again the things and the people she described.

"It was hot despite the fact that it was only mid-April. There were flowers on the table that had been too long in the vase. The air was thick with them. Like incense."

She gave a soft laugh like a sigh. "My mind was working lazily, but I remember clearly thinking that incense fit very well with what Phillip was saying. It was such a shock to us all. He had never spoken one word before that afternoon about going into the seminary."

Still she didn't look at him, and he was not sure yet that it was to him she was really speaking.

"It was just so unbelievable. Phillip, a priest. As soon as he said it I knew it meant some terrible kind of destruction. I saw it in the look on Mother's face."

And now she seemed to remember he was there. She turned to him and smiled.

"We were a very strange family, the three of us. A kind of triangle, Phillip used to say. Our bright, beautiful star of a mother at the top, and we below, the twins, the separate halves . . ."

The words trailed away. He wondered if she were finished. He hoped not.

She was staring across at the portrait now. He watched the gentle rising and falling of the gray silk blouse with her breath. It was all that moved. She didn't even blink.

"Before that moment when Phillip told us he was leaving"

—she was suddenly speaking again—"I had believed that I was becoming independent, that we were finally growing naturally apart. I had met Alfred. I had my music." She made a sad gesture with her head. "An illusion. Just an illusion. And still, after the first shock, and even after Phillip and I had talked that night, I lied to myself that I could stand alone, without him.

"Within two weeks after he left for Catholic University I was ill. Sick as I used to be as an infant. And yet I was glad of it," she said, "the physical illness. It helped to obscure the true sickness till I could get some kind of hold. After a few months I was better, outwardly at least. Inside I always felt torn in half, and disgusted with myself. Understanding an illness is no guarantee of a cure." Her voice was level, but he heard the self-reproach.

"I have no idea why Alfred put up with it. We never discussed what was troubling me; he was just always there waiting. I hated my selfishness in not sending him away. But I understood, even then, that to say anything, to try and influence Alfred, would be the worst kind of insult. I still don't know why he waited all those years. There must be some limit, don't you think? Even to love?"

He hesitated. She was still staring at the portrait. He wondered if she wanted some answer.

"It was Mother's death that changed things." Abruptly she was watching him. The blue eyes seemed almost wholly black, the pupils enormous. "You could not have experienced the kind of fear I felt, Frank. You're very much like Alfred. You have that same *centeredness*. But I had never felt complete within myself. With both Phillip and my mother gone from my life, I believed I would simply die."

She reached down to lift the coffee server. "More coffee, Frank?" She was looking up at him, her face completely composed, as though they'd been chatting about the weather.

"No . . . no, Mrs. Veneé. I'm fine."

She replaced the server and refolded the small square napkin that rested in her lap.

She'd caught him off guard with that offer of more coffee. And he sensed that she knew that. He'd been intent on h monologue. Then it dawned on him that the break in her story had been entirely deliberate. She was bringing him along slowly, building up to something that required some kind of extraordinary readiness on his part.

She placed the napkin on the coffee table, satisfied at last with the new realignment of its folds.

"It's the sweet scent of narcissus I remember most when I think of that day." The brief intermission had ended. "Strange to think that of all that happened, it is the smell of narcissus that I remember most clearly. And there were no narcissus. Narcissus don't bloom in October." She touched the side of her face as though she were making sure she hadn't changed physically in some way.

"When I turned my head on the pillow, there was just the small vase of roses. The pale pink ones that Phillip had put there the day before. But they had no real odor. Roses from the florist rarely do. It was narcissus I smelled. . . ." Her words drifted off, and for a moment he imagined that she wasn't going to say anything more.

"I was so tired after Mother's funeral." She was speaking again. "I remember going up to my room sometime during the afternoon. I must have fallen asleep, because when I woke, the room was dark except for the dim light coming from a bedside lamp.

"I remember floating, drifting in and out, moving somewhere between consciousness and sleep, trying desperately recall what had happened to me that I should feel so terribly, terribly sad. I was very frightened that I had no memory of it, yet I think more frightened that I should remember." She stopped and took in a short fragile breath.

"I don't know how long I remained like that. Lying very still on the mattress of my bed. The smell of narcissus all around me. Watching the shadows stretching wide and dark over the furniture like dustcovers."

She shook her head, waving her hand a little through the . "My thoughts were wild, jumbled images. More fantasy than anything real. Yet . . . yet a part of me understood that something of great importance was finally coming to an .

"But then it was a beginning, too." She touched her temple as though she had a sudden headache, and he noticed that her hand trembled slightly. He was about to call out to her when—

"When I looked up he was standing over me. Smiling. And my eyes followed him as he took one of the small pink roses from the vase and ran it across my cheek. I remember the petals felt very cool against my skin. And then he bent and kissed me, a soft dry kiss on my lips, and my fingers brushed against the corners of his mouth."

He watched her glance down, examine her hands spread like small fans in her lap.

"And . . . And then I was crying, crying so that my breath seemed to get all tangled up inside of me. And I could feel that he was holding me, pressing me against him so tightly that I could no longer tell if it were my heart or his that beat inside my chest. 'It's all right, Margaret,' he whispered over and over again. 'I'm here, my darling. I'm here.'"

She stopped. And he heard what sounded like a small muffled cry, although he was sure her lips had not moved.

"Mrs. Veneé . . . ?"

She glanced up at the sound of her name. Her face was flushed. And he saw that her large blue eyes seemed almost startled. Then she stood and walked toward the portrait of her mother. She remained perfectly still, gazing up into the oil painting as though it were a mirror. Then abruptly she turned and looked across the room.

"No matter what sin God and the world may name it"—her voice was incredibly calm—"I can only remember it as the sweetest single comfort that ever came into my life."

He watched her move slowly back to her chair, resettling the soft gathers of her skirt, smoothing the collar of her blouse. Her hand twisted the single strand of pearls at her throat.

"You see, Frank"—there was finally a smile on her pretty face—"you were right about Alexandra. She is Phillip's daughter. Phillip's daughter and mine."

Frank shut off the overhead light and dropped back in chair seat. The floating hum inside the belly of the plane was putting him to sleep. Still over an hour's worth to D.C. A little shut-eye would probably do him some good.

He closed his lids and saw Margaret Veneé. Strange how close two people could get in just a few short hours. Even if he were a betting man, which he wasn't, he'd never have taken odds on what had happened this afternoon in Margaret Veneé's parlor. But then, Margaret Veneé was never quite what she seemed. . . .

After. . . when she knew for certain that she was pregnant, she thought of telling Alfred. But she knew she could never do such a thing. What, dear God, would she have said? Yet when she told him that things would never work out between them, that too much had happened, and that she was going away for a while, he'd guessed it. Guessed all of it.

In his own quiet unassuming way Alfred understood, had understood all along. Perhaps better than she herself, he'd known what it was that had bound her to Phillip all of those years. And now because what joined them had come full circle, had reached full term, Alfred understood that it must at last be finished.

Yet not a single word did he say against Phillip. He'd merely taken her into his arms and asked her to marry him again. Oh, how she had underestimated him. Underestimated his strength. His goodness. His love for her. And more, how pitifully for so long had she underestimated her love for him.

He heard Margaret Veneé's soft laugh now.

He jerked open his eyes and turned. Crazily he half expected her to be sitting next to him. Instead the brunette in the adjoining seat had slumped over, and her head was resting heavily against his shoulder. He reached to ease her over, but had second thoughts. He snuggled his shoulder closer and settled back, trying to relocate Margaret Veneé's laugh.

She had laughed when she'd finished talking about how wonderful Alfred had been. How beautiful their wedding was. How those months waiting for Alexandra to be born were magical.

"You know, Frank Gregory"—that was when she'd laughed—
"it's because you remind me so much of Alfred that I felt I
could talk to you." And she'd walked over and sat next to him
on the sofa, touching him lightly on the arm. For a minute he
thought she was going to kiss his cheek. But she didn't.
Instead she just smiled at him with those clear blue eyes
that reminded him of those endless summer skies of his
childhood. "You're a good man, Frank Gregory," she said
softly.

So it had been their secret all these years. Hers and
Alfred's secret. Never once until today did she ever think of
sharing it. Certainly not with Phillip. Although sometimes
when she'd seen Phillip and Alexandra together, she'd imagined that he knew. Perhaps Phillip had had his own secret—
allowing her to believe that he hadn't known.

In the early years, when Alex was still very young, it would
happen sometimes. Happen that she would weaken and
become frightened. Full of doubts. And during those awful
periods she would believe that God was going to punish her
for what she and Phillip had done. Punish her through
Alexandra. Make Alex pay the price for that one moment of
completeness she'd shared with her brother.

But Alexandra was perfect. And with each passing year, she
saw her daughter grow more beautiful, more intelligent.
More wonderful. She seemed indeed to be the very best of
both her and Phillip. And after a while she slipped into a kind
of easy acceptance, believing that no punishment would
come, because no sin had been committed. No sin would
ever be tallied against her and Phillip. But she had been
wrong. There always a price to pay. Yet there was one
absolution granted them. Their daughter, their Alexandra,
was perfect.

Alexandra was perfect ... perfect, perfect, perfect....

He must have dozed off because he could feel the cabin's
pressure sucking at him as the plane began to descend. He
looked over at the woman sitting next to him. She was
putting on lipstick. She turned and grinned. "We both fell
asleep," she said timidly. He smiled, then glanced out of the
window and saw the far-off lights of the city signaling up

to him. He was back. It felt good. And the trip felt good, too.

I'll be there if you want me, Alex, he promised her, making the words his own little mantra from now on. Fuck, hard-boiled reporters don't have mantras. Well, maybe this hard-boiled reporter was just going to break the mold. And he leaned back into the seat cushion and let the big jet carry him home.

Now there are two great ways to catch up with your favorite thrillers

Audio:

☐ 45116-2 **Final Flight** *by Stephen Coonts*
Performance by George Kennedy
180 mins. Double Cassette $14.95

☐ 45170-7 **The Negotiator** *by Frederick Forsyth*
Performance by Anthony Zerbe
180 mins. Double Cassette $15.95

☐ 45207-X **Black Sand** *by William J. Caunitz*
Performance by Tony Roberts
180 mins. Double Cassette $14.95

☐ 45156-1 **The Butcher's Theater** *by Jonathan Kellerman*
Performance by Ben Kingsley
180 mins. Double Cassette $14.95

☐ 45211-8 **The Day Before Midnight** *by Stephen Hunter*
Performance by Philip Bosco
180 mins. Double Cassette $14.95

☐ 45202-9 **The Minotaur** *by Stephen Coonts*
Performance by Joseph Campanella
180 mins. Double Cassette $14.95

Paperbacks:

☐ 26705-1 **Suspects** *by William J. Caunitz* $5.99
☐ 27430-9 **Secrets of Harry Bright** *by Joseph Wambaugh* $5.95
☐ 27510-0 **Butcher's Theater** *by Jonathan Kellerman* $5.99
☐ 28063-5 **The Rhineman Exchange** *by Robert Ludlum* $5.95
☐ 26757-4 **The Little Drummer Girl** *by John le Carre* $5.95
☐ 28359-6 **Black Sand** *by William J. Caunitz* $5.95
☐ 27523-2 **One Police Plaza** *by William J. Caunitz* $4.95

Buy them at your local bookstore or use this page to order:

Bantam Books, Dept. FBB, 414 East Golf Road, Des Plaines, IL 60016

Please send me the items I have checked above. I am enclosing $_____
(please add $2.50 to cover postage and handling). Send check or money
order, no cash or C.O.D.s please. (Tape offer good in USA only.)

Mr/Ms _____

Address _____

City/State _____ Zip _____

FBB–6/91

Please allow four to six weeks for delivery.
Prices and availability subject to change without notice.